Lake Oswego Public Library
706 Fourth Street
Lake Oswego, Oregon 97034

[УПЫРЬСКИЙ ЗАГОВОР]
THE NOSFERATU CONSPIRACY

BOOK ONE: THE SLEEPWALKER

KDK 12 Press • Los Angeles, CA

[УПЫРЬСКИЙ ЗАГОВОР]
THE NOSFERATU CONSPIRACY

BOOK ONE: THE SLEEPWALKER

BRIAN JAMES GAGE

2020

Copyright © 2020 KDK 12, Inc.

All rights reserved. This book or any portion thereof may not be reproduced or used in any manner whatsoever without the express written permission of the publisher except for the use of brief quotations in a book review.

First Printing: 2020
978-0-578-62713-7

Also available in electronic format
978-0-615-53095-6

KDK 12 Press
Los Angeles, CA

brianjamesgage.com
nosferatuconspiracy.com
instagram.com/brianjamesgage
instagram.com/nosferatuconspiracy

For my parents, Jim & Linda.

Acknowledgements

Special thanks to the following people who either inspired or supported my journey in writing this novel: Kimberly Roth, Nick Mamatas, Richard Nash, Jennifer Surprenant, Anne Horowitz, Paul Rozvadovsky, Von Doh, Dr. Margaret Trenchard-Smith, Stephen Elliott, Jordan Fried, Stanley Kubrick, Christine Kessler (R.I.P.), LE Gordon, Holly Randall, Humphry Knipe, Suze Randall, Erin Hall, Ryan Hyde, Jon Beauregard, Laura Ivan, and Rosie Colleen O'Neill.

PART I: STĂPÂNUL

Chapter 1

Part I: Stăpânul

1

СОВЕРШЕННО СЕКРЕТНО [TOP SECRET]
"Behold! Eternal night rises with the
blood of men in its cusp."
—Vlad Drăculea, Book of Visions 4:9,
Sfânta Biblie al Strigoiului Viu, 1456
[Holy Bible of the Living Vampiric Witch]

The Buzău River stops flowing at the base of the Carpathian Mountains east of Brașov—a paranormal phenomenon known as *dead water*. It remains inert for the next seventy miles southeast, all the way to the Subcarpathian commune of Berca, where it once again flows with vigor. A sullen understanding hangs over the region, one obeyed by fish, migrating birds, and any superstitious person—that is to say all inhabitants of Wallachia and Transylvania.

This dread, this silent decree, is woven into Romanian lore as far back as the thirteenth century. Secret texts recovered from the Teutonic Knights cite building fortifications across the north and south entrances of the Buzău Pass, not to impede Turkish invaders as history speculates; rather to keep people—all people—from an evil lurking deep within the Carpathians' imperious summits.

The river that slithers below the Carpathian peaks sucks all life and hope into its sinuous network of vessels feeding enriched silt to its heart: the black waters of the massive Loch Dracul. The loch, entrenched by sharp, slate-colored spires, drinks its fill from the surrounding countryside like a vast tar pit eager to swallow any life that happens upon its calm surface.

Chapter 1

At its center hulks a long, lean island that juts upward from the dark water—a geographic aberration historically known as Insula Lui Negru Vodă, the Isle of the Black Ruler. Its grim aspect, born of dark granite, rises from the bottomless murk of Loch Dracul, stilling any heart unfortunate enough to gaze upon it. Atop the island's rocky cliffs grow patches of tall, slim grass before a dense line of black and gnarled trees. They are neither willow nor oak but bear similarities to both. At the forefront of the forest, crumbled stone that was once Vlad Drăculea's fortified citadel lies strewn about, giving the appearance of jagged teeth guarding the tree line.

The limestone bricks eroded in time and moss prevailed, but the human blood spilled upon the island lingers in spirit and lore. From Galaţi to Braşov, locals whisper about the legends: serpentine monsters dwelling in the loch, giant vampire bats roaming the blackwood forest, and the restless souls drowned beneath the loch whose ghostly hymns are heard on nights the wind is silent.

On April 2, 1894, Loch Dracul found two unexpected guests at its mouth.

Four days prior, the Kovenski twins escaped a Bucharest prison and fled to Berca, where they appropriated a six-meter rowboat. After rowing themselves in circles through the Buzău's treacherous capillaries, they sat adrift in the middle of the loch's onyx waters. A sheer fog lifted before them. In the distance, the steep island cliffs seemed to echo the rhythms of their timorous hearts.

"We'll never find our way out."

"Quiet. Do you realize what that is?"

Bela nodded as his brother motioned toward the isle.

"People say this place is just legend."

Bela peered overboard. "Look at those depths, Saren. Pure blackness. I'm rowing out." He leaned forward and took up the oars.

Saren squeezed his brother's arm. "We've come too far," he whispered into Bela's ear. "This is an opportunity. Think about it. We have the hooks and a net."

Bela turned and glared at Saren. "What? In a six-meter rowboat?"

Saren grinned.

"Even if we did catch her," continued Bela. "Even if we did! How then do you propose we tow a ten-ton monster all the way back Buzău?"

Part I: Stăpânul

"Quiet. You'll scare her off."

"No, you be quiet!" Bela stood and thrust his finger at Saren. "Escaping up the Buzău was your idea. We row days through putridness. Through stink and shit only to get sucked into this hellhole, and you're telling me you want to hook the loch monster? We're better off looking for the Impaler's treasure!" Bela wiped the spittle from his mouth.

"Don't be stupid! I'm not stepping foot on that island. It's haunted," said Saren.

"The whole cursed loch is haunted! What's the difference? Least we can go up there and see if there's a box of gold. I hope I find one of his rusty old poles because I'm sticking it right up your ass."

Bela planted his feet on the hull, and held the rim while shaking the boat back and forth.

"Stop!" yelled Saren as he clutched starboard and held on tightly.

Bela's fit subsided and he plopped his weight on the bench. "This is it! When we get out of here, I'm turning us both in. Boat thievery for you. Having the stupidest brother on this wretched earth for me. Guilty as charged, Judgeship!"

Bela produced a small canvas satchel from underneath the bench. He pulled out a bread loaf, ripped off a large hunk, and popped it in his mouth. He turned and faced the bow.

"Bela, just think about it. We catch her, bring her back to port. We'll be the two richest and famous fellas in Buzău. In all of Romania. I bet we even get a pardon."

Bela stood, chewing on his bread. "With what then?" Bela tossed a bread morsel into the black water. "Here you go, loch monster. Come on, girl, there's a piece of bread for you."

He whistled as if calling a dog, then sat. "Keep your stupid mouth shut." Bela crossed his arms and slouched. "Days of backbreak you caused me. And God knows we'll starve to death before finding our way out."

"It's your fault! I told you we—"

"Shut it!" Bela watched the isle's trees in the distance. "You see that?"

"What?"

Chapter 1

"Hanging in the trees. What do you suppose those are?"

"It's those vampire bats."

"Can't be. They're as big as people."

"They are ... even bigger. They'll wake at night and drink our blood dry."

Bela grabbed the oars and rowed toward the island. The water churned white beneath the thrust of his powerful strokes.

"Oh, no," said Saren.

"Come on, just to see if they're real."

"I'm not stepping foot—"

"Me neither. Just need a look. Man the rudder."

Saren stood aft and steadied the rudder. A moment later Bela dipped the oars into the water, and the vessel drifted to a stop.

"Give me that spyglass," said Bela.

Saren reached to a spyglass fastened to the side of the boat by thin leather straps. He passed it off to Bela's fat, eager hand.

"Look at that. They *are* bats. Wonder why they're so pale?" Bela realized his mouth was dry as he scanned the canopy. "Vicious-looking things."

"Let me see," said Saren, impatiently waving his hand.

Bela handed him the spyglass.

"They're almost pure white. This isn't natural, Bela—we should go ... now."

A silence crept across the loch.

Bela sat, stroking his chin. "So if that's true, I bet all the legends are." He closed his eyes for a moment. "You hear that, Saren?"

"No." Saren pulled the spyglass from his eye and cocked his head as if to catch a sound from behind.

"That. Listen. They're singing," said Bela, his eyes alive with enchantment.

"The bats?"

"No. The dead. Drowned underneath the loch." Bela closed his eyes once more and pretended to be lost in some glorious symphony.

"I can't hear it," complained Saren.

Part I: Stăpânul

Bela opened his eyes. "Maybe if you leaned overboard and put your ear a bit closer to the water, you can hear them sing. It's lovely. Eerie. But gorgeous."

"Shut it."

"I understand. You're scared."

"Nothing scares me," said Saren.

"Then lean over and put your ear to the water. Prove it."

Bela snatched his bread, shoved the rest into his mouth, and chewed while loudly smacking his lips.

"Fine!" said Saren. "I'll do it. But then we're going. I'm not waiting to see if everything they say about those bats is true. And if you push me in—"

"Now why would I ever?" Bela smiled.

Saren stood and pointed at him. "Don't you dare do it!"

Saren moved starboard, took one last disdainful glance at his brother, then closed his eyes and leaned overboard. The black water sloshed quietly against the boat. He decided not to lean any farther, imagining Bela's joke would end with a dip into the loch at any moment. Still, Saren listened closely. Convinced he heard nothing, he opened his eyes and peered into the murky water.

Back in the boat, Bela stood slowly and crept toward his brother, intending to push him overboard. He paused when Saren's grip abruptly tightened on the rim.

"What is it? Saren?"

Saren was silent. His body stiff.

"Saren, enough. I was joking around." Bela poked his leg as Saren's body fell limp.

Fear struck at Bela and he slowly sat back upon the bench. Sweating and panting heavily, Bela sat frozen, watching his brother's limp body hanging over the side of the boat.

What should I do?

With a slosh of the water, Saren shot back into the boat and cowered upon the floor, shaking.

"There's a woman in the water," said Saren, pointing overboard. He began panting—the color in his cheeks absent.

"You lie!" said Bela.

"There's a woman in the water." Saren was now visibly shaking.

Chapter 1

Bela looked toward the boat's rim as the fog hovered around them. Saren continued to shiver and crouch into the bow. Bela stood inch by inch and leaned starboard. Fear coursed through him as he gazed into the loch to see a pale figure submerged just below the surface. Her naked flesh appeared to glow in contrast to the murky depths.

The woman's black hair waved unnaturally about her face in the calm water. Her legs were bound by a chain that weighted her lower body downward, and her outstretched arms were tied at the wrists. A brown rope ran from her wrists and connected to the chain at her ankles.

Bela noticed deep red lesions across her body. He looked at her for several seconds with his tongue stuck to the roof of his mouth. She looked so vibrant he believed her eyes might open, that air bubbles would shoot from her mouth, and she would scream for his help. But she was dead. Floating alone in a silent, watery grave.

Bela turned to Saren, who was buckled over, clutching his canvas satchel.

"Get up. We're fishing her out."

Saren shook his head.

"We're doing it," said Bela. "Nobody's going to believe this."

Bela moved astern and opened a locker. After rummaging through its contents, he produced a large rusty hook tied to a thick rope and tossed it onto the boat's hull. He then threw the anchor overboard and watched the line unravel. A few long moments passed and the last of the rope disappeared, its final traces descending quickly into the blackness.

"That's twenty meters of rope," he said, shaking his head. He turned to Saren. "Get up, Saren!"

Saren stood reluctantly next to his brother and looked at the naked figure. A nervous cramp struck his gut, and he averted his gaze. "It's a bad idea."

Bela ignored him and swung the rusty hook by some slack in the rope. He flung the hook toward her body, and it sunk into the water.

"Missed!"

He reeled it in and swung the hook once more.

"What are you aiming for?" asked Saren as he stood behind Bela.

Part I: Stăpânul

"See right there. Where the rope that's binding her hands heads to her ankles. I'll hook her right there."

He tossed the hook into the air and it pierced the water, darting to the bindings near her ankles. Bela tugged forcefully on the rope, jerking the woman's body.

"I hate this," said Saren.

"Just help me pull."

They yanked the rope, and the boat drifted toward her.

"She's too heavy," said Saren.

"We'll get a bit more over her and have leverage. Whatever's weighing her down goes deep, so tug."

The rope tied to her ankles dislodged and they felt a sudden snap on the line. Her body floated gently to the surface.

"Help out, Saren."

Bela grabbed the woman's wrist and pulled her toward the boat. Saren wrapped his hands tightly around the back of Bela's belt.

"Pull me," grunted Bela.

After a few tugs, her lifeless body slumped into the boat with a sickening thud. Saren covered his face with a handkerchief, expecting rotten flesh.

"She's been bitten all over," said Bela, inspecting her lesions.

Vicious bite marks were strewn across her body as if someone had stabbed her over and over with a two-pronged ice pick. Some chunks of her flesh were ripped out entirely. Bela looked up to the tree line and curled his nose at the sight of the pale bats.

"We better get rowing."

"Let's go," said Saren without taking his eyes from her.

Bela looked her over. "Poor girl." He pulled her matted black hair from her face and inspected the bites and bruises around her neck. "What got a hold of you?"

Bela reached to lift her slumping head. As his hand reached the tip of her chin, the woman's eyes jerked open and she gasped for breath. Water expelled from her mouth as she tried to scream. Her panicked eyes glared at Bela, who fell backward, clutching his heart. She clamped her hand around his wrist.

"Help me," she begged. "Help. Please."

Chapter 1

Bela broke her grip and pushed her away. She lay at the bottom of the boat, holding a quivering hand toward him. Her brown eyes, beacons of desperation, tore into Bela as he slowly reached outward.

Saren crept behind him. "Don't touch her. She's a succubus," he breathed.

Thick tears streamed down her face and she whispered, "They did this to me."

Her gaze shifted away from Bela and her mouth grew wide. Short, high-pitched whimpers came from her throat as she tried to scream once more. Her chest spasmed as her lungs sucked in quick erratic breaths. She fell limp.

The brothers watched, frozen in their stance as a fog crept in around her motionless body, and her ravaging bite wounds healed all at once.

Part I: Stăpânul

2

СОВЕРШЕННО СЕКРЕТНО [TOP SECRET]
Diary entry of Alexandra Fyodorovna, empress of Russia
1894–1916

December 1, 1916

Every day is darkness. I am swallowed by it. Trapped inside this palace, this ornate mausoleum. Haunted by these crushing nightmares. I cannot close my eyes for but a moment before they engulf me.

The dream came just before I woke this evening. The same horrid vision. I am restrained to the ground, struggling. Subdued by a stranger with terribly powerful hands, his palms pinning my shoulders to the ground. I try to fight but cannot, my arms and legs are restrained. From the corners of my eyes I can see these terrible creatures—bats I suppose, but they are much larger—swarming upon my limbs, sinking their fangs into my body and neck, feasting upon my flesh and blood. The shooting pains are incredible. I try to scream, but am silenced by my own blood filling my lungs. I am drowning.

The dream ends as it always does.

I am floating underwater, just below the surface, ankles and wrists bound by something. Suddenly I am flung from the water into a small boat. A man, bearded and heavyset, is reaching out to me. Someone is standing behind him. I realize I am naked with terrible mutilations to my skin. And then I remember his eyes—the man who was holding

Chapter 2

me down. The one who started this. I can see only his eyes before I scream and wake from the dream.

I pray these terrifying visions will stop!

They are the only thing I can place in my head as a memory as to what happened to me before I became sickness. The longer I hold them inside, the more real they feel. I am terrified to confess these dark visions to anyone. Not to Anna or Sana. Not even to Felix.

I have nowhere to turn.

I am despised by my countrymen, mistrusted by the imperial court, and blamed for all of this by my estranged husband. I can hear the trite whisperings of the servants calling me a witch, a vampire. Worse.

I am the tsaritsa of Russia!

And yet I am treated like a petty servant, some embarrassment to be kept in the attic. Oh, Nicholas! Why must you abandon me at my weakest hour?

My pain has grown intolerable—a wretched, insatiable hunger that screams from every cell in my body. It is worse for Alexei. I cannot be from his side for too long or he sickens. The child will no longer eat anything but rare meat or animal blood. I feel I should dare not express our unusual cravings within these pages. But it is the only thing that quells our rabid pain. I sometimes wonder if what the servants say about me is true.

We will both die soon. I feel it. I do not believe there is a cure. I have prayed and prayed. I have been healed by mystics, priests, and every other grifter from six continents. Yet I grow sicker. The mere thought of daylight turns my stomach. I've ordered curtains drawn over every window in my wing. All light must be blocked! For even the full moon burns my skin now.

My poor Alexei. Soon he'll be nothing but bones. How many more days can I watch him suffer? How many more hours? The doctors now say it's a rare form of hemophilia. Before it was a strange anemia. They know nothing. They can't stop his bleeding fits, they will never cure him.

Part I: Stăpânul

    I sit here watching him sleep just as I do every evening, wondering if this is the last night he'll awaken. I stare at the iron leg braces propped against his bed. I hate myself for them. The rickety contraptions are nothing more than a grotesque reminder of the disease I passed to my own son.

    I am losing my mind watching the only soul I care for suffer. I can carry this sickness. I can stand before the court and wave and look pretty in my gown, and still be sick underneath it all. But no child, and certainly not my own, should have to live alone in the dark with no father who cares for him.

    Please, God, take mercy on my son. He is innocent. He is kind. I will live the rest of my days suffering if only you will spare him. His sickness and loneliness are damnations I can no longer face! Please send me some shred of hope, so that I do not take his life and with it my own.

*

Alexandra closed her diary, placed it on the floor, and looked to Alexei. The large candles on both sides of his bed were usually enough to wake him—the only sunrise he'd ever known. Tonight, he slept undisturbed. Alexandra agonized over his slight face and the dark circles that loomed under his eyes. She stared at the lump beneath the comforter where his legs rested. His leg muscles had atrophied, too weak to support him but for a few clumsy steps. In the past two weeks, Alexei had been unable to walk unassisted.

    Alexandra's eyes became transfixed upon his chest rising and falling. She silently counted the soft, rhythmic lulls of his breath and fretted over his infantile appearance. He was twelve now, but appeared no older than seven.

    Alexei was born ten years after her marriage to Nicholas, the only male heir to the throne and—unbeknownst to Russia—Alexandra's only child by blood. Early in the marriage, it became worrisome to the royals that her sickness caused infertility after she and Nicholas were unable to conceive a child. Nicholas, with Alexandra's consent, fathered four daughters through a surrogate in hopes of producing a male heir. He'd given up hope until August 12, 1904, when Alexandra began hemorrhaging in the morning. Six hours later, Alexei was born at a near fatal body weight in her bathing quarters. She had been unaware of the pregnancy.

The news of a male heir spread through a populace in dire need of an uplifting distraction. The masses believed Alexei's birth was a sign of a quick victory in Russia's war with Japan.

The cost of war grew, and the pending sea battle spelled certain economic collapse. There were mass desertions, and rumors that the entire Russian navy was led by syphilis-infected scoundrels who were starving and largely drunk on vodka to endure their hellish conditions. All of Russia was awakening to the soreness of autocracy's boot wedged into its back.

Even as his top political advisors either abandoned or betrayed him, Nicholas swore never to retreat from Manchuria despite the impending Japanese victory. As best the royals tried to keep it secret, news of Alexei's illness spread to the people. The superstitious population blamed Alexei for defeat, citing his sickness as a sign Russia was doomed from the start.

Alexei woke and gently reached toward his mother.

Alexandra walked to his bedside. She ran her fingers through his hair, careful of his scalp. His bleeding fits were so chronic she feared the slightest scratch would do him in.

"Where's the shadow man?" Alexei wiped the sleep from his eyes and peered around the room.

"Who?"

"My new visitor."

Alexandra smiled. "Is your imagination treating you to some fun?"

Alexei looked upward and thought for a moment.

"It's not fun."

"You poor dear," said Alexandra and stroked his hair. "Is it nightmares?"

"No. The shadow man is real. He is trying to tell me something bad about Father."

"Oh? Perhaps you should tell me."

Part I: Stăpânul

"I don't think I should. It's scary."

"You can. It's just a bad dream."

"He whispers to me and then I fall asleep. He calls me 'the Bloodchild.' He says I have to kill Father—that Father's blood is infecting me and hurting the others."

"What others, sweetheart?"

"I don't know. He just says 'the others,' then takes me to a dark forest where giant white bats hang in black and gnarled trees. He says they will die soon if I don't kill Father."

Alexandra was silent for a long moment.

"I'm so sorry, child. That is the scariest dream I've ever heard," she said. "Would you like me to start sleeping next to you? Would that help you rest more peacefully?"

Alexei reached to his mother's hands and held them tightly. "I think the shadow man is trying to help us. He told me that what we do in the cellars is fine, but there's a better way. He said he is coming for us and will show us. He also thinks you are beautiful."

Alexandra smiled. "As long as he tells you that, then maybe he's a friend after all."

Alexei squeezed her hands once more. "Will Uncle Felix visit me tonight?"

"I don't think so. Your father is hosting a very important gathering for Minister Makarov, and Felix must attend."

Alexei frowned.

"I'm sure Felix will come to see you soon."

Alexei winced as muscles in his forearm began to twitch. "I'm starving."

"I know. Mama is too."

"Please let me come. I'll be quiet. I want to see the palace at night."

Alexei's fit subsided, and Alexandra caressed his face with the back of her hand.

"Come," she whispered.

Alexei wrapped himself around her robed body, and she carried the frail child from the candlelight into the darkened hallway. They walked to the sweeping main stair and descended alongside the banister until reaching the ground floor. Alexandra's feet fell upon the

Chapter 2

cool marble, and she crept to a narrow hallway that ran parallel to the stair. At the very end of the passage was a heavy, polished wooden door.

Alexandra opened the door to a dark, winding stairwell. She positioned Alexei on her hip, then crept all the way to the palace's wine cellar, where a thick circular door sat at the end of the corridor. She revealed a brass skeleton key from her pocket and unlocked the door.

"Will you hold this for Mama?" Alexandra reached to the floor and handed Alexei a bucket—a tarnished butcher knife rattled within its bloodstained interior.

Alexei rubbed his face as Alexandra lit the candles in the candelabra sitting next to the door. She held it in front of her, illuminating yet another stairwell, this one leading to the deepest part of the cellar—the waterways beneath the Winter Palace that fed into Saint Petersburg's rat-infested sewage system.

*

Archimandrite Gyáva stood in the Winter Palace's Room of Coins before Nicholas's inner circle. They sat in a long row of chairs in front of a slim, empty desk. Each man bowed his head, trying to concentrate on Gyáva as his deep voice bellowed his blessing.

"O Christ our God, who at all times and in every hour, in heaven and on earth, art worshiped and glorified. Who art long-suffering, merciful …"

Minister of Justice Aleksander Makarov fidgeted, searching for comfort in his flimsy oak chair. His eyes locked onto Gyáva's long gray beard. He was impressed by the sheer rigidity of the hairy mass, likening it to a metronome bobbing up and down with every spoken syllable of Gyáva's blessing.

"… who lovest the just and showest mercy upon the sinner, who callest all to salvation through the promise of the blessing to come, O Lord …"

Makarov pinched his weathered fingers to the peak of his brow and tried to calm an oncoming sinus headache. He became aware of Grand Duke Pavlovich's whisperings into his ear.

Part I: Stăpânul

"This is not the place," said Makarov, glaring at Pavlovich's handsome young face. "We will discuss such matters in private."

Gyáva stopped his blessing and scowled at Pavlovich, who sat upright and stared off at the columns that ran the perimeter of the Room of Coins. The other cabinet members shifted about in their chairs, taking notice of Makarov's forceful rebuttal.

"Everything fair, Minister?" asked Prime Minister Trepov from several chairs away.

Makarov shook his head and smiled, revealing his yellow teeth. "Wonderful, Prime Minister. Thank you." He looked to Gyáva. "Please, Archimandrite. Continue."

Gyáva frowned, causing his beard to bend against his chest. He took a deep breath. "Sanctify our souls, hallow our bodies, correct our thoughts, and cleanse our minds ..."

And on it goes, thought Makarov, driving his thumbs more firmly into his sinus area.

The rest sat back in their chairs and feigned comfort as they awaited Nicholas's arrival.

As Gyáva finished his prayer, an Okhrana officer marched into the hall's threshold and slapped his boot to the marble floor. He threw his right hand to his forehead in a forceful salute.

"Rise for Nicholas Aleksandrovich Romanov II, Emperor and Autocrat of All the Russians."

All seven men quickly rose to attention and turned to watch Nicholas approach. Nicholas strode across the floor flanked by Ivor Kashin, head of the tsar's secret police. Both men were dressed in white formal attire. Nicholas stood behind his desk and tossed a folder full of papers onto its center as Kashin moved behind him. Nicholas slammed his fists onto the desk and glared at his cabinet members as his temples and ja-w pulsed. His gaze focused on Makarov. Nicholas opened the folder and pulled out a newspaper clipping, tapping his finger along a featured article.

"I need not express the sheer rage that besieges me when I read of my cabinet's treachery in the newspapers." Nicholas traced a line of text with his finger. "Minister Makarov has promised universal male suffrage for men old enough to fight in war!" His brown eyes shot to Makarov. "How dare you, Minister!"

Chapter 2

The remaining cabinet members relaxed a bit, and stared toward Makarov.

"Emperor, if I may," began Makarov, then paused for a moment.

Nicholas stared wide-eyed at him and jerked his open palm forward. "Well? Say something!"

Makarov cleared his throat. "The promises I make in public are no reflection on my loyalty to this court or your leadership. Please understand, Emperor, we are on the brink of revolution—"

"I understand clearly, Minister. That is why I'm behind this desk, and you are standing there."

Silence pervaded the room as Makarov stared at his shoes.

"Emperor, I beg you. If the public is not told what they want to hear … certainly you see the danger."

Nicholas glared at him for long moment, then bowed his head. "You may sit."

The men shuffled about, and took their seats.

"Not you, Minister," said Nicholas.

Makarov rose from his half-seated position.

"This is for you too, Prime Minister," began Nicholas, pointing at Trepov. "Minister Makarov's point is well taken, but let it be known to you all that I will dissolve the Duma in one instant if any of its members try to assert themselves over this divine autocracy. Is that understood?"

"Yes, Emperor," they said in unison.

"Is it understood, Minister?"

Makarov stood silently. He clasped his hands together and bowed his head, revealing his liver-spotted bald spot. "Understood, Emperor."

"Very well. Be seated."

Nicholas turned to Kashin. "That will be all, Commander."

Kashin bowed and walked to the far perimeter of the room. He stood in the shadows and listened to Nicholas chide his cabinet members over the looming threat of a Bolshevik revolt. Quiet footsteps came from his back, and Kashin turned to see Officer Baylor approach.

"What is it?" whispered Kashin.

Part I: Stăpânul

Baylor handed him an envelope, СОВЕРШЕННО СЕКРЕТНО typed in small letters upon the upper-left corner.

"It's the Khlysts dossier I've been preparing. It requires your immediate attention, sir. They're on the move, planning something big."

Kashin huffed. "I warned you about troubling me over such matters. Our men are poised to assassinate the tsaritsa and her son in a matter of days." He tossed the envelope to Baylor. "The Khlysts can wait in line."

"A large arms stockpile," said Baylor.

Kashin turned to him.

"It was uncovered in a Khlysts temple east of Saint Petersburg. Rifles, grenades. Lots of gasoline. We have a date. December 16. Whatever they're planning will happen then."

Kashin glared at him, then looked to the envelope. He snatched it from Baylor's hand and both men shuffled off behind a curtain leading from the Room of Coins.

*

Dossier delivered to Ivor Kashin

**СЛЕДСТВЕННОЕ ОТДЕЛЕНИЕ ОХРАНЫ
[OKHRANA INVESTIGATION]
СОВЕРШЕННО СЕКРЕТНО [TOP SECRET]
ДЕКАБРЬ 1916 [DECEMBER 1916]
ХЛЫСТЫ: КУЛЬТ, ЧЬЕ ПОВЕДЕНИЕ
НЕ ПОДДАЕТСЯ ОБЪЯСНЕНИЮ
[KHLYSTS: CULT PARANORMAL ACTIVITIES]**

ОПИСАНИЕ [DESCRIPTION]

Khlysts have been immigrating to Saint Petersburg in great numbers beginning in early November 1916. The cult is mostly active around Tobolsk Guberniya and surrounding Siberia, portraying themselves as an excommunicated off-branch of the Russian Orthodox Church.

Chapter 2

ПРОИСХОЖДЕНИЕ [ORIGIN]

Khlysts are comprised largely of Stovâjįk, an ethnic minority from Romania's Wallachia region who became disciples of Vlad Tepes [Vlad Drăculea, Vlad the Impaler] in the mid to late 1400s. The Stovâjįk populace fell victim to genocide once Vlad Tepes was murdered by his own brother and his monarchy overthrown. They fled persecution to Siberia's Tolbolsk Guberniya circa 1480.

ПРИНЦИП РАБОТЫ [MODUS OPERANDI]

Further investigation into the cult's operations and agenda is still underway. They display little interest in recruitment of new members. Infiltration thus far has failed. Interrogations of cult defectors have proved difficult as once approached for questioning, they will commit suicide or disappear.

ПОСЛЕДНИЕ СОБЫТИЯ [RECENT ACTIVITIES]

Февраль 3, 1916, Тобо́льск, Сиби́рь [February 3, 1916, Tobolsk, Siberia]

Upon investigation of a string of child murders throughout Russia linked to Khlysts activity, police in Siberia discovered one child alive.

Mina Minskva, an eleven-year-old girl reported missing from Moscow for seven months after being abducted by her father, a known Khlysts elder, was found wandering naked and disoriented along a country road roughly fifteen kilometers outside of Tobolsk.

She was taken to police headquarters, believed to have been severely beaten. Upon inspection, it was discovered that she was covered in blood that was not her own. Her back was freshly branded with a depiction of a fanged bat. The child was in great pain, constantly clutching her lower abdomen. She was submitted to a surgeon who removed a jeweled amulet lodged inside her cervix.

On the face of the amulet is a hieroglyphic depicting a large fanged bat, its wings outstretched over a naked man and woman (both noted as Strigoi vii), the woman clutching a baby to her breast (Copilul Sângelui is engraved underneath the child). Translations pending.

Around the golden-rimmed amulet is inscribed: *SFÂNTA BIBLIE AL STRIGOIULUI VIU* [translated from Romanian: HOLY BIBLE OF THE LIVING VAMPIRIC WITCH].

The girl was in deep shock, suffering from severe hypothermia. No statement was recorded. The Tobolsk police constable reported her mumbling, "*Sfârşitul lumii, sfârşitul lumii. Nosferatu sfârşitul lumii.*" [Translated from Romanian: "Apocalypse, apocalypse, Nosferatu apocalypse."]

She was returned to Moscow on February 8, 1916. She, her mother, and her infant brother were found brutally murdered the following morning.

The father remains at large.

ИЮЛЬ 17, 1916, Москва [July 17, 1916, Moscow]

Okhrana agents apprehended defected cult elder Sergei Michailovich Trufanoff (a.k.a. Iliodor the Mad Monk), who had been in hiding for nearly twenty-three years.

For the first three hours of his interrogation, he mumbled only, "The darkness awaits." After succumbing to a variety of psychological techniques, Iliodor began sobbing, babbling the following: "The Holy Upir trapped in limbo, the stăpân is coming, the Bloodchild born half-dark, half-light."

The officers attending his interrogation threatened Iliodor with more painful techniques unless he provided them with useful information. They left the room briefly, leaving Iliodor unfettered with only a glass of water. When they returned, Iliodor had broken the glass and cut out his own tongue.

He was sent to a gulag insane asylum where he hanged himself one week later.

ЧИСЛА [NUMEROLOGY]

Numerology is important across all layers of the cult. There are certain dates discovered that repeat in recovered Khlysts literature, falling under the Romanian titles geneză [genesis], naştere [birth], and sfârşitul lumii [apocalypse].

Their significance is yet to be determined; however, it is assumed they are calendar dates: "genesis," 26031894; "birth," 12081904. The final number in the numerological calendar falls under the title "apocalypse," 16121916.

СИМВОЛЫ [SYMBOLS]

Little is known about cult symbology. Barns and underground catacombs investigated for cult activity have turned up several small amulets and charms as well as one unidentifiable wall scroll. Each of the amulets and charms contained scroll-work depicting a large fanged bat.

СОВРЕМЕННОЕ РУКОВОДСТВО [MODERN LEADERSHIP]

SERGEI MICHAILOVICH TRUFANOFF (A.K.A. ILIODOR THE MAD MONK), 1869–93. Left Siberian Khlysts sect after being ousted by GRIGORI YEFIMOVICH RASPUTIN. Deceased: suicide.

GRIGORI YEFIMOVICH RASPUTIN, 1893 – PRESENT. Although the cult is administratively run by several lower-ranking clerics, Rasputin—even in his absence—seems to be considered the cult's rightful leader from within the ranking coven. He has been missing since 1894. Last seen in Bucharest, Romania.

СВЯЗИ С ИМПЕРАТОРСКИМ ОКРУЖЕНИЕМ [IMPERIAL TIES]

****PENDING FURTHER INVESTIGATION****
Many high-ranking Russian officials and aristocracy are rumored to be members of separatist Khlysts sects in

Part I: Stăpânul

Saint Petersburg and Moscow. They operate and meet at random times and locations as a secret society calling themselves the Black Hundred.

The Black Hundred was initially formed in Moscow as early as 1875 as an anti-Semitic conservative movement fiercely loyal to the tsarist regime. The group had strong ties to German aristocracy; one recovered document cites Louis IV of Hesse (deceased; father of Tsaritsa Alexandra) as an active member.

The Black Hundred converted to Khlysts during the mid-1880s. No documents on their history have been recovered since.

CURRENT SUSPECTED MEMBERS OF RUSSIAN ELITE:
1. GRAND DUKE DMITRI PAVLOVICH
2. ALEKSANDER ALEKANDROVICH MAKAROV
3. GENERAL EVGENIY VLADOVICH DRAGUNOV
4. GRAND DUKE GEORGE ALEXANDROVICH [DECEASED: ASSASSINATION IN BUCHAREST, ROMANIA, MARCH 1894]

КОНЕЦ ДОСЬЕ [END DOSSIER]

*

"Minister! Minister!"

Grand Duke Dmitri Pavlovich's heels clacked upon the marble of the Jordan Staircase as he shot after Makarov.

"Minister!"

Makarov stopped and kept his back to Dmitri while continuing to pull on a thick winter coat.

"Yes, Dmitri," said Makarov, positioning his ushanka hat.

Dmitri stood next to him and spoke in a soft voice. "It is simply—"

"It is simply foolish," yelled Makarov, before lowering his voice, "to bring up such matters in the middle of a cabinet meeting. Downright stupid to do it during Gyáva's fat-winded sermon.

Chapter 2

And dangerously careless when the subject of discussion is seated three chairs away."

"I'm sorry, Minister. It will not happen again."

"I know," said Makarov, continuing down the stairs.

Dmitri followed.

"It's just. Why don't we simply kill him? He's a depressive. We can make it appear like a suicide. If the stăpân says he's a threat, we should kill him. I don't want to risk Irina."

Makarov continued in silence for a few more stairs. "The Stăpân has stated he will deal personally with Yusupov. If you would attend a meeting now and again, you would also know the stăpân has made it abundantly clear that no murders will befall anyone of royal blood until it is time. The seers have predicted this action will be effective. Thus the ranking coven has made it a mandate." Makarov's dark eyes turned to Dmitri. "Yusupov will be handled as we have provisioned, and you will be rewarded for cooperating. That is all."

Dmitri stopped and watched Makarov descend to the bottom of the stair.

"It's simply . . ." Dmitri's voice echoed through the hall. "It's simply I do not trust the Stăpân. He tricked us from the start. He has kept us waiting for decades!"

Makarov turned and stared upward at him.

"Yes. Us," began Makarov, speaking intently. "The Stăpân has kept *us* waiting for decades. And the nature of his trickery is not your concern. You were but a mere infant when we put these mechanisms into motion. Count yourself lucky to be one of us as a young man."

Dmitri appeared worried. "I do. I am thankful every day. I—I just do not want harm to come to her. She will be turned. Correct? That is what the Stăpân has promised. She is to be turned. Will you promise me that?"

Makarov looked upward and waved his finger toward the arched ceiling. "Be careful when you boast your misgivings about the Stăpân. He could be watching."

Makarov flashed his yellow smile and walked into the Winter Palace's grand foyer. Dmitri watched him exit into the cold

Part I: Stăpânul

Saint Petersburg night, taking a few moments to notice his own face was dripping with perspiration.

Chapter 3

Part I: Stăpânul

3

December 1, 1916 (OS), night

The Aurora Express barreled through the nighttime countryside. Tomorrow at 7:15 a.m. it would arrive in Saint Petersburg, the architectural jewel of tsarist Russia.

Rodion Kvoss walked through the dining car with his pushcart just in front of him. The food stains on his apron were apparent even in the dim lighting. He watched over the dining travelers, picked occasional pieces of trash from their trays, and placed the rubbish in a small waste bin on his cart. A heavyset man, dressed in an overcoat and cap, squeezed by him and moved toward the front of the car.

"Off to your cabin, sir?"

The man nodded.

"Be sure and lock your door now. Especially after midnight."

The man acknowledged him with a slight nod and disappeared into the next car.

Rodion came to his filling station and poured his trash into a larger receptacle. At the top of the bin, he noticed a discarded copy of the *Revolutionary Gazette* and sat down to read it. The newspaper was folded open to an interior page with several dense articles:

Stovâjĭk Immigration Surges

Saint Petersburg, Dec. 1, 1916— Forgoing their usual home of the Siberian tundra, the Stovâjĭk or "swamp gypsies" have been immigrating in great numbers to Saint Petersburg. There are no economic indicators that explain the sudden spike in Stovâjĭk populace who are known for

Chapter 3

their inclusive ways and affiliation with the Siberian Khlysts.

Since the unexpected growth in Stovâjįk population last month, the Saint Petersburg Metropolitan Police have reported a sharp rise in assaults, theft, and petty burglary for which the gypsies are renowned. The police have advised citizens to be wary of traveling alone in depressed areas of the city.

Several autocratic organizations, including some more conservative factions of the Octobrist Party, have staged rallies and taken up campaigns to rid the city of the Stovâjįk. Even more moderate political factions are recommending a halt to the gypsy population growth unless the tsar's Office of Civil Engineering can determine a solution that addresses the labor concerns of workers native to Saint Petersburg. Both the Trudoviki Party and the Social Democratic Labor Party have sworn to stand by Saint Petersburg's worker unions to ensure that locals retain their jobs during the influx of cheaper labor.

In a stark contrast to his party's political platform, Minister of Justice Aleksander Makarov has promised to fight for the Stovâjįk's rights to stay in Saint Petersburg.

(Cont. A-15)

Rodion flipped the pages in search of the editorial section. Finally his eyes fell on the featured editorial, "Sleeping Beauty 'Celebrates' Anniversary." The accompanying illustration pictured Tsar Nicholas II standing next to his wife, Alexandra, who was seated on a delicate Isabella chair. Tsar Nicholas—chest out, chin up—was dressed in his ceremonial state garb, white-gloved hand upon his saber. Even in the illustration, Alexandra carried an air of faintness about her. Her dress was slight with heavy pearls around her neck, and her dark hair was pulled back from her face.

Saint Petersburg, Nov. 14—"Thank you for coming," was the short and only remark breathed by the apparently ill tsaritsa to those in attendance at her anniversary ball. Tsar Nicholas and Tsaritsa Alexandra gathered with 100

Part I: Stăpânul

close associates in the Winter Palace ballroom yesterday to commemorate their 22nd wedding anniversary. It was reported that the tsaritsa posed for this photo, spoke her short thanks, and quickly returned to her darkened section of the Winter Palace to care for their son, Alexei, who has now been confirmed to suffer from an even rarer and deadlier form of hemophilia.

This marks one of the few public appearances by the tsaritsa, whose reclusive behavior is cause of much concern within the ranking elite. Insiders complain that her erratic and unladylike behavior further entrenches the increasingly unpopular Nicholas, leading his few supporters to view him as a traitor for marrying a woman of Germanic descent.

The tsaritsa was at the center of an international sensation 22 years ago when she fell unconscious and was rushed to a Berlin hospital after her betrothed—Grand Duke George Alexandrovich of Russia—was assassinated in Bucharest, Romania.

Upon hearing the news of her hospitalization, Nicholas II, brother of Grand Duke Alexandrovich, begged his father to bring her to Saint Petersburg so that he could care for her and honor his late brother.

According to the lore surrounding the events, Nicholas traveled to Berlin and sat next to Alexandra on her hospital bed. As he reached to her face, she woke for the first time in ten days upon his touch. She has been by his side ever since.

Facing political upheaval in the embattled Fourth Duma, Tsar Nicholas has threatened to dissolve the body and assert supreme control over Russia and its war with Germany. But it is the opinion this newspaper, and the Russian people in general, that the tsar must first take control of his wife by sending her back to Germany, and marrying a woman of noble Russian blood.

Rodion tossed his head back and laughed. *Poor Nicholas.* If the editors of Saint Petersburg's best-known underground newspaper

Chapter 3

could publish such a scathing editorial and live to tell about it, Rodion imagined Nicholas must be standing on his last political legs. He continued to flip through the paper until disturbed by a figure lurking over him. There stood fat Edmund, the closest thing he had to a friend working the line.

"Guess what, Rodion?"

"What's that?"

"You drew guard."

"Like hell. What's wrong with Kolya?"

"They had to rush him to a hospital in Minsk this morning. He lost his mind on last night's shift."

Rodion shook his head and smirked. "I bet."

"You didn't hear?" Edmund sounded boastful. "He went into blue car number one. Came out insane."

Rodion turned his attention from Edmund's portly young face to the newspaper.

"And guess what? Car one is reserved—the whole thing—all for one man." Edmund crouched toward Rodion and whispered as if he didn't want any nosy travelers to overhear. "But nobody's exited or accepted food in two days. The windows are all covered with black tarp. You know what else?"

Rodion glanced to him. "Thrill me."

"Supposedly, grisly murders have been following this train on every stop along the way—bodies found hacked to bits!"

"Is that a fact?" Rodion sounded bored.

"It's what I heard."

Rodion's apparent lack of concern seemed to disappoint Edmund.

"But the part I find particularly intriguing," continued Edmund, "is that nobody ever showed up to claim car one's reservation. It's been locked tight since Bucharest. The only thing that arrived was a telegram on the morning we left giving the conductor strict instructions to cover the windows in thick tarp, that it was to be locked shut and no staff were to enter the car from the time we left until after we stationed in Petersburg."

"It's *Saint* Petersburg."

Part I: Stăpânul

"Either way—they put up the tarp, locked the car, and then poof! Nobody showed."

"So it's empty?"

"Seems."

"Then how is it Kolya went crazy?"

Edmund began to bounce at the knees a bit, barely able to contain his excitement. "David said Kolya had been complaining of hearing things when he'd come close to car one on his late shifts—voices and such. I guess he must have been too curious, unlocked the door, and went in. When he came out, he walked right to his quarters and cut open his wrists." Edmund pantomimed a razor slashing at his wrists and his eyes widened. "David was there when they took him away. Said Kolya never mumbled a word. Just kept staring ... like he'd seen something."

Rodion rolled his eyes.

"Enough of it," he said. "I'm not the scaring type, so save it for any of the staff who's superstitious."

"I'm serious. We drew guard for you, so you have to go."

"Fine, give me the baton."

Edmund handed it over.

"I mean it, Rodion. Stay out of car one. They say you should have seen Kolya's eyes. He saw something in there." Edmund leaned into him. "Want me to go with you?"

Rodion blinked, surprised by the offer. "Oh, yes—"

"Just kidding," he said, pointing his fingers like a pair of six-shooters.

"Good one, Edmund."

Rodion sat for another moment, then threw his newspaper in the waste bin.

"Fine. I'm guard." He stood up and poked Edmund in his fat gut. The two laughed, then Rodion opened the train door and ventured into the darkened third class.

Rodion opened the car's electric box and flipped the switch a few times. No luck. He navigated the dark passageway by the light of the gibbous moon that cast the corridor in a stark bluish-white hue. The landscape outside revealed they were moving north across the marshlands toward Novgorod. He shivered a bit watching the

Chapter 3

moon paring stalk the train. His fingers tightened around the baton, and he pulled out his Daylo pistol light. The pistol-shaped flashlight was a gift from his mother when he started working the lines. It was from New York City, nickel-plated for an authentic look and feel. Pull the trigger and on came the light.

He kept a brisk pace through third class, appearing like a policeman ready to pounce. Upon entering second class, Rodion pocketed his flashlight. The stark, naked bulbs along the corridor lit his path. He walked from door to door, ensuring each was locked. After finding a door that was unlocked or occasionally ajar, he'd rap on it and encourage the inhabitants to lock up.

A wave of relief swept him as he came to first class—the pride of the line: clean, well lit, and since the inhabitants generally had valuable possessions, they always came armed.

If trouble comes, everyone to first class!

Rodion recited the staff joke once more and took a moment to look over his appearance in the window's reflection. He patted down his wavy brown hair and inspected his on-going and feeble attempt to grow a mustache.

I'm going to look nineteen forever.

The lights flickered on and off, then stayed off. Rodion shot upright. The door slid closed behind him, and he pulled out his flashlight. He walked along the corridor, testing each door with his baton—all locked.

The train began to bounce wildly up and down as Rodion entered car two. He stood in the darkened corridor and shined his light to each cabin door to see if any were ajar.

They're locked. Maybe for a few kopecks more a week.

Rodion turned back as something brushed by his shoulder. He spun around to face an empty corridor.

His flashlight went dead, and he banged it against the window. After a few fleeting bursts of hope, the light was gone. Rodion stood alone, staring down the darkened hall toward car number one. The hallway seemed to breathe his name, to beckon him toward its end. The lights flicked on.

Thank God.

He exhaled, convinced he was brave enough to try the door to car one. Rodion moved down the corridor, tightly gripping his baton.

Part I: Stăpânul

His reflection in the wide windows instilled in him a sense of companionship as the train tracks rattled and repeatedly jerked the cabin.

He crept toward car one, placing each foot on the floor as if he were moving through a minefield. Rodion attempted to open the intermediary door that connected the two cars—it was either jammed or off its rail. He forced it open. Rodion stood on the coupling platform, which bounced up and down in a near frenzy. He pulled the key from his pocket and inserted it into the lock. His pulse quickened as he looked from the keyhole back to the white number one. Too frightened to unlock the door, Rodion pulled the key and pocketed it.

Come on, at least you can tell them you tried it.

With his fingers wrapped around the lever, he took a deep breath and tugged forcefully upon it. Locked.

What a joke. Leave it to Edmund.

The click of the train tracks once again resonated as the tune of his monotonous daily routines. Rodion relaxed and turned around. He started back, forgetting to close the jammed intermediary door.

Come back, Rodion ...

He stopped dead halfway down the corridor and turned to the sight of car one's door standing wide open. He leapt backward as the train's whistle blew overhead.

A strange clicking sensation throbbed through his chest, and his face was struck by a thick, slimy substance that flew from the darkness of car one. His entire mouth went numb. Rodion wiped the glop from his chin and inspected the clear, stringy fluid. He slumped against the corridor wall, barely able to stand.

Something fluttered about the window, and his eyes darted to the glass. His gaze shot back to the darkened door. And then Rodion felt it moving around him—everywhere. He closed his eyes and froze as the shadow slithered its cold across his skin, enveloping the corridor like a fast-growing black moss. The specter crept up his back and hovered for a moment. A burning pain pierced his chest as warm liquid glided down his torso. He opened his eyes to find the corridor was empty, the shadow gone.

Rodion tried to move but his legs were torpid, immobile. A tugging in his torso grew more intense until his sternum cracked—

Chapter 3

tearing cartilage and breaking ribs reverberated through his body; yet there was nothing. No pain, and he stood alone, pinned against the wall in the brightly lit corridor, unable to move.

I'm going mad.

Rodion peered to the window. It was there. Feeding on him in the reflection—soaking his white apron to deep crimson.

Scream. Fight.

Waves of extreme pleasure overcame Rodion and numbed him further to paralysis as its teeth sunk into his left ventricle, devouring his oxygenated blood. He drifted toward blackness as the numbness wore thin and an icy pain shot through his bones. The shadow lifted him from the floor, cradling him like a limp babe. Rodion closed his eyes and embraced its frigid kiss, until he was finally smothered by a dark euphoria.

I am yours.

*

Daylight brought the travel-weary passengers out of their cabins to watch the timid sun skip across the subarctic dawn. The door to car one appeared undisturbed, with no trace of the previous night's events. The Aurora Express bore on across the vast snow-covered farmlands. It would dock in Saint Petersburg in less than one hour.

Far in the distance, the bronzed dome of Saint Isaac's Cathedral and the proud lines of Saint Petersburg's palaces and spires framed their prestige against the deep purple of morning's twilight. The city beckoned the eager travelers as Saint Petersburg came into full view: a metropolis of over one million inhabitants, renowned for its wealth of architecture, palace-lined waterways, and beautiful bridges, halved by the Neva River.

The vision of the city was but a picturesque memory when the rails moved into the filthy outskirts. The passengers impatiently watched the slums roll by, finding it hardly a regal welcome. Pristine snow of the countryside soon turned sullied brown and was indiscernible from the muck of the slum's dirt roads.

The 7:15 came to its final resting point inside the open-air platform of Vitebsk Station. Saint Petersburg, so beautiful from a distance, now revealed its unsightly underbelly.

Part I: Stăpânul

4

СОВЕРШЕННО СЕКРЕТНО [TOP SECRET]
"Thus spoke the Darkness, 'Bring one nation before Me and thou shalt know My eternal kingdom. For he who summons the Nosferatu shall rule in My name over all things living and dead.'"
—Vlad Drăculea, Book of Visions 12:11, Sfânta
Biblie al Strigoiului Viu, 1456
[Holy Bible of the Living Vampiric Witch]

December 2, 1916 (OS), morning

It was still dark when Grigori Rasputin stood on the bustling platform of Vitebsk Station. His sunken, fiery stare absorbed the sporadic movement around him. His broad brow and forehead cast an amplitude of strength onto his otherwise gaunt face. Aside from the insidious gleam in his black eyes, he appeared like any other Russian *strannik*, or religious pilgrim: dark brown hair pulled back from his bearded face, a heavy black tunic that stopped at mid-thigh to reveal black pant legs with worn peasant boots rising to just under the knee, and a tarnished pectoral cross that hung around his neck.

A mother and daughter, dressed too economically for the harsh winter, hobbled toward him, clutching one another to fend off the cold. Rasputin broke his long gaze from the station line and noticed them bobbing their heads toward him. He nodded slightly to welcome their request, then raised his right hand and blessed them. They bowed deeply and continued on their way.

Rasputin looked to the open-air roof, impressed by its once grand construction: rusty beams riddled with chipped paint rose to greet soaring arches constructed with a slim glass ceiling that ran

Chapter 4

the course of the station. Dense globs of pigeon feces stained the glass roof—Rasputin grew disgusted by the filth and neglect. He momentarily focused on the dark morning sky to clear his mind. While mumbling to himself, he looked again to the length of Vitebsk Station.

Swarms of people bustled about and everyone appeared to be in uniform. The train stewards pulled the baggage from the train's side compartments and left the parcels scattered at the edge of the platform. The passengers collected their bags, shuffling them like mother cats positioning their newborn litters, as surly passport officers constantly inspected the commotion.

Rasputin stood perfectly still, sucking deep pockets of air into his nose and exhaling through his mouth. Despite the frigid air, his breath left no vapors. Two direly serious passport officers marched toward him as he stared into the distance. They stopped before him, rigid as two iron rods, and peered at one another, clearly surprised by his height.

"Papers, please," said the leaner of the two. His breath rose into the air. Rasputin watched it slowly dissipate.

"Ah! He sees us. Thought he might have been meditating."

Rasputin glared at him, then at his counterpart. After deciding he had little regard for the two men, he continued to look toward the end of the platform, which opened up into the main hall of Vitebsk Station. At its mouth was a statue of Tsar Nicholas I riding a horse, his mounted figure pointing a saber southeast toward Moscow.

"Hand me your papers!" shouted the passport officer.

Rasputin was quiet.

"Hand me—"

"I hear you," spoke Rasputin, never taking his eyes from the statue.

"Then hand me your papers." The officer held out his gloved hand.

Rasputin pulled his powerful hands from behind his back, patted his chest. "I must have left them in Bucharest."

He smiled broadly and feigned absentmindedness.

"Bucharest?" The officer's face grew red. He pulled his whistle from a small breast pocket and blew into it. Three police officers rushed toward them.

"What's the problem?" asked the first policeman.

Part I: Stăpânul

"Illegal. No papers."

The commanding police officer moved toward Rasputin, taking notice of his manner of dress.

"Excuse me, Father, I have to—"

"I left my papers in Bucharest, or possibly Paris," he began with an air of embarrassment in his voice. "But as you can see, I speak fluent Russian, native Russian I might add, and"—he motioned to his own garb—"am obviously of Russian descent. So then, would it not lend you to believe this is an honest mistake, my good Officer Brams?"

"Yes, Father, but—"

"How long in Romania?" barked the passport officer.

"Years."

"Father, please," began Officer Brams. "Possibly you left them in your baggage?"

"I carry none."

"How long do you plan to stay in Russia?" questioned the passport officer.

"Indefinitely."

"Years abroad, moving indefinitely, and you come back with no bags? Nothing at all to declare?"

Rasputin clasped his hands behind his back and looked to the passport officer.

"Well, Mikhail, I crave no earthly possessions. Therefore, I have none. The cross on my chest is the only burden I choose to declare." He glanced to the police officers. "Officer Brams, Officer Egorov, and kind Officer Peytenik, tell Mikhail this is all a misunderstanding, and that we may move along to enjoy the crisp air of this magnificent morning."

Officer Brams and his men turned to Mikhail and pulled him aside. After a brief argument, they returned to Rasputin.

"Please, Father, carry on. God be with you."

Rasputin swung his arms outward and made a broad motion to bless them. "So very kind of you," he said with an apparent smirk. "You'll be rewarded in heaven's kingdom, my good sons."

He stepped forward, clasped his hands behind him, and walked toward the station's grand exit, appearing like a glorious raven

Chapter 4

strolling among the sewer rats. The officers watched him until his dark figure disappeared down the stairs at the main exit.

Mikhail looked to the policemen's uniforms, noticing no one present wore any name identification.

"How do you suppose he knew our names?"

The police stood quietly, wondering the same.

*

Rasputin walked down Vitebsk's grand arched stairway and cautiously avoided the cracks, corrosion, and occasional beggar that riddled the marble stairs. He exited the station and paused, taking in the drab beauty of Saint Petersburg. Nearly twenty-four years had passed since he last visited, and the deep scars inflicted by pollution surprised him. Filth marred the face of the once pristine city. All the way beyond the peak of the Peter and Paul Fortress, buildings once healthy and thoughtful sat bruised with soot. The industrial smokestacks overshadowing Saint Petersburg's city limits appeared like prison bars sprouting up around a weary captive.

Rasputin looked upward and held out his hand to catch a few small flakes of black snow that sprinkled around him. Closer inspection revealed the particles were ash expelled from a nearby smokestack. The city was drowning in foul exhaust like some fat pressure cooker ready to burst from its own corroded iron gut. Rasputin was home.

His tall figure strode into the gallery where drivers of horse-drawn carriages hustled for passengers. The squat buildings near Vitebsk Station allowed a view deep into Saint Petersburg's skyline. In front of him was Zagorodny Avenue—the station's main artery to the city, where the occasional automobile struggled to swerve around the population of buggies dominating the slush-covered brick.

Alongside the road sat a covered carriage with an imperial insignia on its side and a handsome black steed at its helm. Rasputin walked toward the horse and patted it on the nose. The driver perched atop the buggy gripped the horse's reins around his gloved hands. He wore a purple sikke hat and round-rimmed glasses that were smoked a deep charcoal. His slight face was almost swallowed

Part I: Stăpânul

by the high collar of his black overcoat. The only discernible feature on his face was a long scar that ran from his forehead over his left eye and onward to his chin.

Rasputin stroked the horse's nose for another moment, paying the driver no mind.

"I come back to Saint Petersburg only to find it haunted by the same dreary sky? What sort of welcome is this?"

He looked to the driver, who acknowledged him with a slow, polite nod.

"Is everything prepared?"

"Yes, my Stăpân," replied the driver, his voice monotone.

"Very well." Rasputin entered the carriage and closed the door. He sunk into the red leather seats and pulled down the carriage's window shades. The driver snapped the reins and the horse jumped into motion, trotting along Saint Petersburg's busy boulevards.

The buggy traveled onto Gorokhovaya Street and onward to central Saint Petersburg. It darted across the Palace Bridge and entered the Petrogradskaya side of the city, where gas lamps still burned inside their ornate wrought iron cases. Cast against the dawn, the dancing beacons conveyed an unnatural sense of urgency, as if they were some secret alert for residents to stay off the streets.

The horse-drawn buggy moved steadily around a long semi-circular avenue, stopping in front of a brushed-granite mansion of irregular shape.

The golden address on the arched stone entrance read *1*.

*

Professor Charles Vondling opened the glass door of his balcony overlooking Kronverksky Avenue and leaned against the railing as the buggy came to a stop below. A nervous perspiration broke upon his brow, and his glasses began to slip down his nose. His bony finger met the bridge of his silver frames, and he pushed them back into place. Vondling's scrawny frame shook all over, for inside the buggy sat a man he'd been desperately waiting to meet again. He leaned farther into the cold morning air, hoping for a glimpse of Rasputin. Vondling reentered his mansion and pulled the balcony door closed.

Chapter 4

*

Twenty-two years prior, a thirty-one-year-old Professor Charles Vondling opened the glass door of his balcony overlooking Strada Radu Calomfirescu in Bucharest, Romania. A similar nervous perspiration broke upon his brow, causing his glasses to slip down his nose. He pulled the glasses from his face, placed them in his pocket, and wiped his brow with a silk handkerchief. He had no physiological reason for eyeglasses at his age but wore them anyway, believing they added an air of intelligence and eccentricity that would impress his university colleagues.

Vondling looked to the nighttime clouds illuminated by the moon, and he counted the weeks in his head. Three. It had been three weeks since he'd seen Rasputin.

"Half day to the river, half day to the loch. How long does it take to become a vampire? A day, two? The bats killed him. I know it," he said aloud into the night.

He went back inside his handsome flat and sat at his sturdy oak desk while he scanned a newspaper. There was no mention of any heinous murders on the front page, so he turned to the obituary section. This was his last hope, yet no reported deaths seemed unusual or untimely. He let out a long stress-induced sigh, folded his arms, and placed his head upon them.

Certainly the plan was a failure, he'd convinced himself. He tried to calm his mind, but he knew they'd be coming for him—at any moment.

You conned the wrong death cult this time, Charles.

Vondling sat upright and decided to pour himself a glass of wine. He stood at his bar and had just selected a bottle when a banging at his front door startled him.

"Professor," came a gruff voice from the other side, followed by more banging. "Professor. We know you're in there. We saw you on the balcony."

Vondling hung his head, knowing he'd been caught. He lumbered to the door and opened it, peering at three burly men—all dressed in black—from behind his security chain.

The man in front looked at the chain and then to Vondling.

Part I: Stăpânul

"Charles," he said, looking amused. "I would expect so much more from you."

"I'm sorry, Kir. One moment," said Vondling.

Vondling closed the door and undid the chain.

Kir and his men burst in with the last man closing the door and locking it.

Vondling appeared defeated and led them to his parlor.

One of the men pulled a wooden chair, dragging it loudly over the hardwood floor. He placed it behind Vondling and forced him to sit.

"You know why we've come," began Kir. "Where is your holy man? Alexandra and her party will be leaving in two days. You were supposed to act days ago …"

Vondling was silent.

"Come now, Charles, we paid you extremely well. You promised us a mystic who would lead us to the loch. Our patience was thin then. Now it is nil."

Vondling cleared his throat as the man behind him placed his hands firmly upon Vondling's shoulders.

"He's gone missing," said Vondling.

"Missing! You hear that, gentlemen? We paid Charles a small fortune to deliver us this mystic, and finally the charlatan reveals he's missing. This is unfortunate, Charles. You leave me with few options."

Kir wound up and landed a punch square on Vondling's chin. The man behind him steadied him so he would not fall to the floor. Vondling appeared unconscious briefly, then sat up with tears in his eyes and blood dripping from his mouth.

"No, no, Charles. No time for tears. You did not cry when you took our money and made your promises."

"But—"

"Hold him." Kir pulled a pair of long, lean scissors from his jacket. "Grab his legs."

The other man moved in and held on to Vondling's legs as the man behind him tightened his grip on his shoulders.

"You know what we do with liars, Charles. Don't you?"

Chapter 4

Kir approached Vondling, slowly opening and closing the scissors.

"Please! I'll fix this! Please—"

"Open his mouth," said Kir.

The man behind Vondling held his chin and forced his tongue from his mouth.

"At first I thought I would start with your ears. But I am so very tired of your lies."

Vondling struggled and tried to protest as Kir held his face. He positioned Vondling's tongue inside the scissors and stared at him. "Any last words?" Kir said with a laugh.

Vondling closed his eyes, knowing his time had come.

At that moment, a fierce wind blew open the balcony doors and the parlor erupted in chaos. The men released their hold on Vondling, and he fell to the floor. He closed his eyes and cowered as the sounds of struggle grew more intense, with horrid gurgling noises and screams. Vondling covered his ears only to realize the noise had stopped. He opened his eyes to see Rasputin standing before him, his face covered in blood.

"Stand up, Charles," said Rasputin.

Vondling rose to his knees and looked around his parlor at the carnage. Only bits of the men remained—blood splatter was everywhere.

Barely able to muster the words, he spoke: "Those men … they are Black Hundred."

"*Were* Black Hundred," said Rasputin. "Now stand."

Vondling stood and approached Rasputin, falling to his knees once more.

"Oh, my master. My master! You did it. You found it!"

He wrapped his arms around Rasputin's legs.

"Quit your blubbering," said Rasputin, reaching down to pull Vondling upward. "We have work to do."

The door to Vondling's flat burst open once more as four Stovâjįk men holding handguns moved into the parlor.

"Is everything fine, my Stăpân?" said one with a long scar down the left side of his face.

Part I: Stăpânul

The men scattered about the parlor and inspected the mangled bodies.

"Indeed it is," said Rasputin. "Best wait outside to ensure no more are coming."

Without question, the four men turned and exited the flat.

"But what have you done?" said Vondling. "This will start a war when the coven discovers your actions."

"I did exactly what *we* planned."

"But attacking Black Hundred operatives was not a—"

"I am now the prime vampire," said Rasputin, glaring at him. "And *I* now control these events. The day after tomorrow our men will attack Alexandra's traveling party, murder Grand Duke Alexandrovich, and kidnap her. We will then take her to the loch and proceed with the ceremony. Our time to rule is very near."

"And what about me? When will you convert me?"

Rasputin broke his gaze from Vondling and peered around the room. Deciding he was disgusted by the mess, he extended his hand toward the hallway. "Shall we?"

Vondling led the way down the hall to his kitchen. He then sat at a table and looked up to Rasputin, who remained standing.

"So? When will I be converted? It is what you promised."

"Your time will come," said Rasputin. "Until then we have other problems you must address. Do you know anything about a man named Denis Borovitch?"

Vondling thought for a moment.

"I don't know anyone by that name. Do you know his surname?"

"I do not. Not yet. But I have inquired that our seers figure out exactly who he is. What they do know is he's an undercover Okhrana agent of the highest order posing as a professor at the University of Bucharest, seemingly acting on his own accord. He is masking his full identity with a very weak spell. I believe he has been tracking me since we arrived in Bucharest, and he seems to know quite a bit about my movements. I was able to lose him once I reached the Carpathians, but his interest in me is concerning."

"Indeed."

Chapter 4

"Indeed, Charles? That is all you have for me? A moment ago three very angry men were about to cut out your tongue—I can only assume it's because you talk too much to too many."

Vondling slouched. "I am sorry, my Stăpân." His eyes lit up. "May I call you that? Instead of master? Now that you're the prime vampire. May I call you my Stăpân?"

Rasputin stood in silence. Vondling was saddened by the lack of response.

"My apologies, Stăpân. You must know in order for me to do what I do, and to get the information we require, I must talk. I must be a friend to everyone."

Rasputin cocked his head a bit and considered Vondling. "Well then, Charles, best you see to your *friends* in the parlor. I will call for you when it is time. Until then—find out everything you can about this Denis Borovitch."

A powerful gust filled the room and Rasputin was gone.

Vondling sat quietly and caught a glimpse of himself in the window.

"You dummy!" he yelled at his reflection.

He trembled and wrapped his arms around his chest as he tried to control his rage. Screaming, he burst up from the chair and knocked it to the floor before dashing into the parlor and out onto the balcony.

"You'd better keep your promise, Stăpân! Do you hear me … Stăpân?"

Silence was his answer as he scanned the night sky.

He waited for a few more minutes before returning inside. Looking over the bodies, Vondling noticed a pool of blood on the floor by the remnants of a torso. He knelt, placed his face near the puddle, and inhaled the aroma. He extended his tongue to the blood.

Delicious.

Vondling thrust his face into the puddle and began lapping up the remainder of the spilled blood, growling as he relished the taste. He continued licking up the blood in a near frenzy until the taste of hardwood invaded his mouth. Using his hands, Vondling smeared the rest of the gore onto his face. He stood and walked to a mirror across the room, entranced by his reflection. He fashioned a few poses while hissing and gnashing his bloodstained teeth.

Part I: Stăpânul

Vondling stood upright and smiled into the mirror.
One day ... one day I will feast on them all!

*

The memory of that evening was fresh on Vondling's mind as he emerged from his mansion's arched stone entrance. The frigid Saint Petersburg morning seemed to cut right through him as he pulled a thick sable coat over his nightshirt and approached the street.

Rasputin opened the carriage door and peered down to see Vondling bowing upon the snow-covered sidewalk. Tears streamed from Vondling's face as he reached for Rasputin's hand and planted his lips on broad knuckles.

"Stand up," ordered Rasputin.

Vondling's face was flushed. He panted heavily, sending small puffs of vapor into the cold morning air. Upon meeting Rasputin's eyes, he fell once more to his knees. He placed his head at Rasputin's feet and wrapped his arms around the holy man's boots.

"Oh, Stăpân, Stăpân! I give myself unto you!"

Rasputin looked around to see if any passersby had taken notice. With his boot toe, he flicked a small clump of snow onto Vondling's head.

"I said stand."

Vondling stood slowly. "Of course, Stăpân! Yes."

"The sun is coming and I am in need of rest."

"Indeed, Stăpân. Follow. Follow!"

Vondling held Rasputin's cold hand and attempted to lead him to the stone archway. Rasputin yanked his hand away and walked in front of Vondling, leaving him alone on the sidewalk.

"Now!" beckoned Rasputin.

Vondling shuffled after him and guided Rasputin into his comfortable art nouveau mansion as an early morning fog slowly engulfed the avenue.

*

Chapter 4

Professor Vondling led Rasputin up a wide flight of stairs and down a long hallway to a study with a lingering scent of methanol. Upon entering the modest room, Rasputin was taken by its dense, decorative occult curios: taxidermy bats hung from the oak rafters; stuffed owls and rodents stared back at him from ramshackle bookshelves. Along the far wall, a large wooden desk stationed before a wide-paned window showcased Vondling's love of the grotesque. Various-sized jars and bottles with multicolored fluids were filled with human body parts: severed hands, a woman's fingers still with red fingernails and wedding ring, a heart sliced in two perfect halves, and a human head with its eyes half-open.

Rasputin squinted against the bright morning that began to seep into the room. He raised his hand to shadow his eyes and gagged quietly.

"Oh, how terrible of me," chirped Vondling. "You must be sick all over!" He removed his coat, slung it over a coatrack, and moved his fragile body toward the window. Vondling shut the thick velvet curtains and the room fell to black. Rasputin heard him shuffling about in the darkness.

"I've spared nothing," said Vondling. "I purchased the curtains from the local theater especially for you. They're the thickest you can get. And the most expensive!"

A sudden whiff of sulfur filled the air, followed by a glow emanating from Vondling's hand. He lit two large candles on the side of a modest shrine at his desk's center. Rasputin took notice of a sizable ceremonial book placed upon the shrine's podium.

"I transcribed it myself," said Vondling. "Calligraphy is but a side hobby of mine. Do you like it?"

Rasputin inspected the book and ran his fingers over the thick parchment.

"Inscribed in blood?"

"Yes, Stăpân. I bought it from the coroner. Fresh from the corpses."

"And does the coroner know your reason for buying blood?"

"No. But he's—"

"Who else?"

"Just him. I promise. Just him!"

Part I: Stăpânul

Rasputin nodded and slammed the book closed. It was bound in a thick leather casing with the words *Sfânta Biblie al Strigoiului Viu* inscribed in gold foil.

"I had it inscribed in gold, just for you! Shall we pray?"

Vondling fell to his knees and faced the book. Rasputin remained still.

"Inscribed where?"

"A talented printer on Bolshoy Prospekt. Why? Do you not like it? I wanted you to—"

"Enough," he said.

"Everything is in order, Stăpân. Are you not pleased?"

"My quarters?"

"In the attic," said Vondling, motioning to a narrow door next to the bookcase.

Rasputin stepped over him and opened the door.

"Shall I wake you? At dusk? It would be my honor!"

Rasputin stood with his back to Vondling, who knelt upon the floor with his hands still raised into the air as if waiting to receive some holy sacrament.

"You are to lock this door behind me," began Rasputin, his voice steady and stern. "Never open it again."

"Yes. Of course."

"You will see me when your time is come."

Rasputin walked up the staircase, and the door slammed behind him.

"You haven't forgotten your promise, have you?" shouted Vondling, a small vein pulsing in the middle of his forehead. "Remember your promise? Stăpân?"

Professor Vondling stayed on his knees, listening for the slightest rustle as Rasputin ascended into the attic. He sucked deep breaths into his lungs and scanned the ceiling, hoping for a speck of falling dust from a depressed floorboard. The room fell silent as the candlelight danced mockingly in his glasses. His chin quivered and tears fell down his cheeks.

"Stupid!" He punched himself in the face, knocking his glasses to the floor. "Stupid! Stupid! Stupid!"

Chapter 4

Vondling repeatedly beat himself until his lower lip bled, and he was too breathless to continue. For the rest of the morning, Professor Vondling lay on the study's polished wooden floor, sucking on his split lip and reveling in the salty-sweet taste of his own blood.

Soon, it will be another's.

Part I: Stăpânul

5

СОВЕРШЕННО СЕКРЕТНО [TOP SECRET]
Clipping from the Saint Petersburg *Vedomosti*:

Train Accident Linked to Famed Killer

Saint Petersburg, Dec. 3—Vitebsk Station, nestled on the brim of the Vvedensky Canal and Zagorodny Avenue, was the scene of grisly accident reported on the morning of December 2.

The Saint Petersburg Metropolitan Police have yet to release an official report, but sources tell this newspaper that early in the morning of December 2 the body of a male cabin steward who worked the line from Bucharest to Saint Petersburg was found mangled to pieces and stuffed in a trash bin inside the train's dinner cabin. Reportedly, there were no bloodstains anywhere on board.

Chief Constable Milton Petrov of the Saint Petersburg Metropolitan Police has asserted his department's domain over the investigation, and (despite strong speculation otherwise) has hypothesized that the young man fell between train cars upon docking and was later disposed of in a trash can by an unknown party.

This marks the second body found in similar condition along the route that originated three days ago in Bucharest, Romania. The first dismembered body was discovered underneath a train platform in the downtown station of Chişinău, Moldova, on the evening of December 1. Constable Petrov had no speculations regarding the

Chapter 5

Chişinău discovery or why that body was also drained of blood.

Residents living near Vitebsk have expressed concern that the condition of both bodies recalls the mangled state of the countless string of victims linked to the Sleepwalker, the famous European killer who has eluded capture for nearly a quarter century.

The Sleepwalker murders started in Bucharest, Romania, 23 years ago, victimizing prostitutes and the homeless. The Bucharest killings ceased in April 1894, with reported slayings discovered in rural France thereafter.

To this day, the case remains unsolved with no suspects. Sources speculate that if the newly recovered bodies are in fact mangled and drained of blood, this may be an indication that Europe's Sleepwalker has decided to leave retirement and pay a visit to Saint Petersburg.

*

Constable Petrov stood at the back door of Saint Petersburg's city morgue, hoping to avoid reporters. He banged on the iron door until Coroner Rurik Kozlov emerged, the door emitting a giant creak upon opening. Rurik's narrow face, accentuated by his thick black-rimmed glasses, nodded sullenly. He unbolted the chains and Petrov followed him inside.

Petrov noted the temperature was colder inside the morgue—well below freezing.

"Winter is always best for preservation," said Rurik, looking back to Petrov, who cupped his hands and attempted to blow warmth onto his freezing digits.

Petrov's pale blue eyes scanned the dim corridor. *What a hellhole.*

The sickly green hallway appeared to suffer from the remnants of some horrid plague—brown stains bubbled from the moisture-damaged paint, appearing like dried blood. Various medical tables, each heaped with rusty surgical instruments, were strewn about the cracked and missing floor tiles. Everything was drowned in filth.

Part I: Stăpânul

"It's a real honor to have you here, Constable," said Rurik, rubbing his hand through the gray hair along his temple. "When I heard you were coming in person, I—"

"Thank you. This case is gathering a lot of attention, and I wanted to make sure I have all the facts before assigning any specific detective."

"You won't be taking the case yourself?"

"My time is too important for petty murders. I'm merely here for appearance sake."

"This is definitely not petty. It's unlike anything I've seen. Remember the doctor who chopped up his wife a few years back?"

"Yes."

"Much worse," said Rurik, turning to him. "Much."

Petrov pretended he was prepared for anything, and Rurik led him toward a small room to their right. At its center was a metal table that rose to waist level. A squat metal bin with its contents covered by a white bloodstained sheet sat upon the rusted steel tabletop.

"He came in bits," began Rurik. "So I just threw them in a bin. Didn't seem appropriate to sprawl him out on the table like a jigsaw puzzle." He smiled, revealing his crooked, yellow-stained teeth.

Knock-kneed dolt. "Ah!" said Petrov.

"Shall I pull it off?"

"Please."

Rurik placed his fingertips on the sheet corners, then pulled it from the tub. He remained bent over, away from the bin's contents. Petrov looked away instantly, sucking in fresh air to avoid vomiting. He reached into his coat pocket and pulled out a handkerchief he'd doused in his wife's perfume. After placing the handkerchief to his mouth and breathing deeply, he inspected the body parts.

Only a moment passed before he tapped Rurik to cover the bin. In one small second, he saw it all—the bones and bits, flaps of torn flesh, and something he prayed he'd soon forget: the boy's eyes still wide open, staring at him. Rurik swung the sheet back over the bin and motioned Petrov from the room. They walked to Rurik's office.

"Please, sit," said Rurik.

Chapter 5

Petrov slumped upon the chair, perspiration beads gathering at his receding hairline. He removed his coat and swung it around the back of the chair.

"God, it's hot in here," said Petrov.

"It's freezing." Rurik pointed to the open window above his desk. "I keep the whole place as cold as I can during the winter. You should smell it come summer."

"Hacked to bits," said Petrov with a tinge of disbelief.

"No, sir. Not hacked. He was chewed apart. By something with particularly powerful jaws. I can show you the teeth marks if you like."

"No, no. I believe you."

The two men sat and stared at each other for a moment as if searching for some sort of comfort from the other.

"What do we do?"

"Well, sir. You're the constable."

"It's him, isn't it? The Sleepwalker."

"Only from what I've read. We would need to reach Scotland Yard to understand fully what we're dealing with. Most recent killings were near their purview."

"No!" shouted Petrov. "This is our jurisdiction. You'll see to it this problem disappears. Too much strain on my men as it is. Just help me keep it quiet."

"Sir, but if the killings keep coming, the public should—"

"You're not the police, goddamn it!"

"Yes, sir. I'll simply tell the newspapers that the coroner's office has confirmed the body is not the victim of the Sleepwalker, who is not in Saint Petersburg."

"No! Don't even mention the name. We'll conveniently ignore it. And once I finally deliver the killer it will be more of a…surprise …to the royal family. Just say you confirmed my theory. Kid fell under the train, scared conductor shoved the body in the trash."

Rurik cocked his head, blinking repeatedly at Constable Petrov.

"Are you certain of that, good Constable? It sounds—"

"Yes … it's only speculation about the Sleepwalker. Let's just hope the murders stop, and then we can say we scared him off. Only then admit we suspected him."

"Of course, sir."

Part I: Stăpânul

Petrov's brow dripped with sweat, and he began panting. His plump face grew hot, and he felt ready to burst from within. "I have to go. It's getting late in the uh ... yes. I'm leaving."

"Sir?"

"Yes?" Petrov had one foot in the hallway.

"What if he does it again? I mean, will you be investigating?"

Petrov patted his brow with his handkerchief.

"Why, yes! I will put my top resources into it."

"It's just if he strikes at people of status in the community instead of prostitutes, it will be difficult to explain."

"Great point," said Petrov as he wagged his finger repeatedly toward Rurik.

Petrov quickly threw on his coat and jogged down the hall. He slammed the back door and ran to a darkened corner of the alley, where he expelled the contents of his stomach. While looking down the corridor, he placed his cap back onto his head and straightened it. He left the alleyway and walked into the city streets as several young men were busy lighting gas lamps before dusk.

*

Rurik peered out a front window onto Telezhnaya Street and saw no reporters; however, he'd been coroner long enough to understand reporters had clever ways of making themselves invisible. He walked through the desolate halls, extinguishing any lights, then exited out the back. He locked the heavy iron door and turned toward the street—a dense fog hung just above the gas lamps.

The streets were empty of people.

He looked to the overhead fog and took a deep breath, realizing he was in the exact depressed area of town where the Sleepwalker was likely to prey.

Not a prostitute. Not a drunk. Well, not a drunk yet.

Rurik gripped the blackwood stake he'd concealed inside his jacket and rounded the corner to Degtyarnaya Street. Five blocks away shone his favorite gas lamp—the beacon that led to the Imperial Pub. He pulled his lapels together and walked briskly to outpace the thickening fog. Rurik walked close to the buildings' walls and noticed the gap of an alley just ahead. He had passed it on his way to the tavern countless times, but suddenly it felt like an act of sheer bravery to move beyond it. A small curling sensation crept up along his ear, as if someone were whispering to him. He spun around but saw no one.

Not drunk yet.

He jumped in front of the alley and stared into the darkened pathway. It was empty. Rurik turned and yelped as a dark figure stood before him.

"Professor Vondling," said Rurik with an air of annoyance. "You startled me."

"We must talk," said Vondling, trying to catch his breath.

Vondling pushed Rurik into the alley.

"Listen," began Vondling. "You haven't said anything … to anyone?" Vondling shoved him against the wall, tightly gripping his lapels. "Promise me."

"Of course not."

"Promise me you won't tell anyone. Ever. I'll never ask for more. I paid you well, didn't I?" Vondling looked up to the passing fog and raised his voice. "And you don't know what I was using it for, right?"

"No. I … Charles, I have as much to lose as you."

"Never tell anyone," said Vondling. He let go of Rurik's coat and ran away, vanishing down the foggy street.

Rurik closed his eyes and stayed in the alley for a moment.

Why on earth did you sell him corpse blood?

He shook off the thought, hoping Vondling was just experiencing another of his absinthe-induced episodes. Placing his hands in his jacket pockets, Rurik proceeded to his favorite tavern where he swayed the night with his two true muses: cheap vodka from Moscow's alembic stills, and the plump, buxom barkeep Hedrina Kastayevna.

One day, she will be Mrs. Kozlova.

*

Part I: Stăpânul

Sometime just before dawn, Rurik was seated in front of Orna inside her austere apartment. Her eyeballs swirled underneath her weathered eyelids as she clutched a typewriter ribbon in her hands.

"I have located his typewriter. You may begin."

Rurik, still drunk, began his dictation, badly slurring his words.

Dear Brother,

It is finally here in Saint Petersburg! I would very much like to speak with you over the telephone. However, since you refuse to obtain one, I can only hope you find this letter in a timely manner.

   A body was delivered to me this morning—chewed to pieces and drained of blood. Orna sensed its arrival early yesterday.

   We need you here immediately. Your fruitless search for *Desmodus draculae* has become burdensome to us all. Orna has foreseen the end on December 16—the Khlysts prophecy is unfolding.

   The real fight is brewing in Saint Petersburg.

Godspeed,
Rurik

Rurik sat silently as Orna took in deep breaths and hummed quietly. She opened her eyes, revealing her thick white cataracts.

"The message is delivered," she said.

"Thank you, Orna. I can't stay. I must make my way back to the morgue."

"Of course. You will be seeing a new visitor shortly. One Prince Felix Yusupov. Keep him safe and see that he makes his way to me as soon as possible."

Rurik stood up. "It's finally all happening. Isn't it?"

"Yes."

"Will we win?"

Orna frowned. "Honestly, Rurik. I do not foresee we will. This is troublesome."

Chapter 5

"And what exactly is Yusupov's place in this?"

"That is not clear to me, but all will be revealed soon enough."

"I'll be back in touch with you as soon as I can."

Orna smiled. "Be safe, Rurik."

Rurik exited the apartment and emerged onto the cold city streets.

Far away, in the outskirts of Bucharest, a typewriter sprung into action, typing out Rurik's message to his brother, Dr. Denis Borovitch Kozlov.

Part I: Stăpânul

6

December 4, 1916 (OS), evening

The Yusupov Palace sprawled itself across central Saint Petersburg in leagues with the city's most illustrious buildings. Nestled against the frozen surface of the Moika River, its façade shone like a giant lemon-yellow citrine defiant in the face of the night sky. Prince Felix Yusupov's shadowed figure stood framed in a frost-glazed window on the palace's second story.

At twenty-nine years old, the orphaned Felix was the sole heir to the second-largest personal fortune in Russia and, despite being engaged to Irina Alexandrovna, was renowned for his decadent and reckless lifestyle.

Felix stood in the palace's grand Red Parlor, his back to his late mother's priceless Regency furniture collection. The elegant marquetry inlays and polished rosewood gleamed against the fires burning in the room's twin hearths. Everything shimmered a royal red. In contrast were crème-colored accents of the vaulted ceiling and marble floor, both framed by lavish golden crown and base moldings.

Felix wiped away the window's icy residue and stared at the frozen Moika River. Gas lamps reflected from its translucent surface, and he watched them for a moment. An intense feeling of boredom overcame him. He blew his breath onto the window and watched the frost crystallize over it. The last swig of scotch coated his esophagus with warm shivers, and he rapped his knuckle on the window. He placed his palm against the cold glass, pulled it away, then watched the frost overtake his hand-print.

Just smash it.

Chapter 6

Felix wound up and drove his fist toward the pane, pulling his punch at the last moment. He patted the window with the meaty side of his hand, then placed his forehead against its frigid surface. The cold surge relaxed him and he slowly rocked his forehead left to right, watching small streams of water glide from the tip of his nose toward the windowsill.

Somebody shoot me.

The sound of breaking glass rang out from the parlor's entrance, and he turned to see his lovely fiancée, Irina, kneeling upon the floor with a crystal serving platter and bottle of brown liquor shattered about her feet.

"Don't cut yourself," he said, rushing to her.

She looked to him with her bright green eyes and soft, crooked smile. The vintage scotch stained her white blouse, slowly soaking through.

"Exactly how I like it," said Felix.

"I'm so sorry, Felix, I know it is expensive."

He helped her from the floor, carefully brushing the broken glass from her shoes. Her flesh showed through her scotch-drenched top, and Felix leaned in and bit her firmly on the neck. She winced and held a handful of his thick brown hair as he pulled open her blouse and guided her to the wall. He wrapped his arm around the small of her back and moved his mouth to her breasts, ingesting the essence of liquor from her skin.

"Not now," said Irina, pushing him away. "You're too drunk."

"Dearest, come …"

"It's every hour with you, I swear it."

She finished tying her blouse, then deflected his hands as they moved toward her hips. "After the party. I promise."

Felix shrugged, then gently placed his thumb upon her dimpled chin. "I'll hold you to it. You're gorgeous, you know. Especially when covered in an '88 vintage."

She smiled and kissed him on the cheek. "I must freshen up. I can't be seen again with both of us smelling like a distillery."

Felix watched her slender frame disappear into the Blue Parlor and he sighed. The image of her naked body sprawled upon the parlor's red carpet flashed into his mind. He broke the thought when his eyes caught the shattered serving tray.

Part I: Stăpânul

"Next time let the servants do the serving," he yelled.

He waited for her response. "And bring back a little tube of my favorite color, will you? I want to shock the party with red lips." Felix smiled his arrogant grin, hoping the comment would provoke her. No answer. He peered around the doorframe to see that she was gone, then looked to the shattered glass.

Pity.

The broken bottle still had a slug of scotch resting in its hull. Felix picked it up and sauntered drunkenly to the nearest fireplace. He placed the bottle on the mantel and fished a few pieces of broken glass from the brown liquid. He poured the salvage into his glass and brought it to his nose. The aroma soothed him. Felix tipped the drink to his lips and caught his dashing image in the mantel-to-ceiling mirror. He raised the glass to his reflection and puffed out his chest.

"To you, you handsome devil."

He stared at himself for a long moment, swaying a bit from drunkenness. The feelings of detachment that stalked him welled inside his gut. His body craved escape from the boredom, the listlessness, the anodyne drudgery that somehow pervaded every piece of his privileged life.

It shouldn't be like this.

The boredom grew white-hot like the bite of some vicious parasite ready to chew its way through his stomach. Felix peered to his own eyes in the looking glass, and he became filled with disgust. He wound up, cast his drink into the mirror, and reveled at his reflection shattering to a thousand jaded crystalline shards.

To you, you handsome devil.

*

Olaf sat in a deep high-back chair with his eyes closed. His cozy mahogany study seemed to shine by the light of a small fire crackling in the hearth next to him. He focused on the warmth as he awaited his visitor. Controlling his breath, he locked upon his intended vision and let the events play through in his mind.

"Will it be done?" came a voice.

Chapter 6

Olaf yelped and opened his eyes to see Rasputin standing before him. "You're the only one who could ever sneak up on me!" He smiled, revealing his yellow teeth.

"I take that as a compliment to my skills," said Rasputin, bowing to him slightly.

"And skilled you are, my old friend. Please, sit." Olaf motioned to a small hassock in front of his armchair.

"No, thank you."

"Suit yourself," said Olaf. "I see you are not here for any pleasantries."

"Have I ever been?"

Olaf grinned. "If anything, Grigori, you are consistent."

"I have provisioned everything as you and the seers have predicted. I must not fail. Can you see now?"

Olaf closed his eyes once more and rested his bald head upon his chair.

"And so—will it be done?" said Olaf as his eyes began to move underneath his eyelids and he hummed softly. "The actions around Alexei and Alexandra are perfectly in motion. All in the ranking coven are doing their part. But there will be external interference. Too cloudy to see exactly what that will be." Olaf took a few deep breaths, each time exaggerating his exhale. "Despite these intrusions to our plan, I envision success. The Nosferatu will prevail. But you must not waver or failure is certain."

"Very well. And Yusupov?"

Olaf turned up his nose and frowned. "It seems the sommelier is still interfering with the vision. I warned you he was to be terminated."

"He is too powerful for my skills alone, and there were more pressing details at hand. For now, he will remain in Paris. Alive."

"As he will," said Olaf softly. "Felix Yusupov then. In the short term, I can see your plan will further your goals. But you must isolate him immediately. I warn you to keep your focus on Alexei—Yusupov must remain secondary." Olaf began swaying his head slightly. "Your only hope at controlling Yusupov is to inject him with your venom as provisioned in the book—show him what he is meant to become. And even then … the magic surrounding him is extremely potent … I fear he will become too powerful for you—

Part I: Stăpânul

even me—when the truth is revealed. I simply cannot foresee events shrouded by magic of this magnitude. Nothing. Nothing like this has been seen or attempted since Vlad Drăculea himself."

"Vlad Drăculea himself indeed," said Rasputin, grinning slightly.

"Clever," said Olaf with pursed lips.

"And you're certain you can continue to mask these events surrounding Yusupov? None of the coven is aware?"

Olaf opened his eyes. "My dear Grigori. I have done so for twenty-nine years. This knowledge resides only between you, me, and the sommelier. The only loose end was Yusupov's parents, and I took care of them."

Rasputin stared at him for a long moment, satisfied with his answer. "Tonight's plan then. Shall I proceed?"

Olaf closed his eyes once more and began humming loudly.

"Yes. Proceed," he said. "But be warned—Pavlovich will lash out, and you must return to Yusupov only once the Nosferatu are spawned. And I assert to you once more—the girl must die if Yusupov is to be controlled. He is to be left with no attachments to this mortal coil."

Rasputin reached to Olaf's weathered hand and grasped it.

"Understood. Thank you again, my friend," said Rasputin. With a sudden gust of wind, he quickly transformed into a black mist and disappeared into the shadows.

Olaf stared into the fire, trying to focus on the warmth. He looked to a small side table, where a teapot and two small teacups sat.

"Whatever was I thinking?" he said aloud, shrugging his shoulders. "Vampires don't drink tea."

He leaned toward the table and poured himself a warm cup.

*

Felix and Irina arrived at the sterling palace of Grand Duke Dmitri Pavlovich shortly after 10:00 p.m. They stood at the base of the lobby's grand marble stair, the echo of rollicking music taunting them from the second floor. Two tuxedoed servants bowed as they

Chapter 6

approached the cranberry carpet that ran the center of the pillow-white stairs.

"The grand duke has been expecting you, sir."

"Party's arrived, Borya, my friend," said Felix. "Lead the way to the grand dastard!"

Irina poked him. "You're slurring. Be nice."

Felix looked to her. "They're just servants. Besides—think Dmitri's in any better state?"

He stood at the first stair and bowed, motioning for her to ascend. She smiled and shook her head. "Always the charmer."

Irina removed her fur and handed it to Borya. Underneath her coat was a deep red dress that ran to knee-length on her left and was cut nearly to her right hip. Felix looked her over, then kissed her. "I love you, Irina. You're perfect."

She blushed and flashed her flawless teeth.

Irina glided up the stairs alongside Felix's boisterous bounce. Borya led them down the expansive hall to the Silver Ballroom, where—even in the dim light—everything glimmered. A live ragtime band belted an energetic tune to the pleasure of the dance-frenzied guests. Felix scanned the hall and saw Dmitri's figure exactly where he expected. He held Irina's hand and led her to the far wall, where Dmitri leaned into the bar, engaged in playful conversation with a beautiful young brunette.

"Hi-dee-ho, my dastardly dastard," said Felix, raising his voice above the music.

Dmitri's handsome face turned with a sly glance, and he smirked at the sight of his friend. His blue eyes rolled back to the dark-haired girl. "Pardon me for one moment." He opened his arms and embraced Felix as his eyes turned to Irina. "I thought you'd never let him out again after last time," he said, smiling at her.

"The two of you together is always so scandalous, how could I refuse?"

"My sweet Irina," said Dmitri, bowing and kissing her gloved hand. "So good of you to come."

"I live for your parties, Grand Duke."

Dmitri grinned as he placed his hands on their shoulders—even at twenty-five he looked like an eager teen whenever he smiled.

Part I: Stăpânul

"You know," said Felix, "I can't help but admit the tinge of jealousy I get every time I come here. To think someone four years younger has three ballrooms to my two."

Dmitri stood away from them and ran his palms across the breast of his dark suit, drawing attention to the golden crest on his pocket. "That, old boy, is a benefit that comes with being second in line to the throne." Dmitri looked around the hall for a moment, appearing to take it all in. "Tell you what. Once I'm tsar, I'll give you this entire palace in trade for your perfect jawline and darling fiancée."

"Sold!" said Felix with an uproarious laugh as Irina affectionately slapped him on the shoulder.

"Come," said Dmitri, eyeing Irina. "I want you to meet someone."

He led them to the bar where the brunette, dressed in pearls and a slinky black dress, stood sipping her martini.

"Felix, Irina, this is Coco. She's a dear friend from Paris."

"Charmed," said Felix, kissing her hand.

"Nice to meet you both," she said with a French accent, and cast a lingering glance at Irina.

"What brings you from Paris?" asked Felix.

"The grand duke, of course."

The circle laughed.

"Honestly? Russia will never fall to the kaiser, but I have my doubts about Western Europe. So I thought I would sit out the war in style with Dmitri as my patron."

Dmitri planted a kiss firmly on her cheek. "Such a smart girl. Coco's going to change the world one day. She's a millinery maven."

Coco's eyes shot to the floor.

"Modest too," said Dmitri, wrapping his arm around her. He leaned toward the bar and motioned to the barman.

"What'll it be, my dear?" Dmitri said to Irina.

"Gin and tonic."

"A gin and tonic for the lovely lady in red, and a scotch, neat, for the sir. Give him a drop from my personal reserve."

The barman nodded and moved to his service station.

"How on earth did you get the band?" asked Felix.

Dmitri looked to the stage and smiled.

Chapter 6

"Logistical nightmares, my good man. Logistical nightmares. You have no idea the amount of money it takes to smuggle a ragtime band over a war-torn continent. I believe I've bribed every public official from Saint Petersburg to Chicago." He looked to Irina and his eyes lit up. "Do you like them? They're the toast of the United States."

"I love them." She looked to the party as people danced about every nook of the hall. Even smaller groups gathering around tables and sofas seemed to bounce with an air of exuberance.

The bartender returned. Dmitri handed Irina and Felix their drinks. He and Coco held their glasses high and everyone clinked them together.

"To autocracy!" shouted Dmitri.

"*Na zdorovye!*" responded the rest.

Felix downed his drink in one gulp, then joined Dmitri at the bar. Irina stood next to Coco and the two engaged in warm conversation.

"Another," said Felix.

Dmitri nodded to his barman, who had a drink ready on command. Felix placed the glass to his lips and grew aware of a sudden curling sensation in his stomach. He placed his palm on his gut and pushed inward, trying to quench the feeling.

"You all right?" asked Dmitri.

"I don't feel so well all of a sudden."

"We should have you lie down."

"I'm fine. It will pass."

Felix tried to ignore the pain as the room pulsed and his eyes lost focus.

"Actually, yes. I should lie down."

Dmitri turned to Coco. "Will you excuse us for a moment? Felix has fallen ill."

Irina moved to Felix and placed her hand on his arm. "Darling, what's the matter?"

Felix leaned into Dmitri, who positioned himself to support the weight.

"Perhaps he's too drunk?" asked Coco.

"He's fine. Typical Felix," said Dmitri. "You mind waiting while I lay him down?"

Part I: Stăpânul

Coco shook her head.

"Irina, you should come with us."

"Of course."

Dmitri supported Felix and led him to a slim door at the back of the ballroom. Irina followed them down a lean corridor into a study.

Felix's field of vision melded to blurry pulsations. He looked around the room, barely able to discern the presence of three other men dressed in black along the far wall. Felix's eyes became transfixed upon the man in the middle, who stared back with an unsettling, intense glare. He noticed the man had a black beard.

Two of the men helped Felix stand as his legs gave way. Felix heard voices and believed Irina and Dmitri were arguing. He looked to Irina as his vision fell sideways—sight and sound merged into one. Felix focused on Irina's red dress. It appeared she was hugging the man with the terrible gleam in his eye.

"It's too late, my sweet," said a voice.

Felix stared at Dmitri and tried to focus on his handsome features as they bowed and blurred like a reflection in a circus mirror. A red streak flashed from the corner of his eye, and Felix thought he saw Irina fall to the floor. He tried to move for her but was forced to the ground, too dizzy to struggle. He became aware of a strange suckling noise coupled with the sound of Irina weeping, then shrieking.

Sorry, old boy, came Dmitri's voice.

Felix felt a quick blow to the back of his neck.

Everything was black.

Chapter 7

Part I: Stăpânul

7

December 5, 1916 (OS), morning

Felix shot awake at 10:19 a.m. in his own bedroom—the late, arctic sunrise illuminated the white curtains covering his windows. His head hurt so badly he thought it must have been split open. He ran his fingers over his scalp, searching for a crack in his skull only to find a pronounced lump at the back of his head. He lay in bed and tried to piece together last evening's events. The last solid memory was meeting Dmitri's Parisian girlfriend.

Candy, or Catherine, or something … good-looking girl … I need water.

Felix pulled himself from bed, then walked to his bathing quarters. The bathroom was pitch-black. He fumbled for the light switch, and the Turkish bath lit up before him. His feet dragged across the cool tiles, guiding him to the freestanding sink. He turned the faucet and cupped his hand to collect the water. As he fed himself handfuls of water, his eyes finally focused on his reflection. Blood. He was covered in it. Dried blood soaked his hair, face, and torso. Red streams of it ran from his chin and hands as it mixed with the faucet water.

Christ!

He jumped backward and looked down to his naked body, feeling around for any cuts or stab wounds.

It's not mine.

Felix stumbled from the bathroom and ran to his bed. He pulled back the white sheets to see bloodstains covering his side. Irina's portion of the bedding remained undisturbed—her pillow still fluffed.

"Irina?"

Chapter 7

He ran from the room and down the hall, screaming for her. Forceful voices came from the main lobby, and he sprinted toward them unconcerned about his state of undress. Felix rounded the hallway to see several police officers standing in the hall arguing intensely with his service staff.

His master servant noticed Felix round the corner, and his face fell blank. A policeman turned to see Felix naked, covered in blood. He crouched a bit, then pulled his firearm and pointed it at Felix. The other officers, acting on the pronounced motion, targeted their weapons.

Felix raised his hands.

"Prince Felix?"

"Yes."

The policeman stood upright, his gun pointed at Felix.

"You're under arrest for the murder of Irina Alexandrovna."

*

It was late evening. Felix sat slumped in a wooden chair with his wrists handcuffed to its posts, and a flimsy wooden table placed just before him. His body ached all over, and he craved water. The police had hosed him down earlier to clean the blood from his body, and given him a pair of canvas prisoner skivvies that hardly insulated him from the chamber's permeating cold.

A dagger of a man in a dark suit, low-brimmed hat, and a stiff posture entered the room with several files tucked underneath his arm. He threw them on the table and stared into Felix's puffy eyes.

"Ready to talk?"

"Who are you?" Felix noticed he wore no badge on his blazer. "I didn't do anything."

"You murdered your fiancée. You were covered in her blood, and your bloodied fingerprints are all over the murder weapon, which we have recovered from your residence."

The man opened a file and pulled out a stack of handwritten letters.

"And I would say these are the final bullet."

Part I: Stăpânul

He threw the papers across the table. Felix looked over the stack, not recognizing the handwriting.

"What are they?"

"These, my friend, were found in your dresser, covered with your bloody fingerprints."

Felix looked to them once more. "I have never seen those in my life."

"Allow me to refresh your memory." He cleared his throat and read with an air of mockery. "My sweet Irina. How it pains me that we cannot be together. I think of you every waking second of every waking day. I promise you. When I ascend to the throne, you will be my bride, and you can forever be free from the grasp of that boorish child Felix."

Felix glared at him.

"Remember now, my Prince?"

"No."

"There's much more."

The man thumbed through the letters. "Here's another professing his love, begging her once more to leave you. And another describing a torrid rendezvous in your very own palace while you slept. All signed by the grand duke Dmitri Pavlovich."

"Enough."

"You found out about the affair and murdered her in a fit of jealousy."

"I absolutely did not. I demand to speak with someone from the imperial court. I—"

The man drove his fists into the wooden table.

"You're guilty. That's that."

"This is absurd," said Felix. "I demand to see the tsaritsa! Who are—"

The man swung around the table, landing a punch square in Felix's gut.

"That's my name," he said into Felix's ear. "I'll be back when you're ready to confess. You'll rot in here until you do."

He left the room. Felix sucked in deep pockets of air, trying to gather his wind. Once his stomach muscles stopped aching,

Chapter 7

he sat with his head slumped over and tried to hold back tears of rage welling in his eyes.

*

Over the next several hours, Felix drifted in and out of consciousness, usually waking to the pain of pins and needles in his legs. Occasional voices passed his chamber door, but the conversation fragments he heard were not about him. His mind flashed with terrible ideas about his fate as he tried to piece together last evening's events. The strange man's glare came to clear focus in his mind as fear and uncertainty singed his heart.

I'm doomed.

A click came from the door, and a man wearing a gray wool overcoat and fur hat entered. His face was cloaked by the room's shadows. The man listened at the door for a moment, then turned and sat opposite Felix. The naked light bulb illuminated the stranger's face and Felix recognized him at once—the grand duke himself with a fresh black eye and a swollen lower lip.

"I'm sorry, Felix. I came as soon as I could."

Felix stared at him for a long moment. "What happened to your face?" he asked while lurching forward a bit in his chair.

"I only have a few minutes. You must listen."

"I didn't do anything."

"I know. It wasn't supposed to happen this way."

A shiver crept across Felix's neck. "What are you talking about?"

He looked to Dmitri's blue eyes, but the grand duke quickly broke eye contact, unable to look Felix in the face.

"I don't know how to say any of this, so just listen."

"You were sleeping with her."

"Felix. There's no time."

"You drugged me."

Dmitri clenched his fist and shook it at Felix. "Shut your mouth and listen to me or they'll kill you."

Felix flexed, trying to break his bindings. "You're a dead man when I get out of here."

Part I: Stăpânul

Dmitri reached in his coat pocket and pulled out a revolver. He pointed it at Felix.

"I'm trying to save you. Shut your mouth for once."

He placed the gun on the corner of the table and fished a key from his coat pocket. He knelt behind Felix and loosened the handcuffs to the point where he could slip free. Dmitri moved to the door. He listened intently to the passing voices, then turned to Felix, who was massaging his sore wrists.

"She wasn't supposed to die. He betrayed me."

"Who's 'he'?"

"I'd never hurt Irina. You know that. I can't tell you anything else." Dmitri's eyes grew wide. "Listen to me. Outside, to the left, is the exit to the back alley. The door is ajar."

"Dmitri—"

"Shut up. My driver is waiting for you at the end of the alley. He'll take you to Moscow Station, and you're on the next train out. There's a suitcase inside my limousine with a fake passport and money. The amount should suffice you indefinitely."

"I'm not leaving. I haven't done anything."

Felix stood and forced his chest into Dmitri.

"You're in great danger, Felix!" Dmitri pressed him away with his palms. "Do as I tell you and you might survive. Just promise me you'll go far away. The other side of the world." Dmitri looked deeply into Felix's eyes. "I was told you were only to be drugged and sent away."

"You're worthless," huffed Felix.

Dmitri sat in the chair. "I never wanted any harm to come to her. She did love you, Felix. Giving you one last hope of survival is the only thing I could think of to honor her memory. Take this act as my penance."

Dmitri gestured toward the gun, and Felix grabbed it.

"It's not loaded," said Dmitri. "So don't bother."

"How do I know I won't be gunned down the moment I step outside this door?"

"You don't. Hit me, Felix. Do it."

They stared at each other with a strong sense of emptiness—the hollow feeling of brother turned against brother.

Chapter 7

"Use the butt. Hit here, it's already numb." He pointed to his black-and-blue cheekbone.

Felix stood over him and raised the gun into the air. His chin curled, and he smashed the butt into Dmitri's face. Dmitri fell with the blow, tipping the chair.

"Now go," he yelled, never looking up at Felix. "Leave the gun."

Felix dropped it and dashed from the room. He entered the dingy hallway to see the exit ajar just as Dmitri had promised. He stepped into the cold night and fled along the icy bricks on his bare feet. At the end of the alley was a limousine—Felix could see the imperial insignia on the door even in the darkness. He jumped inside the car, and the driver pressed the gas.

The back seat of the vehicle was piled high with Felix's own clothing. He sorted through it, pulling the warmest garments he could find. Inside a suitcase sat bundles of cash. Felix took the money belt on top of the rubles and strapped it around his waist. He shoved one bundle into the pouch, then dressed himself.

*

Felix stepped from the limousine twenty minutes later, his cloaked silhouette cast against the lights of Moscow Station. The car pulled away, and he stood with the suitcase grasped tightly in his gloved hand. He looked down to the snowy road and leaned back a bit as the packed snow crunched beneath his heels. Just as he was about to move toward the station, four police officers emerged from the front gates. Fear pricked his spine. The officers stood in a single line, chatting about the abysmal freezing wind.

Felix stared at the twinkling station lights for a long moment, finally convinced the police paid him no mind.

Irina's smile flashed through his head.

He dropped the suitcase, spilling the cash. The wind surged through the money and scattered it off into frigid city streets. Felix watched it blow away. As the last ruble whisked off into the darkness, he turned on his heels and walked back into the Saint Petersburg night.

Part I: Stăpânul

8

December 6, 1916 (OS), early evening

"Tell them he was mauled by his printing press," growled Petrov through the phone receiver.

"Sir, nobody's going to believe it." Rurik rolled his eyes and pulled the phone slightly away from his ear.

"I don't care. Bolshoy and the entire surrounding district will shut down immediately if this gets out. Nicholas will have my head."

"Sir, I—"

"It's cause for frenzy, Coroner. Do as I tell you!"

"Constable, with all due respect, the steward-caught-under-the-train story was almost too much. I don't believe the papers will endure a print shop owner shredded to bits by a printing press. Is that possible?"

"That's the story! That's what you'll say, goddamn it!"

Petrov hung up the phone.

Rurik paused for a moment before doing the same. The morgue was quiet as usual. A sudden rapping upon the back door startled him.

Rurik opened his desk drawer and removed his Nagant 7.62 mm revolver. He placed the gun in his lab coat pocket and walked to the back door. The impatient knocking continued. Standing upon a crate, he peered through the small window over the door. A man in the alley stood against the brick, his face concealed by a high collar that almost met his low-brimmed hat.

Rurik opened the door and peeked through four large security chains.

"May I help you?"

Chapter 8

"I'm hoping to speak with Coroner Kozlov."

"I am he," said Rurik with a rising tone in his voice.

"Mr. Kozlov, I am here on orders from the imperial court to discuss the murder of Irina Alexandrovna."

"You're not Okhrana. Who are you?"

"Um. I—"

"Your name?" Rurik feigned a smile, appearing to mock the stranger with his repeated blinking.

"I'm uhh …"

Rurik slammed the door.

Felix stared at the door for a moment, then scanned the brick walls searching for a means to scale to the roof. A loud click filled the alley, followed by the rattling of chains. The door swung open. Rurik leapt into the alley and shoved his gun into Felix's side.

"Hands up!"

Felix threw his hands in the air. Rurik forced him inside and slammed the door behind them.

"You're Prince Felix, aren't you?"

"Look, I—"

"Keep your hands up! Yes or no?"

"I am. Don't shoot."

"Does anybody know you're here?"

"No."

"How did you escape?"

"They … someone freed me. I'm not sure why."

Felix felt the barrel's pressure ease from his back. Rurik uncocked the gun and pocketed it.

"Very brave of you to come. Brave and stupid."

Felix slowly turned around to see Rurik standing with both hands in his lab coat—an odd smirk accentuated the proud laugh lines along his cheeks.

"I can't believe it's you!" said Rurik. "A miracle you're here."

"I was hoping—"

"You can put your hands down. Please, follow me. You're safe for now. I'm Rurik Kozlov, by the way. But apparently you knew that."

Part I: Stăpânul

Rurik locked the door, then led Felix down the hall to his office. Felix sat in a chair at the front of Rurik's desk.

"Have you seen this?" Rurik handed him a newspaper.

Felix looked over the front page. An illustration bearing his likeness sat under the title "Murderer Prince Escapes Jail."

"Someone has it out for you."

Felix perused the first paragraph.

> Saint Petersburg, Dec. 6—Prince Felix Yusupov, famed royal darling and godfather to the tsarevich, escaped from Saint Petersburg City Jail last evening after being arrested for the murder of his fiancée, Irina Alexandrovna. A city-wide manhunt has been underway since early this morning.

Felix felt his intestines squirm. "I didn't kill her. I don't know why this is happening."

"I believe you. Well, actually. There is one small thing you can do to quench any doubts."

"What's that?"

Rurik slid a hand mirror across the desk.

"Turn that over and look into it."

Felix cocked his head.

"It's important," said Rurik.

Felix reached for the mirror. "Is this a joke?"

Rurik shook his head with an eager air about him. Felix flipped over the mirror and looked into it.

"What do you see?"

Felix stared at himself for a moment. "A guy who needs a decent night's sleep?"

Rurik laughed, his large Adam's apple bobbing in his throat. "You see? You're not the killer!"

"Huh?"

"You can put it down."

Rurik moved to a bookshelf piled with random papers.

"If you were the killer, you'd have thrown that mirror down, petrified of your own reflection."

Chapter 8

"I'm not sure what you're getting at, Mr. Kozlov."

Rurik exited the room and shuffled through a large filing cabinet. A moment later, he returned carrying a stack of newspapers.

"Luckily for you, I have been collecting these clippings for decades from far and wide." He plopped the papers on the desk. "This is the murderer of your fiancée. And two other bodies I had in the morgue."

Felix looked at the top newspaper.

"Sleepwalker Strikes in Bordeaux"

He flipped through a few more clippings:

"Famed Killer Mangles Again"

"Possible Sleepwalker Victims Found Near Paris"

"Sleepwalker Returns to Bucharest"

"These are the only ones I managed to acquire. We believed at the time the Sleepwalker was dead and these were merely sensationalist stories. But I wanted a record just in case."

Felix's jawline pulsed as he read through the articles. He looked to Rurik.

"I don't understand what this has to do with me. I just need to see Irina."

"Impossible. Her body—along with those of the other victims—was ordered cremated this morning."

Felix looked to the floor and clenched his fists. "Okhrana?"

"I don't know for certain. It's just a habit of mine. Whenever men dressed in black trench coats show up and order me to do something, I do it. You'd be surprised how many years it can add to your life span. Fortunately, I was able to preserve a portion of one of the bodies without their knowledge."

Felix shook his head and pressed his palms into his face. "How did she die?"

"Do you really want to know?"

Felix gritted his teeth and nodded. Thick tears ran down his face and he looked to the ceiling.

"Her blood was sucked from her body, and she was chewed to bits."

Felix's face flushed as his eyes shot to Rurik. "Chewed?"

Rurik nodded and gestured to the newspapers.

Part I: Stăpânul

"What do you know about this ... Sleepwalker?"

Felix settled for a moment.

"Nothing. Other than the legends. I read about the train steward."

"Well, I will tell you that the Sleepwalker has been murdering people throughout Europe for the past two decades. It was given that sobriquet for slaughtering its victims mostly after midnight. And now this monster is here in Saint Petersburg. It has murdered three people that I know of thus far: the boy from the train, a merchant on Bolshoy Prospekt, and your fiancée. The question is why are you being framed for one of the murders? What's your connection?"

"There is none," said Felix loudly.

"Keep your voice down."

Felix quickly looked over his shoulder. "Is someone else here?"

"No. I would just prefer if you didn't shout."

Felix furrowed his brow, annoyed at Rurik's tone.

"I'm not implying you're directly connected, but somebody out there has framed you for murder. A gruesome killing clearly carried out by this specter. You have no indication why?"

"I don't."

"Do you know who framed you?"

"Yes ... well ... I know Grand Duke Pavlovich is involved ... he freed me from jail, said there are others."

"Interesting. He frames you then frees you."

"He said freeing me was his penance and that her murder was an accident."

"It was no accident. That I can assure you." Rurik frowned and rapped his fist upon the desk. "This complicates things." Rurik suddenly pulled the gun from his pocket—his eyes darted to Felix. "Hands up!"

Felix threw his hands into the air. "Why?"

"*Decembrie şaisprezece, Nosferatu sfârşitul lumii!*" shouted Rurik.

Felix's face lost color as Rurik came around the desk and stood over him, pointing the barrel at his forehead.

"Are you Black Hundred?" shouted Rurik.

Felix turned his head away from the gun and his cheeks began to twitch.

Chapter 8

"I don't know what you're talking about," breathed Felix.

A click reverberated through the room as Rurik cocked the gun and placed it to Felix's head.

"Are you Black Hundred? Lie to me and I will shoot you down!" Rurik pressed the barrel more firmly into Felix's cheek.

"No! I don't know what that is."

"Look at me! Into my eyes." Rurik stood back, pointing to his own eyeballs. "*Decembrie şaisprezece, Nosferatu sfârşitul lumii!* Are you Black Hundred?"

Felix slowly turned his head and stared into the dark circle of the barrel. He looked to Rurik's eyes.

Rurik glared at him, searching for some revealing truth. He nodded, then uncocked the gun and placed it back into his pocket. "You don't speak Romanian."

"No."

"Sorry about that," said Rurik with a chuckle. "Had to be sure. You can put your hands down."

Rurik leaned against his desk and folded his arms—a broad pursed-lip smile on his face.

Felix slowly lowered his hands, and blinked repeatedly as he searched for something to say. *Great work, old boy. Your only ally is a raging lunatic.*

He looked to the office door and wondered if he should make a dash for it. "Mr. Kozlov, I mean no disrespect, but I came here for some clue as to who killed her. If it's this Sleepwalker, then I assure you I will spare nothing to have this man's head on a plate."

"Well, that's just it," said Rurik. "From the newspapers and legends, it seems obvious the Sleepwalker is human. But when you see the remains of the first victim's body, it will become clear to you. This killer is no man."

Felix was slack-jawed.

"Are you squeamish, Prince Felix?"

"I don't think so."

Rurik curled his chin and nodded. "Come with me. I will show you."

He glided from the room as if inviting Felix to a grand ballroom jaunt. Felix sat for another moment, shaking his head.

Part I: Stăpânul

Why the hell did I come here?

Rurik's voice echoed down the barren hall. "Prince Felix, come! There's no time!"

*

Felix sat in a chair next to the autopsy table and peered at the rusty bin covered by a bloodstained tarp.

"Fortunately, my visitors this morning were not entirely diligent in their stay," said Rurik, sorting through the bin. "I will warn you. What you're going to see is incredibly grotesque. But you must look carefully, objectively. I need an open mind."

"Is it—what you're about to show me—is it how Irina died?"

Rurik turned to him. "Yes. We can stop if you think it's too much."

"I want to know." Felix nodded then swallowed, trying to clear his throat. "Show me."

Rurik reached back into the bin and produced a forearm of Rodion Kvoss—the hand still attached.

"Look here," said Rurik, holding the arm out.

Felix took one look at the arm and shot out of his chair. He clenched his fists and stumbled to a utility sink, where he seized upon the rim and lifted with all his strength, trying to yank it from the wall. He grunted and huffed in a rage, finally tugging at the faucet and bending it from its socket. He let out a scream and fell to the floor.

Rurik rushed to him.

"Felix, we can stop. It's too much for you. Please don't destroy my things."

Felix slobbered on the floor, occasionally punching the broken tile. His bloodshot eyes looked up to Rurik.

"I'll kill whoever did that to her." Tears ran down his face.

Rurik placed his hand on Felix's shoulder and helped him up.

"I believe that you will, my friend. Perhaps we should save this for when you are ready."

"No. I want to see it. Forgive me."

Chapter 8

Felix composed himself and returned to the chair. Rurik stood at the bin and turned to him.

"Are you certain?"

Felix nodded, gripping the underside of his chair.

Rurik picked up the same body part and held it before Felix. With a slim metal pointer, Rurik motioned to an area where the elbow was ripped from the forearm. "Pay attention here. These are bite marks. No metal instrument was used. Can you tell it was teeth?"

Felix nodded.

"If you follow the tear through the muscle to the bone, you see right here at this ledge. This is where the killer's upper and lower molars split the bone. You can see the markings here in the marrow and also here. It is clearly a bite—agreed?"

"It … yes. It appears so."

"Very well," said Rurik. "Then you will see here in the bruised flesh. Again, clear teeth marks. The killer in its frenzied feeding then bit higher upon the arm to chew through it, notice the finishing bite here." Rurik made a chomping motion, bringing his teeth together.

Felix blushed.

"I sense you're uncomfortable. Please, I mean no disrespect to you or the body. But it's very important if you are to understand what we're up against. One moment."

Rurik walked to another cast iron sink, where his dinner plate sat with discarded chicken bones. He picked up a leg bone and walked toward Felix.

"Let me ask you, Felix. Have you ever been enjoying ground meat, reveling in the tenderness, and then had it all ruined by a piece of gristle?"

"Yes."

"It hurts. Makes you want to scream as if your teeth have cracked apart."

"Certainly."

"And it's only a tiny piece of bone. Here." Rurik tossed him the chicken bone. "Bite through it."

Felix smiled.

Part I: Stăpânul

"I'm serious. Bite through it ... what? You cannot? It is but a little bone. Surely you can do it!"

"Of course not."

"It would shatter your teeth, no? Then logically you must ask yourself. What manner of man could bite through a tiny chicken bone without hurting his teeth? A madman?"

Rurik removed a tumid remnant of Rodion's upper arm and biceps. He laid it next to the forearm and pointed to the bones poking from the muscle.

"But have that madman try to bite through a human's arm—through the humerus here, through the radius, and also the ulna bone—in one bite. I challenge you to find me a human who could do that. I challenge you to find me a polar bear."

"So it's an animal doing this? Some sort of large wolf?"

"Don't be coy. This was no animal. Then finally you must ask ... What type of weapon could do this? An axe? These marks are too precise for that. This is one crunch of a jaw. You're being framed for a murder with human psyche behind it, but the perpetrator is not human. This was the work of *vámpir*—the living vampire."

Rurik looked as if he had won his case in court and proudly crossed his arms. Felix was silent.

"Let me make sure I understand this," Felix finally said, clearing his throat. "You believe that a member of the imperial court who happens to be my ex–best friend framed me for a murder perpetrated by a vampire?"

Rurik shot his finger into the air. "Exactly!"

Felix hung his head. *I shouldn't have come.* "I mean no disrespect, Mr. Kozlov—"

"Please, it's Rurik. Rurik Borovitch Kozlov."

"Rurik, thank you. It's just, I'm trying to find the man responsible for this, and although it was very nice of you to go through all that—I'm very serious about avenging my fiancée."

"Ha! It sounds far-fetched, I know. But no offense, you are a privileged lad. It has blinded you."

"I don't—"

"Where are you staying?"

"Some rattrap south of Saint Petersburg."

Chapter 8

Rurik snapped his fingers. "Do you have carriage fare?"

"Yes."

He clapped his hands in excitement. "Come! You will see."

*

The horse-drawn carriage traveled to a small industrial area on the brim of south Saint Petersburg. It bounced along a narrow, snowy road before stopping in front of a mesh-iron fence that encircled a barren property. Felix peered into the night and noticed a burned-out building about thirty yards from the roadside.

Rurik exited the carriage and walked to the driver.

"Will you wait?" he asked, extending a handful of money.

The carriage driver held the wad up to his lantern and nodded.

"Thank you," said Rurik.

Rurik rounded the horse and walked to a broken section of the fence. He pulled the opening wide, and Felix followed. They walked toward the fire-damaged hovel. Rurik pulled two flashlights from a canvas bag strapped to his back and handed one to Felix. They flicked on their beacons and trudged through the pristine snow.

Rurik motioned toward the building with his flashlight. "I find it difficult to believe you've never heard of the Black Hundred. You're a member of the same social circle."

Felix shook his head. "I promise you. I know nothing of it."

"Too busy counting your gold to pay attention?" Rurik smiled, then patted him on the shoulder. They continued toward the structure as Felix began to feel annoyed by Rurik's tone.

"You're familiar with Khlysts?" asked Rurik.

"Only by name. The Siberian cult?"

"Cult is too kind. Khlysts are a germ—the living legacy of evil incarnate—lurking in the shadows of every palace in Russia."

"Preposterous," said Felix, looking to him. "Khlysts are peasants, mere swamp gypsies—"

"But the Black Hundred are not. They are royals and top government officials. An elitist Khlysts sect operating in Saint Petersburg and Moscow for over a quarter century. All the best people participating in mass orgies, blood ritual, human sacrifice. Perhaps you've dined with some of them?"

"Easy, Rurik."

"Sorry. I don't mean to be crass, but my hatred of them runs deep."

They reached the outside of the structure, and Rurik turned to Felix. "I simply think it might interest you that one of the sect's highest-ranking members is your friend Grand Duke Pavlovich."

Felix's face grew red. Rurik crouched into the building by forcing himself between two broken beams. He knelt to the floor and peered out at Felix.

"Well. Come on," said Rurik, motioning to Felix with his hand.

"I order you to change your tone about the aristocracy!"

"Order?" Rurik laughed. "I'd be mindful of your circumstances—I'm the only friend you have."

Felix looked back to the carriage, then to the barrenness around him. Rurik extended his hand. "Come. Save your pouting for later."

Felix grabbed Rurik's hand and shimmied inside. He shined his flashlight around the gutted building, tracing his light along peaked beams and rafters that had survived the fire.

"Was this a church?" asked Felix.

Rurik walked ahead of him toward what appeared to be the nave.

"This was a secret worship temple of the Black Hundred. Mind the floorboards," said Rurik, pointing out large holes riddling the charred hardwood. Felix shined his light downward, noticing what appeared to be a shallow subbasement beneath the floor.

"It burned down two years ago," continued Rurik. "After this was discovered." He turned to Felix and handed him a ruby-colored amulet. Felix shined his light on it, and its gold trim cast a halo of light onto the floor. He looked it over for a minute. The face was inscribed with a golden hieroglyphic depicting a large fanged bat.

"That belongs to the people who framed you—the Black Hundred."

Felix turned the amulet on its side and ran his finger along the inscription: *Nosferatu sfârşitul lumii :: Decembrie 16, 1916 :: Copilul Sângelui nascut de Eva, aducatoarea intunericului etern.*

"What does it mean?"

Chapter 8

"'Nosferatu apocalypse, December 16, 1916,' followed by a proverb, 'The Bloodchild born from Eve, harbinger of Darkness evermore.' Take a look at this."

Felix followed Rurik to the front of the sanctuary. They stood at the base of a burned-out altar. Rurik shined his flashlight on the wall. Upon the charred wood were traces of the same pictograph inscribed on the amulet. Felix's eyes caught a portion of the proverb that remained unsoiled: *Sf   l   ii Decemb   16 1916   ilul.*

"The date's in ten days. You're sure this burned down two years ago?"

"Yes. I'm the one who did it."

Felix looked at Rurik, who glared at the wall scroll with an air of stern brutality about him.

"That amulet you're holding …"

Felix shined his light onto it and inspected the pictograph.

"A ten-year-old murder victim—a girl—was delivered to the morgue with terrible mutilations to her skin. While performing the autopsy, I found that lodged inside her cervix."

Felix huffed, disgusted by the thought. "Here, I don't want to hold this," he said, holding the amulet to Rurik.

"It's been washed," said Rurik, snatching the jewel.

Felix relaxed a bit, but still felt uneasy at the thought.

"Her body was found here," said Rurik. "Many children have gone missing over the years anywhere a Khlysts temple is discovered. It's my suspicion they are all victim to this same ritual sacrifice. The only child on record to have escaped was brutally murdered along with her family days after speaking with police."

"I don't believe anyone in the aristocracy would be involved in something this grim."

Rurik let out a long breath, watching its vapor trail.

"As far as the aristocracy is concerned, you're lucky I didn't find you on my slab with one of those shoved up your ass." He held out the amulet to Felix, then pocketed it.

Felix stood for a long moment with a pronounced scowl upon his face. He fidgeted slightly, appearing to silently manage a temper tantrum.

"Relax, Felix. I'm trying to help you."

Part I: Stăpânul

Felix exhaled. "So I have this cult after me?"

"Yes. So it would be wise to stay hidden. You must know something about them or they wouldn't have tried to get rid of you."

"I have nothing to do with them."

"I know. But you're considered a threat for some reason."

Felix shined his flashlight to the fanged bat upon the wall.

"Why the bat?"

"*Desmodus draculae*. God of Khlysts holy doctrine. The crux of their worship centers on these giant bats and their transformation to savage, manlike vampire gods. It is said that he who summons and controls these Nosferatu will rule over all things living and dead."

"And you believe that?"

"Every word," said Rurik, shining his light on a portion of the wall underneath the bat. "Notice there is a man and woman. In her arms a child—see the halo? Above its head ... this scroll is a depiction of a ritual that will bring Nosferatu to the living plane."

Felix traced his light along the faintness of the human figures.

"*Ciclul strigoiului viu*," began Rurik. "The cycle of the vampire. The most sacred ritual in Khlysts doctrine. It preaches that vampires are the pinnacle of might and order over all living things—humans are merely bloodstock." Rurik traced his spotlight to the man and woman. "To initiate the cycle and bring the vampire to its rightful place, a man and woman mate after becoming infected by the bite of the *draculae* bats. See there—bite marks on each neck, fangs in their mouths." Rurik shined the spotlight upon the haloed baby. "If the child born from the union is of human form, the bats will then transform to Nosferatu. The cycle is complete, and the Nosferatu are forever linked and under the control of this child. If the baby is stillborn ... or, *worse* ... the bats will fall dormant until someone tries again." Rurik shined his light on the bat. "They are like locusts—coming from their dark underworld whenever the conditions are right."

Felix flicked off his light.

"Look, Rurik—I don't believe in the Bible. Let alone—"

"You must."

Felix tensed. "You hear that?"

Chapter 8

They crouched at the sound of an approaching automobile and ran to the wall for cover. Felix peeked around a wooden beam to see a limousine pull behind the carriage. He watched a figure in a trench coat exit the back door and stand with his back to the car.

"Felix Yusupov?" yelled the man.

Felix's eyes shot to Rurik, who held his revolver flat against a plank of wood. He cocked the weapon and nodded to Felix.

"Felix? It's Dmitri. I know you're in there. Come out. Make things easy."

Rurik shook his head. "I thought he freed you?"

"He did," whispered Felix. "On the condition I leave forever."

"Advice you should have taken."

Felix kept his voice low. "What do we do?"

"Stay still," said Rurik. He pulled a small pair of binoculars from his coat pocket and looked through the broken wood.

"Felix," shouted Dmitri. "Come out so we can talk."

"How many are there?" asked Felix.

"Just him. And a driver."

"How did they find us?"

Rurik scanned Dmitri and then his driver, who stepped from the vehicle. Even in the darkness, Rurik could see the driver's eyes were closed and his hand was held outward, moving in circles.

"The driver," said Rurik. "He's a seer."

"A what?"

"A witch," said Rurik, clutching his fist. "Well, Felix, for what it's worth, I wholly believe you're not on their side now."

Another automobile and a covered truck arrived on the scene. Two Stovâjĭk men, both identifiable by their tall sikke hats, exited the auto, while two others wearing what appeared to be gas masks emerged from the truck. One Stovâjĭk walked to the carriage driver and shot him in the head. He then freed the horse and fired several shots over the animal as it ran off into the night.

"Hand me the binoculars," said Felix. He brought them to his eyes and saw three men move to the back of the truck and remove a large hunk of metal.

"What are they doing?" hissed Rurik.

Part I: Stăpânul

Felix shrugged. "Can't see. The two in masks are assembling something."

Rurik snatched the binoculars and spied on the men. His eyes widened. "Get down!" He flattened himself to the floor and yanked on Felix's collar, pulling him downward.

Dmitri stood at the perimeter of the fence while the masked men set up a Vickers machine gun just in front of him.

"Come out, Felix. This is your final warning." He paused for a long moment. "Very well. And to your mystery friend with the protection spell masking his identity. We will figure out who you are, and when we do—you and everyone you know will be butchered." Dmitri signaled to the masked men, then turned and walked to his limousine. One of the masked men knelt behind the machine gun, while the other positioned himself to feed the ammunition.

The sound of gunfire ripped through the quiet evening as the wood above Felix and Rurik exploded. They threw their arms over their heads and crawled along the rickety floor as the repetitive thuds of machine-gun fire cycled in the distance. The remaining skeleton of the building collapsed in upon them.

*

The assassins fired for five solid minutes, shredding every portion that remained of the building. They packed up the machine gun, and four men moved in toward the hovel's remnants, each with a canister of gas in hand.

Dmitri stood at the fence and watched his men walk about the wreckage, dumping gasoline on the remaining floorboards.

"Any bodies? Bits?" he shouted.

One of the men looked to him. "No, sir. Nothing."

"Move to the other side—any tracks?"

The man navigated to the opposite side and glanced at the snow. "No, sir. Only the set leading in. I'm certain we got them."

Dmitri nodded and continued to watch from the distance.

*

Chapter 8

Rurik and Felix lay on their stomachs in the slim space beneath the floorboards and watched as the gasoline dripped through the holes in the floor. The sharp smell permeated their surroundings.

"What now?" whispered Felix.

"Wait here."

Rurik crawled toward the brick foundation and looked back to Felix. "This way," he said, waving his hand.

"I can't stand small spaces," said Felix on heavy breath.

Rurik slid his way back to Felix.

"Crawl with me, hurry."

Rurik pulled on Felix's shoulder and helped him forward. They reached the foundation and Rurik ran his fingers along the wobbly cement blocks. He tapped Felix and motioned to the wall. They shoved their weight against two bricks, almost knocking them from the setting. At that moment, footsteps sounded directly above them. Rurik rolled on his back and looked upward as the shadow dumped gasoline over the floorboards, some of it pouring into the sub-basement.

Rurik whispered to Felix, who nodded then planted his back against the brick. Rurik crawled toward a wide opening in the floorboards and peered through. Shadows of the men still shuffled about. He pulled his Kraemer lighter from his pant pocket and struck the flint wheel several times. The wick caught flame and he threw it through a hole in the floorboard. He crawled quickly toward Felix. The remaining floor structure above exploded, igniting the gas that dripped into the subbasement. Rurik reached Felix just as a large portion of the floorboards caved in—flames, smoke, and ash flooded the crawlspace as Felix shoved his weight against the bricks and knocked them from the foundation. He pulled Rurik from the fire.

Both men slithered onto the snow. Felix stood and swatted out a fire on Rurik's pants and jacket.

"Are you burned?" shouted Felix.

"Singed," said Rurik, brushing his shoulder.

They stood back from the glaring heat and watched the flames engulf what was left of the structure—harrowing screams rose into the night.

Part I: Stăpânul

Rurik looked to Felix. "Hoisted by their own petards!" He placed his fists on his hips, impressed as he watched the men twist and scream inside the inferno. "I never thought I'd have the chance to say that literally," he said, smiling.

Felix heard Dmitri's limousine fire its ignition.

"Give me your gun!"

Rurik fumbled through his pockets and handed the revolver to Felix, who took off running around the front of the building.

Felix continued to push his way through the snow as Dmitri's driver slowly maneuvered the limousine around the other vehicles. Felix fired the gun and a bullet shattered the limousine's side window. Dmitri spotted Felix charging through the snow, unloading three more bullets into the limousine.

"Go!" yelled Dmitri, ducking to the floor. The car's wheels spun, unable to find traction in the snow.

Felix shot two more bullets into the back of the car as it lurched forward and gained traction. Another moment and it was off. He threw the gun after the limousine, and it sunk into a snowdrift in the distance.

"Hey!" yelled Rurik. "That's my only revolver."

Felix stood hunched over, trying to catch his breath.

"Sorry. I wasn't thinking."

Rurik scanned the snowdrifts, unable to spot the gun's point of entry.

"There goes that gun." Rurik patted Felix on the back. "Come, we must hide you."

They jumped in the empty automobile and drove away. Felix looked back to the burning building. He thought of Irina and quietly wished he could relive the screams of the men as they burned to death.

Chapter 9

Part I: Stăpânul

9

СОВЕРШЕННО СЕКРЕТНО [TOP SECRET]
Sfânta Biblie al Strigoiului Viu
[Holy Bible of the Living Vampiric Witch]
The Book of Change :: Converting the Living

I

A vampire will need to enlist converts in his campaigns against the living. My findings seek not to understand the differences between converting male and female humans, only to warn of the outcome. The vampire bent on converts must prepare for these events.

II

Silence is the passage to vampirism for males. Upon being bitten, most males will fall to a restful sleep within hours. Others may wander until sunrise, growing increasingly agitated until sleep takes them. All will rest until the next night and wake hungry. It is advised to have bloodstock prepared—be it a pig or a dog, but preferably a child. The taste of fear emitted into its bloodstream will calm the awakening vampire.

The male will act unexpectedly violent toward other vampires until his senses are about him. I have killed many male converts who are too erratic upon waking and recommend this—I will discuss reasons in later verses.

Chapter 9

III

The female becoming period is quite unpredictable compared to that of the male. I have experienced transformation in as short as several hours and as long as one week. The longer transformations are indicative of a more docile vampire upon waking.

As the vampire blood slowly overtakes her own, the female, although asleep, will become terribly violent—fits of body contortion followed by screaming. I assure you the screaming is something that will disquiet the bravest of hearts. If conversion is to take place where it may be discovered by humans, it is advised the female be buried deep underground during her dormancy. As mentioned in the Book of Ritual, I have found keeping them submerged underwater is the best method of silencing the fits.

The waking female is always quite docile, seemingly waiting to be fed. I have experimented with this, and have seen that transformed females will wander for weeks, even months (perhaps longer), feeding only on small animals—never understanding their unusual cravings until shown the delight of human blood.

—**Vlad Drăculea, 1456**

*

The Saint Petersburg night still brimmed with activity. In the Petrogradskaya district, a horse-drawn carriage parked itself in front of the expansive Taneyev residence. The driver walked up the narrow stairs and rang the doorbell. A moment later, a tall servant opened the door.

"I will inform them you have arrived," he said.

The driver returned to the carriage, and two full-figured young women bundled tightly against the cold emerged from the mansion. They giggled and chatted merrily as they hopped into the carriage. The driver secured the door, then snapped the horses into motion. Their hooves striking the cobblestones echoed for several blocks.

The carriage traveled over the snowy streets into the depressed areas of southeast Saint Petersburg, not too far from Moscow Station.

Part I: Stăpânul

It came to a stop in front of a nondescript building distinguished only by a large red candle in the front window. The driver dismounted and opened the door. The Taneyev sisters exited the buggy and entered the building.

They were greeted by a warm foyer with a small fire kindling in a potbelly stove. The circular room was adorned with red velvet drapes. Anna and Sana removed their fur bundles and hung them next to the stove. They sat on a wide bench next to the front entrance. Anna reached to a small golden bell centered on a narrow table to her right. She rang the bell twice, then quickly placed it back on the table.

The sisters smiled at one another as their brown curls settled about their pleasant faces. With cheeks still blushed from the cold, they beamed with an air of healthful radiance. They sat patiently for a moment, peering at the curtains opposite them.

"Where is she?" whispered Sana.

"Shh. We must clear our thoughts."

Anna reached to the bell and rang it once more. Still, no one appeared from the curtain.

"Madam Lenora?" beckoned Sana.

Sana and Anna jumped when a tall, bearded man emerged from the curtains. Upon noticing his manner of dress, they quickly made the sign of the cross.

"Forgive us, Father. We know this is not the place to look for answers."

"On the contrary, my good sisters," he said. His booming voice was playful. "Please, follow me."

He whipped open the curtains to reveal Madam Lenora's candlelit parlor—a darkened chamber with a round, felt-covered table positioned at its center. Atop the table glistened the mystical crystal ball the sisters had come to depend on for answers to all their questions.

"Who are you? Where's Madam Lenora?"

"Forgive me. I am Grigori—Madam Lenora's replacement. She has fallen … ill." He bowed cordially. "I beg you, come into my parlor."

Chapter 9

The starets smiled and revealed what Anna thought were unusually large canines that seemed to shine against the backdrop of the red velvet curtains.

"Why, Father, what big teeth you have!"

"The better to … taste you with, my sweet Anna." He bowed, never taking his dark eyes from her.

Anna blushed and leaned toward Sana. "He's handsome." Sana nodded and the two giggled as they shuffled past Rasputin into the candlelit parlor.

He sat opposite them as they stared deeply into the crystal ball.

"Excuse me, Father," said Sana. "I mean no disrespect, but I thought startsy were forbidden from participating in the occult."

Rasputin looked to her.

"Ahh, my dear Sana, but I am blessed with the gift of foresight. Would it not be a shame in the eyes of our Lord if I did not use my gift? 'If a man's gift is prophesying, let him use it in proportion to his faith'!"

The Taneyev sisters appeared charmed.

"Romans 12:6," said Rasputin. "I have found another path to enlightenment, and that truth makes me no less holy in the eyes of our Lord."

"And certainly never a starets so handsome," said Anna as she covered her mouth and looked toward her sister.

Sana shot upright.

"Wait. How do you know our names? Did Madam Lenora tell you?"

Rasputin smiled and shook his finger at them. "Perhaps I already knew?"

The sisters relaxed, enchanted by his mysterious aura.

"Now, should we discuss your mother and father?"

"How did you know that?"

"Girls! What manner of fortune teller would not know these things?" His eyes grew wide. "I see everything … like a fog hovering in the night that envelops all and can see all."

Almost in unison, the sisters rubbed their hands together and stared at the crystal ball as if waiting to devour a fat roast duck.

Rasputin placed his palms over the crystal ball, closed his eyes, and swirled his lean fingers over the glass.

"You must clear your minds so that we may find the answers you seek."

Anna and Sana fell silent. They huddled together and closed their eyes. Their faces relaxed in true belief.

"You seek answers surrounding the disappearance of your mother and father."

"Yes," breathed Sana. "Can you see them?"

"I can. Your father is a powerful man. Well-connected politically."

"He is!"

The sisters grinned.

"I see they are dear friends of the royal family."

"Yes! Yes!" said Anna while clapping. "Are they safe?"

Rasputin opened his eyes to see the sisters holding hands and smiling broadly.

"Safe?" he asked.

"Yes. Are they safe?"

"No."

Their mouths dropped open, eyes still closed.

"Why?" began Anna. "Do they want to tell us something? Is there something left undone?"

"Indeed there is."

Rasputin slammed his fists upon the table. The sisters yelped and held on to one another. They looked to him as the whites of his eyes seared through the darkness.

"Your father wants you to know he was butchered by a faction of the Okhrana working within the royal palace. Your mother was raped and beheaded. What's left of them is buried behind a barn thirty miles south of Saint Petersburg."

Sana gasped.

"I can tell you the name of the farmer if you like," said Rasputin. "Your father also wants you to know the Okhrana plan to murder you both this very evening."

"You bastard!" yelled Anna and rose from the table. She took her sister's hand and moved from the room, only to be blocked by Rasputin.

Chapter 9

"How did you—"

"Sit," he commanded.

The sisters backed away slowly and sat in the chairs. Sana wept.

"Don't hurt us," said Anna.

"I have no desire to hurt you."

"Why are you doing this?"

"Tomorrow you shall take court with the tsaritsa. Tell her what I have told you, exactly as I have told it to you. Tell her a faction of the Okhrana plan to murder her and her son. If she desires proof, she will find their intended murder weapons hidden underneath Alexei's mattress." Rasputin cupped his hands behind his back and glared at Anna. "I will be here, waiting for your response."

Anna stood.

"Who are you? Do you know who you are talking to?"

"Indeed I do. Sisters who are viewed by the wrong factions as loyal to the tsar. And as your parents have proved, that is, shall we say, the unpopular choice? Your butler took notice that your carriage driver this evening was not your regular. Of course, he did not mention this … did he?"

"This is disgusting," screamed Anna. "How dare you frighten us? What's your name?"

Rasputin bowed. "Grigori Yefimovich Rasputin." He looked up and revealed a glint of his sharp teeth. "But you may call me a friend." He motioned toward the door with his hand. "Your carriage is waiting. You will see I am a man of truth when your carriage crosses the Liteyny Bridge and continues up Bolshoy Sampsonievskiy. Far outside of Saint Petersburg there is a cabin in the woods where your murderers await to hack you to bits."

Anna reached to her sister, who cowered behind her.

"You dog! You'll pay for this cruelness. Come, Sana."

They rushed from the parlor and jumped in their carriage.

"Home!" shouted Anna.

The driver dismounted, locked the sisters safely in the carriage, and they were off into the frigid night.

*

Part I: Stăpânul

The carriage's rhythmic bounce soothed them as they traveled farther away from Rasputin. Sana dried her tears, and Anna stared sternly out the window, which was overgrown with a dense frost. She leaned forward and rubbed it clean with her coat sleeve, keeping an eye on the passing gas lamps.

"We shall tell Alexandra tomorrow." Sana paused for a moment. "Anna," she said, looking to her sister. "It's true, though. I didn't recognize the carriage driver."

"Stop it! We have different drivers often. It's nothing."

Anna sat back into her sister's arms, and they huddled in each other's warmth as the street landmarks grew more familiar. Sana closed her eyes and rested her head on her sister's shoulder, while Anna continued to watch the gas lamps roll past. Anna closed her eyes for a moment, too, relaxing to the sound of the horses' hooves. They would be home soon.

Anna opened her eyes and saw that they were halfway across the Liteyny Bridge. She grew nervous as they neared the other side. Her stomach nearly leapt from her body when the carriage failed to turn left and continued up Bolshoy Sampsonievskiy.

"Hey!" she yelled, rapping on the roof. "You were to turn!"

The carriage gained speed, and they could hear the driver forcefully slapping the horses' reins.

"Anna?" whimpered Sana.

"Someone is playing a cruel joke." She banged on the carriage roof once more.

"What if it's not?"

"I don't know."

Anna tugged on the door handle, trying to open it.

"It's locked from the outside."

Anna embraced her sister as tears fell from her face.

The carriage continued onward for several miles, traveling east beyond Saint Petersburg's city limits. Finally, it reached a small cabin in the woods, where they felt the carriage rise as the driver leapt from his perch. They held each other tightly, shivering and crying as the muffled sounds of men's voices came from outside the carriage.

Chapter 9

A masked man unlocked the door and pulled it open. Someone wearing a white masquerade mask reached in and snatched Anna by her feet. He ripped her from the carriage and forced her onto the crusty snow. She was pinned down by two other men, who threw a sack over her head and tied it around her neck. A moment later Sana landed on the ground next to her. Sana screamed and gasped as the men threw a sack over her head.

The sisters sat bound at each other's backs.

"Please, we're rich! We will give you anything!" yelled Anna.

The masked men walked to an automobile and removed a lantern from its interior.

"Please!" begged Sana.

"Shut them up!" yelled one of the men.

"Shut up or I'll cut out your throats," yelled a masked man.

He placed the lantern in a low-hanging tree branch, and another masked man approached with an axe in his hand.

"Oh, not yet! The itch is upon me," he said, stroking his crotch.

"Make it quick," said the man with the axe.

He forced himself upon Anna and began to fondle her breasts. She huffed beneath the sack.

"Scream and I'll cut you," breathed the man.

He pushed her to the ground, pulled up her dress, and tore open her undergarments as she tried to hold her knees together. Another man pinned Sana to the ground. The two women cried and begged. Anna could hear her attacker unbuckling his belt. He forced himself between her legs, holding her knees to the ground. She felt the warmth of his legs against her thighs, and his coarse hand between her legs as he positioned himself to enter.

Suddenly, the weight of his body was gone.

The sisters lay on the ground struggling and heard only a few gurgling sounds before the quiet of the forest resonated in their ears.

"Sana?"

"Yes?"

"Are you all right?"

"Yes. I think."

"I'm tied up. I can't feel my hands."

Part I: Stăpânul

Anna struggled to loosen her bonds. She felt something brush behind her, and then she was free. After ripping the sack from her head, she crawled to her sister and removed her bindings. They hugged.

Sana screamed at something in the distance.

Anna turned and saw the bodies—what was left of them. One body, pants pulled down around its ankles, lay headless with blood still spurting from its neck, slowly turning the snow a dark crimson. The other three bodies lay mangled among the blood and bits splattered across the pristine snow. Anna covered her mouth and held back a scream. She looked to their carriage. The door was wide open, and the horses whinnied as a thick fog crept in around them.

"Come, Sana. Hurry Someone is still here."

Anna helped her sister into the carriage and closed the door. She picked up her coat and hat, then threw them on. She found the horses' reins and climbed to the perch.

"Kya!" she yelled as she snapped the reins. The carriage was off into the night.

The half moon guided Anna to the carriage's ascending wheel marks in the snowy road. She followed them back into Saint Petersburg, then steered the carriage to the Metropolitan Police Station. She helped her sister into the station, where several officers provided them with blankets and medical assistance. A patient policeman took their statements, constantly assuring them of their safety.

A female officer, one of the few allowed on Saint Petersburg's force, swabbed at Anna's cuts and scratches and wiped the dirt from her face. She pulled back Anna's hair and gasped.

"Dear girl!"

"What?"

"You've been bitten."

"I have?"

"Yes, very nasty bite—like a big snake got you. Here, look."

The officer gave Anna a hand mirror and positioned another in front of the bite mark.

Anna adjusted the mirror to see the back of her neck, then placed her hand to her mouth. Two dark, circular marks sat perfectly in the

Chapter 9

center of a deep bruise. She reached around and felt the nape of her spine.

"Strange," she said. "It doesn't hurt."

Anna repositioned the mirror and looked to her own face. She shrieked and threw it down.

"What?" asked the officer.

"Nothing. I—I saw a monster in the mirror." She turned to the policewoman and feigned a smile. "I'm sorry. I've had a long night, forgive me."

"My dear, you must be seen by a doctor."

"I will see the tsar's doctor tomorrow. I am much too tired, and it doesn't hurt at all."

"May I see it again?" questioned the policewoman.

"Certainly."

Anna moved her hair to reveal the back of her neck. The policewoman shrugged.

"I think we're both having a long night," she said. "It's gone."

Anna ran her fingers over the bite to find nothing but smooth skin.

"I need some rest," said Anna. She lay back on the cot and closed her eyes.

*

Felix liked the looks of the Imperial Pub: the rustic exterior, the stained glass windows that sparkled from the candlelight within, and especially the small bronze pig that hung over the weathered oak door. The pub was nestled at the dead end of Pyra Street.

Rurik stood in front of the heavy oak door and bowed to the establishment as if he were introducing Felix to some imperial majesty.

"Welcome, Prince Felix, to my home," he said with a large grin.

Felix looked around the alley.

"I thought we were hiding me."

"We are! Deep within the seediest establishment in Saint Petersburg."

Part I: Stăpânul

"I'm not so sure this is a good idea. They're clearly following us."

"I'd say our little bonfire put them off for a bit."

Felix looked back to the pig statue, his face heavy with hesitation.

"My likeness is splashed across every newspaper in the—"

"Yes, yes. You're a wanted man. You and every other scoundrel here. Being recognized as a royal is your real concern."

Rurik opened the door and motioned for Felix to enter.

"But—"

He grabbed Felix by the shoulder and led him inside the darkened pub. Felix pulled down his hat and sunk inside his collar as they sifted through the crowd toward an empty table in the back corner.

Laughter abounded inside the small tavern as two musicians—an accordion player and a violinist—played Siberian folk music. Felix peered toward the fire blazing in a stone hearth along the far wall. At that moment he realized he never wanted to see the inside of a palace again.

They sat at the table, and a barmaid approached.

"Good evening, my Rurik," she said.

"Ah, Hedrina. My sweet Hedrina! Allow me to introduce you to my very good friend Fe … Sasha."

"Sasha Ivanov," said Felix, smirking toward Rurik.

"Very nice to meet you," said Hedrina. "Welcome."

"Thank you."

Rurik patted him on the shoulder, then waved to a drunk couple seated at the bar. The noise inside the Imperial Pub seemed to grow more boisterous with the addition of Rurik—the guest of honor had finally arrived.

"My dear Hedrina," shouted Rurik. "The lovely Hedrina. Would you be so kind as to bring us a bottle of your cheapest vodka and two of your tallest shot glasses? My friend and I have had a very rough evening."

Hedrina nodded and walked toward the bar. Rurik's eyes followed her figure the entire way.

"Vodka?" questioned Felix.

Chapter 9

"You don't like?"

"Scotch is my drink."

"Psssh! Scotch? A fancy lad's drink! Trust me. Cheap vodka will salvage your soul. And take off your hat. You look like a spy."

Felix removed his hat and coat and watched Rurik as he bobbed his head to the music. Despite having met Rurik only a few hours prior and deciding he was clearly bound for an asylum, Felix realized he liked him a great deal. Rurik's carefree enjoyment of the tavern gave Felix a fleeting moment in which his life felt vibrant and new, and then he remembered why he'd met Rurik in the first place.

"Rurik."

Rurik snapped from his trance and looked back to the table. "Yes?"

"When do you think he'll do it again?"

"Who? Oh! Yes ... of course ... I haven't the slightest idea."

"It's just ... there are others inside the royal family I'm close to. What if they're at risk? The killer—"

"The vampire," corrected Rurik.

Hedrina came back to the table and set down two shot glasses followed by a clear glass bottle filled nearly to the brim.

"Thank you, my dear!" said Rurik as he stuffed a wad of money into her apron.

She kissed him on the cheek, then attended other patrons.

Rurik again watched her plump figure walk from the table. He placed his hands over his heart and looked to Felix. "One day, I tell you. She will be Mrs. Kozlova!"

Felix shot a curious glance to Rurik.

"What?" asked Rurik.

"I think she's in her mid twenties."

"So?"

Felix remained quiet.

"Well, say it," demanded Rurik.

"Maybe a bit young for you?"

Rurik appeared offended. "How old do you take me for?"

Felix looked over Rurik's deep laugh lines and crow's feet and thought it best to round down. "Uh, sixty-five?"

Part I: Stăpânul

"Sixty-five!" Rurik banged his fist on the table. "You privileged scoundrel. I'm forty-eight and one month!"

Felix raised his hands. "Oh, I'm so sorry. I—"

"Forget it," said Rurik, laughing. "I suppose not living in a palace all my life has taken its toll."

"Rurik, really I'm—"

Rurik raised his hand in protest and grabbed the vodka. He poured two generous shots into each glass. "No more talking!" he said, raising his glass.

Felix followed suit. "What should we drink to?"

"To my sixty-fifth birthday!" Rurik laughed. "No. No. Better—to you. My brave and foolish friend."

They clinked their glasses together and swallowed the alcohol. Felix, not particularly fond of the sharp taste of vodka, coughed as the liquid glided down his esophagus.

"Ha! Ha! You see? Scotch is for the children! Another!"

Rurik poured two more and raised his thimble into the air. Felix followed. "To Hedrina!"

"To Hedrina."

They downed their drinks, and Felix found his second round much more pleasing. Warm shivers spread across his body, and he smiled at Rurik.

"Yes! Yes! A commoner in you after all. One more!"

Soon thereafter, the two men were drunk. Rurik ordered another bottle.

"So ... a vampire, huh?"

"Yes," said Rurik. "Alarming it has reemerged in Saint Petersburg. We thought we killed it long ago in Romania."

"We? So there are more people wandering the streets who believe in this—"

"Crap?"

"No ... I—"

"You meant to say crap. It's fine. I understand this is all nonsense to you, but if we plan to catch this monster in time, there is much for you to learn."

Felix rubbed his face and realized he was sweating. The soft pulse of drunkenness was upon him. He enjoyed the subtle throbbing

Chapter 9

of blood in his face, then looked back to Rurik, who appeared stunningly composed.

"I have to be honest with you, Rurik. I think it's crazy."

Rurik curled his chin. "And coming from someone who was framed for murder by his best friend, I believe you. What's crazy is your ineptitude to see what's right under your nose. Think your pal Pavlovich keeps machine gun–toting goons handy because he has nothing to hide? The military can't get their hands on weaponry like that." Rurik looked up as if an idea struck him. "Oh, yes. You're right. They followed us to an abandoned building and annihilated it because he's merely angry with you. Yes, I'm the crazy one."

Rurik raised his glass and swallowed his drink. Felix let the barb pass and downed another shot.

Rurik became stern. "There is a darkness here, Felix. One that has haunted every single person who is involved in what we do. One we've sworn to thwart. I think your coming to the morgue today was honorable. But if you are to be involved in these dire events, I insist that you must cast away your doubts of the supernatural or whatever it is you call things you do not understand. But I assert—they are wholly natural, biological, and happening as we sit."

"I'm listening," Felix said, reaching for the vodka bottle.

Rurik snatched his wrist and stopped him. "I'm serious, Felix. You're tied into this. Your neck is on the line and your fiancée is dead—butchered to bits. Countless more victims will follow. Soon there won't be just one Sleepwalker but millions. From Saint Petersburg to all the way across the globe."

Rurik held his shot glass and pointed his finger at Felix. "There is a vampire in Saint Petersburg. If we do not kill it, its actions will unleash the weight of mercury upon the back of mankind."

Felix's bloodshot eyes stared at Rurik's stern glare.

"Boo!" yelled Felix, laughing a bit.

Rurik rolled his eyes and downed his shot.

"The world ends in ten days," said Rurik, tossing the amulet on the table. "I'd like to prove this thing wrong."

Felix glanced at the date: *Decembrie 16, 1916*. "Well, at least we have a warning shot," he said, slurring badly.

Rurik stared at him for a long moment, then smiled.

Part I: Stăpânul

"No sense arguing with a drunk."

Felix slid onto the floor.

Rurik threw his jacket around Felix's shoulders. "Let's get you to a safe place," he said, and helped Felix from the floor.

Chapter 10

Part I: Stăpânul

10

December 7, 1916 (OS), late afternoon

Felix woke in an unfamiliar room. It was narrow with a cathedral ceiling, completely barren of furniture, and had only a large oblong window on the far wall that shone with late afternoon's light. Along the ceiling's perimeter ran iron rods that hung heavy with black felt. The curtains were suspended by a weave of ropes that fed behind the rods to a circular candelabra dangling from the ceiling's center.

Felix's body ached from sleeping on the hardwood floor, and he shivered from the cutting cold—a wool rug his blanket and his own socks as a makeshift pillow. His throat ached for water. As he gathered his senses, Felix noticed a large Saint Bernard sitting before him. The dog stared with its head cocked, panting heavily with a broad pink tongue bobbing about its mouth. Felix yawned. "Hi, pooch."

Felix placed his head back on the floor and drifted off for another moment. He was woken again by the dog licking his bare feet.

"Watch it ... too early." He pushed the dog away with one foot.

The Saint Bernard continued, and Felix threw his socks in the far corner of the room. The beast chased the socks and returned, begging for more play.

"Enough, Greta!" said a woman's voice. "Go lie down."

Felix shot up to see an old woman hanging upside down in a doorframe behind him. Her eyes were closed, and in one hand she held a string of ropes that fed to the candelabra.

"What on—"

"Keeps blood in the scalp ... necessary for remote viewing."

Chapter 10

Felix rubbed his eyes and took a closer look as Greta lay down next to her. Her eyelids were closed and twitched occasionally to reveal thick cataracts. She was bundled head to toe in dense winter garb and appeared to be in her late eighties. Her ankles were bound into a homemade device that locked her upside down at the top of the doorframe. The hinged device gave her the ability to sway back and forth, and the curtains on the walls bobbed ever so slightly with her movements, never revealing what lay behind.

"I'm Orna," she said, extending a mittened hand.

Felix shook it.

"How did I get here?"

"Rurik brought you."

"I don't remember that."

"Clearly," she said with a pursed smile. "You're safe here with me. None of your pursuers can see within my walls."

"Great," said Felix with a yawn. "What time is it?"

"Past four, I think. Maybe as late as six. I leave following time to you mortals." Orna giggled.

"I have to go," said Felix, rubbing his cheeks.

"Rurik said that you are to do no poking around. You must see him immediately."

"And who is he to tell me anything?"

"Mr. Yusupov, it's more of a *we* at this point. And *we* tell you no more poking around. You must see Rurik immediately, or we will see to it you're on the next train out of Russia."

Felix thought for a moment.

"I'm—"

"Tch. Tch. Tch. Listen now, Mr. Yusupov," she began with a sharp rise in her voice. "Your title means nothing here."

"Not so certain it means anything anywhere right now." Felix scratched his head, then rubbed his face. "Can you at least give me a clue as to what the hell is going on?"

Orna grinned.

"Exactly that, Mr. Yusupov—hell. A vampire at work in Saint Petersburg. A particularly powerful and slippery one," she said with a tinge of admiration. "Its presence here confirms the spiders are a-spinning! This one has very big plans." Orna laughed. Felix thought it more of a cackle.

She closed her eyes more tightly and took a deep breath.

"My dear Mr. Yusupov. You've been holding out on us!"

Felix cocked his head. "How so?"

"One moment." She scrunched her face. "Why, yes! You've had contact with this vampire. Face-to-face, in fact."

"I'm sorry. I haven't."

"But you have. I see a room with five other people. Dark men. Evil men. A woman in a red dress. Do you know this room?"

Felix thought back to the night Dmitri drugged him, and the glare of the strange man's eyes seared into his mind.

"Yes. It was the night my fiancée was murdered. I was drugged."

Orna remained silent.

"So you were. I can see that now. Our vampire was there in the room with you that night. He killed … Irina was it?"

"Yes." Felix glared at the floor, trying to contain his anger.

"I'm sorry, Mr. Yusupov. I can feel your suffering. Please—one more. The name Grigori, does it mean anything to you?"

"No. I don't think so."

She swirled her eyes underneath her aged eyelids as if she were looking toward a different area of the room. "Oh," she said, sounding disappointed. "I suppose I'll keep looking."

"Why was she killed?"

"One moment."

Orna craned her neck and flared her nostrils as if she were following a scent in front of her.

"Irina's death is cloudy. The vampire is cloaking it."

Felix nodded.

"Can you see why I was framed?"

"That too is masked. But I can sense … the vampire … it possibly fears you … no … wait … it wanted you isolated … it has a plan for you … a dark secret … unbeknownst to its collaborators … I see a bottle of wine … I see Paris …" Orna smiled. "Oh, and I see a sommelier … a dark man with great wisdom … I'm sorry. I've lost it. Slippery one, this devil."

Chapter 10

Felix's eyes widened as he watched Orna's cheeks begin to twitch.

"Then why didn't it kill me?"

"You were to be killed—hanged, in fact. But that was the plan of the men involved. Not the vampire … I keep seeing Paris but still cannot hone in on this vampire's interest in you. I can tell you, though, its interest is very intense. Your escape from jail has these men very worried … I can see—Dmitri, is it? He was beaten viciously—once more—for aiding you. He has sworn to find you. To bring you back to the vampire."

"Orna, please. Why is this happening?"

Orna took in a deep breath. "You'd better sit back down, Mr. Yusupov."

She suddenly appeared confused and her eyes shot open. "Ha!" she yelled. "There you are!"

"Who?"

"Just a moment. Going to give it a tug on the tail."

Felix looked around the room and then back to Orna.

"Tell Rurik when you see him that our vampire should be paying me a visit soon." She outstretched her free hand and plucked the air in front of her face. "I let it know I'm aware of its presence in Saint Petersburg."

Felix placed his fingers to his temples as a sudden headache pulsed outward upon his skull. "Yeah, I'll tell him just that," he said, pushing his fingers into his head.

"Tch. Tch. Tch. Poor Mr. Yusupov. Still failing to see the truth before him." She paused. "You'd better get going. Very little time! The spiders are a-spinning."

"Yeah, sure. Spiders spinning," he said, rubbing his eyes. "You seen my boots?"

"Seen them? No. But they are to your right."

"Ahh."

Felix gathered his socks. He reached to his boots and slipped them on. Orna hung upside down with a content smile. For the moment her eyes stopped twitching.

"Umm, thank you for your … hospitality," he said, then patted Greta on the head.

Part I: Stăpânul

"Always, Mr. Yusupov. Remember—to Coroner Kozlov. I'll be watching over you."

Felix buttoned his coat and looked to her. "I bet you will," he whispered to himself. He moved past her into a small foyer and opened the apartment door.

"Mr. Yusupov?"

"Yes?"

"Down three flights, out the front, take a left. Two blocks up and then right until you see the morgue. You know the rest. I've cast a protection spell over you, and those who are looking for you are busy for the moment. So I suggest you hurry."

"Got it," he said, and slipped out the door.

*

Earlier that morning, just after dawn, Constable Petrov had arrived by automobile to the cabin where the Taneyev sisters were attacked. He and two of his men exited the vehicle and walked toward four Okhrana officers who stood about the perimeter of the murder scene.

Petrov turned to his officers. "Better wait here, men. These Okhrana can get a little mouthy."

Ivor Kashin stood next to three of his men, all of whom were dressed in typical garb of the secret police: patent leather black boots, gray straight-leg wool pants with gray wool trench coats that came to their knees, and black ushanka hats with the ear flaps buttoned up. Constable Petrov noticed that the Okhrana, no matter how cold, never put down their ear flaps. He thought to quickly retract the flaps on his own hat, but it was too late—Kashin turned to see him approaching.

"Commander." Petrov nodded.

Kashin nodded in return with an apparent sneer on his face. The two men stood next to one another and surveyed the scene.

"Disgusting," said Petrov.

"You think so, Constable?" said Kashin, whose mustache appeared to be frozen in place. "It's nothing short of a meat grinder accident."

Chapter 10

"For certain," said Petrov.

"For certain—that's all you can say?"

"I just received the call an hour ago. And let me just mention, Commander, I'm honored to have this opportunity to work with the Okhrana. I admire your work very much."

Kashin looked at him with an open mouth and curled nose. He turned to his officers and flicked his hand at them. They shuffled off to an automobile parked next to Petrov's.

"The women involved have already talked to the *Vedomosti*," said Petrov. "What do we say to the newspapers?"

"We?" said Kashin with a laugh. "Well, *we* don't technically exist—it's up to you. Look out there. That's exactly as we found it. What does your police work tell you?"

Petrov furrowed his brow and puckered his lips, suggesting he was piecing the puzzle together.

"Forget it, Constable. Look—a carriage, I'm assuming the women's, pulled there, and there is where it eventually left. The footprints there imply someone jumped from the carriage, and then a struggle ensued there when the passengers were pulled from inside." He pointed to the body imprints in the snow. His gaze shifted to the black car. "Three men came in that automobile. You can see their footprints from the auto there—three sets. So there are four men—three from the auto, one driving the carriage. At one point all four men hovered about the body imprints there on the ground. And then?"

Petrov looked to him. "Yes?"

"Then apparently everyone exploded." Kashin laughed. "To hell if I know. Somehow the women escaped, a headless body left no tracks to its final resting place, and four of what I thought were my best men are butchered to bits."

"Those men are Okhrana?"

"Yes, but not on Okhrana orders. Not on my orders, anyway."

"Do you think the girls did it?" asked Petrov with a quiver in his voice.

Kashin glared at him. "Are you truly that stupid, Constable?"

"Yes … I mean, no … I mean … what do you want me to do?"

Part I: Stăpânul

"Get to the newspaper. Counter the story. If I see the Okhrana—even a rogue faction—implicated in this, I will be very upset. Very upset. As will the tsar."

"Yes, sir," said Constable Petrov as he saluted Kashin.

Kashin slapped away the salute. "You stupid ass." He turned and walked to his automobile.

One of Kashin's men opened the vehicle's door, and he climbed into the back seat.

"Commander? Uh, what should I do with this?" shouted Petrov, motioning to the grisly scene.

"Be good little police officers and make it disappear," yelled Kashin from inside the vehicle.

They started the auto and were off.

*

Felix appeared sluggish when Rurik spied him through the slim window above the morgue's back exit. He quickly opened the large iron door and pulled Felix inside.

"Come, hurry! Much has happened."

Rurik shuffled him into the morgue, where three bins sat on tables along the far wall. A covered body lay on the center table.

"Four more. The tsar's secret police. The implications of this are incredible." Rurik appeared to be enjoying the moment. "Here, read." He handed Felix a newspaper.

Saint Petersburg Vedomosti
Royal Assassination Plot Foiled

Saint Petersburg, Dec. 7—Sirens rang throughout the city at dawn when an assassination plot aimed at the tsaritsa and her son unfolded early this morning. Late last evening, Anna Taneyev and Sana Taneyev, daughters of the missing ambassador Akexander Taneyev and his wife Nadezhda Illarionovna Tolstoy, were kidnapped and taken to a remote wooded location, where they were assaulted and nearly murdered. The sisters escaped death thanks to a police officer who arrived on the scene to stop the events.

Chapter 10

Upon arriving at the Metropolitan Police Station, the sisters reported overhearing their kidnappers discussing the details of a planned attempt on the tsaritsa's life. Their information turned up a stash of knives and ropes hidden in Prince Alexei's bedroom that were apparently planted on scene to aid in the assassinations.

No information was given on the status or whereabouts of the implicated kidnappers, but Chief Constable Milton Petrov issued a statement saying, "The suspects have been neutralized and pose no further threat."

The Winter Palace was placed on immediate lockdown, and nobody has been allowed in or out since the Taneyev sisters were granted passage at the tsaritsa's request. Several imperial servants have been arrested under suspicion of aiding the attempt.

The kidnapping of the Taneyev sisters marks the second occasion in two months that aristocracy near the tsar's inner circle have been targets of attack and criminal harassment.

The Metropolitan Police have acknowledged that Ambassador Taneyev and his wife may have suffered a dire fate, considering last night's actions taken against their daughters. The police are currently investigating an inside tip on the possible whereabouts of the bodies.

Felix looked up from the paper. "I have to go. I should be there for Alexei."

"That's ridiculous."

"He's my godson."

Felix stood and moved toward the door. Rurik grabbed him by his coat.

"Quit acting rashly. Don't you see? There was no policeman. It's the Sleepwalker. Here, look!"

He pulled the sheets from the bins one by one.

Felix looked into the bins—the mangled state of the bodies shocked him. He nodded, and Rurik replaced the sheets.

Part I: Stăpânul

"And let us not forget!" said Rurik as he went over to the covered body and pulled back the sheet. "Voilà! Off with the head in one bite! Here, look at the teeth marks."

"I see," said Felix, his hangover making it difficult to view the gruesome spectacle.

"No, you don't!" Rurik was ebullient. "These are targeted attacks. Our vampire is revealing its agenda. Starting from its time in Saint Petersburg, each kill has been for a purpose. We have to toast! A toast!"

"What about the Bolshoy Prospekt merchant?"

"Well, I believe there was a reason for that. It's just not apparent yet."

"And Irina?"

"No idea."

Rurik walked to a cabinet along the far wall and came back with a bottle of vodka and two tall glasses. He placed them on the autopsy table and opened the bottle. He poured carefully, then raised his glass.

"To discovery," said Rurik, and downed his drink.

Felix looked at him for a moment, holding his glass at chest level.

"What?" asked Rurik, appearing confused.

Felix's face grew red, and he threw the alcohol on the floor, still holding on to his glass.

"Look!" he said, pointing to Rurik. "Somebody better tell me what the hell is going on around here, or I'm going to take that revolver of yours and shoot us both—"

"You threw my revolver into a snowdrift—"

"I have you trying to convince me that I'm wanted dead by people who believe in sex with mythical bats, then there's an upside-down insane woman telling me things that don't make any sense. There's a goddamn cold-blooded killer loose in the streets. He's murdered the woman I love, and I've been framed for it. And instead of making any headway in understanding anything, I'm playing hide-and-seek with Saint Petersburg's nut commission—"

"Felix, listen, I—"

Chapter 10

"No, you listen, Coroner. I want this son of a bitch dead. If I have to kill ten people to get to him, I'll do it. There's nothing that will stand in my way. Not you, not your cult buddies, not even Nicholas and the imperial court."

"Please, Felix, calm down. You're hurting my feelings." Rurik frowned.

"Huh?"

"My feelings, you're hurting them."

Rurik removed his glasses, patted his eyes with his shirtsleeve, then looked back to Felix.

"Oh, uh … are you serious?" said Felix with an air of concern.

"Yes, I'm sensitive to yelling and bad words cast in my general direction. I have been since I was a small child. And I've never been in a cult." Rurik sniffled and placed his glasses back on. "Now, you were saying?"

"Oh … well, I didn't mean to hurt your feelings. It's just, this is all very frustrating. We're wasting a lot of time."

"I understand. Here, you must drink." Rurik held the bottle to him.

Felix placed his glass on the table. "I'm not thirsty."

Rurik stared at him for a long moment. He poured more vodka into the glass and motioned toward it with his eyes. Felix snatched it and took a deep swig.

"There you go!" Rurik patted his shoulder. "We should move to my office. But I must warn you that no matter your intent, I still offer the same—if you do not believe me or are unwilling to participate, you will find yourself with nowhere to turn. We'll see you on the next train out of Russia." Rurik smiled. "I know you just gave me that tough guy speech, but if we decide you must go, you will go. We're your last refuge. Everyone else in Saint Petersburg thinks you're a murderer or is trying to kill you."

Rurik appeared stern.

"Fine," huffed Felix.

"Please, to my office."

"Oh, and I'm supposed to tell you that Orna is expecting a visit from the vampire. She tugged or tapped him or something."

Part I: Stăpânul

Rurik clapped. "Great news! If anyone, Orna can handle this monster. Come, follow."

*

Felix sat across the desk, looking at Rurik. The coroner's thick eyeglasses gave the impression his face was all eyeballs.

"OK, Felix," he began, moving a small glass to the edge of the desk. Rurik leaned forward and dumped the contents of his bottle into it.

Felix sat back, holding the vodka in both hands.

"Vampires exist," said Rurik. "This you must believe."

Rurik reached into his jacket, removed a flimsy and haggard leather-bound book, and tossed it to Felix. Felix looked at the cover.

Sfânta Biblie al Strigoiului Viu.

"That's the bible of the Nosferatu cult—the Khlysts."

"It's only ten pages or so," replied Felix with an air of humorous disbelief.

"Well, that is all we have," continued Rurik, his cheeks flushing. "We do know that bible is much more substantial. We simply cannot locate the rest of it. But in those pages, we have stories of how vampires convert the living, what will kill them. And also the Bloodchild's birth ritual."

"This doesn't really seem like enough."

"Have you ever read Sherlock Holmes?"

"Of course."

"In how many instances did he solve a crime based on discovering a mere note or artifact passed between accomplices? Handwriting upon a torn piece of paper, perhaps?"

"I understand."

"Then consider that the small piece of evidence is what leads to a more complete understanding of the suspect. That bible was written entirely by Vlad Drăculea just after he crushed his Turkish pursuers in 1456. Victory came to Drăculea only after he sold his soul to the will of the vampire."

Felix slugged on his drink and looked at the weathered book.

"May I keep this?"

Chapter 10

"You may peruse it. But I am bound to keep it on my person."

"Let's say I go with you for a second and accept it's all true."

"You should. You've seen it with your own eyes. Saint Petersburg's new visitor has followed the rituals in that book. His reemergence is for bigger plans than feeding on hookers throughout rural Europe, I can assure you. Why is it a vampire is interested in saving women close to the imperial circle and murdering rogue Okhrana?"

"I don't know."

"Seems our vampire has political aspirations." Rurik pursed his lips. "My brother Denis thought he killed it long ago. But it fooled us, even Orna. Only when I began collecting the news clippings a few years ago did we begin to suspect it was still alive. And now we've only ten days to kill it."

"That seems adequate," said Felix, sounding hopeful.

"It's successfully evaded capture for over twenty years."

Felix frowned. "If Orna really has second sight, why don't you have more answers?"

"Well, she is nine hundred forty-two. That's old even for a witch of her stature."

Felix raised his eyebrows. "Funny," he said. "I thought she was sixty-five."

Rurik let out a small laugh at Felix's joke.

"So where exactly do you fall into this?" asked Felix. "Are you the leader?"

"Me, the leader? How very flattering you'd think that," said Rurik. "No. No. Our leader is ... in England."

"England? How did you meet—"

"But me? I'm a hunter!" Rurik proudly patted his chest.

"A ... ?"

"A vampire hunter. I kill them. I'm quite skilled at killing vampires, you see!"

Rurik smiled. It occurred to Felix that he'd never noticed such pride on someone's face.

"How many have you killed?"

"Well, none. I mean . . . well . . . yes, none. But I know all the methods," he said, motioning to the vampire bible. "My brother has staked many, though, and has told me the tales."

Felix laughed. "So you've personally never seen one?"

"Of course not! A vampire never reveals itself." Rurik rose from the desk, held his hand like a claw, and crept toward Felix. "By the time you see one." He playfully struck Felix in the ribs. "You're already dead." Rurik considered his own statement. "Only a newborn or extremely reckless vampire would reveal itself before a kill."

Felix wore a bemused expression.

"You don't believe it?" Rurik was disappointed.

"Not a word. I'm sorry. I'm just the type that unless I see it myself—"

"A skeptic to the point of self-destruction."

"Something like that. Look, Rurik. I can't thank you enough for helping me. It's just I think I'm best to secretly contact Alexandra. She's my last ally on the inside. I think if I go to her—"

"Insanity! You read the article. The entire Winter Palace is sealed under guard. You think a man wanted for murder is going to waltz up for a chat with the tsaritsa? They'll have you back in a cell before you get down the block."

Felix ran his fingers through his brown hair, then clenched his fists.

"You're a dead man if they catch you. You know that," said Rurik.

"I want revenge. Following you around is getting me nowhere."

Rurik reflected for a moment before finishing off his drink.

"There is only one thing left that you can do."

"Yes?" said Felix.

"Until things cool off your trail, you must travel to Bucharest and convince my brother to return here. I have been unable to reach him, and his contributions will be necessary for us to succeed."

"And how is that furthering *my* agenda?"

"Your agenda? Tell me, Prince Felix. What exactly is that agenda? Revenge? You have no means to exact that revenge, only options that will find you dead or imprisoned. Think rationally for just one moment."

Chapter 10

Felix huffed. "Then what?"

"I told you. The best use of your services is to travel to Bucharest and bring back my brother. We don't know if or when the vampire will visit Orna. My guess is it will choose to avoid her. In the meantime, my brother is the only person alive who has faced off against this specter and survived, and our best chance at flushing it out of the shadows. He is fearless. A genius. He has invented a new weapon to obliterate vampires en masse. We need his skills for this brewing battle. I believe once he sees that I've sent you in person to retrieve him, he will realize it's time to come home and fight by my side."

Felix considered his options. "I'll do it. But how will I make it back in time?"

"My brother's a pilot—all of that is arranged. Our operatives there will assist you in locating him."

Rurik leaned against the wall and looked to the ceiling as if lost in his next thought.

"Well?" said Felix.

"Well, what?"

"Let's get started! I want to be on the first train out tomorrow morning."

"Ah yes! Forgive me. My mind went somewhere else. I can make those preparations this evening. But first, I believe a certain buxom lovely is awaiting my arrival at our favorite pub."

"You're serious? It's barely sundown."

"Excuses, excuses."

Rurik stood at a coatrack, bundling up.

"Rurik, I appreciate it. But I think it's best for me to stay the night here. I don't want to draw any—"

"You won't. Orna has cast a protection spell over you. They can't track you for a bit."

"Still, I—"

"Suit yourself. Spending the night alone in a freezing morgue with a bunch of mangled bodies sounds … charming."

Rurik gave Felix a moment to think it over.

"Shall we, my Prince?" he said with a bow.

Part I: Stăpânul

Chapter 11

Part I: Stăpânul

11

December 7, 1916 (OS), late afternoon

Nicholas sat in the ornate Room of Coins as Alexandra and the Taneyev sisters approached. The women walked alongside the granite Doric columns that ran the perimeter of the room. Sundown was in less than an hour and only a modicum of light was emitted from the massive windows, yet Alexandra pulled her headscarf closer to her face. A large fire roaring in a hearth along the back wall radiated a hint of warmth.

Nicholas walked to greet them, flanked by Commander Kashin and Minister Makarov.

As Alexandra watched them approach, she considered the absurdity of such an expanse housing only one small wooden desk and a smattering of antique furniture.

Nicholas hugged Alexandra. "Is everyone unharmed?" he asked, looking into her eyes. "Alexei, he is safe?"

Alexandra nodded, and her chin quivered.

"I would have come to you both sooner, but I had to direct actions to sweep the palace for any further evidence of assassination schemes. I assure you that your safety comes before mine, my beloved."

He kissed her on the mouth, something he hadn't done in a long time. Nicholas moved to Anna and then Sana, hugging each woman and expressing his concern. Alexandra watched him and felt that the man she loved was back in the room. Nicholas's unwavering sincerity and confidence calmed them.

"I will find and uproot anyone involved. This will never happen again."

Chapter 11

Anna looked behind Nicholas to Makarov, whose official uniform augmented his sagely appearance. Although he appeared regal at first glance, this impression was betrayed upon closer inspection by his yellow teeth and facial liver spots, which he attempted to cover with makeup.

With his usual grandiosity, Makarov outstretched his hands as he approached. "Alexandra, I came the moment I heard!" He pulled her hand to his lips. "Sana, I'm shocked," he said, and reached for her hand. "Anna, I'm—"

Anna turned her back on him when she noticed Kashin a few paces behind.

Makarov stood upright, and his height over Nicholas was noted by all. "I'm sorry if my presence is causing concern," he said. "I will go."

"Stay, Minister," commanded Nicholas. "Anna, please. This is no time for—"

"I'm sorry, Minister. It's not you. I'm not feeling well."

"I understand, dear Anna. Please, everyone." He motioned toward Nicholas's desk.

Nicholas sat with Makarov and Kashin behind him. In front of the desk were two decorative Isabella chairs and a carved giltwood chaise longue upholstered with pink-and-white-striped silk. Alexandra sat in a chair, and the Taneyev sisters sat next to her on one side of the chaise.

"Tell me everything."

"Oh, Nicholas. It's hard on them," began Alexandra. "But there are things. Things we should look into."

"We went to see Madam Lenora, our fortune teller," said Sana. "But she was ill. A new man we'd never seen before was in her parlor. He told us everything just as it happened. He said the carriage wouldn't turn. He predicted where our attackers would drive us to. He even said that Mother and Father are murdered and told us where the bodies are buried."

"Did he?" interrupted Kashin.

"Yes. Behind a barn south of Saint Petersburg. Does that sound familiar, Commander? He said it was orchestrated by Okhrana agents working within the palace."

Part I: Stăpânul

Nicholas and Makarov looked wide-eyed to Kashin, who smiled and pushed his palms outward. "I assure you this is a mistake—pure fantasy. Surprising this fortune teller would dare implicate my officers in your parents' disappearance. They were family to me." Kashin bowed to Nicholas. "Emperor, may I start an initiative to see if this barn story is true? I would be honored to have my security detail lead an investigation."

"Thank you, Commander," said Nicholas.

"You can't trust him!" yelled Anna. "He's practically been implicated!"

"Girls, please," said Nicholas. "My confidence in Commander Kashin and his security detail is implicit."

Kashin stepped forward. "We cannot let a parlor trickster pull apart the fabric of our mutual trust, especially when those close to us all are under attack. I dread the day when my loyalty to Nicholas is ever questioned within this court. Especially by a fortune teller."

"Then how did he know about the knives and ropes under Alexei's mattress?" shouted Anna. "How did he know about what was going to happen to us at that cabin?"

"What was this fortune teller's name?" questioned Nicholas.

"Grigori Rasputin," said Anna.

"It's true! He knew everything," interjected Sana, tears falling down her face. "He said the palace Okhrana were behind it all."

"Please, girls," cautioned Nicholas.

"Where is this fortune teller located?" asked Makarov.

"Madam Lenora's parlor—near Moscow Station."

"Commander," said Makarov. "Send some of your officers to bring this Rasputin in for questioning."

"What?" yelled Sana.

"Absolutely," said Nicholas. "I will see him myself with Commander Kashin present. I believe we should all hear what this fortune teller has to say."

Sana reached to Alexandra for comfort. Anna seemed absent from the conversation and stared at the floor, her body starting to sway slightly. Makarov raised his finger toward Kashin, who clicked his heels and walked off behind the desk, where he spoke

Chapter 11

sternly with two Okhrana officers. They quickly shuffled from the room, and Kashin returned to his position near Nicholas.

"Emperor Romanov is correct," began Kashin. "We should all hear what this fortune teller has to say. I find it difficult to believe that he's not involved in the disappearance of your parents, knowing such intimate details."

"But if he's authentic," said Alexandra, "then what? He predicted the plot around Alexei and me."

Makarov cleared his throat. "We will expose him in front of you all. He won't dare implicate Kashin and his men while they're in the room …"

"That is, if he's even still in Saint Petersburg," said Kashin. "Too often these vagabond types go missing or—"

Everyone turned suddenly to Anna as she screamed and fell face-first onto the floor. Alexandra tried to roll her onto her back but proved too weak to move her.

"She's unconscious," said Alexandra, looking to Kashin.

Sana knelt to her sister and fanned air onto her.

Kashin rolled Anna over and placed his ear to her mouth.

"She's not breathing," he said. "Get the doctor, quickly!"

*

It was dark when three Okhrana officers arrived at Madam Lenora's parlor. They entered the front door and marched to the back room, where Rasputin sat with his eyes closed, playfully rubbing his hands about the crystal ball.

"Welcome, Officer Baylor."

"Grigori Rasputin?"

Rasputin opened his dark eyes and stared at them.

"Yes."

Baylor motioned to his men, who now stood behind Rasputin.

"You're under arrest in the name of the tsar."

"For what charge?"

"Conspiring to commit murder of the royal family."

"You know, as do I, that charge is untrue."

Part I: Stăpânul

Baylor motioned to his men. They thrust themselves upon Rasputin and threw a sack over his head. They pulled him from the chair and forced him face-first onto the floor. Baylor stood over Rasputin and cuffed his hands. Lifting him between them, they marched from the parlor and threw him into the back of a black automobile.

The vehicle drove quickly through Saint Petersburg's boulevards, onward to the outskirts of town. As night settled upon the cold, quiet forest, they arrived in front of the same cabin where Sana and Anna were nearly murdered.

Baylor left the engine running and sat still as the other officers pulled Rasputin from the car. One of the men shoved his boot into the back of Rasputin's kneecap, forcing him to the snow with his hands bound behind his back. Baylor exited the automobile and headed toward him with a pistol in his right hand. Another officer pulled the sack from Rasputin's head.

"Not wise for an outsider to interfere with the dealings of the Okhrana," said Baylor.

Rasputin looked to him and then to the cabin. "Ahh, a familiar sight!"

Baylor punched him in the mouth and stood back. Rasputin was unfazed by the attack. Baylor walked behind him and placed his pistol to the back of Rasputin's head.

A shot rang through the forest and Rasputin slumped forward. All was quiet.

One of the officers spit on Rasputin's back, and they walked back to the car. They drove off into the night as Rasputin's body lay bleeding in the pristine snow.

Chapter 12

Part I: Stăpânul

12

December 7, 1916 (OS), night

"I'm on my way. This is a tragedy. She was a most lovely girl."

Archimandrite Mikhail Gyáva hung up the telephone in his dark study. The room was lit only by a small lamp sitting on the corner of his desk and the last remnants of orange embers smoldering in the fireplace. He walked to a wardrobe along the back wall, then pulled his vestments and a vial of chrism from its interior. He placed the items into a black leather handbag, then buckled it closed. He threw on his over-cassock, took a brimmed hat from his coatrack, and headed into the Saint Petersburg night.

Last rites were usually left to the lower-rung staretsy or other clergy, depending on the class of the deceased. But Archimandrite Gyáva always made a point to travel to the hospital no matter the weather when a friend of the tsar had passed.

He walked down the quiet streets toward Nevsky Prospekt, sucking short bursts of frigid air onto his lower teeth. As he came to the Anichkov Bridge, Gyáva watched the lights of the gas lamps dance in a small center portion of the Fontanka River that remained unfrozen. He disliked walking alone at night and always made a point to count the lamps to pass the time. Gyáva never walked any farther than nine lamps once he reached the bridge—a superstition he based upon the nine saints canonized during Nicholas's rule. Countless souls had thrown themselves from the Anichkov into the icy Fontanka, and Gyáva grew nauseated thinking of the restless spirits drowned just beneath his feet—especially those who were men of the cloth.

He stood at the foot of the bridge, and a thick fog glissaded its way down the Fontanka, further eclipsing his view of Nevsky Prospect.

Chapter 12

Gyáva made the sign of the cross to the Horse Tamers, the statues that guarded the bridge's entrance. After a deep breath, he walked toward the first lamp and nervously ran his fingers through his long, gray beard.

Praise to Saint Theodosius of Chernigov glorified in 1896, amen.

He crossed the lamp's threshold and stopped for a moment. The fog grew so thick that only the slight glow of lamp two was visible. Dread pricked his heart as Gyáva became aware of a woman sobbing just behind him. He turned to greet her.

No one was present.

After another small prayer, he moved into the fog, keeping his eye on the lamp's glow. He believed the fog cut right down the middle of the bridge, and that he'd emerge shortly to the warm glow of the second lamp—only five lamps left to the hospital.

Praise to Saint Isidore Yurievsky glorified in 1897, amen.

Gyáva heard more whimpering behind him as he passed the second lamp.

He looked back, but no one was in sight. Gyáva turned, and his heart nearly stopped at the sight of a hooded female figure in the mist before him. And then he heard her voice.

Mikhail…

"Who's there?"

The shadow slunk toward Gyáva. The click of its heels upon the stone sent shivers across his neck.

"Who approaches?"

The figure crept closer.

Gyáva spun around and ran until he emerged from the fog. Shock engulfed him as he stood in a snow-covered forest with slim black trees that rose into the air. He turned back in hopes to see the bridge, but he was surrounded on all sides by a barren forest.

Mikhail…

He looked through the trees to see a red-robed figure huddled close to the ground in the near distance. His heart pounded, and he clutched at the cross hanging around his neck.

"Rosemary, is that you?" He gripped his cross tightly.

Part I: Stăpânul

Her back was to him as she huddled over something on the snowy earth. Gyáva moved closer, and the snow crunching beneath his feet caught her attention. She turned slightly, revealing only a small portion of her face.

"Dear God. Rosemary?"

Gyáva reached his hand toward her shoulder, and she turned toward him. Sharp fangs hung from her mouth and blood ran from the corners of her lips. He saw his own reflection in her black eyes. She stood to confront him, revealing a tiny gravestone jutting from the snow. In her hands she held a dead baby wearing only a ragged cloth diaper.

Remember us, Mikhail, she said, her lips never moving. *Remember ...*

Gyáva clasped his hands to his heart and stumbled backward.

"Please no. Please ..."

Be with us, Mikhail ...

She held the child out toward him, and Gyáva noticed deep bruises around its neck and face.

Remember ...

Gyáva crawled backward along the snow as she continued toward him. Her robe fell open to reveal her naked body—ravaging strangulation marks encircled her neck. She stood over him and held the baby closer. Just as the child was in front of him, it opened its eyelids to reveal dead, black eyes.

Remember...

The vision faded as Gyáva sat up in bed, panting and clutching his chest. He knelt upon the stone floor, looked to the cross hanging on the wall, and folded his hands together. Gyáva prayed well into early morning, finally falling asleep still kneeling upon the hard stone.

*

Kashin arrived at the hospital at 9:56 p.m.—a swarm of police officers hovered about the halls. They took notice of his manner of dress and shuffled out of his way, some nodding as he strode past.

Chapter 12

As he reached the ward reserved for aristocracy, two police officers stood from their chairs and saluted him.

"Hands down, you idiots. Never salute Okhrana."

He pushed through the door to an empty hallway where Sana sat slumped in a chair. Before her knelt a starets holding her hands and consoling her.

"Sana!"

She looked up and ran toward him. They embraced.

"I'm sorry for how I behaved earlier. I'm just so frightened and confused. I don't know who to trust."

"I understand, Sana. I am here to help. Any word of your sister?"

With tears in her eyes, she shook her head. "Dead," she whimpered.

"I'm so sorry, Sana."

They held each other for a moment, then Kashin looked to the starets. Sana broke their embrace and turned toward him.

"Commander Kashin," she said, drying her tears. "This is Father Rasputin. He arrived just before you did."

Kashin was stiff as Rasputin bowed at the waist.

"Commander, it is an honor. My few instances of seeing the Okhrana at work have left me with the highest regard for their ... professionalism," he said, revealing his striking white teeth.

Kashin stared at him, searching momentarily for something to say. "No one is permitted past those officers. Only Archimandrite Gyáva. How did you get in here?"

"Gyáva has—"

"Father Rasputin was sent in his place," interrupted Sana. "My heart leapt when I saw him enter this hall. I know it is fate for him to bless Anna, Commander. He's the one I told you about. He practically saved us!"

Kashin's face lost color.

"Commander Kashin. Will you stand witness?" asked Rasputin.

"Please, Commander," begged Sana.

"I am honored."

"Please, follow," said Rasputin.

They entered Anna's room, where she lay dead upon a nondescript hospital bed with only a thin white sheet covering her up to the neck. Kashin followed them, never taking his gaze from Rasputin.

Part I: Stăpânul

Rasputin stood over Anna and closed his eyes and hovered his hands over her body. Sana stood on the other side of the bed and cried as she watched Rasputin's hands circle over her dead sister.

"The doctors said it was pneumonia ... they said ..."

"Quiet, my dear," said Rasputin. "I don't believe Anna is ready to go. She has ... she has something she wants to say to you."

Rasputin placed his hands upon Anna and thrust all his weight onto her torso, which induced a dire cracking sound from her ribs. Kashin moved in and tried to pull Rasputin away. Anna sucked in a great breath, and she attempted to sit upright. Rasputin subdued her and she lay with eyes open wide.

"Dear God!" shouted Kashin. He backed away to the door.

Sana screamed, then calmed herself. She crept toward her sister. Anna appeared peaceful, her eyes fixed on the ceiling. She turned her head to see Sana approach.

"Sana," she said, reaching toward her.

Rasputin continued to close his eyes and hold his hands upon her body. Sana trembled as she grasped her sister's hand.

"I thought I lost you, Anna."

Anna smiled at her, appearing weak. She breathed softly, her voice barely escaping her mouth.

"It's beautiful, Sana. So beautiful."

"Anna, please. Stay with me."

"I wanted to come back. To say goodbye. I wanted to say I love you ... and that ... that you must take Father Rasputin to Alexandra. He can save Alexei. He can save you all."

Anna closed her eyes, and her body fell limp. Rasputin looked to Sana.

"Father! Please, bring her back."

"She is gone. It was all I could do."

Sana shivered.

Kashin took notice and led her to a chair along the wall. Rasputin watched them for a moment, then came to her side.

"Give me your hands, Sana."

Sana placed her dainty hands into Rasputin's palms.

"Pray with me," he said, and bowed his head.

Chapter 12

She pushed her forehead into his, and Rasputin began to whisper. Kashin stood near, trying to overhear the prayer—it sounded like a foreign tongue.

Rasputin opened his eyes.

"She is free now," he said.

"Thank you, Father. Thank you," said Sana. She placed her hand upon Rasputin's cheek. "You're a miracle, Father Rasputin. A gift." She smiled. "I beg you to be my guest at court tomorrow. I must introduce you to Nicholas and Alexandra."

"As you command, Sana. Upon your invitation, I will come." He stood, then bowed deeply.

Rasputin held Sana under his arm as they walked from the room.

"Commander, my regards to Officer Baylor," said Rasputin before entering the hall.

*

The City Duma appeared like a rigid watchman over the empty, snow-covered Nevsky Prospekt. Electric lamps shone upward, illuminating the Duma's italianate tower, cutting deep shadows into its subtle motifs and wide eaves. Hidden from below, a hooded figure paced around the outdoor terrace that encircled the tower's pinnacle.

Makarov peered over the gilded railing toward the Kazan Cathedral and then to the near distance, where the Winter Palace's lights twinkled with a sense of optimism. He closed his eyes, sucking in deep breaths of cold, crisp air. Several moments of quiet passed until a brisk gust of wind blew upon his back, followed by intent footsteps.

"Do you have any idea the lengths we've gone to keep your carelessness from the newspapers?" Makarov kept his focus on the Winter Palace.

Rasputin walked slowly toward him, stopping several paces behind his cloaked figure. "This is the greeting you give me after—"

"Almost thirteen years," said Makarov, revealing his face. "I've been counting too. Between the Okhrana butchery and your little feasts, we might as well advertise your presence on the front page

Part I: Stăpânul

of the *Vedomosti*. All of Saint Petersburg is alive with talk of the Sleepwalker."

Rasputin stood next to him and faced outward, neither man looking toward the other.

"The Okhrana are acting alone," said Rasputin.

"Clearly."

"They came to me earlier, arrested me as planned. Imagine my surprise when they took me to the woods and shot me."

Rasputin looked to Makarov's gloved hands as they squeezed the railing.

"If you knew of the attack on the girls, why didn't you inform us? You were merely to tell them of Alexandra's planned assassination. There were to be no more surprises."

"And how would that information have been relayed to Nicholas if the girls were murdered? I foresaw the events and I acted. I need not seek your approval."

Makarov grimaced. "You've demonstrated that for decades. Do you have any idea the rage that will outpour from this? If the coven is made aware you turned Anna to vámpir?"

"Then don't tell them," said Rasputin.

"The seers will know!"

"Olaf has cloaked my actions. Anna was necessary. Bringing her back to life momentarily has solidified an undying trust within Sana. She has invited me to meet Nicholas and Alexandra tomorrow. It will be easier for me to manipulate Nicholas and Alexandra with Anna's unexpected death close to their hearts. Grief clouds better judgment, and I can finally get close to the boy."

Makarov laughed. "And with Archimandrite Gyáva still alive. Who will it be to counsel them? A strannik they barely know?"

"Gyáva will die. But it must not be perceived as murder."

"Very well," said Makarov.

"It was an Officer Baylor who came to me," said Rasputin.

Makarov looked to him. "And you suppose I orchestrated this?"

"Had it been blackwood to the heart, yes."

Makarov's cloaked figure turned away from Rasputin toward the skyline. He exhaled deeply and watched his vapors slowly rise into the night.

Chapter 12

"Baylor is Kashin's lapdog," said Makarov. "They're Bolshevik double agents merely acting in self-preservation. Kashin chopped up Taneyev and his wife for God's sake. It was a grave miscalculation on your part to implicate Okhrana in their disappearance. You were only to disclose the assassination attempt. Your actions have Kashin desperate and angry. That's—"

"I will deal with Kashin. If questioned about the Okhrana involvement, I will simply say it is false. Sana was speaking out of confusion and fear. It will go away."

Makarov beat his gloved hand repeatedly against the railing. "I assure you the body of the Okhrana is loyal to me." He turned his back and walked along the railing. Rasputin followed. "The entire fabric of control is crumbling here. There are many other factions vying for power. And thanks to you, they may just grasp it."

"Mind your tongue," said Rasputin. "For soon you will call me Stăpân."

Makarov turned to him.

"I will call you Stăpân when you have proved to me you are worthy. Do not forget that it's your insubordination that has put us in this position." Makarov paused. "Although I do commend your cunning. Hiding in the shadows far from the coven's sight, keeping the cycle in limbo for decades. Biding your time until Alexandra birthed a halfling—"

"I told you I foresaw Alexei's birth. It was the only way to correct the cycle. Had you simply taken the steps to reunite me with Alexandra before she married Nicholas, all of this could have been avoided."

"You'd have been killed the moment you came back to Russia! The Black Hundred were furious a lowly *mujik* strannik took it upon himself to initiate the cycle—"

"I—"

"And I will remind you that you'd have been hunted and killed just after you disappeared it weren't for my interference. For years I listened to you, believed you were correct to wait for the boy's birth. And so I waited. The coven wanted her throat slit. They knew full well the cycle could be restarted if you and Alexandra were killed. But I warned them they would never find you. I persuaded them to keep her alive and to wait for Alexei's birth, hoping then you'd deliver on your promises. And yet you left me waiting for nearly thirteen more years."

"The boy had to mature. Do you believe a sickly child could commit murder of his own volition?"

Makarov bit his lower lip. "Point taken. But I will not be able to defend you any longer. Your treachery to the Black Hundred has not been forgotten. The man and woman were to be of noble blood—not a peasant and a princess. We delivered her to you. We financed you. You took it upon yourself to betray us. And your disobedience continues."

Rasputin scowled. "Don't forget. It was my spiritual gifts that brought this to fruition. I deserve everything I take."

A smile emerged from underneath Makarov's hood. He turned to the railing once more. "Let us not argue over who owes whom, shall we? Yes, your insight was … helpful. I just hope you remember your promises when the time comes. I will grab Russia's power if you succeed or not. It's eternal life I want." He looked to Rasputin. "And it's what you have promised me—to all of us."

"None of whom do I trust. I've had great reservations from the start, knowing your agenda is counter to my own . . . counter to the book."

Makarov laughed. "Oh, I'd forgotten. You and those Stovâjįk Khlysts believe vampirism should absolve the pure and the weak from their suffering. That they may rise up against their oppressors and purge the world of man's sin. Pathetic. You know as well as I do the Stovâjįk will be destroyed the moment they are no longer useful to us. Be thankful you're in the position you are or you'd die with them."

"This gift is not a divine right of the autocracy."

"Indeed it is. In time, you will see." Makarov looked to Rasputin and smiled. "An undead idealist. You never cease to amuse me, Father Rasputin."

Rasputin stood next to him and they stared at the Kazan Cathedral for several moments.

"Pavlovich seems intent on correcting his wrongs," said Makarov. "He should be spared. Grief clouds better judgment, as you know."

"I assure you. No harm will come to him."

Chapter 12

Makarov nodded. "Very well. Are you still having the visions about Yusupov?"

"Yes, but they are cloudy. He is being protected by a seer."

"We must apprehend him before he reaches Alexandra. She and the boy must remain isolated."

"I assure you, I will deal with Yusupov—"

"What is your interest in him?" asked Makarov, turning to confront him. "It feels to me you are hiding something once more."

Rasputin paused for a long moment. "Yusupov has an important part to play in all of this, and it is not your concern."

Makarov let out a long breath. "But it is my concern," he said, raising his voice.

Rasputin stood closer to him, seeming to tower over the old man. "It is not."

Makarov's eyes shot to the floor. He peered out into the Saint Petersburg night. "Well then, your time is slim," he said, shaking his head. "I doubt you will manage to entice Alexei to murder his own father. Our seers have predicted the boy's death on December 16. The Holy Upir will die, and your heart will stop with them."

Rasputin appeared stern. "I too have had the visions. December 16 will come. The cycle will be corrected."

"I pray it is."

There was a long pause between them.

"My sources tell me the Bolsheviks will revolt within the week," began Makarov. "Since Kashin interrupted our plans, my future is uncertain. I must still be put somewhere safe. Until I am made immortal, my head is as much a treasure to the leftists as the tsar's. I'll see to it Kashin is put into a position where you can eliminate him. With him acting alone, I'm not certain any longer as to who my enemies are." He paused and looked to Rasputin. "Present company excluded, of course … Stăpân."

Rasputin turned and walked away.

"And Stăpân?"

Rasputin's footsteps ceased.

"Turning Anna was a grave mistake. She is to remain buried."

Part I: Stăpânul

A gust of wind came over them, and Rasputin was off into the night. Makarov looked to the Winter Palace once more with a devilish grin upon his face.

*

Professor Vondling closed his eyes and held his bony hand in front of a slim white candle, enjoying the flame's focused warmth. The light emanated a soft glow through his long, manicured fingernails. He opened a drawer in his kitchen cabinet, removed a butcher knife, and placed it upon the tiled counter. Vondling spent a good amount of care selecting the perfect drinking glass from an assortment of fine crystal within an ornate cabinet. He wrapped his fingers around a tall goblet with a fat belly and cradled it against his chest.

He set the vessel next to the sink, then looked to the baby pig that lay bound and struggling in the porcelain basin. Vondling held the butcher knife to its throat. The small animal shrieked as the knife sawed through its puny neck. After using the goblet to catch the pig's blood, Vondling raised it to his mouth. He stood still with eyes closed and let the scent rise as would a sommelier wafting the undertones of a fine wine.

Vondling placed his lips upon the glass and tipped it. The crystal felt cool upon his lips as the warm blood flooded his mouth. A few eager gulps and it was finished. Vondling leaned on his counter for a moment and let the sensation soothe him. He slowly lifted his head and curled his upper lip to reveal bloodstained teeth. A fluttering from upstairs broke his trance as the candles went dark.

"My Stăpân?" He looked upward with blood dripping from his mouth.

Vondling struck a match and lit a nearby candle. With the candlestick outstretched before him, he left the kitchen and walked toward the staircase that led upstairs. A small bubble of light surrounded his figure as he crept down the dark hallway toward his study.

"Stăpân?"

Vondling opened the door to his study. It was empty. He closed the door behind him and placed the candle upon his desk. His eyes scanned the ceiling for the slightest hint of movement. Placing his

Chapter 12

ear to the attic door, he closed his eyes and ran his hand along the mahogany. His hand traced its way to the dragon-shaped door handle, and he tugged on it. As ordered, the door was locked.

"Oh, Stăpân," he said while pressing his cheek against the door like a lovesick teen.

"I am here, Charles," echoed Rasputin's voice.

Vondling stood back from the door and postured upright as if greeting a general.

"I see you have attempted to warn others about my knowledge of them. Are you aware of the repercussions of these actions? Are you aware what they could have caused?"

"Stăpân, please. I was merely trying to protect you."

"Are you aware, Professor Vondling, that those same parties are now working to destroy me?"

"How dare they!"

"They are, Professor. Conspiring to find me. To kill me."

"I can stop them."

"I doubt that. I have begun to doubt my choice in you. Perhaps I should have chosen another? Someone a bit more … trustworthy?"

"Please, Stăpân! Let me show you. It is my honor to serve! Is it the coroner and the witch?"

"I will handle the seer. You are too novice for her powers."

"Then allow me to kill Kozlov for his betrayal."

Vondling stood near the door, hoping it would open. A sullen silence hung about the room.

"There is another," spoke Rasputin. "One you must bring before me."

"I will do whatever it takes." Vondling drove his foot into the hardwood. He breathed heavily, sucking on his lower lip. His fingernails curled into his palms, and he appeared ready to pounce through the door.

"Do you promise to do as you're told?"

"I will obey your every command, my Stăpân."

"Have you studied? Do you know the book by heart?"

"I breathe those words."

"Very well, Charles."

Part I: Stăpânul

A click from the attic filled the cold air. Vondling jumped. The door creaked open and revealed the attic stairs. Vondling stepped forward into the darkness. He crept up the staircase, and the attic door closed as softly as it had opened.

*

Orna hung upside down in the homemade contraption, her hand wrapped tightly around the series of ropes that fed into the candelabra at the ceiling's center. A dense row of candles lined the perimeter of the room, their flames bobbed to the subtle gusts of wind that came from the open window. Greta lay asleep on the floor next to her. Orna's eyes shifted about underneath her eyelids. She held her free hand in front of her, then clasped it.

"I have you now," she said.

A sudden breeze filled the room, nearly extinguishing the candles. The flames recovered, and the warm yellow glow illuminated the apartment.

Greta stood and growled at the shadowy intruder.

"Easy, girl," said Orna.

Rasputin stood in the center of the room, directly underneath the candelabra.

"I knew you'd come," she said with a smile that revealed her gums.

Rasputin stood a few feet in front of her.

"An old witch and a mangy mutt. This is an insult."

"Grigori Rasputin. Finally, I see. You've made a dire mistake in revealing yourself to me."

"Pity you will never breathe my name again."

"You underestimate me." She cackled. "See your wicked self, foul vámpir. Be gone from my home!"

Orna released the ropes, sending the curtains to the floor. A dust cloud settled to reveal full-length mirrors covering each surrounding wall. Rasputin looked to the mirrors to see the reflection of a monster: a lean muscular body covered in a soft patchy fur running from the top of his head all the way to his posterior. He hunched upon the floor on all fours, his slender limbs giving him

Chapter 12

the appearance of a four-legged spider. Bony spikes jutted from his shoulders and elbows, and thin flaps of winglike skin ran along the sides of his body, connecting at both his wrists and ankles. Pointy, fur-covered ears jutted from the sides of his face, and a thick brow gave predominance to a large pug nose and fanged jaws. His gruesome reflection recycled onward to infinity, bouncing back among the surrounding mirrors.

Rasputin closed his eyes for a moment, then looked back to his reflection. A deep guttural laugh resonated through the room as the monster in the mirror once again crawled toward Orna.

"Save your tricks for the newborn," he said.

Orna opened her eyes, revealing her white eyeballs.

"Back, demon!" she yelled, raising her hand and starting to mutter in tongues.

Greta growled, gnashed her teeth, and jumped toward Rasputin. He grabbed the dog by her head and flung her out the window. A sharp, quick whimper rose as she struck the sidewalk three stories below. Orna gasped, then raised her voice and continued shouting her spell toward Rasputin.

In the mirror, the vámpir reflection slithered on all fours toward Orna. Rasputin stopped just before her face. He clenched his fists, and the mirrors shattered. The sound of crashing glass resonated through the room, followed by the quiet of the outside street.

Orna was silent, but breathing heavily.

Rasputin stood over her and snatched her wrist. "Your powers are weak, old woman," he said, twisting her arm sharply and breaking it. She merely let out a defeated whimper.

His svelte frame knelt to the floor, and he caressed her face as she tried to pull away.

"Brave Orna ... foolish girl."

Rasputin moved his sharp fingernails to her chin and slid both hands into her mouth. He pried open her jaw and ripped her entire jawbone from her face—the cracking of bone and a sickening gurgle filled the room. Rasputin threw her jawbone onto the floor, and a stream of dark blood spurted from her face.

"Please give this to Coroner Kozlov for me." He tucked an envelope into her jacket pocket. A fierce gust of wind surged through the room, causing the candles to go dead as Rasputin vanished.

Part I: Stăpânul

Orna hung upside down, struggling to breathe as blood forced its way down her esophagus and into her lungs. Tears filled her eyes while her mind raced for a spell that might save her. Her thoughts became clouded by panic and fear, and her eyes focused on a single twinkle of light outside her window in the far distance. Whether it was a star or lamplight, Orna could not discern. She focused on the distant light, trying to calm herself, but the lack of oxygen became too painful. Orna began convulsing in the darkness—twisting and turning as she tried desperately to breathe. Only another pain-filled moment passed before she fell limp, finally drowning in her own blood.

Chapter 13

Part I: Stăpânul

13

December 8, 1916 (OS), morning

It was 6:04 a.m. when Felix emerged onto the train platform at Vitebsk Station. He wore a low brimmed hat and high collar to conceal his features. Only three hours had passed since he and Rurik stopped drinking, and his puffy, bloodshot eyes gave a clue to his heavy alcohol consumption. Best as he tried to stand rigidly upright, his body still swayed a bit from the lingering drunkenness. Two passport officers approached him. Felix turned toward them, careful not to breathe heavily.

"Prince Felix Yusupov?"

"I'm sorry. You've mistaken me for—"

"Rurik sent us."

"Oh, yes. It's me."

"This way, please."

The officers walked the station line, and Felix followed.

"Rurik said you are to meet your contact at the center of car number three," said an officer, pointing to the train before them.

Felix turned to the officers. "Will you escort me?"

The men laughed.

"No. No. We know about you. The conductor cannot. Four cars up. Wait in the center. You will crawl."

The officer pointed to the gravel underneath the final open vestibule car.

"You're serious."

"Indeed. We'll ensure you go unnoticed."

Felix stood at the edge of the platform, and the officers turned their backs on him—their wide wool trench coats concealed him.

Chapter 13

"Not yet," said one of the officers, who stood watching the patrons pass by. "On three you can go. One ... two ..."

By the time three rolled from his tongue, Felix's boots had crashed onto the gravel below. The officers moved away from Felix's disappearing act and sauntered along the platform next to the train.

Felix crawled underneath the train, his elbows aching as they repeatedly dug into the gravel and rail ties. He continued under the open vestibule car, and then beyond the dining car as the gravel cut more into his elbows and knees.

Is he crawling to meet me? This is ridiculous.

As he clambered along, Felix looked up from the train well to see the passport officers walking along the platform, pacing him. He crawled until he reached the center of the fourth car, as instructed. Nobody was there. He looked up to the passport officers, who nodded to someone inside the train. A loud banging caused Felix to turn on his back and look up to the belly of the car. A rectangle of light opened above him to reveal a young cabin steward looking down at him.

"Prince Felix, I presume."

"Uh, yeah."

The boy extended his hand and pulled him into the cabin. He slammed the opening and covered it with the cabin's carpet.

"Thanks, kid."

Felix looked around the cabin. It was of moderate size with one bed, but much smaller than any he'd ever traveled in.

"Nice place," said Felix.

"Not bad. Toilet's down the hall, though. Didn't have time to muster you one with a private toilet."

"Fine."

"Take off your clothes."

"Pardon?"

"Your clothes, take them off."

"Now?"

"My time is short. Please," he said, and motioned to a folded garment sitting upon the cabin bed.

"Sure."

Part I: Stăpânul

Felix looked to the boy and pointed toward the cabin door. The boy rolled his eyes and turned his back. Felix tightened the money belt he'd strapped to his waist, then changed into the brown tunic. He noticed a thick brown wig underneath the last article of clothing.

"What's this?"

"Your new hair," said the kid, turning around. "Put this on too."

The cabin boy handed him a wooden Orthodox pectoral cross, and Felix strung it around his neck.

"OK, now the wig."

"No."

"You must. If you are caught impersonating a strannik, people will rip your limbs off."

Felix considered the statement, then flipped on the wig. The kid helped him position it until it fit naturally on his head.

"There. Very convincing, actually," began the kid. "And don't shave. You won't arrive until late on the tenth. You're more baby-faced than me, so at least try and look scruffy."

"Right."

"Oh! And no showering either. You have to stink like a strannik if you expect to pull this off."

"I most certainly—"

"Most certainly will listen to exactly what I tell you."

Felix was surprised by the boy's bravado.

"Stranniks commonly go on vows of silence," said the kid. "So if anyone approaches you, do not speak to them. Simply bow and sign the cross. Mostly you will be bothered by peasants requesting a blessing. Nobody of class bothers with your kind."

"My kind?"

"You're a strannik now—you might as well be pigeon shit."

"Great. What if I'm stopped by another priest?"

"Sign the cross and move on. You're under a vow of silence and that's the story you're sticking to. Silently, of course."

"Understood."

"Once you're in Bucharest, you should be fine, but I'd still keep quiet if I were you."

"Are you going to be on board?"

Chapter 13

"No. I'm just here to get you settled. There's a letter for you under your pillow from Rurik. You can read it when I'm gone."

The steward gathered Felix's belongings.

"Oh, hey. Those are—"

"Confiscated. Stranniks have no possessions, so you have no possessions."

"Wait a—"

"This is not a negotiation. Rurik will have them for you upon your return. Relax."

"So are you one of them too?"

"One of what?"

"Like Rurik. A vampire hunter?"

The kid laughed. "No. I work for Rurik. I'm a smuggler," he said. "What'd you think?"

Felix nervously patted down his tunic. "Well, I guess I didn't—"

"Stop. Vow of silence, remember? It's probably better if you don't leave this cabin. At least until you sober up. Toilet is down the hall. Dining car is last before the vestibule, I believe."

"Thanks," said Felix.

"And here," said the kid, pulling a parcel from his jacket pocket. "Bread and jam. Should keep you sustained until you reach Bucharest. Trust me. Stay in your cabin."

"Will do," he said, and accepted the brown bag.

The kid slipped from the cabin door.

Felix lay down upon the mattress. After a moment of stillness, he slid his hand underneath the pillow to feel for the letter. Felix sat up and looked at the envelope. He turned it over to see it had endorsement and tore it open.

Dear Felix,

My apologies for not going over everything in person last evening. I understand all of this must feel terribly jarring, especially when you are asked to believe in something you've been conditioned to think is a ghost story.

Part I: Stăpânul

Because we are uncertain of the vampire's exact whereabouts, I implore you to take all necessary precautions to protect yourself. It could very well be on to us.

You are on a small train mostly reserved for Russian military officers and Romanian aristocracy returning to Bucharest. I believe you will find its comforts pleasing—the ranking officers have a strong penchant for luxury. Posing as a strannik will allow you good cover until you reach Bucharest as it is common for religious pilgrims to board the lines in order to spread their message.

When you arrive in Bucharest, a liaison of ours will guide you to the Inn of Azul on the outskirts of town. The liaison will then help you find passage to my brother Denis. His address is listed below as a precaution. I had Orna telepathically send his typewriter a message about your arrival, but he is an eccentric and curmudgeon at best, so do not expect him to be hospitable to you. Please give him the attached letter. It will convince him that he must come to our aid in Saint Petersburg.

Your traveling papers are also attached. And for your protection, under the mattress we have hidden a large hand mirror and three medium-sized vials filled with crushed-garlic water. There are also a gas mask, two blackwood stakes, and a machete. Use them as I have instructed—especially the hand mirror. Vampires are petrified of their own reflection. Keep it close to you at all times.

We have eight days left. Please return swiftly.

My gratitude,
Rurik

Felix folded the paper and closed his eyes. Then he lifted the mattress and stared at the weapons.

What's with the gas mask?

The train pulled into motion, and he slumped upon the bed, rubbing his temples. When the steam locomotive finally rolled into Saint Petersburg's outskirts, Felix was fast asleep, dreaming of his

Chapter 13

palace bed. He didn't wake until his dreams brought Irina's smile flashing into his mind.

Part I: Stăpânul

PART II:
COPILUL SÂNGELUI

Chapter 14

Part II: Copilul Sângelui

14

СОВЕРШЕННО СЕКРЕТНО [TOP SECRET]
Sfânta Biblie al Strigoiului Viu
[Holy Bible of the Living Vampiric Witch]
The Book of Change :: The Bloodchild

I

1 The Moroii born from the womb of Eve is the Bloodchild—He who forever links the living and the dead.

2 The Bloodchild is the most sacred of all creatures—shepherd of Nosferatu, harbinger of order and might.

3 The Bloodchild must be defended above all else, for His life, His blood bind Nosferatu to the living plane.

4 If the Bloodchild ever shall perish, all Nosferatu will fall with Him. Vámpir will grow weak and take refuge in the shadows evermore.
—Vlad Drăculea, 1456

*

December 8, 1916 (OS), early morning

Alexei was fast asleep in his plush bed when a rumbling woke him. He opened his eyes and looked to the curtains to see morning's twilight poking through. The rumbling continued, and his bathroom door shuddered as someone tugged forcefully on the knob.

Chapter 14

Alexei sat up and noticed the door was framed by a bright light seeping from the other side. His eyes moved to the chair next to his bed, where he expected to see the shadow man. He was alone.

Alexei reached for his leg braces. He strapped them on, then swung his legs over the bedside, wincing a bit as his knee joints buckled. After sliding from the bed, he grabbed two arm crutches nestled alongside his nightstand and balanced himself. His eyes never left the slim beam of light emanating around the bathroom door.

Water flooded from underneath the doorsill.

"Mama?"

The door rattled for another moment, then stopped. Alexei could hear water running, and a woman whimpering. He struck the door with his crutch.

"Mama, is that you?"

Alexei froze as he saw a vision from the bathroom. Blood was everywhere—pouring from the faucet, overflowing onto the white-tiled floor from the raised bathtub. A pale woman floated just beneath the crimson surface, and her body sunk into the red murk. Suddenly, a naked boy stood from the bloody water. Great fangs hung from his mouth and dead, dark eyes bulged from his gaunt face.

Come with me, Alexei.

Alexei closed his eyes, and the splashing water stopped. He opened his eyes once more. The room was black. The bathroom door stood open, revealing nothing. He peered into the room and the white floors and porcelain tub were unsoiled. He shivered for a second, then inched his way back to bed and removed the leg braces. After pulling himself into his comfortable bedding, Alexei tried to relax, hoping his mother would soon be at his bedside.

*

"Nicholas Aleksandrovich Romanov II, emperor and autocrat of all the Russians, I give you Father Grigori Rasputin of Tobolsk, Siberia."

Sana stood beside Rasputin and bowed to him as he gazed at the red and crème floral designs of the sprawling Savonitré carpet. Nicholas and Alexandra sat upon a raised platform and held one

Part II: Copilul Sângelui

another's hands. Both seemed swallowed by their peaked thrones. Above them was a grand crystal chandelier that cast the only light in the room save the candles lining the parlor walls. The chandelier's glass was a deep ruby red, an effect the tsar's glass-smiths created by adding gold to the molten glass just before it was blown into its final setting.

Alexandra's reception parlor exuded a grand coziness from its elaborate antique furnishings. The windows, originally designed to allow ample sunlight, sat draped with heavy cranberry-colored curtains that matched all the fabric within the room. A variety of clocks Alexandra collected stood on the floor, while others hung in any available free space along the walls. They ticked rhythmically, almost in unison. Rasputin's heels clicked on cue as he bowed to Nicholas. He repeated the gesture to Alexandra.

"Rise, Father," spoke Nicholas.

Both Rasputin and Sana stood.

"Please, come forward."

Sana motioned him to move toward the tsar. He walked with an awkwardness about him, uncertain of the protocol.

"You may make eye contact now," whispered Sana.

Rasputin nodded and looked up toward Nicholas. He reached the riser, clicked his heels, and bowed deeply once more. Nicholas walked to him.

"Rise, Father. You have saved the life of my wife and son. For that you will no longer adhere to formalities in the privacy of my family."

Rasputin stood. Nicholas was surprised by his height. "Thank you, Your Highness."

"You may call me Emperor."

"Thank you, Emperor."

Nicholas turned to three chamber musicians seated nearby and nodded. They took his cue, and the room filled with soft sounds of string instruments.

"Alexandra, my darling. Please meet Father Grigori Rasputin."

Alexandra was still in her throne, staring at Rasputin. A warm sensation pulsed through her body as if heat were radiating from her very blood cells. She fanned herself, sweat breaking upon her forehead.

Chapter 14

Nicholas glared at Alexandra. "My darling." He cleared his throat and motioned toward Rasputin.

Alexandra snapped from her trance. She rose and walked to Rasputin, who clicked his heels and bowed at the waist once more.

"Rise, Father," she spoke.

Rasputin stood and stared into her eyes. She quickly looked to Sana.

"I am honored to stand in the presence of Your Grace," said Rasputin.

"A gentleman, indeed," replied Alexandra, smiling at Sana.

"Please, let us sit," said Nicholas.

He led the group to a far corner wall, where a curvature of marble benches adorned with plush velvet cushions surrounded a handsome fire pit. A modest flame crackled in the pit, and everyone stood until Nicholas motioned for them to sit. A moment later, three servants hovered about and left behind a silver serving platter with a variety of sweetmeats, plump cheeses, and bottles of red wine. Sana grasped a bottle and poured everyone a glass. Nicholas raised his glass into the air, and the party followed suit.

"To Father Rasputin and his … gifts."

Their glasses rang throughout the royal reception parlor.

"Na zdorovye," replied Rasputin as the small party began sipping from their glasses.

"Is it foresight, Father?" asked Nicholas. "Sana tells me you predicted everything. She says you brought Anna back to life. Are you a miracle worker?" He sipped from his glass and stared at Rasputin.

Rasputin smiled his bold grin.

"I can see only what God shows me. Through brilliant slivers of light is how he speaks."

"Are we to believe you can talk to God?" Nicholas pursed his lips and stared at Rasputin.

"I assure you, Emperor, there is no blasphemy in my bones. I have been blessed by our heavenly Father. That is all I know. I will use his gifts to comfort all who suffer."

"We … can all use some comforting here. Thank you," said Nicholas.

Rasputin clasped his hands together, and his eyes shone toward Nicholas. "Casting all your care upon him, for he careth for you."

"The Gospel of Peter," said Nicholas.

"Very good, Emperor. Peter 5:7."

Sana smiled and held her hand out to Alexandra, who reciprocated the motion. Nicholas noticed the women relaxing, then placed his elbows upon his knees and leaned closer to Rasputin.

"Thank you, Father," he said. "Despite the tragic loss of our dear Anna, I believe this is the first time in recent memory that any of us has had the inkling to relax. I insist you must stay here in the palace as our official guest. Sana has spoken to me about you being her spiritual advisor, and I too can use a true man of God—one not mired in the politics of Russia. I hope you will accept my offer."

"I am honored." Rasputin bowed his head.

"And you must give the blessing at Anna's wake," said Sana.

"I am at the humble service of the tsar and of any friend of this court."

"Indeed, my friend," said Nicholas. "And that is why I too request your services at Anna's funeral. She was dear to us all."

*

The conversation between Rasputin and Nicholas continued to the sounds of soft chamber music and the clocks softly ticking in the background. The group finished off two bottles of wine while Kashin watched the firelight dance upon the party's pleasantries from the parlor's shadows.

"Anything interesting?" asked Makarov, emerging from the curtains leading to the Okhrana's secret passage.

"You startled me, sir."

Kashin continued to look toward Nicholas. Makarov stood close behind him. "Do you know how bad this is for us?"

"Yes," said Kashin.

"Tell me then."

Kashin was silent.

"It's bad for us, Commander. Bad because this nobody strannik apparently knows very intimate details about our operations. It's bad

Chapter 14

for me because he—over a quaint wine reception—has piqued the ear of a desperate tsar. And it's worse for you because there are rumors floating about that you ordered him taken to the woods and shot."

"He was shot, sir." Kashin swallowed. "My men arrested him. Took him to the woods and shot him."

"They apparently did a great job."

"There's been a mix-up."

"Did your men consider checking the body?"

"Yes. It seems they arrested the wrong person."

Makarov stood closer to Kashin. "Wrong person?"

"Yes, they accidentally arrested the parlor owner. A Madam Lenora. Took her to the woods and shot her dead."

Makarov laughed quietly. "Let me see if I understand this. These men of yours mistook a woman for a giant bearded man? Did you hire the blind?"

"It's embarrassing, sir. I can't explain what happened. They swear it was Rasputin they eliminated. We won't make this mistake again."

"It shouldn't have happened in the first place. Why didn't you address me before acting so drastically?"

"He knows of my involvement with Ambassador Taneyev's disappearance. I had to act."

Makarov rubbed his palm over his face. "Call Gyáva. Tell him we need information on this strannik. Most of them are nomadic, drunken thieves. See if there's any criminal record. And be sure to let Gyáva know the tsar has become very friendly with this newcomer, even inviting him to lead the funeral of their dear friend Anna Taneyev. Isn't that usually the archimandrite's place?" Makarov paused and let Kashin digest the implications of his question. "I'm sure Gyáva can either find a criminal record or destroy any records of his religious past. Impersonating a holy figure before the tsar is punishable by death. Is it not?"

"I believe so. But, sir?"

"Yes?"

"There's something you should know…this strannik is magic."

"Magic?" Makarov said with a laugh.

Part II: Copilul Sângelui

"Yes, I saw it. He brought Anna back to life for a moment."

"Commander, tell me you intend to keep your grasp on reality from this point forward."

"Yes, Minister."

"Good. Now make that call. And the next time you decide to supersede my orders, you'll find yourself joining a certain ambassador and his wife. You see, had Rasputin merely been arrested, do you know where he'd be right now?"

Kashin was stiff.

"In jail." He pointed toward Rasputin as a pleasant laughter rose from the small reception. "Well done, Commander. You've created the new royal darling."

Makarov turned, then stopped. "Rasputin is not to be killed until I order it." He slithered off behind the curtains. Kashin continued to watch the party from the darkness until Nicholas motioned his security detail to move everyone to their sleeping quarters.

*

Sana and Anastasia sat near Alexei on his bed and tickled his stomach. He howled with laughter.

"I gotcha!" they said over and over.

Alexandra entered and rushed toward them.

"Sana, Anastasia, please!"

They looked quickly to Alexandra. Sana's bloodshot eyes took a moment to focus.

"I'm sorry, Alexandra. I was just trying to show him some fun."

"Come, Mother! We were simply playing," said Anastasia.

"Anastasia, you're too old to be playing. Very unladylike. Besides, it's late. To bed immediately!"

Anastasia curled her chin and looked to Sana. She leaned forward and kissed Alexei on his forehead. "See you tomorrow, Alexei."

Alexei smiled.

Alexandra thrust her fists onto her hips as Anastasia scampered by. "And tell your sisters I will be around shortly to tuck them in."

"Yes, Mother." Anastasia disappeared into the hall.

Chapter 14

Alexandra walked to Alexei. She threw the covers from the bed and inspected him.

"Are you cut? Scratched?" A strong, apparent panic in her voice.

"We were just having fun," said Alexei.

Sana and Alexei sneaked private glances at each other and grinned.

"Sana, you know how dangerous any rough play is. The slightest scratch—"

"I'm sorry, Your Highness," she said, and looked to the floor.

"Now," said Alexandra, reaching to Sana's arm. "Don't do that. You know it bothers me. Save the formalities for public."

Sana nodded.

"I'm going to fetch Alexei some water. Can I retrieve anything for you?" asked Alexandra.

"More wine."

"You've had enough." Alexandra smiled at her, then looked to her son. "I'll be right back, Alexei. You behave."

"I will, Mama."

Alexandra looked to them both and shook her head.

"Sometimes, Sana, I feel like I have another child with you around."

She walked from the room. Sana and Alexei started laughing the moment she was from earshot.

"How high do you think I can jump?" asked Sana.

"High!"

"Quick, watch."

Sana climbed on the bed and started jumping up and down on the empty portion of the mattress.

*

Alexandra navigated the darkened hallway toward the servants' quarters. A figure jumped from the shadows.

"Nicholas! You startled me."

Part II: Copilul Sângelui

Nicholas pulled her near and fondled her backside. Alexandra was overwhelmed by the alcohol on his breath. "It's been too long, my sweet," he spoke, and kissed her on the mouth.

Alexandra's heart leapt to feel his strong hands move about her slim body. Nicholas pushed her into a plush curtain and pulled open her gown. He cupped one hand upon her breast and kissed her on the neck while slowly moving his other hand between her legs.

"The servants will see," she said.

"It's too dark."

"My darling … let me just …"

Nicholas kissed gently down her neck. He moved to her breasts and kissed her more firmly. He traced his tongue downward across her stomach as a crash resonated from Alexei's quarters.

"What was that?"

"Forget it," said Nicholas, pressing his lips to her stomach.

"No, it was … something was broken."

"Sana will handle it," he mumbled.

"Nicholas, no!" She pushed him away and tightened her robe.

Nicholas shrugged. "You're icy."

"Me?"

"Yes. The ice empress," he said flatly. Even in the darkness Alexandra could make out his dilated pupils. "All you do is hide out like a recluse spider. I make one attempt to—"

"One attempt?" yelled Alexandra. "You don't acknowledge us at all! We're merely your photo ornaments for the press. Our boy is dying, Nicholas, and—"

"Whose fault is that?" he said, and poked her in the abdomen.

Alexandra turned her back on him.

"You're no father."

She ran toward Alexei's room. Nicholas watched her shadow move down the hall. He shook his head and walked back to his wing of the Winter Palace.

*

Alexei chuckled as Sana thrust more of her weight into the mattress. "Higher!" he said.

Chapter 14

She continued to jump. Her landings bounced Alexei's frail body about upon the mattress. Finally, at the apex of her last jump, Sana threw her legs outward and let the thrust of her weight plow into the box springs. The extra bounce threw Alexei off the bed, into the nightstand, and onto the floor. Sana shrieked as she saw him sitting on the ground, clutching his left shin.

"Alexei, are you hurt?"

Alexei nodded, his chin quivering.

"I'm so sorry. I'm so … oh, Alexei! Let me see."

Alexei's fingers were cupped around his bony shin as a steady stream of blood dripped onto the floor. She coaxed him to slowly open his hands and saw a shard of bone poking through his skin. Sana gasped.

"Alexei, stay here. I'll—"

"What was it?" screamed Alexandra as she ran into the room, tightening the loop on her gown.

Sana stood and rushed to her.

"Please, forgive me, Alexandra," began Sana breathlessly. "I was trying to show him some fun." Thick tears fell down Sana's face.

Alexandra peered to Alexei. He held his knee to his chest and winced, bleeding profusely from the bone protrusion.

"My son!" she screamed, and ran toward him. "How could you, Sana?"

"Please, I didn't …"

Sana felt something brush by her, and she spun around. She turned back to see Rasputin and Alexandra bent over Alexei.

"I heard screaming," said Rasputin.

"Father, his leg is broken." Alexandra was panting. "He's sick. He can die from a simple cut. We need the doctor!"

Rasputin reached to Alexandra. He placed one hand upon her shoulder and another on her forehead. "Relax now, all is well."

Alexandra took a deep breath and sat next to Alexei.

"Hello there, little one," said Rasputin.

"Hi."

"My, my. You have done it this time, haven't you?"

Alexei nodded, tears falling from his eyes.

"Let me see if I can help."

Part II: Copilul Sângelui

"Father Rasputin, he needs a doctor," said Sana, badly slurring her words.

"Sit down, Sana," he spoke firmly.

She sat on the bed.

"May I have a look?" He took Alexei's leg into his palm. "Oh dear."

Alexei continued to whimper.

"What's your favorite food, Alexei?"

Alexei looked to him with warm, concerned eyes.

"Cinnamon crumpets."

Rasputin nodded. "Ahh, very delicious. Now I want you to do me a favor. Close your eyes and think of cinnamon crumpets. Can you do that for me?"

Alexei nodded and closed his eyes.

Rasputin wrapped his hands around the bone protrusion and applied vigorous pressure to the leg. Alexei breathed quick wisps of air through his teeth as Rasputin continued to rub his palms about the wound. A moment later, Rasputin pulled his hands away ... Alexei's leg was healed—no bone, no blood, and no scar.

Sana and Alexandra gasped.

"Where else are you hurt, my boy?" asked Rasputin.

Alexei motioned to his elbow and knees, both with deep purple bruises. Rasputin applied pressure to each area, and the bruises disappeared.

"Stand," said Rasputin. "You may walk."

Alexei stood. He took a few clumsy steps, then walked to his bed and climbed up with ease. Alexandra and Sana watched with their hands over their mouths. Rasputin moved to Alexei's bedside, leaned forward, and kissed the boy's forehead.

"I will rub your legs each day, until they become strong again."

"Thank you, Father."

"Please, call me Grigori."

"Thank you, Grigori."

Rasputin took Alexei's small hands and clasped them in his own. "You are very much welcome, my child. It is not often a humble starets has the chance to heal the tsarevich of Russia. Your mother tells me you have been suffering from bad dreams?"

Chapter 14

"Yes."

"I think I can help with that too." Rasputin took his silver cross from his neck and handed it to Alexei. "Keep this near your heart, and you will dream only of pleasantries."

"Thank you, Grigori."

"Sleep well."

Rasputin rose and turned to Alexandra. She hugged him deeply.

"You're a godsend, Father."

"Please, Alexandra. I insist you call me Grigori."

Alexandra let go the embrace and looked to his eyes. There was an odd familiarity about him, as if she'd known him forever.

"Thank you," she said. "I will tell Nicholas of what you have done. We will have a grand dinner in your honor. You're a miracle."

"I am honored, Your Grace," he said, then leaned forward and kissed her on the cheek.

Alexandra touched her cheek. "Starets are forbidden to—"

Rasputin raised his finger to his lips.

"Good night to you all," he spoke, then walked from the room.

*

It was nearly dawn when Alexei finally drifted toward sleep. Just as his mind neared the cusp, he became aware of a presence in his room. "Is it you?"

Alexei rolled over and looked at the chair next to his bed. The shadow was seated, rocking back and forth. He crawled from bed and knelt before it. Slight whispers escaped its mouth.

"Pray with me, Alexei." Its voice was scratchy and low. "Give me your hands."

Alexei reached to the shadow—a coldness grasped his tiny hands. The shadow swayed, whispering in tongues.

"What do you see, Alexei?"

Alexei closed his eyes and felt the floor move away from him. The presence of the shadow was still near. He opened his eyes and found himself walking alone in a forest dense with blackwood trees. A crackling in the distance caught his attention, and he noticed two men walking along, both wearing gas masks with canisters strapped

Part II: Copilul Sângelui

to their bodies. Alexei crept closer to them, and a wall of fire burst upward in front of him. He recoiled on the ground, holding his face.

Alexei was now alone in the burning forest as smoldering tree limbs fell all around him. He bundled himself into a ball on the forest floor and threw his hands over his ears as the fire's howl grew louder still. As the fire's intensity became too great, he opened his eyes and found himself sitting on the floor in the Room of Coins. His ears fell quiet.

The expanse was dark save a light at its center, where Nicholas sat alone at his slim desk wearing white regal attire. Alexei walked to him. His bare feet crept upon the cool marble until he stood alongside his father. Nicholas was asleep.

"Father?" Alexei pulled on his elbow.

Nicholas shot awake—his eyes were nothing but dark, empty sockets. A stream of dark blood fell from his mouth, staining his pristine uniform.

Drink from me. Make yourself whole.

Alexei shrieked and jumped away. Nicholas slumped to the marble floor, and a guttural laugh echoed through the hall. Alexei turned to see the shadow standing in the entrance. He looked once more to his father to see the naked boy from his bathtub vision hunched over Nicholas, feeding on his neck. Alexei reached for the boy.

"Stop!"

The boy lashed upward and bit Alexei on the hand.

I am you.

Alexei woke in his own bed with the boy's blood-soaked face still fresh in his mind.

The room was dark, but he could see the cross Rasputin had given him lying on his nightstand. It seemed to shine in the darkness. Alexei retrieved the cross and strung it around his neck, wondering why he'd removed it in the first place. He pulled the covers over his head and hoped sleep would soon wash the vision from his mind.

Chapter 15

Part II: Copiul Sângelui

15

December 9, 1916 (OS), morning

A black police wagon met Rurik when he arrived at the morgue's rear entrance. Two officers he did not recognize—one policeman, one Okhrana—stepped out of the wagon and walked to its back. They pulled open the cargo door, where two bodies were encased in black tarp.

"Good morning, gentlemen," said Rurik.

"Morning, Coroner."

Rurik unlocked the back door and pushed it open. The police pulled one of the bodies from the wagon and followed him into the morgue.

"Oh dear," said Rurik as he looked about the room. "It appears we're running out of space. Just set them next to the autopsy table."

The officers flung the body on the floor and left to retrieve the second corpse. After a moment, they returned with the second body tarp and plopped it on the floor.

"OK," said Rurik, rubbing his hands together. "What's on today's menu?"

The officer untied the binding straps of the first body tarp. He pulled away the top, and a redheaded woman in her late thirties appeared beneath. Her pale skin looked supple and vibrant.

"This one's official state business," said the Okhrana officer. "Some fortune teller they found dead in the woods. Petrov on behalf of the Okhrana says to incinerate it. Take no record."

"No problem."

The police officer stood over the second tarp and pulled it back to reveal an elderly woman whose jaw had been torn from her face.

Chapter 15

"Dear God!" yelled Rurik.

"What?" cried the officer, jumping toward his partner.

Rurik calmed.

"Nothing. It's just ... I ... I have never seen such a mutilation."

"We don't know what happened to this one either," began the policeman. "Her body was discovered after neighbors found her dog whimpering on the sidewalk — poor thing must have fallen out the window. By the time we arrived, the old hag bled to death. Not that anyone could have saved her." He laughed. "This was a weird scene. She was hanging upside down in some kind of sex contraption ... mirrors on the walls shattered to pieces. Everything."

"Indeed, gentlemen. Thank you. I can handle it from here."

"Excellent," said the policeman, handing Rurik an evidence log sheet. "If you wouldn't mind logging anything you find on the body into evidence, we'd appreciate it."

"Will do," said Rurik, who then shuffled the officers down the hall and locked the iron door behind them.

Rurik ran back to the morgue and knelt beside Orna. He pulled back the front flap of the body bag and held her mittened hand.

"I'm so sorry, good Orna."

He pulled her hand to his forehead, then looked to her coat, noticing paper was sticking from the pocket. Rurik let go of her hand and pulled out the reddish envelope from her pocket. He opened it to reveal a heavy paper stock with a deep red hue. The top section of the parchment was torn.

> Coroner,
>
> I have left you alive this long for one simple reason: I was in need of your services to help the hapless and cowardly Petrov hide my murders from the newspapers and the royals. But your meddlesome actions with one Prince Felix Yusupov have become a terrible liability to me, and I no longer require your services.
>
>   I would very much enjoy to pay you a visit and thank you in person, but have much larger dealings to attend.

Part II: Copilul Sângelui

My associate will be visiting you soon and will certainly pass on my gratitude.

I wish you luck in all your future ventures—no matter how short-lived they certainly will be.

Sincerely,
S. Walker

Rurik folded the paper and placed it in his pocket. Even in the frigid morgue, damp sweat marks sullied the underarms of his trench coat. A surge of anger and fear pulsed through him, and he slammed his fist to the floor. He scanned the room's small, narrow windows and realized the sun wouldn't rise for another two hours. After covering Orna and the redhead, he ran to the back door and bolted it shut. Running from room to room, Rurik secured all windows and locked every dead bolt, pulling a heavy cabinet or other large piece of furniture in front of any door he could.

When Rurik came to his office, he barricaded it closed with his filing cabinet. He sat at his desk and stared at the cheap walnut door. It was only 8:14 a.m., and he was already digging into his desk for his reserve bottle of vodka. He opened the bottle and poured a helping into a dirty glass upon his desk. After taking a small swig, he pulled the letter from his pocket.

Upon closer inspection, it appeared the paper was part of a stationery letterhead with the top ripped off. He ran his pinky across the finely torn paper, and then rubbed the parchment between the pads of his fingers. A familiarity kindled in his mind. It was a rare paper stock, one he'd seen before.

Rurik slammed the paper onto his desktop and stood forcefully enough to upset his chair. He walked to his filing cabinet. After shuffling through a few files, he pulled out an envelope stuffed with papers. He came back to his desk and carefully withdrew one of the papers from the envelope. He flattened it and with intent precision placed the letter from the Sleepwalker on top of the new document, aligning the bottoms perfectly. A cool perspiration broke upon his brow when he discovered they both had the same deep red hue, clearly from the same stock. The letterhead on the bottom paper read *Professor Charles Vondling, 1 Kronverksky Avenue, Saint Petersburg,*

Chapter 15

with a stark, thin red line underneath the text. Had the Sleepwalker's letter not been torn, the two would have matched exactly. Rurik opened his desk, pulled out a magnifying glass, and inspected the tear, exposing that it had been torn along a thin line of red ink.

Rurik swatted the papers from his desk, and they floated to the floor. He threw his hands to his face and rubbed his fingers through his hair.

"Of course, it's with Vondling," he whispered. "I should have expected this."

He finished off the vodka, swirling the last gulp in his mouth before swallowing. "I must be paying the good professor a visit."

Rurik walked to a wall closet at the right of his desk and opened it, revealing what could have been a witch doctor's wardrobe. He poked about the contents and pulled out a thick leather belt, which he buckled around his waist. Encircling the belt were tiny holsters where Rurik nervously shoved corked vials containing a garlic water concoction. He then wedged two lean blackwood stakes between his belt and his hips. He shoved a hand mirror into his coat pocket and pulled a gas mask from the closet.

Rurik buckled his trench coat and walked back to his desk. He poured more vodka into his glass and downed it in one gulp, then positioned the gas mask over his face. He exited the morgue, ensuring the back door was locked before shuffling down the alley, appearing like a madman ready to do battle with the apocalypse.

*

Rurik arrived at Vondling's residence at 10:19 a.m. The sun had finally cracked winter's perpetual twilight as he stood outside the gate. Assured he went unseen, Rurik unlatched the wrought-iron gate and sneaked toward the mansion's back entrance. The building seemed to hulk over him like a gothic monster waiting to pounce.

He crept to the servants' kitchen entrance and peered through the window—nobody inside. Rurik clenched his gloved fist and punched the small glass pane next to the door handle. The entire pane splintered from the wooden frame and fell inside with a clank.

Part II: Copilul Sângelui

He reached inside and unlocked the door, which opened to a slim hallway. Rurik positioned the gas mask over his face and stepped inside.

The house was quiet. Rurik unfastened his trench coat and pulled the hand mirror from his pocket as he walked into the kitchen.

Dirty dishes and glassware were piled in the open as if Vondling had abandoned last evening's supper. Rurik looked into the sink and curled his nose at the sight of a baby pig carcass. He reached to the crystal goblet sitting on the counter and inspected the dried blood in its hull. A creaking noise from above startled him, and he quickly placed the glass back on the counter.

Again, the floorboards creaked.

Rurik pulled one of the flasks from his belt and uncorked it. He slinked down the hall, gripping the hand mirror. Upon reaching the base of the stairs, he found a small switch and turned on the lights to the second-floor hallway. No sign of motion upstairs. Rurik climbed the marble stairs slowly and steadily.

He reached the top and stood for a moment, restlessly shifting his feet as he stared down the wide, dim hallway. The dark wood paneling seemed to absorb the minuscule light cast from two small electric torch lamps flickering in the distance. Grotesque paintings of historical execution scenes hung along the walls, accented by statues of contorted human bodies that sat upon pedestals lining the hall. The ornately carved doors along the passage were all closed except for one at the very end that stood slightly ajar. From what Rurik could see, the room within was pitch-black. He silently cursed himself for not bringing a flashlight.

"You should leave now, Rurik," he said quietly to himself.

Gripping tightly around his hand mirror, he crept down the hall, ready for anything to pounce. A terrible aching sensation warmed the nape of his neck. He flipped the hand mirror and ensured nobody was behind him.

He stood at the door and pushed it open, creating a dire creaking noise. The house grew silent as his eyes strained for a glimpse of the room's contents.

Rurik noticed a sliver of light upon the room's far wall and shoved the hand mirror into his pocket before making his way toward the window. He bumped into the desk and dropped the garlic

Chapter 15

vial as he swung the plush curtains open. His nerves screamed at the sight of the embalmed human head staring at him from Vondling's collection. He turned to find the room empty. Countless black eyes gazed back at him from a variety of dead birds and small animals. Rurik relaxed slightly when he realized they were his only company.

Vondling's penchant for the occult was renowned among the intellectual circles of Saint Petersburg, yet the bizarre assortment of taxidermy, human body parts, and occult symbols still unnerved Rurik.

Why did I ever agree to sell any of this to him?

An ornate volume displayed on the desk caught his eye. He flipped through the pages, and it was only a brief second before he realized the greatness of the discovery. Excitement surged through him as the words floated by his eyes. Rurik closed the book. *Sfânta Biblie al Strigoiului Viu* was inscribed in gold upon the leather cover. He tapped the title with his finger, almost unable to contain himself.

Footsteps came from above.

They were slow at first. Rurik watched the attic floorboards depress, his eyes tracing their path. He reached in his pocket and pulled out the hand mirror as the footsteps rumbled down the attic stairs. Rurik flung himself against the door.

A quick clicking sound resonated from the other side, and a gunshot exploded, sending a round just above Rurik's head. Wood splinters flew everywhere as a second round blasted through the door near his shoulder. He fell to the floor and dropped the hand mirror. The attic door swung open to reveal a tall, thin man dressed in the simple manner of a Stovâjįk peasant with a large scar running down the left side of his face.

The man reloaded his gun.

Rurik leapt toward him, thrusting his forehead into the man's chin. His vision was engulfed by a white flash from the blow. They both fell to the floor. When he regained his senses, Rurik looked to the unconscious gunman. He took a vial of garlic juice and flung the liquid onto the man's face. The yellow glop ran down his flesh with no effect.

Rurik picked up the shotgun and stood over his assailant, smashing his bootheel into the stranger's face.

Part II: Copilul Sângelui

He stepped over the unconscious man and peered up the attic stairs, pointing the shotgun into the stairwell. A fierce thumping resonated from above, and a powerful gust of wind knocked Rurik to the floor, sending the shotgun from his grasp. He pulled himself up as a freezing sensation invaded his sinuses. His hands fumbled near his belt for a blackwood stake, and he swung around to face the intruder.

His jaw fell limp at the sight of her.

"Help me, Mr. Kozlov. They cut me all up."

Rurik stood silently, barely able to breathe at the sight of the naked girl. She huddled in the corner with severe lacerations gouged into her skin and dried blood caked on her hair and face. She was just as he remembered the day her body arrived at the morgue.

"Is it you?" he gasped.

"It hurts, Mr. Kozlov." She clutched her abdomen and cowered in the corner, weeping. "They're coming for me. Don't let them hurt me again."

Rurik shook his head, dizziness welling inside him.

"What are you holding?" she cried. "Please don't hurt me."

Rurik dropped the blackwood stake and crept toward her, his hands outstretched.

She screamed, cowering from him. "Your mask is scaring me!"

Rurik started to pull up the gas mask. His eyes fell to the floor and he caught a glimpse of her true reflection in the hand mirror. It was the image of a gruesome vámpir.

"Of course, little one. Be still … I won't hurt you."

Rurik feigned removing the mask a bit more. As he neared striking range, he quickly pulled the gas mask down, clutched his last blackwood stake, and lunged for Rasputin, stabbing him in the chest. Rasputin shrieked and flung Rurik on top of the desk.

Rasputin slumped over, coughing blood onto the floor. Rurik's sinuses returned to normal, and he now saw the vámpir before him. He backed away toward the desk, searching for the garlic vial he dropped. Rasputin's head shot up toward Rurik, and he spit a clear, globulous liquid onto Rurik's gas mask as he continued to writhe and shriek while struggling to pull the stake from his chest. The fluid dripped over Rurik's goggles and Rasputin fell to the floor.

Chapter 15

Realizing his opportunity, Rurik tore the gas mask from his face to free up his field of vision. He snatched the vampire bible, held it tightly against his body, and fled down the hall, trailed by Rasputin's shrieks.

By the time Rurik was midway down the stairs, Rasputin had removed the stake. Gobs of bloody flesh hung from it, and smoke from his chest rose into the air. He leaned against the wall as his wound healed. After a few more bloody coughs, he flew down the hall after Rurik.

Rurik jumped to the landing only to have his ankles yanked from underneath him. He fell face-first, and the vampire bible flew from his hands, landing just out of grasp. Head over heels, Rurik dug his fingers into the hardwood floor as Rasputin pulled him upstairs. He reached for the banister and held on by wrapping his elbow around the marble column.

Rurik looked to his feet to see Rasputin levitating, pulling him backward—massive clawed hands were wrapped around his ankles like wolf's teeth. Rurik's grip slipped little by little, and his free hand plucked another garlic vial from his belt. He clenched the cork in his teeth and flung the mixture toward Rasputin—a large clump of it landing on his clawed hands.

The stench of burned flesh immediately permeated the room, followed by a horrid shriek. Rasputin released Rurik's ankles, then disappeared as he transformed into a smoky ether. The black fog fled up the stairwell, sending the paintings and statues smashing to the floor as Rasputin retreated toward the attic.

Rurik snagged the vampire bible, clutching it to his chest as he ran to the back gate. He peered up to the peak of the roof several times as he fled into the street.

An hour later, Rurik was locked tightly back inside the morgue.

Sundown's in six hours. Hurry, Rurik.

He placed the vampire bible on his desk, switched on his desk lamp, and began absorbing the secret doctrine.

*

Anna Taneyev's coffin slowly descended to its final resting place at 3:42 p.m. in a section of the Tsarskoye Selo cemetery reserved

Part II: Copilul Sângelui

solely for the aristocracy. A small party of mourners gathered around the row of earth reserved for the Taneyev family.

Sana stared into the open grave and wondered how much longer it would be before there were two more holes in the ground for her missing parents.

Rasputin stood over the grave and blessed the first patch of dirt shoveled onto Anna's casket. He then splattered a vial of holy water onto her gravestone and handed Sana the empty glass.

"She is with God," he spoke.

The low Arctic sun began to set, never breaking through the day's thick cloud cover. Rasputin was still silently recovering from his duel with Rurik, and despite being well fed from the previous evening, he felt further weakened by the indirect sunlight. He was relieved to feel the daylight wane.

The ceremonial bell for the dead rang over the city. It was to ring five times in honor of those whom Anna had left behind: twice for the tsar and tsaritsa, once for Sana, and twice for her missing parents. Sana knew it should have rung only thrice.

The parties walked beneath the sporadic gas lamps as they returned to their automobiles and carriages. Rasputin walked with Sana under his arm.

"Father Rasputin," called Gyáva as he strode to catch them.

"Sana, please," said Rasputin, gesturing toward the car. Sana nodded and walked to join Alexandra who wore a wide-brimmed hat and scarf that covered most of her face. Nicholas embraced them both as they climbed into their automobile.

"I wanted to congratulate you on your eulogy," said Gyáva. "As you know, I was supposed to be the one who—"

"Yes, I know," said Rasputin, turning to confront him.

Gyáva stared silently at Rasputin.

"You're very well-spoken for a strannik—"

"It's starets now."

Gyáva appeared startled by Rasputin's brashness.

"Might I ask where—"

"Converted at the Verkhoturye monastery. You should be familiar with our forests in Siberia, Archimandrite. You have family buried there."

Chapter 15

Gyáva coughed as Rasputin's dark eyes shot through him.

"Not to my knowledge," he said. "I have no dead family other than my deceased parents, and they're buried here in this cemetery."

Rasputin huffed. "I'm speaking of the girl you impregnated when you were a young monk. The one you then murdered and buried in the forest. You remember Rosemary."

Gyáva's weathered faced blushed a near purple. "You son of a bitch. How do you—"

"She's been asking about you, Archimandrite." Rasputin smiled and flashed his sharp canines. "She wants to reunite the family."

Sana ran back to Rasputin and held his hand. "Come, Grigori. We're late," she said, smiling at Gyáva.

"Oh, Tobolsk!" began Gyáva, pretending to continue a pleasant conversation. "I am very close with Brother Stodovitch and—"

"Indeed." Rasputin turned his back and walked arm in arm with Sana toward the tsar's shiny black automobile.

Rasputin closed the door, never taking his gaze from Gyáva. The car pulled around, and they were on their way back to the Winter Palace. As the vehicle disappeared down the cemetery's windy embankment, Gyáva watched with clenched fists, forcefully digging his fingernails into his own palms and sucking large breaths into his lungs.

*

It was just after dusk when the gravediggers finished packing the last of the dirt onto Anna's grave. Even in the cold of winter, the laborers stripped down to their long wool undergarments as not to overheat while finishing their grueling work. Just as their portable lamps became their only viable light source, they patted Anna's grave with their shovels, took their lamps, and sauntered off into the cold night.

A soft snow fell upon the arched gravestone that read Anna Taneyev, 1892–1916. Inch by inch, damp snowflakes slowly covered the fresh mud of her grave. The falling specks grew in intensity, reflecting the soft orange light of the gas lamps that sprouted aimlessly about the cemetery grounds. A calm serenity overtook the graveyard as night carried itself into early dawn—

Part II: Copilul Sângelui

a silence soon broken by Anna's haunting, muffled screams rising from deep within the earth.

*

Rurik sat in his office, his mind riddled with dreadful thoughts. He poured some vodka into his glass and took a healthy gulp.

"Thank you for coming, Zazlov. I apologize for the urgency," he said, looking to the burly, bald man seated across from him. Rurik took notice of his impeccable all-black double-breasted suit and studied Zazlov's handsome face and unique beard, which had been a matter of silent curiosity for him over the years. It was almost pure black save two silver strips that ran along the outer edge where it was lean and trim around his chin, then ran pointy and sharp to his Adam's apple. Thinking back to a conversation he'd had with his brother years ago, Rurik remembered describing Zazlov's beard as *fanciful* and decided that was likely the best he'd ever do.

"I am happy to come, my old friend—lucky timing, I am set to travel home to Paris tomorrow," said Zazlov with a slight French accent. "I—I am terribly sorry about Orna. She was my mentor in spellbinding several hundred years ago." Zazlov reached over and patted Rurik's hand. Rurik broke eye contact and hung his head.

"You're certain you can do it?" questioned Rurik.

"Absolutely. I will simply need a ribbon from the typewriter."

Rurik slid the typewriter ribbon across the desk to Zazlov, who held it in his hand and closed his eyes. He rubbed the ribbon between his fingers and appeared confused.

"You're certain this is the one from your brother's typewriter?"

"Yes. He sent me two of them. Orna was in possession of one, and I kept the other here, locked away."

"Excellent. One moment." Zazlov gripped the typewriter ribbon and began to hum quietly. "Apologies for the delay. Bucharest is quite far." He smiled after a few more moments. "I have located your brother's typewriter. You may begin."

Rurik downed another shot of vodka and began his dictation.

"Dear Brother. Actually, skip that. Just start with this."

Chapter 15

It is with a heavy heart I send you this urgent letter. Much has transpired since I last messaged you, and I'm afraid none of it is good save my discovery of the Sfânta Biblie al Strigoiului Viu in what appears to be its entirety, including a map that pinpoints Loch Dracul. I will have Zazlov send the map telepathically after this letter. Please be sure to place another piece of paper into your typewriter to receive it.

I believe we still have time to strike this terror once and for all and stop it before it starts. If you can travel to the loch and kill the roosting bats before they can transform to Nosferatu, our chances for success are great.

And now for the terrible news. Orna is gone. Taken from us by this monster. I am still in a deep state of grief over this, so I feel it best to skip any further details. I will see to it she is given a proper burial.

I can report that I now have a solid understanding of the Sleepwalker's actions. I am even prouder to tell you that I have dueled face-to-face with it and staked it myself! Alas, in my haste, my blow was not mortal and the creature lives.

I have managed to digest the vampire bible in its entirety, and much of what we have hypothesized over the years is true. The bats cannot transform because Alexei is a half-breed.

His human blood is poisoning the blood link. But what we never accounted for is that the cycle can be corrected, and it is Nicholas who is central to this.

Their bible speaks of these halfling Morii: children like Alexei born half vampire, half human. The children will grow to puberty and die unless they murder and drink the blood of their human parent, essentially consuming and destroying the blood that poisons them.

I believe our vampire is working to entice the boy to commit this act. Only then can the Nosferatu transform. You must find the bats and kill them. We have seven days. Be swift.

Part II: Copilul Sângelui

Once Felix arrives, I believe it is time to tell him everything. I was hesitant to let him know this centered around Alexei. The boy is his godson. I felt he would certainly act irrationally and worsen matters. Sending him to you to get him out of the way was necessary, but our directives have changed.

Although I will need you both here in the event the Sleepwalker succeeds, I believe it is more important to eradicate the bats before attempting to return. Felix will be able to assist you due to your condition, so I would wait for his arrival if at all possible.

I also regret to tell you that all of the insiders we worked so hard to plant within the Winter Palace have been arrested as a result of a recent assassination attempt on Alexandra, so getting close to the boy will prove difficult if we do indeed have to kill him.

I must go into hiding now, as the Sleepwalker knows I am in possession of its holy book. Please return to Saint Petersburg the moment you have completed your duties. There is still battle at hand.

I eagerly await a time when we can commiserate over a nice glass of cheap vodka—that is, I will drink and you can watch.

Godspeed,
Rurik

Rurik paused. "Speaking of which." He grabbed the vodka bottle and downed another gulp. He looked to Zazlov, who still sat with his eyes closed. "Did you get that?"

Zazlov smiled. "Of course. But you didn't have to speak. I can see your thoughts."

Rurik rubbed his face, then smiled as the warmth of the booze coursed through him. "Ah, yes. I forgot. Poor you." He laughed.

Zazlov opened his eyes. "And now the map to Loch Dracul?"

Rurik took the vampire bible and opened it to a portion detailing a position deep within the Carpathian Mountains.

Chapter 15

Zazlov inspected it and shook his head. "It's been a very long time since I've seen this. Still gives me chills." He ran his fingers through his beard. "I have history with this forsaken portal, you know."

"Portal?"

"Yes. You see here. These markings. It's hidden by an inter-dimensional locking plane."

Rurik appeared confused.

"More simply—it sits on a different dimensional plane, thanks to this portal marking here." Zazlov placed his long fingernail upon a narrow section of the river that branched off from the main artery. "You must enter exactly at these markings, going in this exact direction, or you'd never find it."

"Is there a spell to enter?"

"No. No. Anyone can enter. But the loch is not of this earth. You'd have to know exactly what you were looking for—or be extraordinarily lucky to find it."

"I believe *unlucky* is the word."

Zazlov nodded. "Unlucky indeed. I have wondered for centuries as to who put it there. Inter-dimensional and space-time magic of this order is of the lost arts. Not even the Impaler could have done this. How he found it in the first place was always a mystery to me."

Rurik clapped his hands together. "Please tell me it's possible to close the door to that dimension."

Zazlov stroked his chin. "Well … yes. In fact, I have been searching for that answer myself for a very long time. But it's ancient magic, lost for eons. I do know of a German warlock by the name of Albert Einstein who deals in rediscovering this lost magic, or perhaps my Serbian counterpart Nikola, but …"

"But?"

"It's all very experimental, you see. In attempting to close the portal, they would be just as likely to implode the entire universe as we know it. Best to leave it open for now."

Rurik was disappointed. He looked over the map once more.

"How will you send this?"

Part II: Copilul Sângelui

Zazlov looked thoughtful. "Not too difficult, I suppose. I will just use the characters on the typewriter to etch it out the best I can."

"We need to ensure my brother will understand the instructions. Will it be legible?"

Zazlov smiled. "You're in luck as I am just as much of an artist as I am a warlock." Zazlov placed his hand over the map and closed his eyes. He opened them again after only a moment. "It is done."

"Thank you." Rurik squeezed him on the shoulder. "Listen, I hate—"

"No. No. Remember, I can read your mind. It's no trouble at all. I will show myself out." Zazlov rose and hugged Rurik. "You are in great danger. I cannot see the vampire's intended plan for you. It is riddled with very dark magic. I fear even my spells cannot help you from this point forward."

Rurik stood away from him and looked to the window. "It's funny. We've been preparing for this for decades. And now I feel I have no time."

Zazlov tilted his head and looked to Rurik. "Time is merely a perception of the human condition. Focus your mind. Rest assured, you are prepared. I would stay to assist, but there are some pressing matters I must attend to in Paris."

"I understand," said Rurik.

"And the next time you are in my city, please do visit my haberdashery. A brilliant man such as your self should have equally brilliant attire."

Rurik smiled. "If we make it out of this alive, you can count on it."

Zazlov was enveloped by a black mist. A moment later Rurik stood alone in the room. He sat at his desk and pulled the vodka bottle next to him before taking another swig.

Now what?

"Hi, Nicholas, my name is Rurik. I'm here to stake your son," said Rurik aloud. He laughed, then blew out a distressed sigh. While leaning back on his chair and rocking slightly, he looked to the window above his head and saw the gibbous moon partly hidden behind fast-moving clouds.

Get moving.

Chapter 15

He hastened to the filing cabinet that barricaded his door and repositioned it. Still unsure it would be enough, he pushed his heavy desk behind it. Rurik opened his wall closet and refilled his belt straps. Finally, he turned off the lights in his office, held the vampire bible close, and pushed his chair into the closet. The moonlight flooded the room with a bluish-silver hue.

Inside the closet, he struggled with a large oak beam that leaned against the closet wall, and hung it across two metal clamps, bolting the door shut from within. A coarse brown rope dangled from above. Rurik sat in his chair and tied the rope around his waist, ensuring it was taut.

Now I wait.

Part II: Copilul Sângelui

16

December 9, 1916 (OS), early evening

Nicholas and Rasputin walked side by side near the edge of the enclosed veranda at the Winter Palace. The twinkling, distant lights of Saint Petersburg were their backdrop as they strode past Doric columns that framed the city inside rich, scopic archways. A group of four Okhrana followed them just out of earshot.

"I cannot extend enough gratitude for what you have done for us, Father. Your eulogy for Anna earlier today was very comforting for us all. My duties keep me away from my family, but that does not mean I do not care for them."

Rasputin nodded. "I am honored."

"Is it true you can help Alexei even further by rubbing his legs daily?"

"Yes, Emperor. He can already walk on his own without the use of braces."

"Can he do so for tonight's dinner—for the newspapers?"

Rasputin paused and looked to Nicholas. "He can. Yes."

Nicholas breathed a sigh of relief and rolled his eyes. "Thank God. It will certainly help silence my critics."

Rasputin bowed his head and stared at the marble floor.

"I wanted to speak privately with you in hopes you might be able to confirm what Anna and Sana said. That palace Okhrana were involved in the disappearance of their parents? They said you predicted it."

"I'm sorry, Emperor. I have no recollection of that. I told them only of the weapons planted under Alexei's mattress. I assume the calamity of these events clouded their memories."

Chapter 16

Nicholas placed his hands behind his back and considered the statement. "They were under a lot of stress indeed. I suppose it was just that."

Rasputin and Nicholas continued along in silence.

"You are not the first," said Nicholas, looking out to the skyline. "We have had many holy men and miracle workers come through these halls. You are the only one who has ever produced." Nicholas stopped and turned to him. "Is it truly God working through you?"

Rasputin gazed into his eyes. "It is, Emperor."

Rasputin cupped his hands behind him and walked forward. "I have traveled throughout all the lands. Here in Russia—all the way to England. And I have found God everywhere. It is only when you pull yourself away to a place far from Russia, away from the cities. To a great wilderness and look back. Look back to the crime, to the disease—to the industrial smoke rising like foul breath into the sky. It is then you see what men truly are …"

Nicholas stared at him, intent on the answer.

"Savage dogs. Grappling on top of one another for the biggest scrap of meat, each ready to rip out the innards of the other who tries to take it from him. It is when you realize this you will see God. You will hear his voice. Look up to the sky, and there is God. Only once you are free from all these trifles can you communicate with him. Commit to him. Finding God has nothing to do with Sundays or sermons. God is here—within." Rasputin tapped his fingers to his heart. "Once you feel him, know him, then you too will become capable of performing his will."

"And is that how you do miracles?"

Rasputin nodded.

"My family is indebted to you. All of Russia. With you at my side, Father, I feel we can once again unify this nation."

"It is my calling, Emperor."

Nicholas turned and looked out to Saint Petersburg. "What does your foresight tell you, Father? What will become of Saint Petersburg?" Nicholas radiated a great sense of sincerity as the city lights reflected in his pupils.

Rasputin closed his eyes. "The people of Saint Petersburg—of all Russia—are morally corrupt. Sin is drunk down with sin." Rasputin stared toward the city. "A greater force must govern over

Part II: Copilul Sângelui

the evils of men to redeem them. Russia craves this redemption—all the world seeks it."

"Will it be me to redeem Russia?"

Rasputin looked to him. "You will redeem all of mankind, Emperor. It is the blood that flows in your veins that has become destined to redeem them all."

Nicholas closed his eyes and fell to his knees. "Thank you, Father Rasputin. Praise to you." Nicholas peered upward. "Will you bless me?"

Rasputin held up his hand and made the sign of the cross, the symbol casting a stark shadow across Nicholas's face.

*

"We must separate Rasputin from Nicholas as quickly as we can," said Makarov, sipping from his brandy glass. The shadows cast from the fireplace dug deep lines across his proud jawline and wrinkled brow.

Archimandrite Gyáva sat at his desk, noting Makarov's comments on a thick piece of parchment.

"What you're doing, Mikhail?"

"Taking notes," he said, an air of duty in his voice.

"Well, stop," said Makarov, looking to Kashin. "Commander, would you be so kind?"

Kashin rose from his chair and crumpled Gyáva's paper. He walked to the fireplace and threw it in.

"I'm sorry," said Gyáva. "I wanted to be thorough."

"Fine," said Makarov. "But let us not confuse that with carelessness. Never leave any evidence, my good Archimandrite."

Kashin sat in his chair. "Have you heard from the Holy Synod?" he asked.

"Yes, they're sending more documents. Rest assured we can smear Rasputin."

"Is he really a starets?" asked Makarov.

"A strannik at best. But excommunicated from the church over twenty-five years ago."

Makarov and Kashin looked to him, waiting for an explanation.

Chapter 16

"Oh. Of course. Well, he's a colorful one, this Rasputin—he was famed as the town drunk, a lifelong thief, and a renowned womanizer."

"Or rather a typical strannik," said Makarov. "Has he no real criminal record? Assault, rape?"

"No, but we'll soon have the means to embarrass Nicholas into shunning Rasputin."

"Pray Tell."

Gyáva cleared his throat. "Rasputin was excommunicated for practicing in rituals of an ancient sex cult—the Khlysts. We've investigated them, and although they profess to be protesters of Russian Orthodox dogma, they are known for an obscure worship of a mythical vampire bat. It's very disturbing. Distressing, even the knowledge of such acts ... blood ritual, sex orgies, human sacrifice—horrible things."

"It's true," said Kashin. "We've been investigating the Khlysts for nearly a decade. They're incredibly dangerous. A nihilist cult that preaches all men should be destroyed for their sins."

Gyáva nodded. "My sources have uncovered some of Rasputin's writings and testimonies from his requisition to enter the parish. Also official reprimands from his church superiors. Some records of his sermons, and other accounts of these Khlysts sex orgies. It seems he lured young women into these encounters by preying upon their need for salvation. Rasputin preached that only through committing ultimate sin could one then be absolved of it."

"So you must commit dire sins to be forgiven?" asked Makarov.

"Yes," said Gyáva. "Rasputin believed that to be closer to God, one had to sin to feel his grace. He preached that the pure and the holy were godless."

Makarov laughed. "Oh, that is delightful! Simply cunning. I like this Rasputin after all."

"There are also accounts of these young women going missing after their encounters with him," said Gyáva.

"Can we get any statements from relatives from former cult members?" asked Makarov.

"There are none," said Kashin. "Defectors always end up dead or missing, as do their families."

Part II: Copilul Sângelui

Gyáva patted his brow. "After being excommunicated, he worked as a faith healer and street preacher."

"So we have him for impersonating a holy figure?"

"No, Commander," continued Gyáva. "A strannik's position in the church is largely misunderstood by the populace. They are occasionally called Father. However, they are merely commoners and peasants—apprentices of sorts to the clergy, hopeful starets. So even after his excommunication, Rasputin could have very well been attempting to be absolved and reenter the church. Behaving like a strannik is merely a sign one is interested in pursuing the path of righteousness.

"However, it's clear through his occult interests that he was not seeking grace. He used his manner of dress as a lure. Only gravitated toward prostitutes and orphans. When they disappeared, nobody came looking."

"Then how do you know this?" asked Makarov.

"Rumors, of course, from the Holy Synod. But they are a fastidious lot. I trust their word implicitly."

"The information on the Khlysts is accurate," said Kashin.

"Thank you, Commander," continued Gyáva. "My contact said it was known that if you went to rural Siberia to participate in one of Rasputin's healing orgies, you might not return. Those that did return—some hanged themselves, others cut their wrists."

Makarov raised his brows.

"He's clearly a dangerous con man," said Kashin. "We must neutralize him at once."

"We tried that already," said Makarov with a veiled annoyance in his voice. "And because of your overzealousness in the matter, Rasputin is basically holding hands with Nicholas everywhere the tsar goes, advising him on religious matters. Some say Nicholas has been asking him for advice on governance. All this in under two days. Imagine a week. Imagine a month—this strannik will rule Russia. We must separate them and eliminate Rasputin entirely."

"I know how we can do it," said Kashin.

"Very good, Commander, but let's try mine," said Makarov. "You will stage another assassination attempt at the palace, but one with a body count. Someone high profile, yet insignificant—Nicholas's mother, perhaps? Once the palace is viewed as unsafe,

Chapter 16

you will move everyone but Nicholas to a secure location. I'm sure the boy and Alexandra will want Rasputin with them. Then we will have Nicholas isolated, feeling he must stay behind to rule Russia; the rest of the flock isolated under the watchful eye of our Okhrana agents." Makarov smiled his crooked grin. "Can you do it, Commander?"

"Yes."

"Good," said Makarov. "Once they're separated, we can kill Rasputin, we can say he became drunk and attacked an Okhrana officer. You can shoot him yourself, for all I care. Once Gyáva's information is leaked to the newspapers, nobody will ask any questions. If you succeed in this, I will make you head of state when the Romanovs are toppled." Makarov patted Kashin on the knee. "When can you do it?"

"Tonight," said Kashin. "It can be done tonight. There will be plenty of activity at Alexander Palace due to the state dinner in Rasputin's honor."

"Oh, yes," said Makarov, looking to the ceiling. "I'd nearly forgotten. I'd better get home to change. And you?"

His eyes fell to Gyáva.

"I can offer my support, and any information that I come across. I want Rasputin eliminated. He seems to know too much about us."

"Seems?" questioned Makarov.

"He does … know too much. We have to kill him. He knows things about me that … things that …" Gyáva began to pant. He was perspiring so profusely that it became evident to Makarov and Kashin, even in the dim light.

"Let's not dig into each other's closets and expose the bones," said Makarov. "Each of us certainly has things best kept hidden from others, so I offer each to keep them where they belong. We have a common enemy now—and that spawns the greatest friendships."

Gyáva calmed and sipped from his brandy glass. "Thank you, Minister."

"Will I see you at the state dinner tonight, Archimandrite?"

"Indeed, I intend to arrive just after I hear my clergy's confessions."

Part II: Copilul Sângelui

"Well then," said Makarov. "We have an understanding, and each man a job to do. Let us not stumble in our tasks, gentlemen. Nicholas is on his last legs, and in a matter of days, the streets of Saint Petersburg will be alive with revolutionaries howling for the aristocracy's blood."

"To common enemies," said Kashin.

"To common enemies!" Makarov raised his glass. The others followed suit, and they downed the rest of their brandy.

*

Archimandrite Gyáva despised hearing confession. He believed God purposefully increased the boredom of each session as a means to test his faith and fortitude. As of late, Gyáva had begun looking forward to confession only to catch up on some much-needed sleep. Tonight's confession brought one element of excitement in the form of a .32 caliber snub-nosed pistol hidden in his cassock's right pocket. His encounter earlier that day with Rasputin had brought on intense paranoia and dread. If Rasputin knew about his past, certainly others did—possibly a cabal of enemies out to get him.

Gyáva sauntered through the upper church of the Voskresenia Khristova Cathedral. His black robe billowed out over his shoes and flowed around him so that he appeared to float on a cushion of air. The Blood of Christ Chapel was Gyáva's favorite section of the cathedral. During its renovation in the early part of the century, he had much input to a variety of architectural enhancements.

He slowed his pace to enjoy his contributions to the long, narrow structure. Gyáva particularly liked his inclusion of a lower ceiling. He felt it gave the chapel a more intimate feel than the sweeping openness of the upper church. He sauntered along, taking a moment to admire his favorite painting of the blessed seraphim hand-feeding a bear, then headed to the lower church.

Portions of the inner sanctuary were covered with gold-flecked mosaics that reflected yellow slivers of candlelight upon the sanctuary's apse fresco—a gorgeous depiction of the Theotokos and Christ child. Gyáva purposefully focused on the Virgin Mary, trying to flush his mind of Satan's depiction on the Last Judgment fresco

Chapter 16

upon the back wall. No matter where he moved in the nave, Gyáva was certain the devil's eyes followed him.

Moving toward the altar, Gyáva found himself marveling at the golden iconostasis in the near distance. The depiction of Saint Germogen directly above the iconostasis's ornate bronze gate always gave him pause. He made the sign of the cross, then frowned at the sight of Father Fyodor seated at the confession altar.

Gyáva reluctantly stood next to Fyodor, who nodded, then rested his head next to the Bible.

"Blessed is our God, always, now, and forevermore," said Gyáva.

"Father in heaven," began Fyodor, "forgive me, for sin is a burden inside my heart."

"Carry on," said Gyáva, "for Christ our Lord is ever present."

"Dear Lord, my heart is black. So very black. For I know I am not to mention others negatively during my confession, but I must confide that I yelled at Father Kastovich earlier for refusing to brew coffee for the visiting starets from Kiev. It is his assigned task for the week, and when I saw his refusal, I grew so angry. I yelled at him in front of several pilgrims. I even used a curse word directed toward him, in private, though …"

Gyáva placed his fingers to his head and massaged his temples as he stared at Fyodor's back.

"Go on," said Gyáva.

"And I must confess the sin of indulgence. I have been using extra rations of toilet napkins when I go. And I am spending too much time in the toilet. I find it relaxing. To sit there and go, to get it all out. Some of the visiting pilgrims have complained to other priests about my behavior. And I know it is contemptible, God, but I must confess my sin of gluttony, as I believe it is my right to take longer since I am patriarch of this parish."

The sanctuary was silent.

"Is that all, my son?" asked Gyáva.

"Yes, Father."

Gyáva removed his epitrachelion and placed it over Fyodor's head. "O Lord our God, if during this day he has sinned, whether in word or deed or thought, forgive all, for thou art good and lovest mankind. Grant Father Fyodor peaceful and undisturbed

Part II: Copilul Sângelui

sleep, and deliver him from all influence and temptation of the evil one."

Gyáva placed his hand on Fyodor's back as he became aware of an acute, freezing headache starting at the peak of his own forehead. "The grace of the All-Holy Spirit, through my insignificance, has loosened and granted to you forgiveness."

"Thank you, Holiness," said Fyodor as Gyáva removed his epitrachelion and placed it around his own neck.

Father Fyodor raised his head from the altar and looked to Gyáva with the eyes of an ashamed poodle. He nodded, then walked off into the darkened chapel.

Gyáva's headache became more intense. He pinched his sinuses and closed his eyes as a hooded starets sat at the altar. The pilgrim placed his head next to the Bible and faced away from Gyáva.

"Please remove your hood, my son."

"I fear I am too disfigured in the eyes of the Lord to remove it. I beg your permission."

Gyáva rolled his eyes. "Very well. Blessed is our God, always, now, and forevermore."

"Holy Father. Forgive me, for sin is a burden inside my heart. My last confession was … in truth, oh Lord—I don't recall my last confession."

"Carry on," said Gyáva. "The power of Christ is ever present."

"God in heaven. I have sinned. I have committed sins I do not believe can be absolved."

Gyáva found comfort in the smoothness of this pilgrim's voice—it was deep and calm, almost musical.

"Good pilgrim, it is this act of confession directly to God that can absolve you of all sins."

Gyáva waited for a reply and focused on the pilgrim's deep breathing. He watched the pilgrim's back rise and fall and believed the priest was weeping.

"Thank you, Holiness." He sniffled. "It's just hard for me to confess these sins."

"You must," said Gyáva.

"Well … first … I murdered that boy on the train. I drank all his blood …"

Chapter 16

White fear shot through Gyáva, and he reached for his gun.

"And then I ate up that lonely old man at the print shop. I can't seem to stop."

Gyáva stepped away, clutching his pectoral cross.

"I killed that fortune teller and the tsar's men at the cabin. And now I've come for you, Archimandrite."

Gyáva pointed his gun at the pilgrim—whose head still lay slumped upon the altar next to the Bible.

"Oh, devil! Be gone from my sanctuary. Flee from this place of righteousness!"

The pilgrim sobbed, and his whimpers slowly became feminine.

"Oh, Mikhail," she wept. "Why did you leave us in the forest? It's so cold there."

Gyáva backed to the wall and cocked his gun.

"Please, Mikhail, don't hurt us again. Love us! You promised."

The figure shot up and turned to Gyáva. From underneath the hood emerged Rosemary's pale face. She floated toward him without taking a single step. Her black cassock flowed openly around her naked body, exposing her breasts and the dark purple bruises around her neck. In her arms was their dead son.

Gyáva pointed the gun toward her, and his body contorted with such fear that the pistol shook wildly in his hand.

"Please, Mikhail," she said, her lips never moving.

She hovered closer to him.

"Stay back." He raised the gun toward her chest.

She continued to float slowly toward him, and Gyáva fired a shot into her heart. She stopped cold as pain and sadness swept her face. A perfectly shaped red dot above her left breast streamed blood down her pale body.

"You promised, Mikhail," she said, her chin quivering. "How could you?"

He fired two more rounds into her chest and a final shot at her forehead. She clutched her baby as the hole in her head spurted blood onto her face. Her eyes rolled back, and she fell onto the floor—a puddle of blood quickly spreading around her.

Another priest ran to the scene.

"Archimandrite, what's happening?" he yelled.

Part II: Copilul Sângelui

Gyáva looked to the approaching priest and pointed the gun at him.

"Holiness, don't shoot!" He threw his hands into the air.

Gyáva lowered his gun.

"Dear God! What have you done?" screamed the priest, looking toward the body on the floor.

Gyáva shook his head and looked to the young priest's face. "Forgive me, I …" he began as the priest ran toward the dead body.

"Father Fyodor, dear God!" The young priest cradled Fyodor's head, trying to stop the blood spurting from his face.

Gyáva looked to the ground, stunned to see Father Fyodor lying in a pool of his own blood.

"What have you done?" yelled the priest, embracing Fyodor's limp body. "Murderer!"

"She was … I … he wasn't …" sputtered Gyáva. He then muttered something unintelligible to himself.

The priest wept loudly, rocking back and forth with Fyodor in his arms. Gyáva shook his head as he looked to the floor. He backed away and noticed a figure standing in the nave's shadows. He could see only the glow of two red eyes in the darkness.

"Who's there?"

Rasputin's face emerged into the candlelight—his face bore sharp protrusions on his cheekbones and brow. A deep, guttural laugh filled the sanctuary as Rasputin revealed his large fangs.

Gyáva pointed the gun at Rasputin, who sprung into the air and blended into the shadows, hushing the surrounding candles as he flew. Gyáva felt him flutter overhead, then looked back to the priest weeping over his fallen peer. Horror and sickness consumed Gyáva as the blood crept around his feet. He thought of Rosemary and heard her voice in the panicked cries of the young priest, smelled her perfume in the stench of the blood pouring about him.

Gyáva raised the gun, shoved it in his mouth, and pulled the trigger.

*

Chapter 16

Away from the happenings at Voskresenia Khristova, the guests had arrived at Tsarskoye Selo's Alexander Palace for Rasputin's official state dinner. The elite guests, about thirty in total, gathered in the Imperial Portrait Room. They chatted pleasantly over state affairs and more quietly about the scandals surrounding Prince Felix Yusupov and the recent assassination plot at the Winter Palace. Before them was a grand spread of salty meats, rare caviars, exquisitely prepared mushrooms and asparagus, tiered trays stuffed with delectable confections from the imperial bakery, and bottles of various vodkas distilled from the tsar's private collection.

The adjoining Semi-circular Hall enticed them with a long rectangular table. It was adorned with glimmering flatware aligned perfectly along a lengthy row of squat platinum chafers and decorative sterling fountains sprouting fresh bouquets of yellow flowers at their peak. Beautiful crystal glassware shimmered with glints of rainbow light reflected from the polished iron candelabra that regally crowned the affair.

The male palace servants hovered about the imperial table in their ceremonial livery: black blazers, white ties, white gloves with black breeches and white socks that offset their shiny black shoes. They inspected each piece of dinnerware with a rigid gaze, ensuring every piece was free of even the smallest speck of dust. After putting the finishing touches on the grand setting, they trimmed or pulled any flowers that might have disturbed a guest's view, then shuffled toward the Portrait Room.

Nicholas, dressed in his sterling ceremonial attire, stood in the Portrait Room behind Rasputin and Alexandra, who both sat upon intricately carved Isabella chairs. Prince Alexei, after much coaxing by his father, sat on Rasputin's lap, and they all stared toward a photographer. The flashbulb lit the room as the photograph, set to appear in tomorrow's *Vedomosti*, was snapped.

Nicholas signaled the chamber musicians, and their string instruments accentuated the jovial mood as he strode about the room and mingled with his eager guests.

Rasputin remained seated next to Alexandra only for another moment until Sana ran to him and pulled Alexei from his lap. She led Rasputin by the hand and introduced him to several society women who were jubilant upon having Rasputin's lips meet their gloved hands. One by one, they blushed as he made eye contact with them.

"Handpicked by Alexandra's tailors," said Sana, rubbing her fingers along the sleeve of Rasputin's ruby-colored blouse. His golden sash shone in contrast to the drab vestments of the other male guests.

"The boots too," she said. "A gift from Nicholas himself!"

The women marveled at the gleam of his patent leather boots. Rasputin stood back and posed for a moment as a round of flirtatious giggles erupted.

A small group of men gathered along the opposite wall around Minister Makarov and Grand Duke Pavlovich. Each took a strong, uneasy notice at their wives and daughters doting over Rasputin, whose broad grin seemed to enchant them more each time he spoke. Makarov, aware of his flock's discomfort, spoke first.

"Gentlemen, this reminds me of the time I took my wife to the circus. She was quite intrigued by a large ruby-bloused bear that could balance a ball upon its head."

All at once, the men laughed and raised their glasses to their lips. As Makarov and his cabal relaxed, Nicholas's headwaiter emerged at the threshold of the Semi-circular Hall and rang a small silver bell, signaling dinner was to commence.

The guests promptly placed their drinking glasses and serving plates on the nearest table and waited until Nicholas and Alexandra arrived at their seats at the head of the imperial dining table. A line of waiters—one assigned to each guest—entered the Portrait Room and led the party into the dining hall. Alexei hobbled to Rasputin, who knelt to hug him.

"I want to eat with the adults."

"If it were up to me, you would. Soon. Soon enough you too will feast on splendors."

Alexei let go the embrace and looked to Rasputin, whose broad face eased the child.

"Will you read to me after dinner?"

"Of course, child. Late tonight. I have but a few affairs to tidy up, and then I will read to you for as long as you desire. Pick your favorite book!"

"I will."

Chapter 16

Alexei's nanny took his hand and led him away.

Rasputin stood and faced the Semi-circular Hall to see everyone standing at the table, waiting for him. His waiter led him to a chair next to Nicholas, who then motioned everyone to sit. A quick, thunderous clamor filled the hall as the guests positioned their chairs and settled all around the table. The staff moved in and filled each person's glass with a pouring of champagne.

Nicholas stood rigidly at the head of the table with his hand on Alexandra's shoulder. He raised his champagne glass into the air, and the bubbly liquid shone like a golden, watery beacon.

"In honor of our new friend, Father Grigori Rasputin. A man of God, a blessing to my family, and a friend to all of Russia."

Champagne flutes shot into the air, and the party followed suit as Nicholas slowly sipped from his drink. Warm applause erupted after the glasses were placed back upon the table. Nicholas sat and signaled for Rasputin to stay standing when the applause continued. Rasputin raised his hand to the guests, then bowed before sitting. The waitstaff removed the champagne glasses and returned with bowls of rich cream soup as the hall bustled with polite chatter.

Next to Rasputin sat Sana, who smiled at Alexandra, then looked to Minister Makarov, sitting at Alexandra's left. She feigned a smile at his hello. She looked to Makarov's beautiful young wife and nodded pleasantly toward her.

"I'm so sorry about dear Anna," Mrs. Makarova offered.

"Thank you."

At that moment, a servant wheeled Nicholas's decrepit mother into position and locked her wheelchair in place next to Mrs. Makarova.

"Mother," said Nicholas, nodding toward her.

"Welcome, Mother," followed Alexandra.

Nicholas's mother was barely coherent but managed to nod slightly toward her son. Makarov rose from his chair.

"Good Maria," he beamed, reaching to kiss her on the cheek.

She became invigorated by his presence and smiled at him.

"Sweet Aleksander. How is your darling wife?"

"Eleanor is right here," he said, holding his hand toward her.

Part II: Copilul Sângelui

Maria squinted toward Mrs. Makarova and revealed her tarnished false teeth.

"Oh, I certainly wish my Nicholas would have married you instead of that strange German woman." She reached toward Mrs. Makarova and squeezed her forearm. "She didn't even come with a dowry!"

"Why ... thank you, Mrs. Fyodorovna," she said, careful not to make eye contact with any guests.

"I imagine your womb would have produced a healthy heir for my son, not like my sickly grandson." Her boisterous tone attracted the attention of several party guests.

Nicholas's soup suddenly became of great interest to him as he tried to ignore his mother's comments. Alexandra did the same, closely inspecting her plate of asparagus prepared for her special diet. The remaining guests within earshot did their best to feign ignorance of Mrs. Fyodorovna's remarks.

"Always charming," said Makarov, squeezing Mrs. Fyodorovna's hand before moving to his chair.

Mrs. Fyodorovna looked around the table and gasped at the sight of Rasputin.

"Dear God, what is that?"

The surrounding party grew silent.

"Mother, this is Father Rasputin. He is the one who saved Alexandra and Alexei. The starets I spoke of."

"Starets?" she shouted. "Why not invite prostitutes to dine? Where's the kind Archimandrite Gyáva?"

Makarov looked down the table to Gyáva's empty chair. "I assume His Holiness will be here soon, your grace."

Nicholas cleared his throat and leaned toward Rasputin.

"You must forgive my mother," he said. "She is ... old ... and opinionated."

"I am honored to be at your table, Emperor. No matter the situation."

"Thank you for your grace, Father."

"Where are you from?" growled Mrs. Fyodorovna as her bony finger pointed toward Rasputin.

"I was born and reared in Siberia, Highness."

Chapter 16

Mrs. Fyodorovna fanned her hand at him. She turned to her soup and slopped it into her mouth, seeming to forget about Rasputin.

"Beautiful land, Siberia," said Makarov. "I have toured it three times now."

"Ah, so you know my home?"

"Very well. It is the heartland of our nation. The bloodline to feeding our growing cities."

"Thank you for your compliments, Minister."

Makarov noticed Rasputin's hands were placed on his lap.

"Father Rasputin, certainly you must have an appetite for such a fine dinner prepared in your honor."

"Indeed," said Rasputin. "I must humbly admit I have a strong aversion to shallots." He motioned toward his bowl of soup. "And cream of shallot soup would certainly do me in. My deepest apologies to you all."

"Please, Father," said Nicholas. "It is we who beg your forgiveness. You should have been asked about any dietary restrictions."

"Thank you, Emperor. I unfortunately have severe allergic reactions to onions. Garlic too."

"Think nothing of it." Nicholas raised his hand and motioned toward his head servant, Karl, who was a relic left over from Alexander III. Nicholas proved too loyal to decommission the old man, even though he suffered through poor service in the company of his guests.

"Your Highness?" wheezed Karl.

"Please ensure our guest of honor is put on the same diet as Alexandra. It seems he shares her aversion to garlic and onions," whispered Nicholas.

"Yes, Your Majesty."

Karl carried a bottle of wine and tried to pour some into Nicholas's glass. Nicholas leaned forward to support the old man, whose arms were too weak to suspend the bottle. He then rose from his seat and followed Karl to help him pour a glass for Alexandra.

"Very good, Karl. Thank you," said Nicholas. The old man sauntered off toward the tunnel that led to the kitchen.

"I believe I should alert a waiter a tad speedier," said Nicholas, smiling.

Part II: Copilul Sângelui

The immediate circle laughed.

Nicholas motioned toward Rasputin's waiter, who jumped on cue.

"Sasha, see to it that Father Rasputin is put on the same menu as Alexandra for the evening. In our haste we forgot to ask our guest of any allergies. No garlic, no onions."

"Yes, Emperor." He clicked his heels and trotted off.

The bowls of soup were soon pulled from the table and replaced with the second course: Risotto al Barolo served with a fillet of Arctic char fished from the frigid lakes of northern Russia. The smell of white pepper and paprika filled the air as the lids were pulled from their chafers. The dinner party sighed in collective pleasure at the sight of the plump fillet, and many glasses of wine were emptied and refilled as they delved into the second course.

Mrs. Fyodorovna had fallen fast asleep, and Nicholas motioned for Kashin to wheel her away.

Rasputin leaned into his dish and inhaled the fine aroma. He nodded approvingly, then grabbed a fork and began cutting the fish. Makarov nudged his wife and motioned toward Rasputin.

"Possibly they don't have knives in Siberia?" he whispered to her, prompting hushed laughter.

Rasputin, vaguely aware of Makarov's barb, looked to the other guests, who used a knife and fork to cut their fish. He quickly picked up a knife with his free hand and mimicked their motions.

"So tell me, Father Rasputin," began Dmitri Pavlovich, who was seated next to Mrs. Fyodorovna's empty space. "What brings you to Saint Petersburg?"

"God told me to come."

Makarov coughed on his fish and looked to Dmitri. The two exchanged a sarcastic glare.

"Oh, I see," recovered Dmitri. "So God said you were needed in Saint Petersburg?"

Rasputin, aware that the surrounding party was waiting for his reply, started slowly. "I had a vision that the royal family needed my help, and so I came."

"And so you came," said Makarov, slurring his words slightly. "How lucky for us all."

Chapter 16

"Aleksander, please," snapped Alexandra.

"I mean no disrespect, Empress. Certainly I think Father Rasputin is a blessing to us all—the savior of Russia." He shoved a helping of fish into his mouth and stared at Rasputin.

"Father Rasputin is gifted," said Sana. "He brought Anna back to life and gave Alexei the ability to walk. I have witnessed his powers."

"Powers? You speak of this simple peasant as if he were Jesus himself," said Makarov. "Certainly Father Rasputin will entertain us with these … powers."

"Enough," commanded Nicholas.

Rasputin smiled. "I would be glad to."

"Well then," said Makarov. "Let us start with something simple. Perhaps you can make a prediction? Tell us what the main course will be? Should we expect white or dark meat?"

"Unfair," moaned Dmitri. "Certainly it will be dark meat to accentuate the lightness of the fish!"

The nervousness of the surrounding party seemed appeased by the little game, and everyone stared at Rasputin with eager eyes. Even Nicholas seemed absorbed by the lighthearted challenge.

"That's for Father Rasputin to predict," said Makarov.

"Oh, come now, Aleksander—it is too easy. He has a fifty-fifty chance," said Dmitri.

"It is true. What do you think, Father? Too easy? Something more challenging, perhaps?"

"It's your game, Minister," said Rasputin as an unexpected laughter rose from the party.

"So it is. I'm satisfied with this. If it pleases Father Rasputin, white meat or dark?"

The guests stared at Rasputin, who closed his eyes for a moment.

"It will be both," said Rasputin.

Sana looked to the others, smiles all around.

"You see! Father Rasputin plays with a rigged deck," said Makarov, a broad smile upon his face.

"You will see. A bird. White meat is the breast. Dark meat, the legs."

Part II: Copilul Sângelui

Just as he finished speaking, the waiters removed the fish and placed gleaming silver domes in front of each guest.

"Now wait," spoke Makarov. "His first."

Rasputin's waiter lifted the silver dome to reveal only thin slivers of very rare meat.

A disappointed sigh rose from the table.

"I'm sorry, Father—it seems your powers have escaped you this evening!" said Makarov, throwing his hands outward.

"It's bison," said Sasha to Rasputin. "Tartare. Very delicious. No garlic. Rare and chilled. Here is your mustard or horseradish if you prefer." He motioned to two small dipping trays.

Rasputin looked up from his plate and smiled.

"It's exquisite, Sasha. Thank you."

Nicholas signaled the waiters, and they removed the remaining silver domes like an orchestrated dance. Upon the white china sat plump hazel grouses, roasted to a lovely brown perfection.

Sana clapped at once and leaned into Rasputin. Mrs. Makarova smiled at him as jovial applause swept the table.

"Well done, Father Rasputin," said Nicholas, smirking toward Makarov.

Rasputin looked to Alexandra, who had also been given bison. She nodded toward him in a fashion that conveyed a sense of camaraderie.

"It was luck," said Makarov.

The excitement died down, and the patrons began their main course. Minister Makarov, well into his sixth glass of wine, glared red-faced toward Rasputin.

"Tell me, Father." Makarov hiccupped. "What is it about you rural men that seems to get these society ladies all worked up under their ball gowns?"

Nicholas looked to his setting with pursed lips. "Aleksander, I warn you!"

"Come now, Emperor. This is important. I'm certain the men here would love to know the secret."

"My secret," said Rasputin, "is I speak only when spoken to."

"Really?" questioned Makarov.

Chapter 16

"I believe silence is a gift from God," continued Rasputin. "And there are no words from my mouth that will ever find such grace as those spoken from the Holy Book."

"See, now I would have thought it was from you not bathing. You know, your pheromones working them all up."

"Minister!" barked Nicholas. His fist slammed into the table and upset his plate.

"It's fine, Emperor," said Rasputin. "I find Minister Makarov's interest in me to be flattering."

Nicholas nodded toward Rasputin, then continued with his meal. His temples pulsed as he chewed on his food.

"I find staretsy intriguing," said Mrs. Makarova. "So brave and committed."

She smiled and Rasputin reciprocated. Makarov glared at her, and she returned to her plate.

"I too find Father Rasputin intriguing," he said, slurring his words. "Why, with all his parlor trickery." He purposely chewed with an open mouth, glaring at Rasputin.

Nicholas banged on the table once more and stared wide-eyed at Makarov.

"Minister, you are out of order!"

"My good Minister," began Rasputin. "Let us not chew on bones of the dead in such gracious and glorious company. Indeed there will come a time when you and I may speak over such matters."

"Indeed," said Makarov. "Forgive me, Emperor."

"I will not stand for another moment of this behavior toward my guest. Certainly not in my presence and certainly not at the imperial dining table."

Makarov stood.

"I have offended you, Emperor. My apologies."

Makarov wobbled from his drunkenness. He held his wife by the wrist and clumsily pulled her from the table. The dinner guests turned to watch Makarov stride along the dining hall. As he and his wife disappeared from the adjoining Portrait Room, the party looked toward Nicholas.

"Please," he said. "Carry on. The minister's wife became suddenly ill."

Part II: Copilul Sângelui

The guests accepted the excuse and happily returned to their feast.

"My apologies, Father," said Nicholas. "He's—"

"Planning to overthrow you."

The surrounding party stopped at Rasputin's comment. An impatient silence hung over Nicholas's section of the table.

"Excuse us for a moment," said Nicholas, looking toward Alexandra and Sana. He stood and motioned Rasputin to follow him. They walked a good distance from the imperial table and stood closely together, Nicholas leaning in toward him.

"Father. I—"

"Emperor. May I speak frankly?"

"Indeed, that is why I pulled you aside. No one must overhear this."

"Minister Makarov is an ambitious man, eager for more authority over the Duma and in turn Russia."

"Agreed."

"I have foreseen your demise at his hands. He is working with the Bolsheviks, who are planning a revolution that will topple you. Makarov has much of your military and secret police already with him."

"What else have you foreseen, Father?" Nicholas was intent.

Rasputin closed his eyes.

"He plans to use the Bolsheviks as a means to attack you. And he will betray them once they have served their purpose. I'm afraid if Makarov is not placed under arrest immediately, Russia will suffer dire disgraces. And you, my brave Emperor, are endangering your own life and family."

Nicholas brought his thumb to his mouth and chewed on his thumbnail. Sweat beads appeared upon his forehead. He looked back to the dinner party to see the guests at ease, talking freely among one another. Only Grand Duke Pavlovich seemed to take an interest in Nicholas's conversation with Rasputin.

"What do you suggest?"

"Now is when you must be bold," said Rasputin. "Avoid the shadows, for there are knives waiting to be stuck in your back. You must dissolve the Duma and arrest Makarov for treason. It is no secret his forces are working to undermine your dynasty. I

Chapter 16

foresee it is time for you to tighten your grip on power, Emperor. Do it swiftly."

Rasputin clicked his heels and bowed.

"Thank you, Father," he said, and warmly squeezed Rasputin's biceps. Nicholas and Rasputin walked back to the dinner party.

"Everything fine, Emperor?" questioned Dmitri.

"Yes, Dmitri. Thanks to Father Rasputin, everything is clear now."

After countless bottles of dessert wine, the grand dinner wound down and the guests filtered from Alexander Palace.

*

"Kind Commander, is that you?" asked Mrs. Fyodorovna, squinting in the darkness.

"Yes, Mrs. Fyodorovna," said Kashin as he neared her.

She sat near the base of a red marble staircase leading to the back entrance of her sleeping quarters. The staircase was carved with decorative banisters on each side, casting a deep shadow across her upper body. Kashin noticed her fidget a bit as he approached.

"Will you be so kind as to pull me up the stairs, good Commander? My servant is keeping me waiting. I've been sitting here since you left me."

"Certainly, Mrs. Fyodorovna."

Kashin pulled a pair of gloves from his jacket pocket and slid them onto his hands as he stood behind her. He grabbed the handles on the back of her wheelchair and positioned her at the base of the stairs.

Mrs. Fyodorovna gripped her armrests and braced herself for the ascent as Kashin pulled upward and leveled her off on the first step. He repeated the action methodically up thirteen more stairs, ensuring Mrs. Fyodorovna was tilted as not to tip forward.

At the last step, Kashin held on to her chair with one hand and used his other hand to swing open the heavy oak door that led into her quarters. Kashin pulled her to the top of the landing, then locked her wheels and left her facing the open staircase. He walked away,

Part II: Copilul Sângelui

and Mrs. Fyodorovna could hear him dragging something heavy toward her.

"Commander? What are you doing? I command you to summon my bed nurse so that I may be put to rest. At once!"

At that moment, Kashin dropped a body at her side. Mrs. Fyodorovna looked downward to see a wide-eyed young man bound at the legs and wrists, his mouth stuffed with a blood-soaked cloth. He was badly beaten about his face and neck.

"Why, who is this?"

Kashin crouched behind her and spoke into her ear. "That, my dear Mrs. Fyodorovna, is the young assassin who cut the throat of your servant just as you were pulled to the top of this landing. The same assassin who then dumped you down these stairs. The one I shot in the back just as I entered this room when I heard your screams for help."

Mrs. Fyodorovna appeared sour. "My servant boy is nowhere to be found, the lazy—"

Kashin tipped her chair and sent her tumbling to the bottom of the hard marble stairs. Her neck snapped as she struck the cold stone floor, and she gurgled her final breaths.

He pulled the young man from the ground and forced him to stand behind the wheelchair. The boy, seemingly resigned to his fate, stood with no struggle. Kashin moved to the front of the room, stepped over Mrs. Fyodorovna's servant whose throat he had cut moments earlier, and aimed his gun at the would-be assassin. Kashin fired two shots into the boy's back. The young man slumped forward and tumbled with the wheelchair down the hard stairs. Kashin cursed and quickly followed. He dashed to the bottom of the staircase and unraveled the ropes around the boy's ankles and wrists, then pulled the bloody cloth from his mouth. He then ensured Mrs. Fyodorovna was dead and bolted back up the stairs.

Kashin hid the remaining evidence underneath Mrs. Fyodorovna's mattress. He placed his whistle to his lips, and a shrill erupted from the room. Moments later, the entire castle was abuzz with secret police. Sirens rang over Tsarskoye Selo, alerting all to the danger within Alexander Palace.

*

Chapter 16

"You startled me," said Alexandra, placing her fingers to her chest.

"I'm sorry, Your Highness," said Rasputin. "I thought you saw me exit my room."

Alexandra leaned against the railing upon the palace's grand upper veranda. The light from her sleeping quarters lit her face as she turned to greet Rasputin.

"Please don't take me as rude. It's just nobody ever comes to this side of the palace."

"Highness, I will leave."

"No, please. Stay. I enjoy the company."

Rasputin stood beside her, and they looked out toward Saint Petersburg.

"Beautiful city," said Rasputin. "From a distance."

"From a distance."

Rasputin looked to Alexandra to see she was wearing only a long silk gown.

"Your Highness. It is freezing. Please, allow me to return to my quarters and find you a coat."

"No, I'm fine. Thank you. I don't know what it is, but no matter the weather, I never feel the cold. And I prefer it when you call me Alexandra."

Rasputin became aware of soft cello music rising from behind them. He looked to see a tall wooden table with a phonograph atop it. He closed his eyes for a moment and absorbed the music.

"Dvořák," said Rasputin.

"Cello Concerto in B Minor," replied Alexandra. "You know Dvořák?"

"Indeed. My mentor in Siberia played the cello. I unfortunately have not the skill for musical instruments, only the ear."

"Alexei is the same."

"The violin is the third arm of every peasant farmer in Siberia. As badly as I wanted to, I could never make it sound like anything other than a sick cat. My poor mother—all she wanted was a little virtuoso."

Alexandra laughed. "Is she still in Siberia?"

"No, she's … she was murdered when I was very young."

"Oh," gasped Alexandra. "I'm sorry. I didn't—"

Part II: Copilul Sângelui

"Please, Your Grace. It is nothing."

There was a long silence.

"I play," she said. "The cello and violin. Just a hobby."

Rasputin watched the sparkling lights of Saint Petersburg. "I would love to hear you play."

Alexandra looked to him.

"You would?"

"Of course," said Rasputin.

The two stood quietly, looking out into the crystal-clear night. The sliver of moonlight cast long, lean shadows across the topography of Tsarskoye Selo. A low-hanging cloud glided briskly along the landscape, spreading out into the trees.

"The moon. It's nice tonight," said Alexandra. "Usually it hurts—even burns my skin."

"That is because of your diet," said Rasputin with a smile.

"Oh?" she said, and looked toward him.

"You have much to learn, Alexandra."

"Father Rasputin, I don't know how to take that comment." She gave him a playful smile.

Rasputin looked to her as his ear caught a familiar stanza from the phonograph.

"Do you dance, Empress?"

"With my husband."

"As any devoted empress should. Certainly you would not refuse me one dance on a night so ... radiant?"

She turned to Rasputin to be more firm with him, and he pushed into her. Alexandra folded into his arms as if she'd longed for his touch.

"Stop," said Alexandra.

"It is only one dance," he said, pulling her in step to the rhythm of the cello.

Alexandra thought momentarily to push him away, but was too entranced. Since her arrival in Saint Petersburg, she had been given the finest dance instruction from the most revered teachers in Russia, and she swayed with Rasputin in a manner implying she predicted each of his graceful steps.

"You dance well for a starets," she said.

Chapter 16

"I dance well for a king."

Alexandra blushed and looked to her feet.

At first she and Rasputin took wide, playful steps, giving the sense of a polite courtship. Their hands intertwined, the gap between their bodies closing with each step. Alexandra soon found herself with her head resting upon Rasputin's chest as they swayed in the moonlight to the sounds of Dvořák's cello.

"I see you already have quite a following among the women," said Alexandra.

"They seek answers. They believe I have them."

"That's very modest of you."

"It is true, Your Grace."

They swayed and turned to the cello and intermittent flute medleys.

"May I speak frankly with you, Grigori?"

"Certainly, Your Grace."

"Is it possible that we have met before?"

Rasputin paused before answering and pulled Alexandra close.

"Of course. Everything in the universe is entwined with everything else. It is almost certain that we knew each other once before. Perhaps, even in *this* lifetime."

She pulled back and looked to his face.

"It's just when you are around, I feel healthy. My sickness dissipates. Alexei is the same. But there's something else, something I can only describe as a memory."

Rasputin smiled with pursed lips and nodded. "If you must know, our meeting was not by accident. However, it is too soon to reveal everything to you."

"You must."

"My sweet Alexandra, all that you can know now is that we are bound to each other ... by destiny and by something much, much deeper. In time all truths will reveal themselves."

"Do not be cryptic with me. I—"

"Your Grace." He looked into her eyes. "All things will be revealed soon."

Part II: Copilul Sângelui

She felt calm and placed her head upon his chest. Alexandra looked downward and grasped Rasputin when she saw they were floating above the veranda floor.

"Grigori!"

"Do not be afraid. Move with me."

She held him more tightly, and Rasputin continued to lead the dance in midair. With the gibbous moon as their backdrop, they swayed above the floor in perfect unison with the rising concerto. Rasputin moved them from the veranda into the open night, and they danced above the sheer drop of the palace façade. Below them Tsarskoye Selo sparkled like a mirror of the night sky.

"Please stop. I'm terrified of heights."

Rasputin flashed a devilish grin. "My dear Alexandra, didn't you know you can fly?"

At that moment he spun her away, and she flew toward the hard brick of the palace façade. Alexandra floated freely, spinning and screaming through the air. She flew toward the wall, covering her face for impact. Just before she slammed into the palace, Alexandra threw her palms outward and floated gently toward the wall, her hands clutching a dense row of ivy. She slipped slowly while struggling to maintain her grip. She looked to the lights far beneath her and screamed for help. Rasputin's voice floated to her from below.

"Let go, Alexandra. Come with me."

Rasputin's call echoed to her once more, and she became aware of whistles rising from the veranda. She looked downward as the vision faded. Alexandra found herself sitting in bed as three Okhrana officers burst into her room. With guns drawn, they dashed toward her balcony, past the singing phonograph, and closed the sweeping glass doors.

"What's the matter?" she cried.

"Mrs. Fyodorovna has been murdered. Bolsheviks have breached the palace."

"Where are the children?"

"Everyone is safe, Empress."

"Take me to them!"

Alexandra looked back to the glass doors, thinking she saw Rasputin standing in the shadows. Upon second glance, she realized no one was there. As she leaned forward to stand from bed, strands

Chapter 16

of dried ivy fell from her grip. She watched them fall to the floor and looked back to the large glass doors, hoping for a glimpse of Rasputin.

*

The Okhrana, followed by Alexandra, burst into Alexei's room to find him sitting peacefully on his bed, tucked into one of Rasputin's arms as they shared a storybook. They were surprised by the sudden disturbance.

"Alexei!" yelled Alexandra as she ran to him.

"Yes, Mama. What's wrong?"

The Okhrana men searched the room and confirmed it was safe. Alexandra looked to Rasputin and forced an awkward smile. "Come, we must get to safety," she said, and picked up Alexei from the bed.

"Father, please follow us," said an Okhrana officer.

Rasputin rose from the bed and followed them to a room across the palace in Nicholas's quarters, where Kashin and several Okhrana officers waited. Nicholas rose from a chair and embraced Alexandra and Alexei.

"Everyone is safe," said Kashin before securing the door.

"What are we to do, Nicholas?" asked Alexandra.

Nicholas raised his eyes to Rasputin.

"Father?"

*

Madam Lenora's body lay still on the morgue floor. It had been a week since the unknown visitor arrived in her parlor and bit into her spine. She woke a few days afterward confined inside a coffin. Upon hearing her wrestle about inside, the stranger opened the lid. His presence calmed her.

"Do you remember your name?" He stroked her hair gently.

Lenora shook her head.

She had no previous memories. She knew only the intense hunger—one driven by every cell in her body. The stranger con-

Part II: Copilul Sângelui

tinued to stroke her hair, and she leaned into him. Lenora peered around the dingy room. It appeared to be an attic from its pointy ceiling and exposed wooden beams. Her eyes came back to the strange man, and he moved his wrist to her mouth.

"I am Grigori. Drink from me."

Lenora looked to the faint purple veins underneath his pale skin. She sunk her teeth into Rasputin's flesh and drank feverishly from his veins. Never had she experienced such ecstasy as the billowy, warm liquid rushed onto her tongue. She hoped the sensation would last forever. Rasputin pulled his wrist away and waved his hand over her face.

"Sleep now."

Lenora closed her eyes, lay back into the coffin, and fell to a deep sleep. She had been unconscious ever since—even as Constable Petrov recovered her hooded body, face-first in the snow where Rasputin was supposedly assassinated.

The window to the morgue gave sight to a starry night that was slowly overshadowed by a dark fog hovering outside. The fog poured its way through cracks in the window frame and slowly filled the morgue, circling around Lenora's body, lifting her into the air. She jerked alive, sucking in a deep breath. Her body bag fell to the floor, and she floated freely—the fog continuing to swirl about her. The mist finally positioned her feet softly on the floor, and she stood with her hands outstretched, appearing to accept communion from it. She opened her eyes, taking in the night.

"Yes, master," she whispered.

The fog slithered toward the window and exited the room in the same wispy manner by which it had entered. Lenora stood alone, invigorated. Her long velour robe draped over her body, and she pulled away the deep hood to reveal her vibrant hair and skin. She closed her eyes as the fangs in her mouth grew, causing her jawline to protrude from her face. Saliva dripped from her mouth as she hovered just above the floor tiles, drifting from the morgue toward Rurik's office.

*

Chapter 16

Many hours had passed since Rurik locked himself inside the closet. He had dozed off several times. Shooting pains in his legs woke him from one of his short naps, and he stood to let the blood circulate to his feet, wincing at the sensation.

The morgue was quiet.

He sat once more, folded his arms, and propped his feet upon the oak barricade. Never in his life had he so eagerly awaited morning.

Rurik was startled by a clawing sound at his office door. The noise built in intensity until Madam Lenora burst through the barricade, sending the filing cabinet and desk to the far side of the room. She ripped the door entirely off its hinges and made her way for the closet.

Rurik stood and pulled a garlic water vial from his belt. Madam Lenora ripped a hole in the door at chest level. Rurik fell toward the back of the closet and reached for a gas mask hanging on the wall. Lenora yanked a few pieces of wood from the hole, then started to gnaw the door to pieces with her powerful jaws. Rurik uncorked the garlic vial and expelled its contents onto her face. Smoke rose into the air as she shrieked and fell backward.

Silence.

Rurik listened intently for the slightest sound as he toiled with the gas mask straps. The door shattered to pieces as Madam Lenora burst through. She forced herself upon him, and he dropped the gas mask. She pinned him to the back of the closet and spit in his face. Her jaws chomped toward him as his appendages went numb.

Rurik lost his footing as Madam Lenora plunged on top of him. The rope tied around his waist pulled taut, spilling a bucket filled with garlic juice from above. Lenora growled as the liquid doused her head. She writhed and shrieked, crawling backward from the closet. Acerbic smoke filled the air.

Rurik lay paralyzed on the floor. His arms and legs felt like dense, heavy balloons. He blinked and watched a black moss grow quickly upon the walls. Madam Lenora's shrills pierced his ears, and suddenly it was gone. He blinked repeatedly, watching the moss fade.

The room was empty.

Part II: Copilul Sângelui

Rurik stood and his legs buckled. He fell to the floor. The room spun in all directions. He fumbled with his hands and wiped away the thick, stringy fluid from his face.

Where is it?

Rurik pulled a large hand mirror from the closet wall and scanned the room in its reflection. Madam Lenora was there—lying at the room's center, trembling and shaking as the garlic concoction melted her flesh. He crawled toward her, breathing deeply to quell the noxious effects of her saliva as his limbs slowly regained sensation. He hobbled a bit before finding his balance.

Rurik used the mirror to position himself over her. He pulled a blackwood stake from his belt and drove it through her back, into her heart, and completely through her sternum. Lenora emitted a final ghoulish shriek, then slumped dead upon the floor.

Rurik flicked on the lights as the feeling in his limbs returned. His vision slowly faded back to reality and he dropped the mirror. Lenora's body lay dead before him.

She had already begun to decay—deep purple veins protruding through her pale skin, slowly blossoming to black. Rurik kicked Lenora onto her side and knelt beside her as she crumbled to dust.

He sat on the floor for another moment, breathing heavily, still dizzy from the lingering effects of her saliva. He wiped the remaining spit from his mouth and looked to where his bottle of vodka lay on its side. There was only a small swig left. Rurik picked up the bottle.

"That's how it's done, my boy." He downed the last of the vodka.

I need a safer place.

He gripped the empty bottle and the solution became entirely apparent. A few short moments later, he was ducking through the streets of Saint Petersburg, heavily armed underneath his coat with the vampire bible clutched firmly against his body. Soon he would be warmed by the fire and jubilant crowd inside the Imperial Pub—the only place he felt truly safe.

Chapter 17

Part II: Copilul Sângelui

17

December 10, 1916 (OS), early morning

Ominous clouds rolled across the dark morning sky as the steam locomotive at Tsarskoye Selo Royal Rail Station was being prepared for its journey. It was coupled to three cars: one for security, the royal car for Alexandra and the children, and a third car reserved for recreation and guests of the royal family. Everyone shuffled from the access tunnel across the platform. Commander Kashin helped Alexandra into her car, then did the same for Alexei and his four half sisters. Rasputin pulled himself up by the railing as Kashin stood in the doorframe.

"Sorry, Father. This car is for—"

"I insist," said Rasputin, pushing by him.

Alexandra, nearly too sick to stand, looked to Kashin.

"It's fine, Commander. Alexei needs him. Sana is welcome too."

Sana was already halfway up the stairs and followed Rasputin into the imperial car—its windows painted black to block out all sunlight.

Kashin saw them to safety, then leaned out from the car and signaled to the engineer, who set the locomotive into motion. The train slinked through Tsarskoye Selo until it met with the main tracks of Russia's master rail system. Soon they were pressing at top speed toward the royal summer retreat in Livadia, Crimea.

*

Minister Makarov arrived in the very early morning to his office inside the City Duma. His head was ringing from a terrible hangover,

Chapter 17

and he walked toward the windows to close the shades. Outside, the Kazan Cathedral loomed large against a cascading ashen sky. He thought back to the previous evening, convinced his ruse with Rasputin was a success. He pulled the blinds and sat down at his desk to review some documents. After flicking on a small desk lamp, he was disturbed by an intense banging at the door.

"Yes?"

The door swung open to reveal Constable Petrov followed by two policemen and four Okhrana officers. Makarov suppressed a grin as the men entered the room.

"Constable? This is an odd time to visit."

"Minister, I'm here to place you under arrest."

Makarov stared up from his reading glasses.

"On what grounds?"

"Treason. We hope you will come with no incident."

Makarov looked to the Okhrana to see their guns were drawn.

"Certainly this is some mistake. Where's Commander Kashin?"

"Minister, please."

"Oh, by all means," he said with an undercurrent of annoyance in his voice. "Arrest me."

Makarov stood and placed his hands behind his back. Constable Petrov moved in and wrapped handcuffs around Makarov's wrists.

"Is that too tight, Minister?"

"It's fine. Tell me, has Nicholas lost his mind?"

"Please, this way," said Petrov, taking Makarov by the elbow and leading him gently away from the desk.

"I just find it quite odd Nicholas would commit political suicide. I am the last leg he has in the Duma."

"Duma's been dissolved," said Petrov. "The tsar has asserted his supreme command over all of Russia. He's ordered anyone associated with the Bolsheviks to be arrested en bloc."

Makarov spit an exaggerated laugh.

"If Romanov wants to sign his own death certificate, then I'll gladly relax in jail and watch the show. Does he really think this will stand?"

Petrov was silent.

Part II: Copilul Sângelui

Makarov walked calmly with Petrov along the halls of the City Duma. As they passed the Hall of Sessions, Makarov peered into the open doors and cast a lingering glance at the grand podium at its center. Petrov walked just behind him with his hands on Makarov's wrists. The two policemen led the way, and the Okhrana officers followed flank. They moved onto Nevsky Prospekt, where an unmarked automobile waited for them at the bottom of the stairs. They assisted Makarov into the back, and the vehicle puttered off.

*

Grand Duke Pavlovich stood at attention in the Room of Coins before Nicholas. Dressed in his navy blue military attire hanging heavy with medals, Dmitri saluted Nicholas with his right hand. Tucked under his left arm was a round white hat with a long white feather sticking from its brim.

Nicholas paid him no mind and continued to scribble his signature onto some documents. Dmitri grew uneasy and cleared his throat.

"Just another moment," said Nicholas.

Nicholas finished signing the documents, then looked to Dmitri with impatient eyes and a forced grin.

"Well then," he said. "That puts a stop to the wretched Duma."

Dmitri was rigid.

"Relax, Dmitri. You are family. I have called you here as friendly counsel."

Dmitri breathed out and looked to Nicholas.

"Nicholas, are you sure this is the right thing to do? I—"

"With every drop of blood in my body." He walked slowly to the front of his desk. "No more will my enemies dictate how I rule this nation. They have taken too much. And now they have taken the life of my mother. If they're brutal enough to murder a helpless old woman, there's no telling where they'll stop. I will hang them—all of them."

Nicholas leaned into his desk and crossed his arms. Dmitri bent downward and placed his cap on the floor.

"All of them?"

Chapter 17

"Yes. The Mensheviks, the Octobrists, anyone who dares stand against me. This is war."

"Understood, Emperor. You have my full support."

"Good. Then you will enjoy helping me on the front lines."

"Absolutely."

"Fine. I was planning on overseeing the battle myself. However, I have sent Alexandra into hiding, and I am needed here in Saint Petersburg. Which is why you will go to the Galician front and see that Brusilov's campaign results in victory. We must spare no resources."

Dmitri's face grew red.

"My gracious Emperor, I—"

"You are grand duke and magistrate over Russia's military. You will act accordingly."

"I haven't seen combat since my military training four—"

"This is not a debate. This is your duty. A threat against me is a threat against you. Do you believe the Bolsheviks will keep you in power if they overthrow me? Minister Makarov, perhaps?"

"I see your point. Of course I'll go. It's just Makarov's arrest will enrage the far right—they are at least loyal to our way of life. And I fear a direct attack on the Bolsheviks will have revolution pouring out into the streets by nightfall."

"Fascists or Bolsheviks no matter. I have the Okhrana, the military, and I deputized the entire Metropolitan Police, who are now under direct orders from me. Nothing can stand against my might."

"How is Alexandra?"

"She and the children are safe. Commander Kashin is personally overseeing their safety."

"And have the Okhrana located Lenin?"

"He's still in Switzerland. And so you know, I have taken great lengths to ordered Makarov held in a secluded cell. He will be useful to us again—once he understands who rules this nation." Nicholas stared at Dmitri. "It is my divine right to rule Russia, and I will once again assert that right. Any dissension will be quashed. You are dismissed."

Dmitri clicked his heels and saluted Nicholas, then turned and exited the room.

Part II: Copilul Sângelui

Chapter 18

Part II: Copilul Sângelui

18

December 10, 1916 (OS), dusk

Felix woke inside his train cabin. His body ached and his mouth tasted stale. He'd been largely asleep, never leaving the compartment, since boarding.

The steam whistle screamed overhead, and Felix thought it sounded vaguely like a woman screaming. He pulled open the blinds to view the passing landscape. Outside was a boundless stretch of cow pastures. The winter was apparently more forgiving in this region of Moldova, and an occasional cow or goat stood grazing on some stale grassy patches in the near distance.

The train neared a station stop south of Chişinău, and Felix stood at the window, watching the pastures roll by. He craned his neck to get a better angle and noticed something odd in the field ahead—a black hump of a cow lay dead in the pasture. More followed. As the train slowed, he saw masses of livestock slumped dead in the nearby fields. The vessel creaked to a stop at a tiny freestanding station as pressurized steam blew backward across the tracks like a fleet, passing fog.

A tractor pulling a flatbed full of dead livestock came into view, and a group of farmhands worked to lift the lifeless animals one by one, struggling to hoist them onto the bed.

Felix pulled the hand mirror from underneath the mattress and ensured his wig was in place. After sliding the mirror back, he exited his cabin. Felix stepped down from the blue car—the crisp prairie air invigorated his lungs. He walked to a vantage point on the platform to get a clear look at the dead animals and saw a group of people moving about a small cemetery just beyond the train platform.

Chapter 18

Several tombstones were in ruin—their graves appearing haphazardly dug up. Mangled body parts of the newly dead littered the muddy grass.

Felix stepped down from the platform and walked toward the cemetery. He stood at a wire fence opposite the grounds and watched the gravediggers dump the dead back into the earth. A bearded man in a dark robe stood over the graves, speaking in a language Felix did not recognize.

"*Ustrel, ustrel.*" He repeated it over and over as he tossed holy water over the shallow graves.

The priest looked to Felix and slowly shook his head as visible tears ran from his face. Felix looked away.

In the distance sat a dark, dense forest hidden behind a slim patch of fog. Trees of obsidian bark dominated the forest, their gnarled and twisted limbs intertwined to create a thick, seemingly impenetrable canopy.

Where the trees grow midnight black. Beware to Jill. Beware to Jack.

The surrounding quiet seemed to amplify Felix's heartbeat as he repeated the nursery rhyme.

The conductor shouted for all to board, and Felix turned to see that he was the only person who had exited the train. He thought it peculiar, and a small shiver crept across his flesh.

He walked back to his cabin and locked the door. As the train pulled forward, he gazed into the evening sky and watched the pastures roll by until blackwood trees dominated the foliage in the near distance. For a brief moment, he thought he heard a woman screaming. Deciding it must have been the steam whistle once more, he lay back in bed to relax.

*

Felix stared out the window into the darkness as the train barreled into a hillside tunnel.

Christ, I'm starving.

He pushed on his stomach and foraged in his empty bread bag in hopes to find a lingering scrap. Too hungry to stay in his cabin any longer, Felix headed toward the dining car.

Part II: Copilul Sângelui

He shuffled through first class and walked past a small, circular lounge that sat just before the entrance to the dining car. The table was filled with an assortment of fine breads, cheeses, and several emptied bottles of wine. A portly military officer leaned into his date and kissed her playfully upon the neck. She giggled and ran her fingers through his dark hair. She and Felix made eye contact, and she slowly licked her lips. Felix looked to the floor as he passed them.

Upon entering the dining car, Felix took in its lush interior. Red velveteen curtains hung from the walls and ceiling, and a line of ornate electric lanterns dangled over the tables. Their bright tangerine tablecloths struck a stark yet pleasing contrast against the red interior.

Felix looked down the long row of red velour high-back chairs framed by sturdy strips of varnished oak. He counted the tops of three patrons' heads and looked to the far side of the cabin, where a waiter leaned into the very last chair on the left, apparently taking the order of a fourth patron. They didn't seem bothered by Felix's entrance, so he turned his back and sat in an aisle seat near the entrance.

Just sign the cross and press your gut. He's bound to bring something.

Felix rocked back and forth in motion with the train's rhythmic lull, and he noticed a newspaper wedged in between his seat and the one next to him. He opened it and feigned reading.

While turning the pages, Felix heard the back cabin door open, then close. By the time he thought to look back, a stranger brushed past and sat directly across from him at the table. Felix pretended to read the newspaper. In his peripheral vision, he could see the stranger was tall and thin, wearing a dark gray suit and matching top hat. Upon his chest was a bright ruby-colored kerchief that popped from his blazer pocket, and a white carnation pinned to his opposite lapel.

"Any striking news from Saint Petersburg?" asked the man, a high-pitched curiosity punctuating his question.

English accent. What's he doing here?

"I say, good Father. Any striking news from Saint Petersburg?"

Chapter 18

Felix lowered his newspaper and looked to the stranger. Shiny silver frames imbued his green eyes with a sturdy sense of mischief. Felix looked to his well-manicured long fingernails. His gaze moved to the stranger's top hat, then to a shiny black walking stick that rested on his lap and stuck into the aisleway. Felix bowed his head and tapped his lips.

"Oh, I see!" said the stranger.

Felix nodded and raised his hand in the air to bless the stranger.

"Well then, do you mind if I take a look at your newspaper?"

Felix folded the paper and handed it over.

"Oh, how very interesting! I hadn't heard of the assassination attempt at the palace." His voice seemed purposefully loud, as if he were trying to earn the attention of the other passengers. The man suddenly folded down the paper and glared across the table. Felix quickly looked to the dining car's floral carpeting to avoid eye contact.

Certainly this jackass is done staring.

Felix looked back to see the same bold smile and bright green eyes.

"Hi, there," he said, waving his fingers at Felix. "I suppose I should introduce myself. I'm Charles. Vondling. Professor Vondling, if you wish. I don't imagine you know of me yet."

Felix cupped his hand to his ear.

"No more games, Felix. You can hear me."

Felix glared at him. "How do you know my name?"

"Oh, come now. You've piqued the master's interest. He has sent me to bring you back to Saint Petersburg. But see—I don't like that idea. The master is mine and *only* mine. So I am here to see that you never return."

Vondling sat still, smirking at Felix, whose eyes moved to the window in search of the communication cable.

"They've all been cut." Vondling revealed his sharp canines.

"I'm armed," said Felix, reaching his hand below the table.

"Are you?"

"I have a gun."

"Show me then. Better yet … shoot me." Vondling pointed to his own head.

Part II: Copilul Sângelui

Knowing his bluff was called, Felix shot out of his seat and dashed toward the back of the dining car. He turned to see that Vondling was watching him but remained seated. Felix walked by the other three patrons and made it to the waiter, who was still leaning into the last chair on the left.

"Excuse me," he said, nearing the waiter.

Felix noticed an acrid smell as he rounded the chairs to see gouts of blood splattered upon the table. He looked to the seated patron—his head was slumped over with white lapels drenched in blood. Felix's eyes shot to the waiter's throat—completely chewed apart, his spine protruding from the shredded flesh. He leaned lifelessly into the chair, supported partially by the seated man's back.

Dread swept through Felix as he looked to the other patrons sitting dead in their seats—each with deep bite marks on their throats. They stared back at him with their final moments of terror frozen in their eyes. Felix dashed for the exit behind him only to find it locked.

"Ah-ah! Not that way," said Vondling.

Felix turned to confront Vondling, who stood in the aisle blocking the opposite entrance. His top hat accentuated his perfect posture as he planted his walking stick firmly on the floor between his legs. Felix breathed heavily, scanning the surrounding tables in hopes for a makeshift weapon. Vondling smiled at him, and Felix could see the silvery-white glint of his sharp teeth.

"Now what, Felix?"

Felix backed to the waiter's serving station and grabbed a steak knife from the dirty dishes. Vondling crept toward him with dead, dark eyes as the deceased patrons bobbed about to the train's movement.

"Did you kill Irina?"

"Heavens no," said Vondling, never breaking his slow pace.

"You're him. You son of a bitch!"

"I am not the one you seek." Vondling wagged his finger at Felix, staring at him with a queer sense of benevolence.

Felix held out the knife. "Stay back."

"Now, now," said Vondling. "I'm simply toying with you. I cannot kill you myself or the master would sense my deceit.

Chapter 18

He would then destroy me. But soon I will have my own army of the undead … and accidents will happen."

Vondling stood next to a dead patron and studied his neck wound.

"Delicious," he said, shifting his gaze back toward Felix. "This party's gotten a bit stale, wouldn't you say? How about some guests?" Vondling made an exaggerated motion and clapped his hands together.

At that moment, the patrons sat up in their chairs and glared at Felix with dead, black eyes. The waiter lashed upward, reaching clumsily toward Felix. The rest hissed at him as fangs grew in their mouths and they became aware of their surroundings.

"So tell me, Felix. When you came to the dining car, did you know you were to be the main course?"

Felix charged toward Vondling with the knife in his grip. Two of the patrons became incensed by his motion and tried to grab him as he ran by. Just as Felix reached him, Vondling stepped out of the way and tripped Felix, sending him stumbling to the floor.

"If you wanted to leave, my Prince, all you had to do was ask." Vondling curtsied.

Felix took one last look at Vondling as the undead patrons lumbered into the aisle, clumsily sauntering toward Felix like newborn animals just learning their environment. He stumbled from the dining car and slammed the door shut, unable to locate a locking mechanism. Upon entering the next car, he shielded his eyes from the portly officer's mutilated carcass seated in the circular lounge. The left half of his chest cavity was ripped to shreds with cracked rib bones poking from fresh muscle. Felix clutched his knife, wondering where the female vampire had slithered off to. He moved by the lounge and noticed the man's right hand still gripped around a wine stem—his other arm lay chewed to bits upon the floor.

As he came into the corridor, screams and struggle emerged down the hall. Felix looked to a cabin window next to him to see a gruesome blood splatter dripping from inside the glass. He steeled himself and walked toward the end of the hall. Suddenly, a man fell from one of the cabins into the corridor with two vampires seized upon him. Felix stopped for a moment and clutched his knife. The man screamed in terror as the vampires proceeded to tear him

Part II: Copilul Sângelui

apart with their jowls, feeding on his heart and jugular vein. Behind him, the posterior door to the car slid open. The five newborn vampires from the dining car emerged and dashed toward him. One of them spit its noxious fluid at Felix, who ducked as it flew overhead. With no other options, Felix turned and ran toward the opposite opening. He leapt over the vampires feeding on the man, and they paid him no notice until disturbed by the pursuing vampires. They hissed and swatted at one another, then all seven joined the pursuit.

Felix darted down the next corridor as the lights flickered on and off, finally going dead. He sprinted to his cabin at the end of the hall, just as the pursuing vampires emerged from the car's posterior. He slammed his door and locked it, turning quickly to confront anyone who might have been waiting for him. The cabin was empty.

His mind flashed to Rurik's note and then to the weapons concealed under his mattress. He dropped his knife and ripped the mattress from the frame just as the electricity flicked back on. Felix's stomach curled at the sight of the empty wire bed frame—*someone* had removed all his weapons. He placed the mattress back on the bed, then tore the carpeting from the floor. The trapdoor's circular iron handle rattled up and down from the train's movement. Felix pulled it open to see the gravel and railroad ties passing quickly below.

He stood over the hole for a moment.

Just jump.

Felix knelt over the hole, watching the earth move rapidly beneath him.

OK, on three. One ... two ...

He stood up and ripped the wig from his head.

"That is the dumbest idea you've ever had," he said aloud, peering to the streaks of railroad ties passing below.

In all his haste, Felix had failed to notice that just outside his cabin's window floated the female vampire he'd seen in the lounge, intently watching his actions. Her white gown flowed about her as she drifted gracefully with the motion of the train. Felix stood from the trapdoor and looked to the window to see the woman—her long fangs jutting from her mouth as she scratched at the window.

"Let me in, Felix," she taunted.

Chapter 18

Felix turned to the door and threw back its curtain. Outside stood the seven vampires from the dining car, who began to attempt to break down the door with intense savagery, banging their heads into the glass as it fissured.

In that moment, the outside window to his cabin imploded. The female vampire flew in and thrust herself upon him. They struggled feverishly about the perimeter of the cabin as she tried to sink her fangs into his throat. She flung him onto the bed, and as she attacked, Felix raised his foot, knocking her in the face. The vampiress fell into the open trapdoor and held Felix's feet, pulling him down with her. Felix gripped the bed frame and hung on tightly as her legs dredged along rail ties. She pulled upward on him, opening her sharp jowls—her teeth intent on Felix's shinbone. Just as her mouth was poised to strike, he kicked her in the face and she fell downward. The force caused Felix to lose his grip, and she pulled him deeper into the hole. He threw his forearms onto the floor as the rest of his body hung into the darkness below. He could feel her body jerk as she struck the rail ties over and over. Suddenly, she was gone. Felix heard her wails as she bobbed about underneath the train—the wheels of the massive vehicle claiming her soul.

The cabin door window shattered open as the other vampires began to force their way through the opening—blood dripped down their rabid, fanged faces. One of the vampires spit at Felix, missing his face and striking him on the hand. He shook his hand to dislodge the fluid, which had no discernible effect on him. Then, with every ounce of strength left in him, he swung his feet from beneath the cabin floor and sprawled his body across the open hole. He rolled to the side nearest the train's window as two vampires fell into his cabin. They stood, revealing their innards torn by the shattered glass.

Without another moment's thought, Felix moved to the window. He stuck his head outside to notice a slim metal beam that ran along the side of the train just below its roof. He swung his arm out the window and clutched the beam, hoping it would hold him.

The door gave way to the blunt force of his pursuers, and the five remaining vámpir pushed their way into the cabin, knocking the first two into the open trapdoor. Felix could hear their screams as they were dismembered by the train's wheels. The vámpir dashed toward him and with all his might, Felix pulled himself out the window, desperately clinging to the train as it bounced about. He managed to place his feet on a small ledge toward the bottom of the train and felt momentarily stabilized. Felix looked ahead to see the coal tender and the locomotive and began to shimmy his way toward them, mere meters above the gravel rushing by below. As he inched closer and closer to the coal tender's coupling, he looked back to the window to see a vámpir stick its upper body outside and attempt to grab him. He was barely out of reach. Suddenly, Felix was surrounded by darkness. The train barreled into a tunnel, the brim of which sliced the vampire in half. Felix clung to the train as it shot through the darkness, and the tunnel walls occasionally skimmed his tunic. Just as his forearms burned to numbness and his fingers grew too exhausted, the train emerged back into the night. Felix felt invigorated by the night sky and once more held on as tightly as he could. He continued to shimmy toward the coupling that led to the coal tender. As he reached it, he held on to the railing and placed his foot on one of the railing's chains. He pulled himself over and slumped onto the coupling. After taking a moment to gather his breath, Felix stood and peered into the window of the trailing car, only to see the hallway swarming with a dozen vámpir sprinting toward the door.

"Did he convert the whole damn train?" Felix shouted into the night.

Felix watched as three vampires exited his cabin and glared toward the end of the corridor. Certain they saw him, Felix turned and hopped onto the ladder leading to the coal tender—the black night and glint of the locomotive just ahead of him.

Felix stumbled over the lumps of coal and, in the short distance, could see the interior of the locomotive lit by the glow of the firebox. He slipped on the coal rubble and threw his hand down to steady himself. He stood and hobbled toward the locomotive.

Finally reaching the platform, he jumped to the coupling between the coal tender and the locomotive and stared at the girth of the boiler. A figure lay to the right of the boiler on top of another body. Felix assumed they were the engineer and the fireman. He looked to the coal bin and grabbed the fireman's shovel.

"Hey!" He banged the shovel against the floor.

Chapter 18

The engineer lashed upward, revealing fresh blood dripping from his chin. Beneath him lay the fireman—a deep gash across the front of his neck. The vampire hissed at Felix and shot upright.

Felix steadied himself and accidentally stepped on the firebox treadle. The boiler's door swung open, and the vampire placed its hand over its eyes to shield from the intense heat. Felix swung the shovel wide, the sharp tip slashing across the vampire's neck. It gasped, clutching its throat and stumbling backward. In one forceful motion, Felix plunged the shovel into the vampire's gut and pushed it into the firebox's small oval opening.

The vampire screeched—its legs and torso sticking from the firebox. It clutched for the surrounding instruments as the hot embers devoured its wool uniform. Felix released the treadle, stood back, and wound up. He drove the shovel into the vampire's midsection, forcing the rest of its body into the firebox's tight fit. Felix's eyelashes curled from the intense blaze. As the firebox door slammed shut, the vampire thrashed about, emitting a horrid high-pitched wail. Felix doubled over, covering his ears.

The train rocked from its tracks as the firebox grew white-hot. The jerk in momentum sent Felix falling backward. He regained his footing and watched instrument dials rise and twitch erratically behind their fat, round glasses. Felix's eyes moved to the bevy of levers around the boiler.

One of these has to be the brake.

He noticed a long lever with a red grip rising from the floor. With no other options, he clenched the handle and slammed the lever forward. The locomotive's brakes screeched into place. The train buckled before the massive momentum once again pushed the locomotive forward with incredible force. The disquieting scream of metal on metal gave the notion the brake shoes would fail at any second.

Felix peered to the tender, then to the shadow of the train behind it. The motion of the train pushing then pulling against itself almost threw Felix to the floor once more. In the deep shadows, he could make out the train's very last open vestibule car. He decided to climb up on the train's roof to reach it. As he hopped on the coal tender's ladder, Professor Vondling appeared over him.

Part II: Copilul Sângelui

"My dear Felix. It seems you've nowhere left to run!" yelled Vondling. "There are still fifteen or so friends of mine in the next car. Or! I envision you could escape by leaping overboard and breaking every bone in your body." Vondling smiled at him. "Which shall it be?"

Felix looked to the quick-moving landscape and then back to Vondling, realizing he was doomed.

"Do you see what lies ahead?" asked Vondling, motioning toward the front of the train.

Felix looked to see Bucharest's night lights sparkling in the distance as the train rounded a bend.

"I'd say we're set to arrive shortly," said Vondling.

Felix hung on the ladder, expecting Vondling to kick him in the mouth. Instead, the thin man looked up to the sky and then back to Felix.

"Well, my sweet Prince. For now I bid you ... adieu."

Vondling hissed at Felix, striking him in the face with saliva. Felix's body fell numb at once. He slumped to the locomotive's floor, and his eyes moved to the white-hot firebox. He looked up to Vondling, who still stood over him at the brim of the coal tender. At that moment Vondling shrieked and leapt into the night sky as another shadow emerged at the top of the coal tender.

Felix could no longer keep his eyes open as the effects of Vondling's saliva took hold. He twitched about as the shadow stood over him. Felix's entire body seemed to meld into the metal floor, and his heartbeat became indiscernible from the thumping of the thundering locomotive. He looked once more to the shadow above him. As it reached toward him, Felix noticed a large silver ring on its hand. The shadow neared as a thick black moss seemed to envelop everything around them. Felix's breathing deadened despite his attempts to suck in fresh air, and he could feel the shadow lifting him from the floor. The rumbling steam engine rocked Felix to blackness just as the train's brake shoes shattered from their couplings in a shower of molten metal.

The train, now at full throttle with no means to stop, thrust onward to its final destination.

Chapter 19

Part II: Copilul Sângelui

19

СОВЕРШЕННО СЕКРЕТНО [TOP SECRET]
Clipping from the Bucharest Adevărul:
Gara de Nord Train Disaster Kills 83

Bucharest, Dec. 11—What was believed to be a German artillery attack on Gara de Nord has proved to be a deadly and mysterious train crash that destroyed a large portion of the station, killing 83 people including all 57 passengers and staff on board.

The passenger train, filled mostly with Russian military officers, left Saint Petersburg on December 8 and met an explosive end at its final destination of Gara de Nord on December 10 at 10:17 p.m.

Bucharest transportation officials have only recently tamed the fires that engulfed the station for over six hours, and are still piecing together the happenings surrounding the crash.

Eyewitnesses reported seeing the locomotive engulfed in flames as it entered the final stretch at an incredible speed. An engineer on site believed the train was moving at well over 100 kilometers per hour when it struck the barrier of the main platform, causing the train's boiler to explode. The explosion killed all passengers on board and another 26 bystanders waiting to board other trains. The fire that ensued consumed all three wooden passenger cars, and those of two other trains docked at the main station.

Chapter 19

The train was last seen leaving a small substation south of Chişinău, Moldova, on schedule, and seems to have lost control shortly before its final approach into Bucharest.

From Saint Petersburg to Bucharest, officials have deemed the crash one of the worst train disasters in European history, and are blaming Tsar Nicholas II for ignoring their warnings to update rail communications between borders and modernize Russia's passenger cars to steel frames.

*

Felix shot awake. He was in the same ratty bed where he'd slept the previous night. An incredible soreness pervaded his entire body. As best he tried, he'd been too exhausted to pull himself from bed since arriving. He had no idea where he was or how he had arrived. His sleep had been shoddy at best, owing to several German artillery attacks near Bucharest's outskirts, and the recurring lucid nightmares of his toils at the hands of Charles Vondling.

A mortar flare flashed in the distance, and Felix took a deep breath, trying to calm himself. As the room fell to darkness, the stench and numbing sensation of Vondling's rancid saliva swept over him.

Everything started to spin.

He found himself once more struggling against half consciousness as he tried to repel the multiple vampire attacks. He remembered Vondling fluttering off into the night and then the shadow moving on top of him, pulling him from the train floor. He remembered the large silver ring upon the shadow's hand as it reached out to him and pulled him upward. Felix woke from the fever dream as the wail of the train's wheels resonated in his mind.

His fingers ached as he remembered gripping the coal shovel and shoving the vampire into the tender. Felix dug his thumb into his forearm and tried to release the muscle soreness. The pain brought back the explosion, the harrowing screams, and the helpless sensation of watching the train barrel full speed into Gara de Nord as someone very large and strong carried him away from the scene over his shoulder. Then Felix was suddenly on the ground again,

Part II: Copilul Sângelui

reeling from the explosion's aftershock, landing face-first into slush and gravel before passing out once more.

His next memory was waking in bed.

Felix realized trying to rest was useless and that he had to find Rurik's brother. He sat up in bed, massaging his temples as the vision disappeared. He thought to Professor Vondling once more.

So his master orders him to bring me back to Russia, and he tries to kill me anyway. I'm in way over my head.

His stomach pulled at him.

Felix missed his palace. It had been five days now since he'd met Rurik, and in that time he hadn't showered, shaved, or eaten much save the bread from the train and two bowls of potato soup someone had left at his bedside.

Felix stood from the rickety bed and emerged into a dim hallway. Upon entering the hall, he noticed all the doors were numbered. Down one flight of stairs, he found a burly man dressed in simple clothing, seated upon a comfortable chair next to a warm fire.

"Hello," said Felix, guessing this was the innkeeper.

The man was startled and shot up to confront Felix.

Felix backed away when he took in the stranger's size. He was nearly seven feet tall with deep scars circling his forehead, neck, and wrists—his skin appeared ashen. The massive man simply glared at Felix, breathing heavily.

Felix noticed a large silver ring on his hand.

"It was you. You saved me."

The innkeeper grunted and nodded. He stood closer to Felix and, after a few moments of lingering silence, reached out and embraced him. Felix, struggling to breathe, forced his way free and took a step backward.

"So ... thank you for that. And ... um ... I'm supposed to meet Professor Kozlov," he said, a strong air of uneasiness in his voice. "I assume you can help?"

The giant man hulked over him, not saying a word. In the shadows, Felix could make out what appeared to be stitches in the man's eyeballs. A rustling from the next room caught Felix's attention, and a woman emerged from the door.

Chapter 19

"Sebastian! That's no way to treat our guest," she said with an English accent.

Felix was immediately taken by the woman's beauty. She was in her late twenties with bright blue eyes and dark hair.

"I'm so sorry. I'm Mary," she said, extending her hand. "Please forgive Sebastian. He is very protective. Sebastian! Please sit. You're alarming our new friend."

Sebastian remained unmoved.

"Do you need your dollie?" she questioned.

Sebastian smiled and nodded. Felix noticed his teeth appeared stitched into his gums.

Mary walked to a small wooden bin by the fire and retrieved a worse-for-wear rabbit sawdust doll fashioned from wool—a chipped black button was its only eye. She handed the doll to Sebastian, who returned to his chair by the fire and softly grunted in a singsong manner as he held the rabbit by its arms and made it dance upon his lap.

"Very good, Sebastian," said Mary.

"Is he all right?" asked Felix.

Mary looked to Sebastian. "He is. It's a very long and very tragic story, but as you can attest—he comes in handy. Especially when dealing with the undead."

Felix relaxed. "That he does. He saved me from the … wait. How did he get on the train?"

Mary smiled.

"Mr. Yusupov, do you really think Rurik would send you all the way to Bucharest without our people watching over you along the way? We were assigned to meet you at the final destination, but our associate telegraphed from Chişinău, citing you were the only passenger who exited during the stop. I felt something was amiss, so I consulted my seer, who alerted me to Vondling's presence aboard. Sebastian and I then came to the train as quickly as we could. Good thing too. A moment later and I don't believe we'd be having this conversation. I'm actually quite impressed you survived as long as you did."

"Me too," said Felix. "So you were there?"

"I was. We arrived just as Vondling cornered you."

Part II: Copilul Sângelui

"And how is it you both managed to board a speeding train?"

Mary seemed coy. "You'd be incredulous if I told you. All you need to know is Sebastian and I stepped in and pulled you to safety."

Felix was silent, wanting to press her further. "Thank you," he said instead. "Will you be taking me to see Rurik's brother?"

"No. Sebastian and I have much bigger problems to attend to, thanks to your friend Charles Vondling. A menace, he is. We have an associate with a carriage who can take you to Professor Kozlov. I will send word for him. Two hours."

"Any sooner?"

"No."

Felix frowned. "I'll be in my room. Will you notify me?"

"I will."

They held eye contact for a long moment. Felix felt uneasy in his gut—the last time a woman had this effect on him was when he met Irina for the first time. He nodded at Mary, then smiled before taking one last look at Sebastian, who still sat caressing his rabbit doll.

"Thank you," said Felix. "And thank you both for saving my life."

Felix turned and shuffled back to his room.

"It certainly won't be the last time, Mr. Yusupov," came Mary's words from behind him.

*

It was several minutes past midnight when Felix stood upon the cold, well-lit doorstep of Denis's rustic brick home. The behemoth structure loomed just outside Bucharest's city limits on the edge of the university's agricultural grounds. A squat, dilapidated barn sat in the distance.

Felix stared at the front door, which had a full-length mirror embedded in its wood. Wet, heavy snowflakes fell all around him as he looked over his haggard reflection. He rang the bell, then stood for several moments blowing warmth upon his freezing hands.

"Come on, come on …"

Several more attempts at the buzzer, still no answer.

Chapter 19

"Hands up!"

Felix swung around to see a man bundled heavily in winter garb, his face protected by a modified gas mask with a wide glass faceshield and dual filtration system near the chin. From the top of his coat poked two slim canisters that fed hoses into a long steel rod he was gripping with one hand. At first glance, Felix believed it was a cattle prod. The man poked the rod toward him.

"Put your damn hands up!"

"Christ!" Felix threw his arms upward.

"Who are you?"

Felix looked to the gas mask. The man's face was barely apparent through the foggy glass.

"I'm Felix ... I ... are you Denis?"

The man was silent.

Felix could see the left half of his face was badly disfigured beneath his thick black mustache. Felix's eyes moved to the cattle prod. It was some sort of spray-nozzle mechanism: two narrow rods welded together, attached to a modified rifle butt; at the tip of the device, one of the rods bent downward, then angled up again to meet the straight rod. Felix noticed a metal hook on its trigger jiggle ever so slightly. He traced the hook to a sharp wooden stake that poked from the man's coat sleeve.

"Rurik sent me. You're Denis?"

"Possibly." He positioned the mystery rod between his right biceps and chest, then fumbled inside his coat pocket. "Drink this," he said, extending a vial to Felix.

"Uh—"

"I said drink it!"

Felix took the vial, and the man quickly repositioned his rod device.

"What is it?" Felix uncorked it and the strong smell of garlic invaded his senses.

"Garlic water. Drink."

"I'm not drinking this."

"Then pour it on your hand." He poked the rod at Felix. "I'll shoot."

"Fine! Go easy."

Part II: Copilul Sângelui

Felix held out his hand and poured the garlic over his palm. The masked man watched with wide eyes as the mixture ran from Felix's hand and dripped onto the snow. He pulled up his mask, revealing his face—the left side was terribly disfigured by burn scars, the right side identical to Rurik's.

"Put your hands down. I am Denis." He sounded disappointed.

Felix relaxed and studied Denis's face.

"Sorry about that," said Denis. "I can never be too certain."

"You're twins?"

Denis mumbled something unintelligible and limped past Felix. When he reached the front door, he turned and said, "You mean Rurik never mentioned his twin brother?"

"No. Not that you were twins."

Denis let out an angry sigh and opened the door. He lumbered down a long staircase toward the building's lower floor. Felix stepped inside and closed the door. Mirrors, large and small, were scattered about the walls.

"Lock it please," said Denis.

Felix flipped several large bolt locks, then followed Denis. When he reached the lower floor, Felix was greeted by a warm sitting room stuffed with furniture custom-made from blackwood. Denis stood in the corner, hanging his jacket and gas mask. His back still hung heavy with the canister contraption.

"May I ask what you're wearing?"

"No."

"Is it a gun?"

"Not now."

Felix was nervous. He scanned the room for a place to rest and sat in a nearby chair.

"Nah! Stand up. You stink!"

Felix shot up. "Sorry."

"Until you bathe, I'd rather you not touch anything."

Felix nodded, trying not to stare at Denis's slim, wooden prosthetic forearm—a silver hook embedded in its sharp tip.

"He really never mentioned me?" asked Denis.

"Just briefly. He did say you were a genius."

Denis grunted and swatted his hand into the air.

Chapter 19

"How did you get the name Denis?"

Denis squinted toward him, appearing agitated. "What do you mean?"

Felix smiled, trying his best to convey a sense of good nature. "Well, it's just not very Russian."

"Oh … our father was Russian, mother was English. Rurik was gifted the Russian name, I was left with the English one."

"I see."

"And the looks of course are mine," he said, motioning to his burn scars.

"Of course," said Felix. He looked to the floor when he noticed that in addition to the scars, Denis was missing his left ear.

Denis relaxed in a plush chair, massaging his arm above the prosthesis. "When I heard of the train disaster, I assumed you went with it. Mary is notoriously uncommunicative with me, so I heard nothing of your survival. I'm pleased to learn you're alive."

"Barely."

"You will have to tell all about that."

"Oh! How thoughtless of me," said Felix, snapping his fingers. "There's a vampire. Here. He followed me from—"

"A particularly careless and destructive one. That much I know." Denis stood and limped down the hall. "Follow me. We must hurry."

"To catch him?"

Denis looked back.

"No. You are in dire need of a bath."

*

Felix drifted awake at dawn to the smell of fresh roasted coffee and savory meat. He rolled over in his single bed and peered at a railing that separated the small loft from the interior below. From the ceiling's center, morning's light poured in through a circular skylight and lit the warm cedar paneling that fed from the ceiling to the surrounding walls. Felix noticed fresh clothing laid out for him on a small iron chair. He dressed himself, surprised the garments fit perfectly.

Part II: Copilul Sângelui

He moved down the spiral staircase into a warm library furnished with blackwood bookshelves and a matching desk at its center. Every piece of wooden furniture Felix had seen thus far was constructed of blackwood, and all available wall space was adorned with mirrors. Books sat littered everywhere about the room—stacked to chest height, stuffed on shelves, and piled aimlessly on the large desk.

"In here, Felix." Denis's voice came from a wide hallway.

He walked down a corridor hung with large mirrors, occasional aviation photographs, and decorative frames furbished with military medals. In one photograph, several generals stood around Denis, who had no burns on his face at the time. Another officer in the photo was pinning a medal onto Denis's uniform. The remaining photos were of Denis in pilot's gear, always standing next to a similarly dressed woman. Felix took note that his face was scarred in the photos.

Felix continued to take in the photographs until he came to the very last picture frame, which housed a tarnished page:

**MOBY-DICK;
OR,
THE WHALE.
BY
HERMAN MELVILLE,
AUTHOR OF
"TYPEE," "OMOO," "REDBURN," "MARDI,"
"WHITE-JACKET."**

**NEW YORK:
HARPER & BROTHERS, PUBLISHERS.
LONDON: RICHARD BENTLEY.
1851.**

Felix came into a kitchen that opened to an unexpected brightness. The ceiling and far wall were entirely of glass. The floors sprouted with a plenitude of exotic plants, giving it the feeling of a live-in greenhouse. Denis stood at a long black stove, cooking something

Chapter 19

savory in a large pan. The mystery canisters were still harnessed to his back—the rod device hung from a hook welded to the canister frame.

"Please sit," he said, motioning to a flat metal table at the room's center. "There is coffee."

Felix sat in a chair that faced the outside window.

"May I ask—who's the woman in the photos?"

"That's Elda. My wife."

"Oh, is she around?"

Denis continued to scramble the eggs in his pan, never looking up. "She died last year. Plane crash."

"I'm sorry," said Felix.

"It's fine. She was a magnificent pilot. Just not that morning."

"I wasn't aware we allowed women pilots."

"No. No. Years after I was decommissioned, I took to flying as a hobby, and she followed."

"Were you involved in a crash too?"

"No," said Denis. "Whatever gave you that idea?"

Denis turned around and smirked. Felix blushed and shifted his gaze to the large kitchen window—it opened up into a wider greenhouse that harvested an abundance of green plants with lean stalks rising to tiny caps of white spiderlike flowers.

"Cow parsnip?"

"Giant hogweed," said Denis, returning to his cooking duties.

"Hogsweed?"

"Hogweed. No *s*."

"Looks like cow parsnip."

"Much taller. And much nastier, I promise you."

"What's it for?"

Denis turned off the stove and tipped the pan's contents onto two plates. "That's probably the safest room in the world. Its sap will melt vampires on contact. Leave you with some permanent scars too."

Denis hobbled to the table and placed a plate in front of Felix. He caught a glimpse of a tattoo on Denis's right forearm: *I AM MADNESS MADDENED*. Denis limped back to the stove and returned with his own helping. Felix stared at his wooden prosthesis as Denis gracefully maneuvered his setting.

Denis looked up suddenly. "My arm is missing below the elbow. It's something I am used to." He raised his wooden prosthesis and rolled up his sleeve, exposing where his flesh met the harness below the elbow. The hook gleamed in the morning light.

"It's blackwood," said Denis, tapping his finger to its sharp tip.

"May I ask how it happened?"

Denis chewed on his food, smiling.

"Sure you may ask how it happened." He swallowed.

Denis bent over slightly and reached underneath the table. He fumbled with something for a moment, then sat up.

"This," he said, thumping his wooden arm on the table, "and these"—he motioned to the raised burn scars along the left side of his face and neck—"and this"—he reached below, produced a prosthetic leg, and stretched it out upon the table—"are what happens when you tangle with the wrong vampire."

Felix's mouth fell agape.

He studied the well-fashioned leg—a wooden calf and mid-thigh met with a rather complex metal knee joint. He looked to Denis.

"Was it—"

"Yes … it." Denis pursed his lips. "Our encounter burned down the entire village of Vernești."

"You're lucky to be alive," said Felix with the air of an impressed schoolboy.

"Am I?" Denis stared at him with cool, dark eyes. "Took my leg above the knee in one bite. Same," he said, motioning to his left forearm. "One bite."

Felix looked to his plate. It was overloaded with plump sausages and scrambled eggs. Denis pulled his leg below the table and re-fastened it.

"The fire unfortunately cauterized my wounds and left me alive."

Felix swallowed, trying his best to maintain polite eye contact.

Chapter 19

Denis grabbed his fork and stabbed a sausage. "But now it's back. And this time I . . . 'I will dismember my dismemberer.'" Denis smiled—the left side of his face hung limp.

Felix leaned toward his plate. "Damn. That's a lot of garlic."

Denis huffed. "That and several other nasties from the Allium genus—all deadly to vampires. Dig in." Denis popped a large piece of sausage in his mouth and stared at Felix. "Russian sausages and scrambled quail eggs—in case you were curious."

"This is the closest thing I've had to a decent meal in days," said Felix with a mouth full of food. "Say, you don't happen to have any scotch? I could use a drink."

"Never touch it," said Denis. "I leave that to Rurik."

Felix shrugged it off and finished his meal, stopping just short of licking the plate. He pushed his dish to the side and looked over the table. A large scrapbook with a news clipping sticking out lay to his right. He pulled out the paper and inspected the accompanying photograph: *Tsar Nicholas II, Tsaritsa Alexandra.*

"What's this?" asked Felix.

"Oh, umm ... that's ... just a hobby of mine."

"She's a dear friend of mine—Alexandra."

"I have a whole scrapbook of her—the lady of the loch. The tsaritsa of curious origin."

"I think you're confused. She's—"

"A vampire," interjected Denis. "A weak one who likely has no idea about the true nature of her illness. But she's a vampire nonetheless."

"There's no way."

"There's every way. You're her friend. Haven't you ever questioned her curious behavior?"

"She does have this strange aversion to mirrors," said Felix, scratching his head. "And daylight."

Denis flipped the scrapbook to its center. He pulled out an article and slid it to Felix.

Part II: Copilul Sângelui

**ОХРАННАЯ СЛУЖБА ЕГО
ПРЕВОСХОДИТЕЛЬСТВА ГОСУДАРЯ
ИМПЕРАТОРА АЛЕКСАНДРА III
[OKHRANA OPERATION IN SERVICE
OF EMPEROR ALEXANDER III]
СОВЕРШЕННО СЕКРЕТНО [TOP SECRET]
АПРЕЛЬ 1894 [APRIL 1894]
ВСЕ КОПИИ ОБНАРУЖЕНЫ
И УНИЧТОЖЕНЫ
[All COPIES ARE LOCATED AND DESTROYED]**

Berliner Tageblatt, April 1894
Princess Alix Found Alive

Bucharest, Romania, April 6—After going missing more than two weeks ago, Princess Alexandra of Hesse and by Rhine has been found alive in a Bucharest hospital on the morning of April 4. She is reportedly in stable condition though suffering from severe hypothermia and amnesia.

The princess disappeared after her traveling committee was ambushed on a diplomatic mission to Romania along the southeastern Carpathian Mountains on March 19. She was feared kidnapped by Bosnian separatist factions operating in Romania who murdered the remainder of her traveling party including her betrothed, Grand Duke George Alexandrovich of Russia, son of Tsar Alexander III. Prince Wilhelm II and Alexandra's brother Louis spared no expense on an extensive search to find her before declaring her lost.

Princess Alexandra was dropped off on the hospital's doorstep in the early hours of April 3 by two men who fled the scene. She collapsed upon entering the hospital and has been in and out of consciousness ever since.

Prince Wilhelm has accepted assistance from the tsar, who has offered to bring Alexandra back to Saint Petersburg to ensure her health and safety at the behest of his son Tsarevich Nicholas II.

Felix looked up from the article. "This is false."

Chapter 19

"Certainly not. It was censored."

Felix squinted, conveying doubt.

"I should know. I was the Okhrana agent in charge of locating the copies."

Felix grimaced. "Come on … I'd know about this."

"Even when missing several limbs, I was very good at my job. She was fished out of a loch deep within the Carpathians after being converted to a vampire, then returned to Saint Petersburg under Nicholas's care soon after. You're probably under the belief she nearly died in a Berlin hospital."

"That's true."

"A lie. I made it up."

Felix was silent.

"The men who found her gave their statement at the hospital, then fled … never to be seen again," said Denis, accentuating his words with wide eyes.

"Come on." Felix raised his eyebrows, and in a brief second absorbed the fact that Denis was much more somber than Rurik. Denis exuded a certain thoughtful sternness that escaped his brother.

"So wait a second," said Felix, shaking his head. "Rurik showed me a barn scroll that illustrated the vampire cycle." He paused for a long moment. "This revolves around Alexandra, doesn't it?"

Denis nodded.

"And Alexei. He's the offspring," said Felix.

"Yes. But he's half vampire. His human blood, passed on by Nicholas, is keeping all of this in limbo."

Felix shot out of his chair. "I must get back to them."

"Sit down!" shouted Denis. "You have no means to travel back to Saint Petersburg. There are no trains in or out—remember, you blew up Gara de Nord? You are here until we finish our duties."

Felix ground his fists into the table as Denis pulled away the scrapbook.

"There is still time," said Denis. "The only way this cycle can be corrected is if Alexei kills his father and consumes his blood, making himself whole. Until then we are moderately safe. The Nosferatu cannot transform to the human plane so long as Alexei remains a halfling."

Part II: Copilul Sângelui

"Rurik kept this from me on purpose, didn't he?"

"Yes. Imagine that."

Felix stilled himself as a wave of anger came over him. "He tricked me into coming here ... so you're my babysitter now?"

Denis was silent for a moment. "You are a member of this aristocracy. That is where your loyalties ultimately lie. So yes, we had to keep some things from you. Please, sit."

Felix slumped in his chair. "I should have been informed."

"No. As you continually demonstrate, you are prone to losing your wits. You would have run to the palace and been thrown in jail immediately for a murder you did not commit. Then, who knows? Likely sent to a gulag asylum when you tried to explain that the tsarevich of Russia is a half vampire who must murder the tsar and consume his blood so that magical vampire bats can transform to an army of darkness for a death cult operating within the ruling elite." Denis laughed. "I'm certain all your royal friends would have believed you and then staked Alexei just to be safe. Are you hearing yourself, Felix?"

Felix ran his fingers through his hair and let out a heavy breath.

"Maybe now you understand why we operate in the shadows," said Denis.

"Denis, I must insist. I've come to bring you back to Saint Petersburg. The prediction is December 16. We have to go now!"

"No," said Denis, slamming his hook to the table. "I can make it to Saint Petersburg just fine on my own. But now you are here in Bucharest, and we have more pressing duties. To that you must be clear. Our directives have changed."

"How about a clue, then?"

From his pocket, Denis pulled the map that had been sent telepathically to his typewriter by Zazlov. He unfolded it and passed it to Felix.

"That is our agenda," he said, pointing to a position on the map. "We are traveling there to thwart this menace at its root."

Felix looked at the map and raised his brows. "What is it?"

"A rocky island in the center of Loch Dracul. A place of rather dismal history. I have been searching for it for ages. The loch is surrounded by very dark magic—impossible to find even with the assistance of a seer. But now we have the map from the vampire's

Chapter 19

holy book. And once we finish there, you can return to Saint Petersburg and track the vampire. Kill it if you wish—just know that I'll be one step ahead of you."

"Fine, let's go."

"Not so fast. We must prepare."

Denis rose from the table and placed the scrapbook on a crammed bookshelf.

"What is it you do, anyway?" asked Felix.

"After being decommissioned, I became a doctor of chemistry. I also study cryptozoology and reanimation in my free time."

"So it runs in the family?"

"Is that an air of doubt I detect? Aren't you the disbeliever who recently survived a vampire attack by blowing up an entire train station?"

"Fair enough," said Felix, breaking eye contact. "What monsters are you looking for?"

"Not monsters—biological creatures. One of my most coveted hunts is about to reveal itself to me—*Desmodus draculae*. The giant vampire bat. Or what our enemies call the Holy Upir."

Felix nodded.

"We will travel to Loch Dracul and kill them before they can do any harm ... they're much less dangerous in their present form." Denis paused and returned to his plate. "We have a half day's travel ahead of us," he said with a mouthful of food. "I'll save the rest for then. This way." He wiped his mouth, then hobbled into the outer greenhouse. Felix followed.

*

"Mind the stalks," said Denis as they pushed through the dense row of giant hogweed plants.

Felix followed him to the end of the greenhouse, where what appeared to be a giant juicer sat along an ivy-covered wall. In the far left corner was a table with beakers and Bunsen burners surrounded by rows of gas canisters.

"Put these on," said Denis, handing Felix a canvas jumpsuit and a pair of thick rubber gloves.

Part II: Copilul Sângelui

"Why?"

"The sap will burn your flesh. Gas mask too," said Denis, pointing toward the wall.

Felix put on the suit and gas mask, following Denis's lead.

"You must ensure no skin is exposed," said Denis.

Felix pulled the suit's hood over his head and tightened the drawstrings.

Denis hacked a few stalks of hogweed with an axe and moved to the juicer. He shoved the hogweed into the machine's mouth, forcing the stalks deep into the opening before closing the lid.

"Hand me a canteen," said Denis.

Felix looked along the wall to see a line of canvas-covered canteens with silver caps. He handed one to Denis, who unscrewed it and placed it to a valve protruding from the juicer. Denis began to crank a metal lever on the side of the mechanism, and a clear, viscous liquid oozed from the valve into the mouth of the canteen. He filled it halfway, then moved to a stationary sink and filled the rest with water.

"Oh, a good thing to remember. See the big X?" Denis motioned to the canteen, where a black X was drawn on its canvas.

Felix nodded.

"You don't want to drink out of these by mistake."

"Got it."

After the canteen was full, Denis capped it and handed it to Felix. "For you, my friend. Use it wisely."

"What's it for?" asked Felix, pulling up his gas mask.

"The sap is phototoxic. Dump it on a vampire—it will turn night to day and burn right through their flesh even in darkness. Oh, you'll want to shake it up first."

"Can't we just stick to holy water and crosses?"

Denis pulled up his gas mask.

"They don't work. Silly if you think about it. Why wouldn't a vampire simply move somewhere, say to India with a large Hindu population? Feast upon a defenseless populace." Denis shook his head. "Much to the chagrin of the Holy Synod—a Christian and his charms are no safer against vámpir than the rest of us.

Chapter 19

No religious iconography will harm them." Denis smiled. "Only the living suffer from religion."

Felix continued to shake the canteen.

"How do you know this stuff works?"

"I've used it."

"On vampires?"

Denis shot him a bemused look. "No, on kittens."

Felix rolled his eyes.

"Vampires are still around, left over from Drăculea's time, although I think I've exterminated just about all of them in Romania. There are some left in Paris and London—possibly as far as New York, but they're nothing more than rodents of the night, scavengers. Despite their unusual powers, without the might of Nosferatu to protect them, most vampires prefer to stay hidden."

"Not the ones I encountered."

"They were newborn—hungry."

"So the Nosferatu are truly that vicious?"

"From what we have recovered from the vampire bible and know of Drăculea's summoning, yes—incredibly vicious. Imagine the cunning of a fearless predator, one that must consume its own weight in blood every night. Then add the ruthlessness of a deranged human psyche. They are insatiable, callous killers. You cannot reason with them—you can only destroy them."

Denis continued to juice the stalks until they both had three full canteens strung around their shoulders. He limped to his lab bench and pulled out another harness with small gas canisters attached.

"Strap this on."

Felix inspected the device, then swung it around his back. He noticed a long rubber tube and nozzle running from the canisters.

"It's simple. Turn it on." Denis reached over his shoulder and turned a hand dial at the top of both canisters. "Now you're pressurized. Left canister is hogweed gas—it stays fully open. Right is compressed oxygen. Open or closed depending on how much power you need. After that, simply point and shoot. Pull down your mask."

Felix obeyed. Denis also positioned his mask, then aimed his rod toward the wall, pulling the trigger with his hook. A dense,

Part II: Copilul Sângelui

streamlined smog shot from the nozzle, coating the cement wall. Denis turned back to Felix as the gas poured in around them.

"Pressurized for all your killing needs!"

He released the trigger.

Felix could see Denis's proud grin behind his mask's steamy glass.

"We should pack," said Denis.

He brushed by Felix and disappeared into the stalks. Felix looked down to his iron nozzles and pulled the trigger. He reached around and turned the canister dials. A small hissing sound emanated from his back, and the hose snapped taut. He quickly resealed both cylinders.

You really are in over your head, old boy.

*

Denis and Felix arrived to Vernești at the foothills of the Carpathian Mountains at 10:46 a.m. The trip had taken nearly two hours, and Felix, unused to automobile travel along dirt roads, managed his best to hide his motion sickness from Denis.

"How much longer?" asked Felix.

"Mere minutes. Try not to vomit."

"I'm fine."

Denis looked at him and noticed his pale complexion. "No you're not."

After another few moments of bumpy travel, Denis turned the vehicle to a side road that led to the Nișcov River. He stopped in front of a large, dilapidated shack that sat before a series of docks with a variety of small fishing boats tied to the planks.

"This it?" asked Felix.

"You ask very obvious questions," said Denis flatly as he exited the vehicle.

Felix shrugged and watched Denis try to crack his back into place before bending over to position his leg prosthesis. Felix opened the auto door and was glad to plant his feet on the ground. He bent over, taking in deep breaths to quell his motion sickness. Denis walked toward the shack—Felix stood and followed.

Chapter 19

Denis turned to Felix. "My friend … he and I used to be fishing buddies, but the last time I saw him, I left on … rather unfortunate terms, so stay alert."

"Alert for what?" asked Felix. Denis did not answer.

As they approached, a figure emerged at the front door, which sat open despite the cold. Felix noticed he was a lanky man with striking white hair.

"Come to burn down my village again?" said the man. "Lot of nerve showing up here, Kozlov."

Felix could barely understand his broken Russian.

"Hello, Florin," said Denis, continuing toward the shack. "Long time."

"Now hold it right there," said Florin, spitting a gob of tobacco onto his porch. "Best get back in that fancy auto of yours and turn back now. Figured you'd learned your lesson last time." He sauntered down the porch's splintered wooden stairs and stood with his arms folded as Denis neared him.

"You mean when I saved your entire village from the clutches of death incarnate?"

Florin smiled. "I suppose that's one way of looking at it." He peered down at Denis's leg. "Pretty impressive how well you get around on that thing. Last time I saw you …" Florin made eye contact once more with Denis. "Well, I'm pleased to see you standing."

The two men embraced.

"Back from the dead," said Florin, releasing the grasp.

"No rest for the wicked," said Denis, looking toward the shack. "Is Elena here?"

"No. Daniela has been accepted to university. Elena is visiting."

"Glad to hear your daughter is pursuing higher study. Very challenging in these times."

Florin nodded. "She is a very bright young woman."

Felix was surprised at Denis. His usual cold and calculating nature was absent in his demeanor toward Florin. He realized Denis was much more complex than he'd first considered.

Florin glanced at Felix. "Who's this?"

"This is Felix. He's my apprentice of sorts."

Part II: Copilul Sângelui

Florin held out his hand to Felix, who could barely muster the strength to counter Florin's handshake.

"Quite a grip you have there," said Felix.

Florin pointed his thumb over his shoulder toward the docks. "Lifetime of boating will do that to a man." He looked Felix up and down, trying to figure him out. "You sure you know what you're getting into with this one? Seems everywhere he goes ... lots of destruction."

Florin laughed as Denis nudged his shoulder. "Well," he said, "I can only assume why you've come. And I honestly don't want to know the details. Let's get to it."

Florin led Denis and Felix to his docks. He walked to a newer boat with a small motor affixed to its stern.

"This is the one you want. My prized baby. See that lever?" said Florin, gesturing to the boat. "All you have to do is drop that, fire up the motor, and a propeller will scoot you right along. She's called a Dippy—disappearing propeller boat. The prop will retract in shallow waters or for when you need to row. I imported her from Ontario, Canada. Will save you hours in time and a lot of back pain. She's a bit noisy, though, so I advise you only use her under the right conditions, if you get my meaning."

Felix knelt to the boat and looked it over. "It's brand-new. You sure we can take it?"

Denis raised his hand to silence Felix. "Very generous of you, Florin. Thank you."

Florin nodded. "Well, just count yourselves lucky I have such a strong passion for fishing and, more so laziness. Cost me just about all I had left in my savings. I do owe you one, but promise you'll return my boat in one piece?"

"You have my word," said Denis.

The two men shook hands.

"Let me show you how it works."

*

The last time Denis stood on Florin's docks, he and Rurik had just returned from a journey deep within the Carpathians. Florin sat at

Chapter 19

the end of one of his docks with a fishing pole in hand as they rowed near.

"You find him?" yelled Florin.

"We did," called Denis.

"You kill him?"

Denis shook his head as Rurik continued to row toward the dock. Florin stood, threw Denis a line, and soon thereafter the three men were gathered around a table in Florin's sturdily constructed shack.

"We lost it here," said Denis, pointing to a map.

Florin shot a long glance at the position as he placed tea on the table for Denis and Rurik.

"You Kozlov brothers are really something else. A Russian spy and a medical doctor who hunt vampires. If my wife ever found out I'm helping out a couple of crazies like you, she'd leave me in a moment."

Florin walked back to his teakettle, poured himself a cup, then sat at the table with Denis and Rurik.

"Brother, I'm telling you—the entrance to the loch is right in this area," said Rurik, pointing to a position just north of Denis's marking.

"Well, had you ducked when I told you, we might have seen where he went. Glass on binoculars is reflective, remember? Guaranteed he saw us." Denis glared at him and let out a long breath, then turned to Florin.

"Rurik caught his attention, and we hid behind some rocks. Next time we looked, both he and his rowboat were gone. There has to be a portal. Boats don't just vanish."

"Well, then," interjected Florin, "if what you described to me is true, there's a very good chance he's coming back as a vampire, right?"

"Very good chance, indeed," said Denis.

Rurik continued to scan the map. "It has to be one of these outlets. We have to go back."

"It's not," said Denis. "We scoured the whole area. Very well hidden, wherever it is. We must have Orna send him a message telepathically. Start preparing."

Part II: Copilul Sângelui

"Message?" questioned Florin.

"Get this," said Rurik, shaking his head.

"What?" said Denis. "We have to get his attention. Draw him out."

"You're planning something foolish, aren't you?" asked Florin.

"Not foolish. We know of a witch who deals in such things. I will simply have her bait this vampire, and then destroy it once it emerges."

"Don't tell me you're letting him know you tracked him to Vernești," said Florin.

Denis looked up from the map. "I am letting *it* know I tracked *it* to Vernești."

"You're crazy."

"Don't worry. If this works, it will meet me at Biserica Buna Vestire. I'm not putting your family in danger."

"So then what? You're just going to wait at the Annunciation Church every night?" asked Florin.

"It's abandoned, is it not? Perfect to wage battle."

"I don't think it'll come back here. Vampire or not," said Rurik. "Why risk it?"

"I'll tell you why. Because it believes it is operating in secret. Once it knows there is someone or someones out there on to its actions—it and whomever it works with will be very keen to silence me. And I will be ready." Denis motioned to two canisters against the wall.

"You ready to spill what those are for?" said Florin.

"Hogweed gas canisters," said Rurik.

"No, no," said Denis. "I still can't figure out how to gasify the sap. That, my friends, is a flamethrower. Man or vampire, I'm leaving nothing to chance."

Florin let out a giant laugh. "You even come equipped with Greek fire. Unbelievable." He downed the rest of his tea and left Rurik and Denis, who sat around the table arguing for the next several hours.

*

Chapter 19

Orna arrived from Moscow nearly a week after Denis and Rurik lost track of Rasputin in the Carpathians, and the brothers were eager to consult her. They met her that evening in an abandoned barn outside of Bucharest. Denis and Rurik assisted in tying Orna's feet to a low-hanging beam and sat before her as she hung upside down.

"Well?"

"Do not rush me, Denis," said Orna. "I need more blood to the scalp."

Rurik poked him and the two remained quietly seated in front of Orna as she swayed slightly back and forth. Her face twitched a bit and her eyes began swirling underneath her eyelids. She hummed softly.

"Alexandra of Hess is alive," she said. "It was Stovâjįk mercenaries posing as the Armenian Revolutionary Federation. And a morally corrupt man named Charles Vondling. They kidnapped her and delivered her to our vampire here in Vernești, as you surmised."

"How did you not foresee this?" asked Rurik.

"Slippery, slippery devils," said Orna, panting heavily. "Too many webs! Too many webs! I simply cannot see! I should have stayed in Moscow. Travel has worn me thin."

Denis appeared annoyed and let out an audible sigh. Rurik reached to Orna and held her hand.

"Just be calm, Orna. You can do it."

Orna reached out with her other hand and caressed Rurik's cheek. "Always the kind one, Rurik. Thank you."

Denis rolled his eyes. Rurik sat back and Orna continued to take in deep breaths.

Her face began to twitch. "I see now! I see! Charles Vondling has betrayed the Black Hundred. He and this mystery mystic are initiating the vampire cycle themselves. This mystic has now become the prime vampire instead of Grand Duke Alexandrovich. It intends to produce a child with Alexandra. Once the child is born, it will slaughter the Black Hundred and rule with the might of the Nosferatu."

"Can you see who the mystic is?" asked Denis.

"I cannot. He is protected by a continually shifting cloaking spell. He certainly works with some very dark and powerful warlocks." Orna breathed in deeply through her nostrils. "I can almost smell his deceit. Very clever, this mystic. With the assistance of Charles Vondling, he tricked the Black Hundred to deliver him a woman of royal German blood, knowing once this all unfolded he would at minimum have a foothold in the German Empire with her at his side."

"Has she been converted?" asked Rurik.

"I cannot see the loch. Until our vampire reemerges, I'm afraid all we can do is … wait a moment …" Orna craned her neck and opened her white eyes at Denis. "The vampire knows who you are."

Rurik looked to Denis, who held back a thin smile.

"Then bring it to me," said Denis.

"Is it aware of my presence?" asked Rurik.

Orna swayed her head side to side. "It only knows of Denis. He and the vampire have become psychically linked. Very troubling … very troubling."

"What is it?" asked Denis.

"I can see Rurik had Zazlov cast a protection spell over you both."

"I did," said Rurik. "Just before I left Saint Petersburg."

"Now wait—that doesn't make any sense. Oh, how terribly amateur!" Orna let out a distressed sigh. "It seems Zazlov, in his haste, only cast the spell upon Rurik. Denis has remained unaffected, except he did manage to mask your last name. Not much good that will do." Orna clenched her fists. "I almost don't believe it. I told that young man decades ago that spell-binding is not effective at far distances. Denis needed to be there. How very careless. So the vampire now knows one Denis Borovitch is tracking him."

Denis and Rurik remained quiet.

Orna frowned and shook her head. "Its seers are aware of Denis as well. They know he is on to their plans. As a means to protect their interests and the vampire, they have exposed you to their entire network. It's only a matter of time before they know your full name. This could cause problems for you with the Okhrana if any are Black Hundred."

"I will worry about that later," said Denis.

"Can you protect Denis now?"

"It's too late," said Orna.

Chapter 19

"Then it's coming for me either way. I need you to see this through, Orna. I am skilled enough to kill it. You must call it into the open. Tell it exactly where I am and exactly who I am."

Orna closed her eyes once more. "If I do this ... it will be coming for you."

"Then proceed."

"Normally I would need a garment or something else personal from the vampire. But—"

"But?"

"There are other ways ... it's all webs, you see. Spiders spinning. The thoughts we weave, actions we entwine—all tie together in a web of psychic energy. Those of us sensitive to this realm can read the webs, even manipulate them to a degree. It's much like writing and reading braille, I suppose. I could very easily insert some information into the channels surrounding these events and lead the vampire right to you if you wish."

Denis was stern. "I wish."

"I don't think so, Denis," said Orna. "I am here now. I should face this creature."

Denis reached out to her and took her hand. "Orna. You are too valuable to us. I will not see you put to risk. You are travel-worn and your powers may not be ready. This fight is mine and Rurik's."

Orna grinned. "You're a brave man, Denis. But I see grave danger for you. You have not faced an opponent such as this, and I cannot foresee if you will make it out alive."

Denis stood and placed his hand upon Rurik's shoulder. "Bring the demon to me, and I will send it back to hell."

*

It was midnight. Rurik was off at some tavern drinking as Denis sat in the graveyard at Biserica Buna Vestire with his back against a tree. He had camouflaged himself via a net constructed of woven garlic fibers and garlic leaves. In his experimentation, he had discovered that the hull of the garlic plant and its leaves held the same amount of organic esters, which was what he assumed caused a vampire's aversion. He reached up to scratch his chin underneath

Part II: Copilul Sângelui

the Stenhouse gas mask that covered his mouth and nose and repositioned the device, ensuring it was taut.

Tonight's the night.

He looked to his timepiece, hoping Rurik remembered to meet him at 12:15 a.m., giving them forty-five minutes to prepare for the vampire's arrival.

Orna had delivered a message earlier in the evening, assuring them the vampire had exited the portal from the loch. It was alone and looking to feed. She had sent it some psychic "static," as she put it, that would push it toward the church at 1:00 a.m., when Denis and Rurik would strike. Denis was a bit perturbed that Rurik had decided on drinking instead of helping him set up the ambush, but it was Rurik—the only person he knew who seemed to perform better at most things while inebriated.

Just before dusk, Denis had scoured the interior of the abandoned church and ensured he knew the layout by heart. He had taken note of all appropriate places to hide and escape, and closely inspected the various booby traps he had set within the structure. He was convinced the outcome would favor him. After gathering some firewood and lighting a large fire within the main sanctuary's hearth, he had exited the church and placed a lantern at its doorstep with his thin copy of the vampire bible positioned just before it.

The ground had grown cold and hard, and Denis shifted a bit underneath his netting. As he settled, he became aware of footsteps to his left. He removed a vial of garlic juice from his belt loop and placed his hand firmly on a blackwood stake also in his belt.

Seems odd a vampire would make footsteps.

From the corner of his eye, Denis noticed a man's shadow walk past the tree toward the ramshackle graveyard. He had seen the mystic he was tracking only from a distance, but was certain this scrawny, beardless figure was not the same man. Denis could make out that he was wearing a gray suit and seemed to be weeping.

The man walked toward a gravestone.

"Oh, my Shelly! My Shelly!" the man whimpered and fell to the ground. He was mere meters before Denis, who remained as still as possible.

English accent …

Chapter 19

The man's whimpers grew louder, and Denis began to believe he was behaving theatrically.

"Why, my Shelly? Why? Oh boo-hoo-hoo." The man stood. "Boo-hoo-hoo ... Oh!" He turned to Denis with a cocked revolver drawn. "Boo! Surprise, Denis Borovitch!"

Denis tensed and realized he had no defense against a gun.

The man neared with the revolver pointed directly at him. "Did you actually think you could ambush my Stăpân?"

Denis remained quiet.

"Well, then. I am Charles Vondling. And I will be the master of ceremonies tonight. Now remove whatever feeble attempt at camouflage you're wearing and stand ... slowly."

Denis removed the net woven of garlic strands and dropped it on the ground.

Vondling howled with laughter. "What is on your face? You look like a circus act ... take it off."

Denis unstrapped the gas mask from his face and tossed it on top of the net.

"Now turn around," said Vondling, lackadaisically waving the gun. "Remove the garlic vials and blackwood from your belt."

Denis complied and raised his hands in the air.

"Anything else?"

Denis shook his head.

"Lift up your shirt and jacket, and spin around. And while you're at it, how about a little dance?"

Denis scowled at Vondling as he lifted his garments and turned around.

"That seems adequate," said Vondling. "Now remove your boots, and lift up your pant legs."

Denis remained unmoved. Vondling pointed the gun firmly at him.

"I assure you, I will gun you down right here. Do it now."

Denis glared at Vondling for another moment, then sat on the ground and removed his boots. He stood and pulled up his pant legs.

"Very good," said Vondling. "Now take all your little weapons and place them in the net . . . excellent. See! We can be friends after all."

Part II: Copilul Sângelui

Vondling motioned to Denis to walk forward. Denis bent over to retrieve his boots.

"No boots for you," said Vondling as he walked behind Denis and grabbed the net full of his weapons. "Now forward. Exactly four paces in front. Any more, any less—I shoot."

Denis walked in front of Vondling as they neared the church. While crossing the threshold, Denis noticed his lantern was extinguished and the vampire bible was gone. Vondling led him into the sanctuary, where Denis saw the shadow of a tall, almost burly man standing in front of the hearth embedded in the nave. He knew it was *him*.

"Denis Borovitch! So glad you could come," said Rasputin.

Denis glanced back to Vondling as he continued toward Rasputin.

"Come. Sit," said Rasputin, pointing to a pew near the front of the nave.

Vondling guided Denis to a pew at the left of the aisle, and sat across from him on the right, placing the net full of Denis's weapons at his feet.

Rasputin looked at the net. "What's this?"

"A very bad attempt at camouflage, my Stăpân. And some of his weapons."

"Charming," said Rasputin. "I see you've read the book. What little you have of it." Rasputin thumbed through the few pages and tossed the vampire bible at Denis. He caught it in his lap.

"How many more know about me?" asked Rasputin.

"Just me."

"False. Who's the one sending me psychic messages?"

Denis remained silent.

"Very well," said Rasputin. "I will find out soon enough." He looked at the netting on the floor. "Let's see what you brought for me."

Vondling unfolded the net and dumped the weapons on the floor.

"Blackwood stakes … garlic juice vials … and what is this?" questioned Rasputin, pointing to the gas mask.

"He had it on his face, my Stăpân."

"Toss it here."

Chapter 19

Vondling threw the mask to Rasputin, who inspected it. "A Stenhouse gas mask, I believe." He looked to Denis. "You are a cunning one. I see you've dealt with my kind before."

"Many times."

Rasputin tossed the gas mask into the fire, then turned his sunken stare back to Denis. "Sadly for you, past victories are not indicative of future success. I may be newly converted, but you are far too ill-prepared for this encounter."

"Just wait," said Denis.

Rasputin laughed, prompting Vondling to join him.

"You have so much to learn, my new friend," said Rasputin, "and no more time to learn it." He glanced down again to Denis's weapons. "Such a feeble attempt. Quite shameful."

Vondling placed his gun on the pew, then reached down and grabbed the net made from garlic. "Did you really think you could hide from his sight with a net made from grass?" He stood up and held it wide, mocking Denis, then threw it over his own head. "Look, Stăpân! Nobody can see me."

"Enough, Charles," said Rasputin, who reached out to snatch it from Vondling's head. He shrieked and recoiled as his hand touched the net—smoke erupted from his skin and he appeared dazed from the pain.

"Not grass," said Denis, who shot up and tore the net from Vondling, then immediately cast it over Rasputin's head and torso.

Rasputin hissed and wailed as the strands touched his face. He tried to remove the net as it melted into the flesh on his scalp and hands, sending more smoke into the air. Denis turned back and socked Vondling square in the jaw, knocking him unconscious. He then pushed all his weight into Rasputin and forced him toward the open hearth. Just as they neared the fire, Rasputin untangled the net and removed it—his face and hands were badly scarred. With one more aggressive push, Denis shoved him into the fire, nearly falling in himself.

Denis lay on the nave just before the hearth and watched Rasputin twist and turn as the flames quickly devoured his wool tunic. A great wail emerged from the hearth, and Denis was blown backward into the pews by a powerful gust. He stood to see Rasputin emerge from

Part II: Copilul Sângelui

the flames as a fully transformed vámpir, hissing and screeching as he tried to extinguish the flames burning his body.

Rasputin dove toward Denis, who ducked as the vampire flew into the pews. The old, dry wood caught flame as Rasputin tumbled into them.

Denis stood and ran to the front of the church. Instead of exiting, he dashed up some stairs to his left that led to a walkway encircling the sanctuary. As he reached the top, he jumped over a trip wire he'd set and moved to an adjoining room located just below the bell tower.

"I see you, Denis Borovitch Kozlov. I know who you are!"

Denis barreled into the room, trying to ignore the wood splinters stabbing at his bare feet. He grabbed a pump attached to a gas canister.

"Then come and get me, devil!" he shouted from the room.

Denis began pumping gasoline toward the room's entrance and all over the floor. He then took a few steps backward until he reached the flamethrower he'd positioned earlier. While swinging the canisters over his shoulder, Denis pulled the device from the floor, then waited at the bell tower's stairs.

Meanwhile, back in the sanctuary, Vondling came to and watched as Rasputin stood from the carnage. The flames slowly extinguished themselves from his muscular body but continued to devour the wooden pews. Vondling crouched to the ground and crawled around the perimeter of the sanctuary.

Rasputin closed his eyes and seemed to breathe deeply as his wounds healed. His massive jowls dripped with saliva as he lumbered toward the stairs. He tried to levitate himself to the walkway but was too weakened from Denis's attack. Instead, he growled, knocked several pews from his path, and proceeded up the stairs as Vondling escaped into the night.

While ascending the stairs, Rasputin noticed Denis's trip wire. He stopped momentarily and ran his clawed hands across it, his eyes following the line.

"Not this time," he said, pulling the wire. From the top of the stairs, a blackwood stake swung from a catapult contraption that, had he moved forward, would have struck him square in the chest.

Chapter 19

"Clever," mumbled Rasputin. He then hobbled along the walkway, regaining his strength bit by bit as he approached the door on the other side.

Denis stood with his back to the stairs, never taking his eyes from the opening across the room. Rasputin's shadow emerged. He had transformed back to his nude human form.

"Come on," yelled Denis, igniting the pilot on his flamethrower.

"Gasoline? I think you see now the effects of fire don't kill as expediently as you hoped."

Denis stood quietly, but breathing heavily.

"My wounds heal," continued Rasputin. "Yours will not." He leaned against the doorframe, considering Denis. "I believe it is time to reevaluate our … friendship, Denis. I could use an impassioned and clever man like you. My other associate is, well, a bit obtuse in—"

Denis pulled the trigger, igniting the floor and surrounding area in flames.

Rasputin growled and ran toward him with giant teeth growing from his jowls. Denis focused the stream of flames on Rasputin, who howled as they tore into his flesh once more.

Rasputin's flame-engulfed figure neared and Denis spewed more flames onto him. The fire grew too hot and Denis buckled over, shielding his face with his left arm. In that moment, intense heat once again surged upon him and he realized his left arm was missing just below the elbow. Denis fell to the floor as the fiery vampire stood over him, drinking the blood from his severed arm. Rasputin tossed the arm away, and the flames creeping across his body slowly extinguished.

Denis let out a wail as blood spurted from his arm, dousing the floor beneath him. He unbuckled his belt with his right hand while sliding away from Rasputin. Just as he reached the stairs to the bell tower, he looped it around his left arm and pulled it taut.

Rasputin snatched Denis's right leg and tossed him back toward the fire. Denis landed face-first and felt his eyebrows singe from the nearby flames. He turned on his back and aimed the flamethrower at Rasputin, who reached out and bent the nozzle. With one claw

Part II: Copilul Sângelui

on Denis's left ankle and the other on his left thigh, Rasputin lifted him into the air.

While upside down, Denis watched the horrific creature as it opened its mighty jaws and clenched down upon his left leg, separating it from his body in one bite.

Denis howled.

Still holding on to his left thigh, Rasputin tossed the rest of Denis's leg into the fire, and walked toward the flames, standing just at the perimeter.

Rasputin's dead black eyes stared down at Denis, and then at the blaze.

"Do it," said Denis.

Rasputin flung him into the inferno.

Denis landed on his left side and moaned as the heat cauterized his amputations and seared the left side of his face. He screamed once more as his weight pushed through the burning wood, causing the rest of the flooring to collapse. Both he and Rasputin fell to the story below in a shower of splintered wood and fire.

With his right hand, Denis extinguished the flames on the front of his jacket, and rolled on the floor attempting to exterminate the rest. Shards of flaming wood lay all around him as the church's interior ignited. He grew alarmed that the canisters on his back would explode at any moment. Denis rolled over to see Rasputin's figure lying a few meters away. He appeared still.

To Denis's surprise, Rasputin sat up with a plank of flaming wood sticking through his center chest. The vampire coughed and choked as it tried to remove the plank. Rasputin stood, wailing and clutching the timber. He turned to Denis one last time and hissed at him. With the stake still lodged in his torso, Rasputin dashed toward the wall, crashed through it, and ran off into the night.

With his remaining arm, Denis was able to mostly shield the right side of his head from the flames. He sat up and pulled the canisters from his back, then tossed them as far away as he could to a small area of the floor not consumed by fire. Using his right leg to shimmy along the floor, Denis pushed himself toward the opening Rasputin had created, occasionally dragging himself across hot embers and flaming planks of wood. He made it to the opening and,

Chapter 19

with every bit of strength left in him, pushed himself away from the burning structure.

Denis opened his mouth wide to drink in the fresh air. Lying on the ground and staring into the night sky, he became aware that he felt intense pain only in certain areas of his body. It was clear to him then the fire had seared the majority of his nerves. He looked to his severed arm and leg, and his eyes filled with tears.

Goddamn you, Rurik.

*

"No! No! Only one more drink if you remove it all. Just the blouse doesn't count!"

Rurik lifted his glass into the air as laughter abounded all around him. The topless woman pretended to remove her bra for a moment, then pulled Rurik close and hugged him. She then snatched his beer and downed it in one gulp.

The tavern patrons erupted in cheers.

"She stole my heart and then my beer! A Gypsy soul in every Romanian woman!"

An older gentleman at his table with a giant black mustache leaned forward. "My friend, your Romanian is terrible!"

"I didn't even know I spoke Romanian," shouted Rurik with a giant smile.

Another round of intense laughter rose from the crowd. Just then, a young man burst into the tavern.

"The Annunciation Church is on fire!"

Rurik immediately felt sick. He pulled out his pocket watch and flipped it open: 1:32 a.m.

Denis!

*

Orna hobbled from the barn as Rurik approached on horseback. The horse was harnessed to an open-air cart that carried Denis wrapped in wool blankets.

Part II: Copilul Sângelui

Twenty minutes earlier, Rurik and some townspeople had found Denis unconscious at the side of the church just as the fire spread to the surrounding dry grass. Upon finding he was alive, they moved Denis to the street to avoid the brush fire and summoned a nearby farmer who had a horse and cart.

They loaded Denis onto the cart, wrapped him in wool blankets, and began arguing over where to take him. Rurik made out that the closest hospital was over an hour away.

"He doesn't have that long!" shouted Rurik as he jumped on the horse's back and slapped the reins on its backside.

After a momentary attempt to chase after Rurik, the locals turned their attention back to the fire as it overtook the surrounding foliage and other buildings in the area.

"Bring him to me. Quickly!" yelled Orna.

Rurik jumped from the horse and ran to the cart, using all of his strength to lift his brother.

Denis moaned.

"I have you, brother. Orna is here."

"No," wheezed Denis. "No …"

Rurik laid Denis on the ground and peeled the blankets away as Orna rushed to their side. In the moonlight, Rurik finally had a moment to see the damage. Tears fell from his face as he looked to his brother's missing arm and leg and the horrid charring all across his body. None of Denis's hair had been saved.

"I'm so sorry, Denis," he said, weeping into his hands.

Orna placed her hands on Denis's chest. "There's still a chance. Back away."

Rurik slid a few feet back and watched Orna chant and wave her hands over Denis. He reached up and grabbed her with his right hand.

"Let me die!"

"Silence!" shouted Orna, moving her hand before Denis's face. He fell unconscious.

As Orna spoke in tongues, an illuminated cyclone appeared over Denis and surged upon him. It whirled around him, lifting him slightly off the ground and spinning him with its motion. Beams of green and blue static shot across his body as he twitched and groaned.

Chapter 19

With one last great wail, Orna raised her hands into the night and slammed her fists into the earth. Rurik was thrown back from the concussion, and the whirlwind scattered into nothingness. Denis floated softly to the ground.

Orna sat back, winded. She crawled to Denis and rested her hand on his chest.

"He will live," she said, looking to Rurik.

Rurik walked toward her and gave her a deep hug. "Thank you." He sat on the ground. "I failed him. I failed him."

Orna touched his knee. "Had you been there, your fate might have been worse. I warned you both. But the past is ether—it is now that matters."

"I will stay here then, and look after—"

"No." Orna stood over him. "I will stay and finish healing your brother. I know of several witches in Romania highly skilled in healing magic. We will piece him back together the best we can."

"Then what?"

"This is only the beginning. I cannot see the vampire any longer, but I am not certain Denis claimed its life. Find this Charles Vondling. He does not know of your connection to Denis. Befriend him and track his every move. He is the crux of this evil. The vampire feeds on his weakness and greed. If it reemerges, it will show itself to Vondling first."

"And once I find him?"

Orna looked up into the night as a soft spring breeze blew her gray hair from her face.

"Call to me and I will appear. Our darkest hour is yet to come."

*

The eighteen-foot disappearing propeller boat was forty-seven minutes into its journey when it reached the base of the Carpathian Mountains. Denis had a difficult time navigating and breaking through the occasional ice patches of calmer waters, which Felix did his best to break apart with an oar.

Part II: Copilul Sângelui

The first leg of boat travel had been sheer hell, and Felix believed he would soon vomit from bobbing in the rapids. He was relieved to see Denis guiding the boat toward calmer waters.

"That's it," Denis yelled, pointing ahead. "The water stops dead."

The boat traveled without much strain up the last of the vigorous rapids and floated freely into the still waters that lay beneath the Carpathians. The striking difference was apparent immediately from the surrounding foliage. As if there were an invisible line drawn some

where in the dirt, the trees near the dead water grew black and gnarled—ready to fall under their own rot.

"It stinks," said Felix as the boat floated into the stagnant, algae-covered river.

"It's cursed," yelled Denis, projecting his voice over the noisy motor.

Felix peered overboard and watched the boat cut through the dense green scum.

"Will it slow down the propeller?"

"We should be fine."

The trees grew blacker and more gnarled as they drifted underneath the imperious mountain spires. The twisted greenery near the river embankment became thicker the farther they traveled—no birds or insects were heard anywhere.

"It's almost humid," said Felix, removing his jacket.

"The closer to hell, the hotter it gets."

A fog writhed in and out of the branches, occasionally crossing their path until they were finally immersed in the opaque mist.

"You sure we can find this portal?" asked Felix.

"My friend, we already did." Denis pointed to the slate-colored rubble and loamy embankment.

Through the heavy fog, Felix watched their surroundings fade to monochrome gray as if all the color in the world had wilted away. Even the air became fetid. Felix shivered.

Their slim boat arrived at the loch as the first signs of dusk appeared over the peaks. It had grown so warm that Denis removed his coat as well. Felix expected they had an hour and a half before

Chapter 19

the light slipped fully from the sky. The greenish waters of the Buzău morphed instantly to black as the massive loch opened itself before them. In the distance sat a rocky island with a gnarled and expansive blackwood forest upon it.

A hopeless sensation swept over Felix as the boat pushed steadily toward the island. It was incredibly vast. Denis cut the engine as they neared the sheer cliffs and stood over the device that retracted the propeller. He pulled on the lever and locked it into place.

"Now we row," he said, motioning to a long paddle next to Felix.

Denis sat in his seat and grabbed the paddle next to him.

"No, no, Felix. Opposite sides. I row starboard, you row port. One arm, remember?"

Felix nodded and leaned portside with his paddle in hand. He dug the plank of wood into the water and pulled with all his might.

"Go easy," said Denis. "I'm not exactly sure what we're looking for."

Felix pulled his paddle from the dark water.

"Why am I exerting myself then?"

"Just keep rowing. There will be some sort of dock or stair to the top of the rock. I'll steer."

They rounded the island, and Felix could see over the sheer cliffs to the canopy of blackwood trees.

"Are those native to Romania?"

"They're practically the national tree. It's just not something discussed ... with blackwood forests being notoriously haunted and all," said Denis. "Bad for tourists."

"Don't imagine the Germans are helping."

"Insightful analysis, Felix. Very helpful. Now row."

They rowed for several more minutes until Denis guided the boat closer to the island. Felix scanned the base of the cliffs and saw what appeared to be a flat stone barely breaking the surface of the water—it extended from the cliff into the loch.

"That it?"

"Either that or a loch serpent taking a nap."

Felix looked back. "Not really funny at this point."

"I'm serious."

Part II: Copilul Sângelui

They rowed until hearing the faint slosh of water slapping against the stone dock. It was so low to the water, it was almost impossible to see—certainly not visible from any distance. They paddled the boat to the left of the stone slab. Denis jumped on the dock and hobbled along.

"Throw me the rope."

Felix snatched the docking rope and tossed it to Denis. He pulled the boat to a small cylindrical rock and tied it down. Felix looked overboard, expecting to see the loch's shallows—pure blackness. The face of the cliff ran downward until it faded into the murk.

"How deep is this thing?"

"Apparently bottomless," said Denis.

Felix jumped from the boat and looked to the cliff wall. The dock appeared to run right into the sheer rock.

"It's a dead end."

"Seems so. But we will climb," said Denis.

Felix took a long look up at the cliffs.

"I don't know, Denis. It's—"

"The stairs."

"What stairs?"

"See for yourself. Walk toward the end."

Felix walked toward the gray stone wall and stumbled backward when a steep flight of stairs appeared to his left. He stepped back a few feet to see the crevice morph back into the cliff.

"That's incredible."

"Drăculea was a master of optical illusions. It's only visible after you cross it."

Denis walked to Felix and stood next to him. He took in a deep breath as he peered up the stone stairway. "This is very exciting for me to see this—it was only legends. The island is apparently full of surprises like this."

"Can't wait," said Felix.

"Come, we must hurry."

Felix followed Denis to the boat and helped him unload several large gas cans.

"Why the gas?"

Chapter 19

"To burn down the forest," said Denis flatly. "What did you think?"

"To power the boat."

"You royals are too practical," he said, shaking his head. "For a man who destroyed an entire passenger train to escape a vampire, I'd expect a little more ingenuity."

"I'm plenty ingen...besides, the train was *full* of vampires. And like I told you, I had to shove that one into the boiler."

"Sure you did."

Felix curled his nose.

"Come on. I'm teasing. I am very impressed by your destructiveness. Cleverness, I mean."

"Yeah, yeah. Let's get moving."

Felix moved the last gas can to the stone dock, then looked to the top of the cliff. A shiver shot across his body. He stood dazed, staring at the rocks.

"Hey!" yelled Denis, snapping his fingers at him. "Hey!"

Felix shook his head. "Sorry, I—"

"What's the matter?"

"Nothing. I just had this sensation that I've been here before."

"Well, you haven't—so arm up," said Denis. "Each of us carries three gas cans. Here," he said, handing Felix three canvas belts. "Strap them around the handles and swing them over your shoulders. You'll want to keep your hands free."

"That going to be enough?" asked Felix as he held a gas can. "The air's damp."

"This is plenty. Once that canopy catches, that forest will come down quickly."

"What about the canister backpacks?"

"Too combustible, now that I think about it. Won't kill them anyway—not until they transform."

"So we go unarmed?"

"You should know me better by now. Machetes for the bats, blackwood stakes in case of vámpir, and the rifle for anything else."

Each man took a canvas satchel containing three blackwood stakes and a machete.

Denis handed Felix a gas mask.

Part II: Copilul Sângelui

"Wear this. They're spitters," he said, pointing upward. "Paralyze then kill."

"That much I know."

Felix looked over the gas mask. It was the same as the one Denis had worn before—a wide viewing glass across the front with two charcoal filters that hung from the mouth.

"Custom-made," said Denis. "Can't see a damn thing out of the others."

Felix pulled on the mask. Denis followed suit and strapped a bolt-action rifle across his back. They stood for a moment, looking at the steep incline as a low-hanging cloud moved in overhead.

"What do you suppose is up there?"

"Just be prepared for anything," said Denis, who cocked his rifle and placed his hook on the trigger.

"You sure you can climb this? Your leg—"

"I'll worry about my leg." Denis nudged Felix. "You first."

"Me?"

"Yes. You're faster."

"Yeah, but—"

"I insist."

"Fine, just be careful. Don't shoot me in the ass or anything."

"I'm the least of your worries."

"I wonder," said Felix.

Felix paused for another moment, then took the first step. They continued slowly upward, eyes locked on the brim of the stairwell.

"So what kind of optical illusions should I be expecting?"

"Hard to say. The island was Drăculea's fortress. Supposedly there are many traps to be sprung."

"Can you at least give me a hint? Spikes shooting from the walls?"

"I don't know. The legends say Drăculea's citadel was constructed of many optical illusions to disorient attackers . . . and prisoners."

"Great. I'll just keep an eye out for any stairs that bend sideways."

"Your humor is helping. Keep at it." Denis poked Felix in the back with the gun barrel.

Chapter 19

"Watch it," said Felix, never looking back.

After a long climb and Denis taking several rests to massage his leg stump, they reached the last several stairs, where Felix's head was nearly flush with the top terrain.

"Here, help me up," said Felix.

He dug his fingers into the top of the sidewall and pulled himself up with Denis's aid. Felix peered over the brim of the stairwell to a sparse field of ecru smug-grass that cut a clean path to a dense area of tall blackwood trees.

"Anything up there?" whispered Denis.

"Not that I can see."

"Anything that might have been a castle?"

"Just some flint rock. Nothing else, though."

"Wolves?"

"None."

"Bats in the trees, anything?"

"Nothing. Can't tell about the trees, but it looks safe."

"Good."

Denis lowered Felix, and they looked to one another with a sense of reassurance. Felix pulled off his gas mask.

"It's deserted. I'm sure of it," said Felix as he tried to catch his breath.

"Then we go on five. Only ten or so stairs left. We charge up, run to the forest, deploy gas, burn, run back. Sound good?"

"As good as any, but why five?"

"It's my lucky number."

Felix looked to the last remaining stairs.

"Fair enough," he said and strapped on his gas mask.

"Ready?"

Felix nodded, and Denis began the count. On five, Felix leapt from his stair onto the next—his gas cans clanking along the slim walls. As he reached the eighth to the last step, Felix's foot broke through the stair, and his body lunged forward. He quickly used the strength of his back leg to launch himself upward and managed to grab on to a dense portion of thick grass hanging from the top of the stairwell. The final stretch of stairs crumbled to pieces underneath his weight, revealing a deep pit below. Felix held on tightly

Part II: Copilul Sângelui

as his body hung into the well. He wedged his feet along each side of the well, which gave him some needed leverage.

Denis, unable to stop his momentum, leapt forward on his right leg and clutched on to a gas canister hanging from Felix's shoulder. The canvas strap tightened around Felix's neck, choking him. As Felix slid farther into the well with Denis's weight, the grass roots began to give. Felix held on to the well's brim.

"Quit flailing! You're pulling me down!" yelled Felix. "Use the walls! It's slim enough. Wedge yourself."

"Easy if you have four limbs!"

Denis continued to flail about.

A moment later, Denis's weight was much less burdensome. He'd managed to press his back into the left of the well with his right foot braced against the opposite wall—his prosthetic leg dangled below him. Felix pulled himself higher and managed to grab some smug-grass planted more firmly in the soil.

"You hurt, Denis?"

"I'm fine. Wedged for now, but I'm slipping."

"You lose anything?"

"Leg is hanging on for now!"

"Can you shimmy up?"

"I think, but I'll need to pull on your clothes."

"Fine, not too hard—use your back and leg for leverage."

Denis leveraged himself first on Felix's gas can straps, then his jacket collar. The grass started pulling from its roots.

"Denis!"

Felix clung more tightly as the grass continued to uproot, sliding him lower into the well. "I'm slipping!"

Felix dipped deeper into the well and held the brim of the stair once more—his body fully hanging into the pit. Denis wedged his right foot over the sidewall and released his weight from Felix. He grunted, pulled himself up, and walked toward the front of the stair. Denis dropped his equipment and grabbed Felix's sleeve.

"Here, use me to climb."

Felix took Denis's hand, then turned sideways and wedged himself into the well. He pulled up slowly until he could swing a leg over the top. Denis pulled him to the landing.

Chapter 19

"Christ!" yelled Felix, lying on the ground, staring into the sky.

Denis knelt on the ground, breathing heavily.

Felix dragged himself to the edge of the stairwell and looked into the pit. The shattered remains of the final eight stairs were constructed of thin flint rock. Felix believed even the weight of a small child would have cracked through.

"There goes our only way down," he said.

Denis stood over him. "How far to the bottom?"

"I can't see. Maybe twenty stories?"

Denis was quiet.

Felix reached into the well and cracked some of the flint rock away to reveal a modern metal fastening and shiny screws drilled into the wall.

"Look here," he said.

Denis observed fastening.

"The metal is new—screws too," said Felix.

Denis stood and looked to the dark canopy. "Someone's expecting us."

Felix rolled over and sat up. "They certainly don't want any visitors. Let's burn it down and go."

Denis nodded and collected his equipment. He then sat and refastened his prosthesis.

"Help me up," said Denis, extending his hand.

They entered the forest perimeter, staring at the impenetrable canopy. Generations of overgrowth entwined the branches. The overhang grew so thick, the forest was nearly pitch-black.

"Looks like a cave," said Felix.

"Let's not go too deep. We only need to douse a few."

They walked farther into the forest, their feet making quite a ruckus upon the dried leaves mixed with flint rock.

"You see any bats?" asked Denis, scanning the tree branches.

"None. So how is it they live in blackwood forests, but it also kills them?"

"Blackwood kills vámpir for certain—regular wood will not. I currently do not know the effect of blackwood on Nosferatu. Nobody's seen one in five hundred years. My assumption is blackwood forests spawn them, and in turn it is their weakness."

Part II: Copilul Sângelui

"Perfect. So we're not entirely sure how to kill a Nosferatu yet?"

"No, we are not. But I'm certain my hogweed gas will work," said Denis. "I will need to read Rurik's unabridged vampire bible for such answers to be certain. In the short term, we assume they are vulnerable in the same ways as vámpir."

"So these bats—do they feed on humans?" asked Felix, looking to the canopy.

"Mostly livestock. They must exit this realm to feed—farmers as far as Bucharest have reported livestock slaughtered and drained of blood. But until the bats transform, they behave like ustrel—ancient vampires too timid to feast on the living. There are legends the bats will dig up fresh graves and feast on the dead. That's all I'm aware of."

Felix stopped and pulled off his gas mask. "The bats are migrating north."

Denis looked to him.

"At a station stop. There was a blackwood forest in the distance. Piles of dead livestock in the fields. A nearby graveyard was desecrated with body parts strewn about—they had dug up the dead."

Denis shook his head. "And now is when you decide to expel this information?"

"Well, Professor, I didn't have a frame of reference before."

"Clearly not."

Felix bit his lip and looked to the trees. "Let's just burn it down anyway. This can never happen again."

"A bit deeper," said Denis. "The fire has to take hold. Put on your gas mask."

Felix pulled down his mask and looked to the forest's opening. The light appeared like a safe haven. He turned forward again and heard a popping noise followed by a metallic ding. Looking down, he noticed one of his gas canisters had a small hole in it and was leaking gasoline onto the ground.

"Denis?"

"Yes?"

"Stop for a minute, look," said Felix, removing his gas canister and placing it on the ground. Denis knelt to inspect it. Another pop

Chapter 19

came from the distance and a puff of dust enveloped Denis's canvas satchel.

"Get back!" yelled Felix, noticing the circular tear in Denis's satchel. He slung his arm under Denis's armpit and pulled him behind a tree as two more bullets ripped into the bark.

"Stay low," said Felix, pulling up his gas mask.

Denis crouched behind him as Felix peeked around the tree.

"Can you see anyone?" asked Denis.

"I saw one shadow. There may be more."

"At least they're human. Day guardians for certain."

"So it seems."

Another pop rang out and the bark near Felix's face splintered in all directions. He recoiled behind the tree.

"I see where he is," said Felix. "Do you trust me, Denis?"

"Not for a minute."

"Good. Here's what I need you to do. I need you to run to the forest's opening when I say go. Hand me the rifle."

"You're out of your mind. Can you even shoot?"

Felix took another quick peek from behind the tree. "I graduated from military academy. Top of my class in marksmanship."

"I'm not running out into the open. We don't know how many there are."

"Five shots. That's it. Can't be more than two of them or we'd have been riddled with bullets. And they're not very good, so I can get them first. A true rifleman—we'd be dead on the ground."

"I—"

"No choice. You have to trust me."

"Don't miss."

"I won't." Felix steadied himself against the tree and held the rifle to his side. "On five …" He counted down, and Denis began to hop-skip toward the opening.

Felix swung around the tree and aimed his rifle. Scanning the shadows, he noticed a man pop out from behind a tree, kneel, and aim his weapon at Denis. Felix fired off a shot and the shadow fell to the ground. Another man emerged from behind the tree, attempting to retrieve his fallen comrade. One more squeeze of Felix's trigger, and the man fell limp.

Part II: Copilul Sângelui

"Keep running," yelled Felix.

Denis hobbled toward the light. Felix waited to ensure there were no more attackers. He flung the rifle over his shoulder and ran to the gas canister he had dropped. After dumping the rest of the liquid onto the forest brush, he reached in his satchel, retrieved some matches, and lit the brush on fire. He stood and ran.

"Denis! Light a tree!"

Denis stopped in the near distance, fumbling with a gas can. He managed to loosen the cap and douse a tree trunk. He threw the can down and started with a second can.

"Hurry," yelled Felix, arriving next to him as both men continued to dump gasoline onto several blackwood trees.

"Nice shooting," said Denis, looking back into the forest.

"Told you."

Felix lit several matches and ignited the tree bark. A bullet hole suddenly shot bark into Felix's face. He fell backward and looked to the forest to see a third man charging toward them, firing a rifle.

"Go!" yelled Felix.

Denis ran for the forest opening as another bullet whizzed past Felix's ear. He knelt to the ground and took aim at his pursuer. A shot rang out and the man dove to the ground, quickly getting back up.

Realizing he had missed, Felix turned and ran past Denis, who had stopped at the cliff's edge.

"Come on, Denis!" yelled Felix as he shot past him, leapt into the air, and sailed into the loch below.

"Crazy bastard," said Denis. He looked back to the forest to see the rifleman sprinting toward him. Denis took a few steps backward, then ran toward the cliff, springing from his good leg and following Felix into the murky water below.

Felix steeled his body for the impact, crossing his legs and folding his arms across his chest as he entered the water. Denis landed just shy of his position. Felix surfaced as quickly as he could, taking notice of the water's warmth. He spun around to see Denis surface.

"You hurt?"

Chapter 19

"No," Denis groaned. "But that impact sure knocked the wind out of me." His wooden leg rose to the surface, causing him to float on his back.

Their clothes dragged them down as they swam toward the stone dock. Felix pulled his satchel from his shoulder and let it sink. Denis continued to paddle on his back with his gear attached—the wood from his false appendages kept him buoyant.

Felix took a few more strokes and screamed, splashing the water before him. Denis turned.

"What is it?"

"A body!" Felix swam back a few paces. "Someone's under the water!"

Felix could see a pale figure submerged just below the surface in front of him. He looked to his left to see another. Denis yelled, noticing a pale figure submerged next to him and the glimmer of another just before him.

"They're everywhere!"

Another bullet spiked into the water, sailing just between Felix's legs. "Goddamn it!" he yelled, looking up to the cliffs. The marksman knelt at the edge and positioned himself for another shot. Felix swam to Denis and removed the rifle from his shoulder. He tipped it forward to expel the water from the barrel, then removed a bullet from the chamber and inspected it. It was dry.

"I need you to take a big deep breath and hold it," said Felix, placing the bullet back in the chamber.

"What?"

"Big deep breath. Hold it. Now!"

The rifleman at the top of the cliff fired off another shot and a splash erupted near Denis's head. Denis breathed in deeply and held it, causing his body to become more buoyant. Felix used a small kicking motion to stay afloat and rested the rifle's barrel on Denis's stomach, aiming upward at the man on the cliff. He pulled the figure into his sights and took a deep breath. As the sight sunk a bit downward, Felix pulled the trigger. A scream was heard from above as bloody mist erupted from the man's knee. He fell to the ground, out of their view.

"What a shot!" said Denis.

"To the dock. Go!"

Part II: Copilul Sângelui

Felix dug into the water and swam toward the dock, moving around the submerged pale figures as they appeared before him. Occasionally, he'd accidentally bump one, disgusted by the sensation of touching their limp heads and hair as he'd push them downward into the depths. He expected one to grab him and pull him under. Felix reached the dock and stood with his hands out toward Denis.

"Take my hands!"

Felix pulled him forcefully upward, nearly flinging him onto the dock. They ran for the boat. Denis fell forward as his leg harness slipped from place. He fastened it and pulled himself up before slumping into the back of the boat.

Felix untied the rope and pushed the boat from the dock before jumping inside.

Denis huddled over the engine, yanking on the ripcord several times until the engine roared to life. He lowered the propeller into the water, then manned the rudder.

"Any more ammo?" asked Felix.

Denis reached down to a satchel on the floor and produced three bullets.

"All I need is one," said Felix.

Denis tossed him a bullet. Felix pulled the rifle from his shoulder and loaded it. He squatted into the hull and pointed his weapon up at the cliffs as Denis navigated away. After scanning the rocky embankments for another moment, Felix relaxed and placed the rifle on his lap.

"I definitely got him with the last shot," said Felix as they navigated out of range.

"I'm impressed," said Denis.

Felix peered overboard to see more submerged, naked bodies—lifeless and pale, floating with the motion of the disturbed water.

"They're everywhere."

"It's a harvest!" said Denis, looking over the side.

He steered the boat and they headed from the loch—a bump sounded from the bottom of the boat as they plowed over a submerged body. Felix looked back to the isle as the fire started to consume the blackwood canopy. By the time they were at the mouth

Chapter 19

of the loch, the forest was engulfed in flames—tree limbs cracking apart, falling to the forest floor.

"It's going to be dark soon, you have a lantern?"

"In the box." Denis motioned toward the engine.

Felix moved to a utility box next to the engine and pulled out an electric lantern. "Can you navigate in the dark? I'll do point to ensure we're on track."

"We have to navigate by moonlight. Forget the lantern," said Denis.

"Fine … but don't cut the engine until it's fully dark—about an hour. We need to get—"

"Believe me, I fully understand."

Felix looked back to Loch Dracul. In the distance, he could see the forest fire beacon as a thick column of black smoke ascended into the sky.

"What's with the submerged bodies?"

"Incubating women are buried underground or submerged underwater to silence their screams. Someone is building an army."

There was a moment of silence between them.

"That is by far the worst thing that has ever happened to me," said Felix.

"Worse than the train?"

"Much."

Denis shook his head. "Well buckle in, my prince. I have a suspicion it's about to get far worse."

Part II: Copilul Sângelui

20

СОВЕРШЕННО СЕКРЕТНО [TOP SECRET]
"Thus spoke the Darkness, 'For blood is power. To feed upon it, divine. Bring your blood unto the lips of others, vampire or mortal, and ye shall enthrall their will evermore.'"
—Vlad Drăculea, Book of Blood 6:9, Sfânta Biblie al Strigoiului Viu, 1456 [Holy Bible of the Living Vampiric Witch]

СОВЕРШЕННО СЕКРЕТНО [TOP SECRET]
Diary entry of Alexandra Fyodorovna, empress of Russia 1894–1916:

December 12, 1916

We arrived early this morning, just as dawn cracked over the distant hills. Even though the Okhrana generally unnerve me, Commander Kashin has been wonderful in overseeing every minute detail of our safety. Both our private train cabin and the automobile waiting for us at the station were prepared to block out sunlight. I found it surprising that Grigori was so adamant about traveling in the compartments with us. He stated it was to comfort Alexei, but I believe he suffers from the same affliction toward daylight shared by Alexei and me. I must summon the courage to ask him.

All of us slept soundly through the day.

Grigori read to Alexei as we rolled across the hillsides into Crimea. Watching Alexei and Grigori together fills me with feelings of conflict. I am happy that Alexei has

Chapter 20

found a surrogate for Felix, but it pains me this cannot be his father. Except for our argument a few nights ago, Nicholas has been wonderful and brave through the course of these events, but it is more apparent to me than ever that he does not view Alexei as his son and certainly not worthy of his crown. But Rasputin's effect on Alexei is remarkable—my boy is walking again, almost able to run. Although it is more of a clumsy hobble.

Poor Sana is trying her best to cope with the strong sense of loss she is most certainly feeling. I know she feels we are her only family now. I can tell by the way she clutches on to my arm when I am near, or how she won't sit alone for any stretch of time. She is probably more frightened than any of us. I don't believe her heart can withstand any further loss. She clings to Grigori like a desperate child at all times. I admire the steady nature with which he treats her. I do worry about her excessive drinking as of late. She thinks I don't notice, but she is constantly sipping wine from a small perfume bottle she keeps hung around her neck. I have known Sana for years and have never witnessed this behavior. It is unbecoming on her.

Brave, sweet Grigori—I have been aloof toward him, and I know he senses it. I feel he can sense everything around him. He is the manner of person who seems to know the words from someone's mouth before they utter anything. I know he can feel I am growing uneasy about my feelings. I am drawn to him—more so than any man I have ever met. The vision, or should I call it dream, I had on the balcony still sends shivers across my body when I think to it. I am certain it was real, but cannot explain how I was suddenly upon my bed after flying through the air the previous moments.

Perhaps my mind is finally slipping, but I do believe he is from my past. I simply cannot scratch the memory. When I look to him, I am comfortable in a way that suggests I have known him always. His eyes imply the same. Although I am happy he is along with us for Alexei's sake,

Part II: Copilul Sângelui

I must confess my own reservations, for I cannot be certain of my actions in his presence.

It is well after dark. Due to our hasty travel, the palace staff will not arrive for another two days, so we all will look after one another. Alexei and the girls must be awake by now. I must attend to them.

*

It was night when Rasputin and Alexei walked along a darkened dirt road toward a small abandoned chapel that sat on the Livadia Palace's sprawling estate. A large white willow sprouted from the grounds behind the chapel, and farther back still was a quaint peasant cemetery that had been neglected for nearly a century.

Alexei reached up and held Rasputin's hand. "May I ask you something, Grigori?"

"Certainly."

"Do you think Sana likes me?"

Rasputin looked to him.

"Why, I'd say she likes you very much."

"I don't mean like that. I—"

"Ah!" said Rasputin. "Our young prince has finally noticed the fairer sex!"

Alexei blushed and stared at the ground, letting go Rasputin's hand.

"Be proud!" said Rasputin, patting his head. "You have started along one of life's greatest mysteries."

Alexei looked up to him.

"Women, my boy! The most curious of all creatures. You will find that women are often the sole reason men have for living. I can say for myself—I don't believe I'd bother to comb a hair on my head if it weren't for the loveliness of women."

Alexei felt soothed by Rasputin's words, and they continued along the path, nearing the church's façade.

"It's just I'm too small for her. I look like a little boy. I hear what the adults say about me."

Chapter 20

"I think she will notice you in time, though she may be a bit old for you. You are the tsarevich, one day to be emperor. That alone will win the hearts of many."

"But what if I look like a boy forever?"

"You won't."

"I want to be a man. Like my father, so Sana will like me. But my sickness—"

"It is no sickness," said Rasputin as a gust of wind swept over them.

Rasputin disappeared. Alexei looked to the front of the church as Rasputin's voice fell upon him from above.

"And being a man is nothing to be desired," called Rasputin.

Alexei looked upward to see Rasputin standing on the peak of the church, using one hand on the steeple for support.

"Hey!" Alexei clapped. "How did you get up there?"

"Come with me! The view is gorgeous," yelled Rasputin. "I swear I can see all the way to the Black Sea. Come up, Alexei."

"I can't."

Rasputin balanced along the skinny peak of the chapel like a tightrope walker and quickly spun around to face Alexei.

"You'll hurt yourself! Come down."

"Not until you come up!"

"But I can't."

Rasputin wobbled back and forth. Alexei laughed at his animated gestures. He leaned too far and fell down the opposite side of the roof.

"Grigori!" Alexei hobbled around the front of the chapel, expecting to see him lying in the grass.

Alexei scanned the moonlit grass for Rasputin's body, but found nothing. He looked back to the steeple, hoping to see Rasputin hiding on the other side.

"Where are you?"

"Up here, my King. Come and get me!"

Alexei swung around to see Rasputin seated in the largest branch high up in the white willow.

"Hey!" yelled Alexei. "You scared me almost to death. Come down from there."

Part II: Copilul Sângelui

"You have to come and get me."

Alexei took a breath, then smiled and ran for the tree. He peered upward to see Rasputin wave. With a strong determination, Alexei reached to the first low branch and pulled himself up. He looked to Rasputin's branch to see he was gone.

"Perhaps you need a lift?" said Rasputin, appearing suddenly behind Alexei.

Alexei was startled and nearly slipped from the branch. Rasputin helped him climb down.

"How did you do that?"

"You can do it too," said Rasputin. "You just have to try."

"How?"

"I'll tell you what. If you can catch me, I'll tell you. Fair?"

"Fair!"

Alexei reached out for him, and Rasputin jumped away, disappearing behind the willow's trunk. Alexei gave chase. Sensing Rasputin was just around the bend, Alexei stopped and faced the opposite way in hopes of tricking him. He waited for another moment, then poked around the tree trunk when Rasputin did not reappear. He looked to the cemetery and saw Rasputin rising slowly from behind a tombstone.

"If you think I'm chasing you in there, you're crazy."

Rasputin opened his eyes wide. "Why? Are you afraid of ghosts?" He accentuated "ghosts" with a playful vibrato in his voice. Rasputin made a humorous ghoulish cry and sunk slowly behind the tombstone.

"Then how about here?"

Alexei spun around to see Rasputin's shadow standing in a field of dried cornstalks. The two jogged through the field, laughing. Alexei almost caught up with him despite his pronounced hobble. Just as Alexei was upon him, Rasputin tumbled to the ground. Alexei reached downward to tag him, only to grab a clump of dirt as if Rasputin had melded into the earth itself. The small boy stood and peered around the field.

"Fine, you win!"

The field was silent.

Chapter 20

Alexei squinted, looking for the slightest movement. A field mouse ran across his path, and he jumped backward, startled by the small creature.

"Alexei," Rasputin's voice echoed from the distance.

Alexei looked around the field. No sign of Rasputin.

"Alexei, this way."

Alexei perked up his ears, then turned left to follow Rasputin's voice. In the distance, he noticed the shadow of a tall structure and limped toward it. As he neared the shadow, Alexei saw the skeletal outline of a rickety iron water tower that had been built by his grandfather's men. He stood back, marveling at the reservoir tank's girth.

"Hello down there!"

Rasputin appeared on top of the tower.

Alexei grinned and noticed a ladder constructed into one of the tower legs. He limped toward it and began climbing up the tall tower. It was a great challenge to lift his legs to each rung, but after a few rests, he found himself at the top. He made his way to the catwalk that encircled the tower and leaned against the hull to rest.

The catwalk was enclosed with an iron railing that came to Alexei's neck. Alexei peered over the edge to see a secondary rod several feet below the catwalk. Occasionally, a slim steel support beam connected the two.

Alexei tiptoed around the walkway to see Rasputin standing with his back to him. He took a deep breath and slowly crept toward Rasputin. With only a few steps between them, Rasputin ducked under the support railing and jumped over the side.

"Grigori!"

Alexei ran to where Rasputin had vanished. He looked over the edge to see Rasputin hanging upside down, his knees wrapped around the lower support rod—his upper body dangled freely.

"Are you crazy?"

"Climb down! It's fun. You can do it."

"What if I slip?"

"You won't. You can pull yourself back up! Come down."

Alexei reached to a vertical support rod that connected the upper and lower beams. He swung his body around it, then descended slowly,

Part II: Copilul Sângelui

using the rod like a fireman's pole. His feet gently found the top of the bottom rung.

"That's it, my boy! Now hang with me. Just sit down and lean back!"

Alexei sat carefully, hooking his knees around the steel beam. With one hand on the support iron, he leaned upside down until he finally let go and dangled his hands in the air.

"It is fun, no?" Rasputin laughed.

Alexei smiled and swung back and forth a bit.

"Here, watch!" yelled Rasputin, who used his weight to cause the rod to bounce.

Alexei swung his hands back to the pole for support and enjoyed the ride. Rasputin stopped, and the two hung for a moment.

"Act like a vampire bat," said Rasputin.

He closed his eyes and crossed his arms to his chest. Alexei giggled at the sight. Rasputin peeked at him with one eye open.

"What, you don't think me scary? You try it."

Alexei released his hands and hung more deeply as his arms crossed his chest.

"Very good!" yelled Rasputin. "The perfect vampire bat."

Alexei opened his eyes.

"Alexei, do you know what is the most fun?"

"What?" he said, noticing his legs starting to strain.

"This."

Rasputin released his legs and dropped to the darkness below. Alexei screamed as he watched Rasputin fall from sight.

"Grigori! Grigori!"

He hung from the rod and twitched about. Alexei tried to swing his hand upward to grip the rod for support, but his abdomen had grown weak. His knee joints burned. He once again tried to sit up and hold on to the pole. The strength in his legs vanished.

"Let go, Alexei! Have faith! You will be safe."

Alexei whined a high-pitched scream and desperately tried to grab upward. With no strength left, his legs gave way and he fell head-first toward the ground. He tumbled in the air as the shadow of the earth and the moon spun in his vision. Only another second and he'd smash into the dirt. That's when it happened—a strange

301

Chapter 20

sensation warmed in his gut, some hidden instinctual urge that forced a great energy through his body. He watched to his own surprise as he suddenly floated upright and coasted gently to the ground, landing just before Rasputin.

"Holy hell!" yelled Alexei, looking to his hands.

"Close," replied Rasputin, standing over him.

"How did I ... what? Let's do it again!" Alexei jumped up and down.

"You can do it as much as you wish," said Rasputin. "What you call a sickness is your strength. You simply do not understand it yet."

"How do you know?"

"Because I have it too. So does your mother."

"And Sana?"

"No, but she could." Rasputin smiled, then threw his palms toward the ground, lifting himself into the air. He landed behind Alexei.

"Come, we must get home. Your mother will be looking for you."

"How can I do it? As easy as you?"

Rasputin walked by him.

"There is much to learn. And very little time to learn it. For now, it is the same—conjure that feeling in your gut and then push," he said, gliding into the air once more as he pushed his palms toward the ground.

He continued to float into the air, and Alexei ran to catch up with him.

"Feel the sensation surge through you—then push."

Alexei took a deep breath and threw his hands toward the ground, mimicking Rasputin. He floated into the air for a moment and landed softly again upon the dirt. He repeated the action until he could hover in the air for several seconds.

"Why can't I do it like you?" he asked.

"Because to be like me, you must be well-fed," said Rasputin as he shot higher into the air.

Alexei jogged along the field as quickly as his legs would go, scanning the sky for Rasputin.

"Then feed me!" he yelled into the night.

Part II: Copilul Sângelui

*

Alexandra came to Alexei's quarters to find them empty. She ran to his window that overlooked the stables. Across the moonlit yard, she saw Rasputin and Alexei just at the front of the barn. Her heart sunk when she saw Alexei climb onto the railing of the corral and stand on the very top rung, balancing himself. She turned and ran from the room.

*

"You're him, aren't you?" said Alexei, stretching his arms to keep his balance.

Rasputin looked up to the child's face.

"Him?"

"The shadow man. I figured it out, finally. You're the one who's been telling me secrets."

Rasputin folded his hands behind his back and walked alongside the corral fence. Alexei followed him, arms outstretched, gently teetering as he walked along the top of the fence.

Rasputin peered up to Alexei. "And what would you do if I told you I am him?"

"It's all right. I like the shadow man, but I wish you'd tell me."

"Fine then," said Rasputin. "You've found me out. There are no more secrets between us."

Alexei smiled. "I knew it! Don't worry. I won't tell."

"It does not matter any longer," said Rasputin.

"Does Mother know? About everything?"

"She will."

Alexandra came running from the darkness with Sana behind her.

"Alexei, get down from there! Grigori, get him down!"

"Oh dear," said Rasputin. "Someone's in trouble."

"Should I show her?"

"Not yet. Let's wait until tomorrow night."

He held his arms up to the boy, and Alexei leapt to his hands. Rasputin placed him on the ground.

Chapter 20

"Father Rasputin, I'm shocked at you! You know—"

"He is fine, Your Grace."

"It's fun, Mama!"

Sana caught up to them finally, panting to catch her breath.

"Let him play, Alexandra," she said, wheezing.

"I'm having fun! Grigori is teaching me things."

"What things?" Alexandra sounded stern.

"Secrets. Fun stuff."

Rasputin smiled and held out his hands. "Why don't we all head inside for a nice cup of cocoa?" He bowed politely, and they headed toward the sprawling palace.

Commander Kashin and several Okhrana officers emerged from the night to check on the commotion.

"Is everything well, Empress?"

"It is fine, Commander. Thank you for your promptness."

They continued toward the palace, and Rasputin was sure to stare down Kashin as he walked by.

"Commander," he said and tipped his fingers to his brow.

Alexei jumped on Rasputin and rode piggyback the rest of the way. Alexandra took notice of their ever-increasing bond. She felt a great sense of gratitude toward Rasputin, and smiled as she watched her son wrap his arms tightly around Rasputin's broad shoulders.

*

They sat at the center of the large kitchen around a small circular table—each with a steaming cup of cocoa.

"Grigori," said Sana. "When can we go back? Can you foresee it?"

Rasputin closed his eyes. Alexei reached to him and held his hand tightly.

"I foresee something will pull us back to Saint Petersburg—sooner than it is safe."

"What of Nicholas?" asked Alexandra.

Rasputin opened his eyes.

"I cannot say," he said.

Alexandra frowned and bit her lower lip. "Is there nothing we can do? Just sit here like helpless fawns, waiting for dire news?"

"Saint Petersburg will be changed soon, and all of us in this room will have a heavy hand in the events. I have foreseen this."

"What events?" asked Sana.

"It is too soon to say."

A listlessness swept the gathering.

Alexandra stood and walked to the sink. She dumped the remainder of her cocoa down the drain. "You must excuse me," she said. "I'm terribly tired."

"Alexandra?" questioned Sana.

"I'm fine. I need to lie down and think this all over."

Alexandra hurried off from the kitchen.

"What's wrong with her?" asked Sana.

Rasputin watched Alexandra's figure as she walked down the hallway and turned to climb the stairs.

"She's fine," he said, gazing after her. He looked to Alexei. "It's bedtime for you too."

"But it won't be dawn for hours. I want to stay up with you and Sana."

Sana yawned. "I'm going to rest as well."

"Well, it seems that everyone is heading off to bed," said Rasputin.

Alexei pouted for a moment.

"Good night, sweet Grigori," said Sana, who leaned in and planted a lingering kiss on his cheek. She moved toward Alexei and patted him on the head. "Good night, my special little man."

Alexei jumped from his chair and stormed off.

"What did I do?" asked Sana, looking to Rasputin.

"I will speak with him," said Rasputin and rose from the table.

*

Rasputin entered Alexei's room to find him hidden underneath his blankets. He moved to the lump on the bed and sat beside it.

Chapter 20

"She likes you," groaned Alexei from beneath the covers.

"Stop it. I have said that in time all of your desires will come true if you listen to me."

Alexei sat up and removed the blanket from his head.

"Earlier you said I can have your powers, but I had to feed. What does that mean?"

Rasputin stared at him. "When I came to visit you previously—when you called me the shadow man. How do you think I did that? I was not in Saint Petersburg—far, far from it. And yet it was like I was there in your very room. That was a mere parlor trick compared to the true power that awaits you. But you must do whatever it takes to retain the gifts I have shown you and to acquire more. Will you do it?"

Rasputin motioned his hand toward the door and it slammed shut. He twisted his hand, locking it.

"How did you—"

"I thought it."

Alexei stared at the door with wide eyes.

"You can do it too. But only if you do as I tell you."

"Yes. Make my sickness go, and I'll do whatever it takes."

Rasputin pointed a lean finger at him. "I have told you. It is not a sickness. You will quit calling it such. Do you understand?"

"Yes."

A warm sincerity exuded from Rasputin's face. "You will come to know in time that the means and measures you need to remain healthy are quite natural. The way the world should be."

"What must I do?"

Rasputin smiled, revealing his fangs to Alexei. The child recoiled.

"It is time to show you the true pleasures your body seeks."

Rasputin held out his wrist and sliced it open with his sharp fingernails.

"Drink from me."

Alexei let out a whimper and tried to crawl from the bed. Rasputin held him by the back of his neck and forced him to stare at the cut. A fresh stream of blood ran from Rasputin's wrist and soaked his sleeve. He held it to Alexei's mouth.

Part II: Copilul Sângelui

"Don't hurt me," he cried, looking to Rasputin. His fear dissipated when the smell of Rasputin's blood drove an intense urgency inside his body. He pressed his lips to Rasputin's wrist. Rasputin winced as Alexei's teeth sunk into him. The boy closed his eyes and reveled in the taste. Rasputin pulled away and Alexei's mouth followed. He licked his lips, sensing tiny fangs had grown from his teeth. He raised his fingers to his teeth, feeling the sharp protrusions.

"I need more," he said. "It's delicious."

He reached for Rasputin's wrist.

"And you will have more," he said, pulling away his arm. "But not from me. Not until you have proved to me that you are committed. That you are faithful."

Panic washed over Alexei's face. He peered to Rasputin's wrist and saw blood dripping from his hand. Rasputin was pleased at the sight of Alexei's cheekbones protruding beneath his flesh. Alexei's eyes fell to black as he stared at the blood.

"Will you kill for it, Alexei?" he said, holding his wrist to him.

As Alexei's fangs grew from his face, a terrible dismay swept through him—the thought of missing another drop of blood was an atrocity. He nodded and sucked in deep pockets of air through his protruding jowls. Rasputin walked to the large window on the far wall. He motioned his hands to the glass, and it swung open as a strong breeze filled the room.

"Then show me."

Rasputin turned to the window and disappeared through it.

Alexei sat for another moment, the intensity in his stomach growing as the urge to consume more blood invigorated him. He focused on the burning sensation growing in his gut. Alexei leapt from bed and ran toward the window. The next moment, his bedroom was silent. The window slowly crept shut.

*

Alexei flew after Rasputin all the way to the outskirts of Yalta. He grew quickly adept at chasing Rasputin and matching his playful dips and curves. Rasputin climbed steeply into the air and shot straight for the earth, pulling upright just before hitting the ground. Alexei drifted carefully to his side.

Chapter 20

Rasputin knelt behind a dirt mound that sat a short distance from a farmhouse. The grounds were lit by periodic freestanding torches. His gaze focused on a nearby grain silo.

"What is it?" asked Alexei.

"Watch."

They waited for another moment until a farmer and his young son rounded the silo—a mule at their side pulling a cart loaded with firewood. They walked to the back of the farmhouse.

"Nelli. Sofiya!" The farmer turned and glared at his son. The boy shuffled off into the house and returned with his mother and younger sister.

"I told you we'd be back at dark!" scorned the farmer.

"I am sorry, Ambrus. I lost track of time," said the farmer's wife. "Nelli, help your brother."

"I don't want her help," he said.

"Pavlo! Do as you're told." Ambrus shook his head and shot a stern eye to his son, who pouted as he sifted through the heavier wood. Sofiya gathered an armful of firewood and placed it in the pile behind the house.

Rasputin leaned to Alexei. "Stay here."

*

Ambrus was busy loading wood into his daughter's arms when he noticed Pavlo walk past him and stare off toward the dirt mound.

"What is it, boy?"

"Can you hear it, Papa?"

Ambrus shook his head.

"A clicking. I can feel it." He motioned to his chest. "Someone's out there." Pavlo turned and walked toward the dark field.

"Go to your mother," said Ambrus to Nelli. He walked to the mule, grabbed a chopping axe, then moved toward his son.

Pavlo dropped to his knees.

Ambrus ran to him and cradled the boy as he fell backward into his arms—his left chest cavity was torn open, blood soaking his clothing. The boy's face was covered in a clear slimy fluid.

"Run!" he shouted, turning to Sofiya.

Part II: Copilul Sângelui

She looked to Pavlo's gored body and screamed. She held Nelli's hand and ran off into the field behind the farm.

Ambrus turned toward the dark field and raised his axe—his severed limb lay twitching on the ground before he finished the thought. He backpedaled slowly, unable to see his attacker. He looked to the blood spurting from his torn biceps and let out a wail. Rasputin's noxious spit struck him in the face, and he slumped to the dirt, paralyzed.

*

Alexei watched from the shadows as Rasputin's gruesome teeth ripped open Ambrus's torso. The child covered his mouth and ducked to the dirt, hoping Rasputin had forgotten him. A moment later, Rasputin stepped over the mound—his face dripping with blood.

"Your turn."

Alexei looked to the field to see Sofiya and Nelli running into the night.

Rasputin held out his clawed hand. "Come."

Alexei shook his head and wept. He gathered the courage to speak, but Rasputin was already gone. Alexei listened as screams echoed in the distance. He scanned the sky for Rasputin, then ran in the opposite direction of the screaming—his usual hobble was gone. As he fled from the scene, Alexei stopped occasionally, looking back to see if Rasputin was behind him. The distant cries suddenly ceased. He turned around and stared into the darkness.

The night's silence crept in around him, and the only noise apparent was his own breathing. Sofiya dropped before him. She groaned and twitched as the force from the landing punched the air from her lungs. She lay on the dirt with Rasputin's saliva covering her face. Alexei walked toward her.

"Little one," she said, trying to reach out to him. Her arm fell languidly to the dirt.

Rasputin appeared behind her. He pulled her from the ground and positioned her body to face Alexei.

"She is for you."

Chapter 20

A curious arousal swelled inside Alexei as he watched her head bob limply in Rasputin's grasp. Her pale skin seemed to glow in the starlight. Alexei became aware of a voice in his head—Rasputin was talking to him, possessing him.

Take her life, child. Do it now.

Alexei stood over her as the moon cast a deep shadow across her neck, exposing the hump of her jugular vein. As he neared Sofiya, Alexei could hear her heart beating, beckoning him like some hypnotic drum. Her flesh melded to darkness as pathways of red luminescence coursed through her veins. Rasputin gripped her more firmly, and Alexei stuck his face near her neck—the fangs in his mouth fully apparent.

"Please. I can't see anything," she whispered. "Don't hurt me."

Alexei pulled back slowly and looked to Rasputin. "She's crying."

"Free her from her miserable existence."

Her head lolled in Rasputin's lap as she blabbered incoherently. Alexei's face streamed with tears.

"Don't make me." Alexei closed his eyes.

The woman let out a muffled whimper as Rasputin's fingernail cut upward along her jugular. She tried to struggle, but her body stayed limp. Her blood spurted onto Alexei—the smell entranced him.

Rasputin dug his claws into her rib cage and tore open her chest cavity, exposing her beating heart. It shone to Alexei—a glowing bauble of ruby delight. He leaned into her and tore through her sternum. The adrenaline in her bloodstream shot waves of intense pleasure through Alexei's body as his teeth sunk into her heart. Suddenly, the world around him no longer existed. Every earthly sensation disappeared like a wave of transient static until his mind knew true silence and purity. Gravity itself seemed to dissipate, lifting him into a great heaven of silvery weightless existence as the sweet taste of blood cradled him in its arms.

Sofiya struggled only for another moment, then relaxed as a euphoria swept through her.

"Thank you," she gasped. "Oh God, thank you."

As Sofiya drifted toward death, she reached to Alexei and ran her fingers through his thick hair, pulling him more deeply into her. She fell completely limp.

Part II: Copilul Sângelui

Alexei looked to Rasputin, then to the woman's mangled body on the ground. He stood quietly, watching the rest of her blood trickle onto the dry soil.

"I need more. I can do it myself this time."

Rasputin grinned, then shot into the air. Alexei took one last look at Sofiya's dead body and followed.

*

Nelli Eltsina hid against the knot of a large tree root and gripped her hands together.

Dear God, please let me live. Please. Please, God.

She tried to still her breath while focusing on the silent forest.

Maybe it missed me. Maybe I escaped.

Her body shivered as she scanned the shadows for the slightest movement. Nelli almost let out a scream when a child her own age walked near her hiding place. He stood, looking around in the darkness—a sweet innocence about him.

"Little boy," she whispered. "Little boy, over here. There's a killer on the loose. What are you doing in the forest at night?"

He turned to her, appearing concerned. She held out her hands.

"Here. You can hide with me."

He crept toward her and accepted her embrace as they ducked against the tree.

"We'll keep each other safe," she said, looking to him.

The glint of his silvery fangs was the last thing she would ever see.

*

Hours later, Alexandra walked down the hallway and noticed the light from Alexei's room. She peeked in through the crack in the door and saw him leaning into Rasputin, whose arm was wrapped around the boy. They were immersed in a storybook. Alexandra leaned into the door, and it made a creaking noise. They looked up at her.

"Hello, you two," she said.

"Hi, Mama!"

Chapter 20

"It's going to be dawn soon," said Alexandra. "You should cover the window."

"I will, Mama. Grigori will do it for me."

"Well, good night."

"Good night," they said in unison.

Alexandra walked down the hallway to the sound of her son's laughter. It filled her with relief.

Grigori is a gift from God.

Part II: Copilul Sângelui

21

December 13, 1916 (OS), early morning

The sun cast a surprising radiance through a blanket of dense clouds rolling over the Subcarpathian hills. Despite the cold, Felix's skin beaded with sweat while he lay curled up at the bottom of the propeller boat. The exhaustion pressing into his head made him unsure how long he'd slept. He guessed twenty minutes. Felix peered to the back of the boat. Denis was gone. His footprints led from the sandy riverbank to the snow-sprinkled grass. Felix closed his eyes once more and listened to the sound of the water as it rushed over a series of rocks in the distance.

Felix stood and leapt overboard, his boots landing on the sandy embankment. His shoulders ached from the previous night's rowing, and he twisted and turned at the waist trying to click his spine into place. His eyes traced the boat's trail leading to where he and Denis had pulled it to higher ground. Felix looked toward the mouth of the Carpathians, feeling much less intimidated by the towering rocks.

He sat on the river's embankment and tore off his boots. It felt like a rebirth to remove the putrid socks encasing his feet. Felix cast them into the river, then stripped and tossed his clothes into the boat. He walked into the frigid waters. The froth from the rapids poured in around his shoulders. The cold penetrated through him. He splashed the water to his face and took deep, slow breaths as the sensation pulled him from sleep.

Felix felt surprisingly well.

Chapter 21

If I make it out of this, I'm going to spend more time in the outdoors. Maybe move closer to the sea.

"Felix!" called Denis.

Felix snapped from his spell and looked to see Denis standing near the boat.

"What are you doing?"

"Oh," yelled Felix. "Just refreshing myself, I guess. Where'd you hobble off to?"

"To Berca—not far. I bought us some bread and jam. Dried meats." He held up a parcel and a small loaf of bread. "When you're done with your beauty bath, come and eat your breakfast."

As Felix walked from the river, the mud from the banks clung to his feet. Deciding not to brush it free, he grabbed his boots and flung them into the boat.

"You mind?" he said, motioning to Denis to turn around.

"Why? I just watched you walk from the river."

Felix cupped himself and motioned his head toward the distance. Denis shook his head, then turned as Felix finished dressing himself.

"You're going to freeze to death," said Denis, moving to the back of the boat. He opened the parcel and pulled out some soppressata.

"I feel incredible," said Felix. "The water is amazing."

"Well, Incredible, eat up. We have roughly seventy-two hours left until this situation explodes, and it's going to take us at least half that to get back to Saint Petersburg."

Denis handed him the parcel and bread. Felix snatched it and tore into the bread.

Denis stared at the Carpathians with a stoic look in his eyes. "Never thought I'd find it," he said. "I want to thank you for what you did back there. I couldn't have done any of it without you."

Felix looked up from his meal and wiped his mouth. "Of course. I—"

"That's all." Denis looked to his boots.

"Do you think we'll survive?" Felix raised his brow.

"No. Not if the bats are already on their way. They're psychically linked to your godson. The time is come."

Part II: Copilul Sângelui

Felix swallowed his bread. "So what was all that for?" He motioned toward the dark mountains.

"We did everything we could. Leave it at that." Denis looked up toward the mountain peaks. "The seers have predicted it for a decade now. We failed. But I'll be damned if I don't take a few hundred with me." He forced a smile and bobbed his hooked hand.

"I think we can do it," began Felix. "We—"

A sudden sternness came over Denis as he raised his hand to silence Felix.

"We can't." Denis pointed toward the Carpathian spires. "Vlad Drăculea and his small army were trapped inside those very mountains by 175,000 Turkish invaders on the north and south entrances to the Buzău Pass. Trapped by Muslim holy warriors, who were rested, well-fed, and eager to kill. Drăculea and his men dwindled to less than one hundred—most of them savage Stovâjįk peasants.

"So the Ottomans wait, maybe some in this very spot, for nearly ten months for reinforcements. They want boats to row up the Buzău and invade Drăculea's stronghold. I can only assume they had a map to the loch.

"When the reinforcements finally bring the boats near Mărăcineni, they are greeted by their fellow soldiers impaled on metal stakes lining both sides of the river all the way into the mouth of the Carpathians, where they found the rest: 175,000 armed men—butchered, drained of their blood, and impaled en masse along both entrances of the Buzău Pass. In the ten months it took to send *reinforcements*, Drăculea converted to vampirism. He and his Nosferatu armies slaughtered 175,000 armed men overnight. We can't win, Felix. All we can do now is resist."

"Well, he died, right? Somebody managed—"

"From what has been passed down from the seers, he was betrayed and beheaded by his own brother Radu, who then slayed the Bloodchild, sending the Nosferatu back to their dark realm. But for nearly fifteen years, nothing could stand against Drăculea and his black army. Nothing. They enslaved king and beggar and feasted on men like cattle."

"What happened to Radu?"

"No one knows." Denis looked downriver.

"So Alexei has to die—to stop this?" asked Felix.

Chapter 21

Denis nodded. "But there's no chance of reaching him. We can still make it back to Saint Petersburg, though."

"Then there's still time."

Denis frowned. "Not really." He glanced to the water.

"Then what's the point of going back? There's a vampire here. Converting the living. We should—"

"The point is I'm going to stand next to my brother and fight. For my life. For his. Get my revenge any way I can. It's up to you to find your own reasoning. Stay here and fight your vampire, for all I care."

Felix's eyes moved to the snowy grass.

"We should get moving," said Denis.

Felix crawled from the boat and pushed it into the river as Denis manned an oar. Felix pushed until he was knee-deep in the water, then flung himself inside.

Three hours later, after returning Florin's boat unscathed as promised, Felix and Denis were in their automobile and headed to Bucharest.

*

СОВЕРШЕННО СЕКРЕТНО [TOP SECRET]
Diary entry of Alexandra Fyodorovna, empress of Russia 1894–1916:

December 13, 1916

My greatest fears have come true! Revolution has spilled onto the streets of Saint Petersburg! I was wakened this afternoon from a terrible dream by Commander Kashin knocking at my bedroom door. He told me Nicholas was on the telephone. I went downstairs to my study to find him and two other officers standing at attention around the telephone. I thought this behavior rather formal until I put the device to my ear. It was Nicholas. His voice sounded so uncertain. I have never heard such a tone from him.

Attempts to breach the Winter Palace have been thwarted thus far. Thank God the military and Okhrana are remaining loyal to us.

Part II: Copilul Sângelui

I cannot stay here any longer. I will order Commander Kashin to take us back this evening. I will stand with my husband in his most pressing hour. If he is to die at the hands of his own people, then so am I.

Nicholas was adamant about seeking advice from Grigori.

He told Nicholas that he'd foreseen this, and that, if we are to survive, any remaining militia are to surround Saint Petersburg and build barriers around the city. He said Nicholas was to order the militiamen to shoot anyone who tries to leave. I found his advice grew stranger when he advised that anyone at all should be allowed into Saint Petersburg.

If Grigori did foresee the revolt, I wonder why he didn't mention it last night. He was vague in his prediction. Maybe it was a means not to worry us? With Minister Makarov in jail, I'm afraid not even the right will stand next to us. Oh, I pray that we will make it out of this alive!

These events have brought such misery into my heart. I can barely sleep, and when I do, I am bedeviled by terrible nightmares. My memories from last night's dream are foggy, but they left a strange impression on me nonetheless. I will try to recount them as best I can.

I dreamt that I was hiding in the stables, feasting on a small hamster. Dawn was near, so I decided to head back to the palace. On my way to my quarters, I noticed light in Alexei's room, so I peeked in to see him and Grigori reading peacefully. But there was something about them. I could feel them harboring a strange secret. I looked them over and they seemed innocent enough, so I moved down the hallway to my quarters.

When I entered, I was startled to find Sana asleep in my bed. I nudged her, and she sat up from the sheets to reveal she was naked. I have never felt anything other than kinship toward her before, but I found the sight of her nude body thrilling.

She seemed to speak to me without moving her lips, begging me to caress her. I crawled in bed and began

Chapter 21

kissing her on the lips, running my hands over her soft skin. She wore the small perfume bottle she keeps around her neck. It was nearly empty. I knew then it was not filled with wine, but Rasputin's blood.

Sana and I kissed passionately, and she slowly removed my robe. The sensation of my flesh on hers was exhilarating. I started kissing her neck, even biting her gently. I looked into the darkness to see Grigori standing in the shadows, watching us. He had great fangs in his mouth, and I could almost hear him speaking to me. Saying something. "I brought her for you," or "She is for you," I don't remember, exactly.

I grew so aroused by his eyes on our naked bodies that I bit deeply into Sana's neck, wanting her to moan more loudly. My bite drew blood. At first I was concerned, but she moaned and pulled me into her. The taste of her blood warm in my mouth was the most thrilling experience of my life. Dark blood streams dripped downward across her pale breasts, and I could feel warm beads of it dripping onto my thighs. Sana began panting, pulling my head into her neck, and I drank even more blood from her.

I remember thinking I'd gone too far when Sana let out one great scream. This is where the dream fades. I woke suddenly and caught myself closing my eyes to try and continue the dream with no success. I eventually fell asleep until Commander Kashin rapped on my door just before dusk.

I believe I will be a little embarrassed when I see Sana later this evening.

*

Alexandra closed her diary and walked toward her bedroom upstairs. She felt exhausted from the news of Saint Petersburg. She walked to her bed, pulled back her comforter, and shrieked at the deep bloodstains blotched across the white sheets. She flung the comforter over the mess and ran for Sana's room. Alexandra burst

Part II: Copilul Sângelui

through the door to find the room empty. Sana's bedding was perfectly undisturbed from the previous night.

"Sana!" she screamed.

Alexandra rushed to the back of Sana's quarters, her mind racing with outlandish ideas of where she might be hiding. Alexandra paused when she heard the bedroom door open. Rasputin moved in and pulled the door behind him, locking it.

"Grigori, thank God," said Alexandra, running toward him. "Something terrible has happened. Sana has …" Alexandra froze as the dream came back to her. "You …" she said. "This is real."

Rasputin remained quiet and walked toward her with steady, seemingly threatening eyes. She snatched a vase from a nearby table and jabbed it toward him.

"Stay away from me!"

"Alexandra, stop."

Alexandra backed away. "One scream and I'll have Kashin in here …"

"I beg you, sit." He motioned toward the bed.

Alexandra opened the back entrance, which led to a long hallway. Rasputin followed her.

"Where is she? What did you make me do?"

"Her body is … hidden," said Rasputin.

Alexandra inched backward, never allowing Rasputin closer than six or seven feet between them.

"You did this."

"Put the vase down, Alexandra."

Alexandra retreated to the hallway's end, never taking her eyes from Rasputin. She placed the vase on the floor and opened a door to a dark staircase that twisted upward. She stepped through, then slammed the door and locked it. With her ear to the door, she listened for any sign of movement, then ran to the top of the stairs, which exited to the palace's Florentine tower. Realizing there was no escape, she placed her back against the railing as a sudden gust of wind surged upon the tower.

Rasputin materialized before her.

"How did you—"

Chapter 21

"Don't be coy, Alexandra. There are no more secrets between us. You know what you are now. You've always known, haven't you?"

Alexandra leaned slightly over the tower's railing and looked to the sheer drop below. She peered back to Rasputin and shook her head. "It's not possible," she said, looking over the railing once more. "I'm a God-fearing woman—not a monster."

Rasputin's eyes were steady and hard.

"You did this to me, didn't you?"

"Yes."

Alexandra raised her fists and crashed them into his chest. Rasputin held her wrists and let her struggle.

"Why?" cried Alexandra.

"Do you truly not remember? Those memories are seared into my soul."

*

Olaf's cloaked figure stood over Rasputin's mutilated body in the permeating dark of the blackwood forest. He held a torch in one hand and the vampire bible in the other. Dozens of giant vampire bats surrounded him on the ground.

"O Darkness, bring your might unto this willing soul and cleanse him from the weakness of humanity. Hark, O Darkness, for he is now your servant! Breathe life eternal back into his bones. The Holy Upir have consumed his body and communed with his blood. His life, an offering unto you, O mighty Darkness. He is anointed! Allow him now to do your bidding—to bring your order and might unto this earth! Salvage him, O Darkness, so that he shall rise once more!"

Olaf stared into the night. Silence.

He closed the vampire bible, placed it upon the altar, and looked to Rasputin lying on the stone slab. The mystic's face was entirely chewed away and even in the minuscule light cast by Olaf's torch, it was apparent the giant vampire bats had chewed out his eyeballs. Olaf felt deep concern at the sight of Rasputin's naked skull with bits of torn flesh hanging from it. For a moment, he wondered if he'd gotten it wrong and thought to invoke a healing spell to reverse

Part II: Copilul Sângelui

the damage, but knew from the sight of Rasputin that he was too far gone.

What if my summoning powers are diminished? What if I mishandled the ceremony?

Olaf waited for some response from the darkness as the mighty vampire bats still surrounded him—growling and chirping as they feasted on torn bits of Rasputin's flesh. Some took to flight, returning to their roosts in the canopy above, while others slithered over the ground and ascended the blackwood tree trunks with their clawed appendages. Olaf held his torch over Rasputin, inspecting the rest of his body. After nearly a century in dealing in dark arts, he found himself experiencing the closest emotion he'd ever felt to fear upon seeing the mangled corpse before him—it appeared more like a devoured skeleton than a man, with only tiny bits of muscle, flesh, and organs clinging to various parts of his bones.

They ravaged him.

Olaf looked to the canopy and knelt to the ground. He raised his hands to the bats, now hanging upside down in silence. A further quiet settled upon the forest.

"He shall rise!" shouted Olaf, raising his torch into the dark. "He shall rise!"

Olaf stuck his torch into the earth next to Rasputin and waited for some sign the ceremony had been a success. Becoming aware of sweat breaking on his forehead and his heart rate raising, Olaf sat on the ground, pulled his cloak's hood more deeply over his head, and held his hands to his face.

I failed him.

A shrill emanated from above and Olaf saw one of the vampire bats shaking a bit as it emitted a near deafening cry from its fanged mouth. The entire canopy erupted with a horrid wail as thousands of giant vampire bats joined the chorus. Olaf covered his ears and lay back on the ground. The bats began to quiver and shake violently as waves of blue electric shock crawled across their bodies, illuminating the dark forest.

Olaf rose to his knees, keeping his hands over his ears as he watched the blue luminescence expand across the camp of bats. A turbulent wind picked up through the forest, and the electricity sparking from the bats left their bodies and united into a ball of

Chapter 21

white lightning. It hovered just above Rasputin, then flowed into his body, briefly appearing to light his bones from the inside out. Olaf closed his eyes to avoid being blinded by the brightness.

The forest fell dark.

Silence permeated the forest as the trenchant winds ceased. Olaf opened his eyes, grabbed his torch once more, and held it over Rasputin.

Rasputin's flesh began to materialize over his body—first with torn and shredded pieces of muscle connecting as his skin grew back over his wounds. His face was the last part of his body to heal before Olaf's eyes. Olaf stood back as intense excitement pervaded his gut. He held the beacon over Rasputin, whose eyes shot open.

"My friend!" yelled Olaf.

Rasputin looked to him. "That was … extremely painful," he said calmly.

Olaf helped Rasputin sit upright, then bowed before him.

"My Stăpân. Praise to you."

Rasputin stood, his nude figure contrasted against the shadows. "Rise," he said.

Olaf stood and embraced him. "I thought I failed you."

Rasputin broke the embrace and walked from the slab. "Hurry," he said. "I must feed."

Olaf followed him out of the darkened forest.

*

Princess Alexandra stood at a window in the third story of the Royal Palace of Bucharest, where she'd been residing for nearly two weeks. She was homesick for Berlin and felt unusually anxious. A fresh bouquet of white gerbera daisies sitting on a mahogany table next to the window caught her attention. She leaned toward the vase and inhaled the pleasant smell. A sensation of calmness swept through her.

Looking out the window, Alexandra noticed a line of horse-drawn carriages traveling up Piața Palatului. Grand Duke George Alexandrovich had arrived. She turned around and stood in front of a mirror, ensuring her makeup was fresh and her clothing was in

Part II: Copilul Sângelui

place. She then took a hat from her boudoir, placed it upon her head, and exited the room. On her way down the expansive hall, Alexandra was greeted by Mila, her head of staff and acting chaperon in the absence of her brother Louis.

"Your Grace, Grand Duke has—"

"I know! I know!" she said, accelerating her walk into a near sprint.

Alexandra had been engaged to Grand Duke George of Russia for nearly three months, but had met him only two times. She had always fancied his younger brother Nicholas, as she found him to be kind and soft-spoken. George had always frightened her a bit due to his short temper and deceptive ways, but her family exerted an extreme amount of pressure upon her to marry him, knowing that one day soon she would become empress of Russia. Alexandra was hopeful that after she spent three full weeks with George, touring Romania and furthering her campaign of scarlet fever awareness, the two would become closer and she would find trust for him in her heart and possibly even real love.

She glided down the sweeping main staircase with Mila tailing her and ran out into the semicircular thruway. Alexandra pushed herself beyond the line of servants, who were dressed in red and white regal attire and awaiting the procession of carriages. She jumped up and down and waved as George's carriage neared. Mila finally stood behind her.

"Your Grace," she whispered. "Please, your behavior is unladylike."

Alexandra calmed herself and stood still as the carriages neared.

The horses slowed and two palace servants approached George's carriage. One placed a stair riser at the carriage's door while the other opened it. Alexandra's heart leaped at the sight of him.

"My beloved!" said George, exiting the carriage. His mustache and navy blue formal attire imbued him with the aura of a mature statesman despite his youthful face.

Alexandra nearly jumped into his arms as the two embraced.

"I'm so glad to see you again," she said.

"They're watching," said George.

"Oh, yes. My apologies."

Chapter 21

Alexandra quickly broke the embrace and bowed to George. He held his white-gloved hand to her, bowed, and placed a kiss on her delicate knuckles.

"Beautiful as ever, my sweet," he said, while looking up to her eyes.

The bevy of servants then lined the stairs to the royal palace. The rest of his traveling party followed as George led Alexandra by the hand to the grand entrance, where King Carol I and Elisabeth of Wied waited to greet them.

*

George sat at the end of a comfortable patent leather sofa in his personal quarters. He relaxed a bit, thankful he had shirked joining Alexandra, King Carol, and Queen Elisabeth as they toured the royal garden by blaming his nonexistent pollen allergy.

He shot a stern glare at Kir.

"Keep your man outside the door at all times," said George. "Anyone comes within earshot, knock upon the door to alert us."

"My Stăpân," said Kir, bowing.

Kir walked to his operative and whispered into his ear. The man in all black then exited the room and closed the door.

"Now then," said George, lighting a cigar, "we begin in two days. Is everything prepared?"

Kir was silent.

"Kir!"

"My Stăpân, we have reached a snag."

George puffed on his cigar and exhaled slowly as he watched the smoke rise. "A snag you say? Do you have any idea the amount of money I have spent on this operation?"

"I do. Vondling has been paid and promised the mystic who would lead us to the loch. He has been dodging us ever since."

George bit down on his lip. "Where's the old wizard?"

"I am here, my future Stăpân," said Olaf, materializing on the sofa across from George.

"Late as usual," said George.

Part II: Copilul Sângelui

"I always arrive exactly when needed. And I'm a warlock—not a wizard."

"Same difference." George shook his head and chomped down on his cigar.

"Well, actually, wizards don't exi—"

"Shut up, Olaf!" commanded George. "You're the only one I allow to speak to me in such terms. You know that, right?"

Olaf nodded.

"And from this point forward, you will call me Stăpân. I am mere days away from victory."

"Of course," said Olaf.

George appeared agitated as the laugh lines around his mouth tightened. "Also, you know I hate it when you do that sneaky appearing act. Use the door and show up on time like a goddamn mortal for once."

"Relax, my Stăpân," said Olaf. "Everything is in order. You will succeed. We will locate the mystic and he will guide us to the loch. I can then proceed with the ceremony. I suggest sending Kir and his men to visit Vondling this evening and put a scare into him. That should be enough to produce—"

"Should be enough!" yelled George. "Millions! You hear me? I have spent millions on this campaign. Not an easy feat to embezzle a sum of such magnitude from my father. And now I come to Bucharest to proceed with the ceremony, only to find you both have failed in your duties? I will become the prime vampire."

"And so you will," said Olaf. "I have foreseen this."

"Then why can't you foresee where this damn loch is located? How has this mystic hidden it from you?"

"My Stăpân. It seems only he has procured a version of the Impaler's bible with the exact location. The portal is invisible even to my sight."

George looked to Kir. "Then get your men to this Vondling and beat it out of him."

"Stăpân," said Kir, bowing at the waist. He turned and exited the room.

George continued to puff on his cigar as he stared at Olaf. "Two days," he said. "Tomorrow, I must attend to Alexandra and some

Chapter 21

other official details with King Carol. The day after, Alexandra and I are supposed to leave for Braşov. That is when we will disappear in the Carpathians. Correct?"

"It is, my Stăpân."

"So this mystic. Have you met him?"

"I have not. Only Vondling has."

"I am entirely displeased at the fact that nobody thought about the importance of meeting such a man first. We're being tricked, Olaf. I can sense it. My patience with you and the rest of the Black Hundred has grown thin. Pray I forgive you all once I am turned. And when fortune favors us and Alexandra births the Bloodchild, know then my patience will give way to my ruthlessness with the Nosferatu at my command."

Olaf stood and bowed. "Understood, Stăpân."

"That will be all."

Olaf dissipated into a thin black mist, and George once again found himself alone in the room.

"Use the door like a goddamn mortal!" he shouted into the air.

George shook his head, then walked to the door and rapped upon it. "You may leave now," he said to Kir's operative on the other side.

"Highness!"

George listened to the operative's footsteps move down the hall, and twisted his cigar between his thumb and index finger. He pulled it to his mouth and walked to the room's double-pane window. He stood, puffing on his cigar and watching over the royal palace's courtyard. While observing King Carol follow Alexandra and Elisabeth as they engaged in pleasant conversation, he found himself disgusted at the servants laboring among the grounds. George tapped his cigar and plopped a cylinder of ash onto the carpet as he spied Alexandra bending over to smell a bushel of white roses.

Pollen allergy, indeed. Soon he would inflict a scourge so great upon all the weakness he saw before him. He would purge the world of these commoners, purge the world of his father, weak brother, and that arrogant Wilhelm. He would become the darkness. He would rule this earth.

George looked down to the ash from his cigar and smashed it into the carpeting with his perfectly polished shoe.

Part II: Copilul Sângelui

*

It was just after 11:00 p.m. when Mihaela Nistor stood on the corner of Bulevardul Dacia and Strada Polonă. She positioned her blouse, leaned up against a lamppost, and lit a cigarette. Nearly two hours had passed since she arrived, and her feet were beginning to cramp in her tight laced-up boots. From behind her, a clicking resonated on the cobblestone and she turned to see the shadow of a well-dressed man approach.

"Hello, kind sir. You alone tonight?"

"Out of the way, hag!"

The man brushed by her in a hurry, and she leaned against the lamppost once more. This was the third evening in a row without any takers. Mihaela thought to her younger brother and wondered how she was going to afford food for them both over the coming days. She heard a strange clicking noise and what she believed to be a muffled scream from behind her. Mihaela spun around to see that the man had vanished from the streets. She watched the lane for a moment, then shrugged as her eyes scanned the other side of the avenue. It was time to leave—nobody was out tonight. After crushing her cigarette on the cobblestone, Mihaela began her journey home.

She had just passed by a small alley when she heard the voice.

How many leus, Mihaela?

"Pardon me?" she said, turning into the alley. She couldn't see anyone in the darkness.

Mihaela's arms were suddenly pinned to her sides.

"You're mine!" said the voice.

Mihaela broke the hold and turned to see Andrei. He was visibly drunk as usual.

"You scared me to death!"

"Sorry," said Andrei. "Just trying to lighten the evening. I assume you had as much luck as me?"

Mihaela nodded.

"Well, look at the positive side—at least if you're arrested, you'll be released. I'll be beaten and hanged. How's that for irony? Considering my best clients are all in the royal family."

Chapter 21

Mihaela looked to Andrei's handsome young face and to the vertical scar that ran center of his upper lip. She thought back to the time she found him beaten on the street, unconscious, and assisted him to the hospital for medical attention. Her heart warmed toward him as she realized for the first time that they were friends.

"Irony indeed, Andrei. Let's get off the streets before we're either harmed or detained. Will you walk me home?"

"I would be honored," said Andrei, holding his arm to Mihaela.

She hooked her arm under his, and the two walked off into the night.

*

Marius Mateescu kept a brisk pace as he walked along Strada Polonă. Where he was heading was still unbeknownst to him. After arguing with his wife for the better part of the evening and finally beating her, he needed some air—he simply had to get away from his house to clear his thoughts. As he continued along the avenue, he noticed a woman leaning against a lamppost in the near distance. Her short knickers and open cleavage were visible even in the lamplight.

I hate these streetwalkers.

"Hello, kind sir. You alone tonight?" she said as he approached.

"Out of the way, hag!"

Marius brushed by her and continued on his way. He walked a short distance farther and her buxom figure flashed into his mind. Reaching into his pocket, he silently ensured he had money. Marius stopped and turned to her, noticing she was facing the other direction. He pulled out his leus and counted them. Certainly he had enough.

Marius became aware of a strange curling sensation in the back of his neck.

Someone is watching me.

He turned to a slim opening between the buildings to his right and was struck in the face by a slimy substance. He let out a quick, muffled scream and slumped to the cobblestones before being violently dragged into the alleyway by his shadowy attacker in a fraction of a second.

Part II: Copilul Sângelui

*

Rasputin's hulking, vampiric figure knelt to the ground over the mutilated remains. Bits of Marius lay strewn about every part of the grimy brick alleyway—some of his blood ran into a nearby gutter. Bone-cracking and sucking sounds filled the air as Rasputin feasted on Marius's thigh, drinking as much blood as he could from the torn limb. While watching a stream of blood drip into the gutter, Rasputin became aware of a presence in the alley and dropped the remains of the thigh onto the brick.

"That was quite a frenzied feeding," came a voice.

Rasputin stood and faced the voice—fresh blood splatter about every portion of his fanged face.

"Not polite to watch a vampire feed," said Rasputin as his face returned to its human form.

"Apologies," said Olaf. "Curiosity got the better of me." Olaf briefly regarded the mangled remains before him and stared at Rasputin. "Vondling needs you immediately."

"What now?"

"George's men are on their way to his flat. They're intently looking for you."

"Then find me they shall."

"Careful what you do here. I met with George earlier today. They are set to travel to the Carpathians the day after tomorrow. Anything that seems suspicious may upend our progress."

"He trusts you, correct?"

"Yes."

"Then let's just say some of his little Black Hundred minions go missing. I assume it would be very simple for you to put his mind at ease."

Olaf frowned. "Please do nothing rash. Our Stovâjîk mercenaries will be ready to strike just as their caravan moves from Bucharest."

"Why risk it when I can begin to thin the herd now?"

"Grigori!" warned Olaf.

Chapter 21

"I will try my best," said Rasputin, bowing. "And I will see you back at Loch Dracul for Alexandra's conversion. The night is finally ours."

"Indeed it is, my Stăpân. Best see to Vondling before it's too—"

Rasputin shot upward into the night.

Olaf stood alone in the alley and looked over Marius's remains, noticing the small pool of blood running into the gutter. Knowing deep down Rasputin would not obey his request to leave the operatives alive, he envisioned the mess he'd be cleaning up later.

Well, at least there's not a lot of blood left.

*

Alexandra held on to George's gloved hand as their caravan of three limousines and two horse-drawn carriages traveled along the deciduous tree–lined roadway just south of Tâncăbești. Silently, she rehearsed her speech about the dangers of scarlet fever and looked forward to delivering it to the commoners in Brașov with the aid of her translator. Alexandra peered out the limousine's left window and enjoyed the lush greenery as it rolled by.

"I love the trees after a fresh rain. Reminds me of Westerstede," said Alexandra.

George continued to stare out the window on his side.

"I spent time there as a child. It's beautiful and quiet," she finished.

George paid her no mind.

"Darling, what's the matter?" Alexandra placed her hand upon George's cheek and pulled his attention toward her.

George snapped into focus, gripped her hand, and smiled. "Nothing, my beloved, I was—"

A white flash and concussion blast erupted before them, causing the limousine to tip on its left side. Alexandra had the wind knocked out of her as George's weight fell onto her.

"Are you harmed, Alexandra?" he said as he tried to pull himself upright.

"No. I don't think so," she said, trying to catch her breath.

Four more blasts and gunfire surrounded their vehicle.

Part II: Copilul Sângelui

"What's happening?" shouted Alexandra.

"I've been betrayed!"

George moved off Alexandra the best he could in the confined space, placing his feet on the door. "Stay still," he said.

Gunfire and horse whinnies came from outside, and Alexandra heard their hooves striking the dirt road as they trotted away.

"The horses have escaped!" she said.

"Just be still."

George stood upright and placed his foot on the driver's side headrest. He looked to the front of the cab—the windshield had been blown out and the driver lay unconscious against the door with blood dripping from his ear. Leveraging himself on the headrest, George pulled himself upward and managed to open the vehicle's door. The moment he popped his head outside, a gunshot rang out and his body fell on top of Alexandra. She screamed and squirmed while trying to move herself from under his weight.

Alexandra shimmied from underneath his limp body and saw blood gushing from a bullet hole just above his left eye. She held back another scream, and shifted to peer out the shattered front window. One more gun blast resonated through the air and the surrounding countryside fell quiet. Muffled voices of a tongue Alexandra did not recognize came closer. She positioned herself for a clear view through the front of the vehicle.

At first she could see only that the limousine in front of hers was also on its side—smoke and fire whirring about its charred metal skeleton. Then, through the smoke and chaos, she saw him—a bald elderly man in all black walked toward her vehicle with his hand outstretched. The smoke encircling him parted as he approached, and Alexandra could see his eyes were pure white, almost glowing.

Sleep now, Alexandra.

She shook her head as the voice came to her—a ripe sense of terror filled her lungs as she took in a deep breath.

Sleep now …

She tried to shake the voice from her mind as her field of vision was overcome with blackness.

*

Chapter 21

Alexandra woke to find herself completely nude, lying on a stone slab that sat low upon the ground. She was gagged and bound by the wrists and ankles. After struggling momentarily, she resigned herself to her fetters.

It was nearly pitch-black save a torch beacon fluttering right next to an altar that stood just at her feet. She heard an unusual clicking and the sound of leaves rustling all around her. *Something* was out there in the dark. Alexandra looked to her left, and in the shadows, the forest appeared to be moving, some giant blob of darkness swarming and shifting all around her. She looked upward and could make out black and gnarled tree branches above.

A man appeared at the altar. From his bald head and all-white eyes, she knew it was the man from the limousine.

"Please stop," she said through her gag, struggling a bit more.

The man held out his hand to her. "Hold her down," he said.

Alexandra looked up to see the shadow of another man reach down and pin her shoulders. In the torchlight, all she could discern was his giant black beard. The man with white eyes began speaking in tongues, and the forest around her seemed to move closer. A whiteness emerged from the corner of her eye, and she turned to see the face of a large fanged bat hissing at her. She let out a great scream when she realized they were all around her.

The bats slithered closer, and two of them hovered directly over her. She tried to break free of her bonds, but the bearded man forced her shoulders to the slab. She felt only an icy pinprick for a moment as one of the bats bit into her shoulder—the other nipping at her thigh. The bats crawled away and more took their place, taking small bites of her flesh. They swarmed upon her, feasting on every portion of her body. Finally, when the pain became too great, Alexandra fell unconscious. Her last vision was the sight of her own ribs as a bat tore her rib cage and sunk its fangs into her beating heart.

*

"Will she fully heal?" asked Rasputin, staring into the murky waters—Alexandra's nude pale figure was submerged just below the surface.

Part II: Copilul Sângelui

Olaf stood in the small rowboat and looked overboard. Even in the early twilight, he could make out the scars and contusions strewn across her body.

"She will. The process often takes longer for women."

Rasputin nodded and sat down.

"What's the matter, my friend?" asked Olaf.

"I feel for her. I almost couldn't go through with it."

"What's done is done. You can worry about mending your relationship with her once she awakens. In time, she will come to see you as an ally. Perhaps even in a loving light when she realizes the gift you have given her. Eternal life—eternal youth."

"I believe it so," said Rasputin, looking to the sky.

"We have achieved a wonderful thing, through your insights—something no one has accomplished since Vlad Drăculea … Soon she will wake and you will show her the ways to survive. After you mate with her, nine months or so from now, your son or daughter will be born and bring the Nosferatu back to this mortal plane."

Rasputin was silent. "And then the real work begins."

"Most certainly. But the world will be ours."

"Do you believe she will remain undetected until I return?"

"With absolute certainty. The loch is very well hidden. And you must act swiftly. I foresee great strife for you if this Denis Borovitch is not killed."

"Are you able to sense who has been sending me these messages?"

"Not yet. It seems to be a witch in either Saint Petersburg or Moscow. Very clever, this one, in masking her location, but from her dialect—she's absolutely Russian. I must travel back at once to discern more. Sadly our nation is nothing but a hive of do-gooder witches and warlocks. We'll squash this soon enough. You see to this Denis Borovitch. I'll keep the Black Hundred placated, and deal with anyone else meddling in our affairs once I'm back in Russia."

"Very well then, my friend. I will see you soon," said Rasputin as Olaf dissipated into nothingness.

Rasputin stood and looked to Alexandra once more.

"I'm sorry, my lady," he said. "You were necessary."

Rasputin hovered into the night, transforming into a black ether. Soon he would be in Vernești to confront one Denis Borovitch.

Chapter 21

*

Upon the tower, Alexandra was sobbing. "I remember the explosion on the road and then that wretched lake. Being pulled out of the water by those men in the boat. And … it was you. You were the one—holding me down as those monsters tore into my flesh."

"Yes," said Rasputin.

Alexandra reached to the floor and sat with her face in her hands.

"It was not to be like this, Alexandra. I assure you. You were willed into these events by your brother and Kaiser Wilhelm, cast into a secret alliance meant to bring vampirism to elite factions of Germany and Russia."

"Blasphemy!"

"It is true. They believe vampirism is a wine only to be tasted by the lips of the elite. But I stopped them by converting myself before Grand Duke Alexandrovich could be converted—he had to be stopped. And once we had you, I intended to complete what they started. You were my rightful mate. And our child was meant to bring the vampire to its rightful place—to purge the wickedness of man from this earth."

Alexandra looked up to him.

"But as you were incubating, I left to quell a pressing matter and was taken by surprise and nearly killed," said Rasputin. "That's when you were discovered by those men in the boat. I failed. Never again, Alexandra."

"So you were to rape me and use my life as your pawn?"

Rasputin folded his arms and knelt closely to her. "Search your heart, Alexandra. Do you truly believe I would have forced myself upon—"

"It's what you did with those creatures! You could have saved me. You didn't have to—"

"What's done is done. And we now share a deep bond as the prime vampires," continued Rasputin. "That bond would have flourished upon your awakening. We were to fall in love. I have treated both you and Alexei with nothing but kindness. We are kin now."

Part II: Copilul Sângelui

"You are sick if you think what you have done to me is kindness." Alexandra appeared exhausted, tears streaming down her face.

Rasputin reached out to her. "Come," he said.

Alexandra swatted his hand away. She stood and walked to the railing.

Rasputin moved next to her and they stared out over the rolling farmlands as nighttime settled.

"Fate spared us all when Alexei was born, but he is not whole. Not yet."

Alexandra stared at him in silence.

"If you had to choose between the life of your son and the life of your husband, which would it be?"

Alexandra's chin quivered as she took in the implication of Rasputin's question. "I'll kill myself before I have to."

"Alexei is not whole. He has your vampire blood and Nicholas's human blood. If the link to the human blood is not destroyed, Alexei will soon die. So will you. And so will I."

"So I must kill my husband to save my son?"

"No. Alexei will kill him. He will drink the blood that poisons his body. Only then will a chain of events started long ago be set right."

"Alexei will never—"

"He will murder Nicholas. That I guarantee … I control Alexei now."

Rasputin pulled up his sleeve. He closed his eyes and tiny bite marks materialized on his wrist.

"You fed him. Your blood?"

Alexandra's eyes grew alive with anger. She raised her hands to strike him, but instead clenched her fists and turned away. She moved to the corner of the tower.

"Enough dramatics," said Rasputin, standing behind her. "It is what we are. It is our right. In time you will come to forgive me."

"I will not allow this to pass. I will inform Nicholas in—"

"No one will believe you. If you try to explain this to anyone, your already tempestuous marriage will crumble. The royals will finally abandon you and cast you off as insane. Your only option is with me."

Chapter 21

Alexandra slumped forward.

"Alexandra?"

"I trusted you."

"Alexandra, please."

"You made me a murderer."

Rasputin placed his hand upon her shoulder, and she shrugged it away.

"I wish you never came," she said. "You're the devil."

A sudden gust of wind came over them, and Rasputin was gone.

*

Rasputin marched along the second-story hall to see Alexei peeking from his bedroom, his sisters crowded behind him.

"Is Mama all right?" asked Alexei.

"Stay in your room," said Rasputin. "Don't open the door for anyone but me."

Rasputin descended into the stairwell and found Kashin waiting for him on the first floor.

"Everything well, Father?"

"Fine, Commander," said Rasputin as he walked away.

Kashin pulled out a bottle of wine from behind his back. "Father Rasputin," he called.

Rasputin turned to him, focusing his eyes upon the bottle.

"I'm afraid that you and I have started off badly," said Kashin. "Allow me to make amends."

"Red, no less? How did you know?"

"I too am from Siberia and know we cannot resist a bottle of the red gremlin."

Rasputin smiled.

"Very well, lead the way. I may have a place for you yet, Commander."

"How's that?"

Rasputin placed his hand on Kashin's shoulder and patted him firmly.

Part II: Copilul Sângelui

"There's a surprise waiting for us in Saint Petersburg. You will see."

Kashin led him to the kitchen, where two other Okhrana officers sat around the dining table loaded with cakes, bread, and a pan of seared meat.

"Father Rasputin has decided to join us for a drink. Possibly some dinner too, Father? We would be honored."

"Would you?" questioned Rasputin.

Kashin cracked open the bottle and poured servings into two glasses as Rasputin sat.

"Na zdorovye!" said Kashin, raising his glass into the air.

"Na zdorovye," replied Rasputin and downed his drink.

Rasputin reached for the small cakes and devoured one after another. Kashin held a pan toward Rasputin, which held a plump beef fillet resting in succulent juices and spices.

"Care for meat, Father?"

Rasputin placed his nose to the dish.

"No garlic," said Kashin.

"I would love some," said Rasputin.

Kashin motioned to an officer, who sprung from the table and made a setting for Rasputin. He grabbed his utensils and dug into the dish. The officer returned a moment later with a pan full of roasted potatoes.

"Potatoes, Father?"

"Please."

The officer scooped a helping onto Rasputin's plate.

"Here, Father, have some more wine," said Kashin, pouring him another glass.

Rasputin gladly took the glass, swallowed the alcohol, then dug into his meat. He finished the helping in several bites and was halfway through the potatoes when Kashin shrugged toward his officers. Rasputin, too immersed in his meal, failed to notice the gesture. The officers continued to stare as Rasputin sat back, stroking his belly.

"Absolutely delicious!"

Rasputin took note of the suspicious stares cast from Kashin and his men.

"What is it, Commander?"

Chapter 21

"Uh ..." stuttered Kashin, "I'm just surprised at how quickly you devoured it."

"Oh, I thought you might be astounded by the very large volume of cyanide I just consumed. 'Enough to kill ten horses,' as you said to your men earlier."

Kashin shot up from the table with his pistol drawn. He nodded to an officer on the other side of the table, who picked up the heavy cooking pan and slammed it into Rasputin's head. He slumped over, unconscious. Kashin placed his gun back into his holster and looked down the hall to ensure no others had seen the assault.

"Take him to the basement. I'll get the rest. You," he said, pointing to one of his men. "Light the curtains and the carpeting—I want this whole damn palace up in flames."

"Yes, sir!"

The others moved around the table and dragged Rasputin out the back door.

They opened external doors to the basement and dragged Rasputin below, where they fettered him to a heavy wooden chair. Rasputin raised his head, looking dazed. One of the officers pulled his pistol from its holster and brought the butt down across Rasputin's face. At this moment, two other Okhrana officers entered the room. Rasputin looked to them.

"Officer Baylor! So good to see you again."

Baylor ignored Rasputin and handed a rope to his cohorts, who strung it over a thick rafter and let it hang just before Rasputin's face.

"Kashin says kill him," ordered Baylor.

The men flung the noose around Rasputin's neck, unfettered him from the chair, then yanked on the rope until he was bobbing about with his feet hovering just above the ground. Baylor held his gun to Rasputin.

"No more parlor tricks," he said and fired three rounds into Rasputin's chest.

Rasputin fell limp. They continued to pull on the rope for several more seconds before dropping his lifeless body onto the mud floor.

"The bonfire's burning," said Baylor, brushing his hands. "Bring him up. I'll meet you there with the boy and the women."

Part II: Copilul Sângelui

Baylor began up the stairs when a strange gurgling sound came from behind. He turned, taking in the grisly scene all at once: bony, fleshy bits and chunks of body parts strewn next to the toppled chair; another body entirely ripped in half with its mangled spine sticking into bloody entrails; and finally the third body left relatively whole save its mangled arm and missing head.

Rasputin had vanished.

Shock surged through Baylor's body, and he drew his gun, pointing it toward the basement's shadows. Certain nothing lurked in the darkness, he turned up the stairs and ran square into Rasputin, who was now standing before him. Baylor fell to the muddy floor and aimed his gun upward toward Rasputin. He shot two rounds into Rasputin's stomach.

"One left, Officer Baylor," said Rasputin.

Rasputin spread his hands wide and moved them in circles in front of Baylor, who became mesmerized. Officer Baylor slowly turned the gun toward his own head. With the barrel square in his forehead, Baylor pulled the trigger.

*

The fire had already consumed the interior of the palace's first floor by the time Kashin and his remaining men had bound Alexandra, Alexei, and his half sisters. The Okhrana men pulled them a distance from the burning palace to a larger bonfire near the barn. Kashin walked to the barn and returned with a long stock of straw. He came near the fire and recoiled from the great heat. He tried once more and lit the straw. He ran toward the barn and threw the burning straw onto the floor. Kashin watched as the wood quickly caught fire.

"The horses, they'll—"

"Shut her up!" yelled Kashin.

An Okhrana officer smacked Alexandra across the mouth and clutched her hair, pulling her closer to the fire.

"Mama!" yelled Alexei, struggling with his bonds as his sisters yelped and wept.

Alexandra continued to struggle as Commander Kashin came near.

Chapter 21

"How could you?" she yelled.

"Autocracy is criminal."

"Traitor!"

Kashin looked to the four other officers who stood behind Alexandra. He motioned to them, and they stood behind the sisters, moving down the line and shooting each in the back of the head. The frail bodies of Olga, Tatiana, Maria, and Anastasia lay slumped the dirt, blood pouring around their heads. One by one Kashin's men picked up their lifeless bodies and threw them into the fire.

Alexandra was in hysterics, sobbing on the ground. Kashin stood over her.

"Mercy?" he asked his men, while pointing his gun to Alexandra's head.

"No mercy! Burn her alive!" The men laughed.

"No mercy then," yelled Kashin.

He placed the gun back into his holster and held Alexandra by the wrists. Another officer moved in and grabbed her ankles, pulling her closer to the fire. Kashin momentarily looked back to Alexei, who had broken free of his bonds and stood hissing at them. Kashin placed Alexandra on the ground and nodded to the other officer. They drew their guns and walked forward as the remaining three officers pinned Alexandra to the dirt.

Alexei stood with his eyes closed, the bones in his face bulging outward as fangs began to grow from his jowls.

"What the hell is wrong with him?" asked the officer.

Kashin shrugged his shoulders, then whacked Alexei across the forehead, knocking the boy unconscious. Alexandra screamed, and Kashin turned to see the officer who had just been standing next to him fall to the dirt, headless.

"Dear God!" screamed Kashin, throwing his hands over his face.

The three officers pinning Alexandra released her and ran.

Alexandra turned away and closed her eyes as gurgling and screams filled the air. The horrific commotion stopped, and fear struck her heart as she looked to see Rasputin as a blood-soaked vampire hulking over the butchered bodies. All of them were dead save Kashin, who lay on the ground, trying to shove his entrails back inside his torn stomach. He coughed up several mouthfuls of blood and fell limp.

Alexandra loosened her fetters and ran toward Alexei. The boy lay unconscious in the dirt with a pronounced lump in the middle of his forehead. Alexandra cried and held him close, rocking back and forth.

Rasputin stood over them.

"They murdered the girls. The savages!" she screamed, looking to their remains burning in the fire. "Save Alexei, please!"

Rasputin waved his clawed hand over Alexei's face.

"Awake, child," he said.

Alexei's eyes shot open, and the lump on his forehead slowly disappeared. He looked around at the carnage, seemingly unaffected by it. "Where's Sana?" he asked.

Rasputin motioned toward the palace as the fire engulfed its façade. Alexei watched the flames consume the charred skeleton of the estate as heavy oak beams crashed to the ground. He squinted with angry black eyes for a moment, then leapt upward into the night. Alexandra gasped at the sight of Alexei shooting into the air.

She looked to Rasputin, backing away from him.

"Thank you for saving my son," she said.

Rasputin ignored her and followed after Alexei.

Alexandra's eyes scanned the night sky for a trace of Alexei when she became distracted by horse whinnies. Behind her, the burning barn started to crumble in upon the trapped horses. She ran inside beyond the flames. The intense heat and smoke overwhelmed her, yet she trudged to each stall and freed the horses. She led them to the opposite side of the barn where the fire had not spread, and they bolted into the night.

Alexandra stumbled from the barn, coughing and trying to rub the smoke from her eyes. She continued along the dirt road that led from the estate, occasionally turning to watch the sprawl burn to the ground. She thought to her beloved surrogate daughters and felt that a knife had been stuck into her heart. Alexandra sank to the cold earth and sobbed—her world had finally collapsed. From above, she heard Alexei calling for her. She looked upward.

"Come with us, Mama."

"Alexei, I can't," she yelled, scanning the sky. "I can't see you."

Chapter 21

From the depths of the night, a dark figure dipped toward her—a moment later she was lifted from the ground, falling unconscious in Rasputin's grasp.

Six hours later, Rasputin, Alexei, and Alexandra were aboard the imperial steam train and en route back to Saint Petersburg. Alexei was already fast asleep when Rasputin tucked him into bed. He then came to Alexandra, who was lying on a plush sofa.

"I'm sorry for the loss of your daughters," he began.

"Stop," she replied, turning away from him. "We must send a telegram to Nicholas—inform him of Kashin's betrayal."

"We'll be back in less than thirty-six hours," said Rasputin. "We will inform him of these dire events then."

"And then what? You'll have him murdered? I wish you would go."

Rasputin waved his hand over her head. "Sleep," he said, and her body fell limp.

*

Felix and Denis arrived at Denis's home late on the thirteenth and slept until midmorning. When Felix finally awoke, his body ached in places he'd been unaware had muscle. He pulled himself gently from a large blackwood couch in Denis's sitting room. Denis entered the room and threw a newspaper on his stomach.

"The Germans have taken Bucharest," said Denis.

Felix flipped over the newspaper and looked to the featured article: "Bucharest Falls."

"We're screwed," said Felix.

"We've *been* screwed."

Felix shot Denis a scowl.

Denis shrugged his shoulders. "No sense in worrying now. We're leaving immediately."

Denis left the room, and Felix continued to thumb through the newspaper.

A few minutes passed, and a sudden ding filled the room as Denis's typewriter sprung into action. Felix was stunned to see it typing all by itself.

Part II: Copilul Sângelui

"Denis?" he called.

Denis limped into the room, his immediate focus being the typewriter as it continued to move on its own.

"What's happening?" asked Felix.

"It's how I communicate with Rurik. Our seers send me messages telepathically. How do you think I got the map to Loch Dracul?"

"Just a bit shocking to see it in person, I suppose," said Felix.

After a few lines of text, the typewriter began inserting a variety of characters, slowly building out a picture of a man's face.

Denis watched it for a short moment before it stopped. He pulled the paper from the typewriter to inspect it.

> It is with the boy. You must return immediately. Here is the monster we face. —Rurik.

The illustration below the text was of a bearded man with a strong brow and terrible gleam in his eye.

Felix leaned in to view the message. "Son of a bitch!"

"What?"

"This is him!" yelled Felix, thrusting his finger to the illustration. "The Sleepwalker! He was in the room the night my fiancée was murdered."

Denis placed the paper upon the table, bit his thumbnail, and studied the illustration. He rubbed his false arm as the memory of his duel with Rasputin flashed to his mind. "And so it is."

"He's with Alexei!" yelled Felix and swatted the paper from the table.

"I told you, Felix. We failed. Fate has already chosen the outcome."

Felix stood back and kicked the table. "We're out in the middle of nowhere! I could have been there."

Denis thrust his chest into Felix. "And you'd be dead."

"What's the difference? I'll be dead in two days anyway." Felix sunk into a chair.

"You'll be dead the next time you kick furniture in my home." Denis corrected the table.

Felix looked to him. "I'm sorry, Denis."

Chapter 21

"It's fine."

"This whole thing happened right underneath my nose. I let it happen."

Denis patted him on the shoulder. "Let's pack our things. You can pout later."

*

Denis led Felix to the barn on the perimeter of his property just before noon. Both men were bundled in heavy fur and leather jackets.

"I finally get to see this airplane of yours?"

"*Airplanes*, my friend. I have several."

Denis opened the barn door and Felix assisted with the other side. The face of an Airco DH.4 propeller stared back at them. Felix noticed that several other planes sat behind this one.

"I'm not getting inside that thing. I can't stand small spaces."

"The seat is small, but the sky is big. You'll be fine." He hobbled past Felix. "It's the newest, fastest plane in the world."

"Can you fly it? With your—"

"Your main concern is keeping warm."

Felix blew out a long breath, taking in the plane's streamlined beauty. "How'd you get it?"

Denis turned to him. "When you know all the dirty little secrets about the elite on several continents…lots of interesting things just show up on your doorstep."

Denis walked to the plane as Felix stood at the barn's threshold.

"How long?"

Denis stroked his mustache. "Well, it'll do one hundred knots comfortably. If we're lucky? Twelve to fourteen hours of air time. Close to two days with stops and rest. Flying at night is not an option. I have secured several airfields along the way that will assist in refueling and rest."

Felix looked again to Denis. "How long have you been planning this?"

"Long time," said Denis.

"We'll get shot down, you know."

Part II: Copilul Sângelui

"Probably," said Denis with a smile. He threw Felix a pair of goggles. "Hop in."

*

December 16, 1916 (OS), 5:02 a.m.

Minister Makarov lay upon his narrow prison bed in the small, single-person cell. It had been six days since his incarceration. The boredom was more unbearable than the permeating cold. His only entertainment was the endless parade of imprisoned Bolsheviks marched by his cell door and the occasional explosion heard off in the distance.

He walked to the slim window and pressed his fingers to the reinforced glass. He wiped the frost from the window and stared at the starless sky, momentarily watching the wispy clouds pass against the darkness.

Today.

Makarov fell back in bed and slung his arm over his face. He drifted in and out of sleep for another thirty minutes, eventually rolling to his side and peering out the cell door. His eyes moved to the shadowy corner of the cell—something was there with him. Makarov sat up and placed his boots upon the floor while squinting toward the far corner.

He fell to his knees.

"Is it time?"

Rasputin towered over him.

"I will need you this evening after Nicholas is killed," he said. "But first you will bow to me as your Stăpân. Do you swear allegiance? Our meeting on top of the Duma left me … with doubts."

Makarov reached to Rasputin's hand and pulled it to his mouth. He planted a firm kiss on his knuckles.

"My actions were for our safety. My anger … my crassness, only frustration. I am in awe of your precision in these matters … in honor of your success, I submit myself unto you, Stăpân. I beg you—grant me eternal life!"

Rasputin stood over him, staring into Makarov's eyes.

Chapter 21

"Are you not satisfied with my duties, Stăpân? I beg that you are."

"You have performed flawlessly," said Rasputin.

"Thank you. Praise to you."

Makarov held Rasputin's wrist once more, pulling it to his face. He rubbed the back of Rasputin's hand against his cheek for a moment, relishing the touch.

"Rise," said Rasputin.

Makarov stood and looked to Rasputin. He closed his eyes and slowly spun around, exposing the cervical portion of his neck. Rasputin leaned in and sunk his fangs deep into Makarov's atlas vertebra. Intense pleasure surged through Makarov's spine, and Rasputin wrapped his forearm around him as his legs gave way. A short moment later, Makarov was alone, lying back in bed with a gaping bite wound at the back of his neck.

December 16, 1916 (OS), 6:12 a.m.

Dmitri knelt before a handsome mahogany altar in his darkened study. The Sfânta Biblie al Strigoiului Viu lay before him. He folded his hands close to his face and prayed as his knuckles grew white.

For victory, oh Darkness. I pray unto thee. I give you my life, my soul—yours eternally. Grant me—

A presence in the room startled him. Dmitri opened his eyes.

"I thought you retreated to Livadia," he said, never taking his eyes from the soft candlelight reflecting from the bible's pages.

"Everything unfolded as the seers predicted. Alexandra's train is set to arrive back shortly. Everything is in place."

Rasputin stood behind him and placed his cold, lean fingers on Dmitri's back. He reached to Rasputin's hand and gripped it, placing his cheek on Rasputin's clammy skin.

"I surrender myself to you, Stăpân."

Dmitri leaned forward, exposing his cervical vertebrae.

"Will you obey?"

"With absolute assent."

Rasputin patted his shoulders.

"You will travel to Bucharest. Vondling has gone rogue. You must rein him in and take control of our operations there. And—"

Part II: Copilul Sângelui

"But I ... I must be here. I pray I may witness the Nosfer—"

"Very well. I must return to Alexandra before my absence is noticed. I will deal with you later," said Rasputin as he turned and took a few intent steps toward the window.

"Stăpân, please. Wait! I misspoke."

Rasputin stopped. Dmitri fell to his knees and raised his hands.

"Forgive my insolence." He bowed and pulled down his collar, exposing the back of his neck. Rasputin stood behind him.

"You will wake in Bucharest." He asserted his grip on Dmitri's shoulders. "If you fail, do not return."

"Yes, Stăpân."

Rasputin bit into Dmitri's neck, injecting venom deep into his spinal fluid.

PART III:
SFÂRŞITUL LUMII

Chapter 22

Part III: Sfârşitul Lumii

22

СОВЕРШЕННО СЕКРЕТНО [TOP SECRET]
"No mercy unto man. For man is the enemy
of all things living and dead."
—Vlad Drăculea, Book of Governance 11:16,
Sfânta Biblie al Strigoiului Viu, 1456.
[Holy Bible of the Living Vampiric Witch]

December 16, 1916 (OS), 7:19 a.m.

The Room of Coins was dark save a warm bubble of light at its center. Nicholas sat at his slim desk, a wide-eyed impatient expression about his face. He stared at Prime Minister Trepov, then to several cabinet advisors seated in front of him. A force of thirty soldiers and ten Okhrana stood at attention along the shadowy perimeter of the hall.

"Palace Square is impregnable as of 4:13 this morning," began General Dragunov. "All bridges along the Neva are drawn. No resistance from the north can reach us. Snipers on all bridges along the waterway if they try."

"Very well," said Nicholas.

"Most of Nevsky Prospekt is under control. At sunrise we move forward street by street, push resistance south past the Fontanka. Central Saint Petersburg will be completely impregnable by sundown."

Gunfire echoed through the hall, followed by a white flash from a distant explosion. Nicholas blinked repeatedly, appearing annoyed. "Are the barricades complete?"

"All major roadways and railways have been sectioned off. I have also ordered riflemen scattered throughout the countryside and

Chapter 22

along the ridgeways to the east and south to eliminate anyone fleeing by non-conventional means. The snipers will remain positioned at various points around the city until commanded otherwise."

"Excellent work, General," said Nicholas.

"Emperor," said Trepov. "May I ask the strategy behind not allowing anyone to flee?"

"I spoke with Father Rasputin on the telephone. He foresaw victory if we didn't allow anyone to flee Saint Petersburg."

"Very well," said Trepov. "Although he's only a starets. Certainly—"

"Certainly I trust Father Rasputin's vision implicitly. He has saved my family's life."

"My Lord," said Trepov, bowing slightly.

"General," said Nicholas. "What of the Octobrists? Will they lend me their support?"

"Emperor, if I may speak freely."

"I insist."

"The right is infuriated by Makarov's imprisonment. I have substantial influence and will be able to keep them from splintering until we destroy the Bolsheviks. I am concerned about the party's actions if Makarov is kept in prison without trial."

"I promise you, General, keep the Octobrists and Nationalists loyal to me, and I will reward you a thousandfold after the Bolsheviks are quashed."

Dragunov nodded.

Nicholas smiled at him, and his eyes suddenly darted to the distance.

"Father Rasputin!" he yelled and stood at once.

Rasputin strode through the Room of Coins with Alexei limp in his arms. A soldier followed, carrying Alexandra's unconscious body.

"My family!" Nicholas ran toward them, noticing Alexei had pronounced cheekbones. "Is he ill?"

"He is, Emperor."

"Place her on the sofa, gently," said Nicholas, looking to the soldier carrying Alexandra. "Where are the girls?"

Part III: Sfârșitul Lumii

"The Okhrana, Emperor," began Rasputin. "They attempted to kill us. Burned down the estate, murdered Sana and your daughters."

Nicholas held his hands to his heart. His knees became weak and he reached to the floor, finally slumping upon the cool marble. "My innocent girls," he said, shaking his head. He looked to Rasputin with anger in his eyes. "Where is Commander Kashin?"

"He orchestrated it."

Nicholas appeared dazed, and held his fist to his mouth.

Rasputin walked to the sofa and placed Alexei next to Alexandra. Nicholas, aware his cabinet members were watching him, rose from the floor and composed himself. He walked to the sofa and held Alexandra's hand. "Father, how is it you have returned? I wasn't informed. The railways are supposedly barricaded." Nicholas cast a scornful glance to Dragunov. "How did you—"

"After we were attacked, we departed immediately. I felt it wise to keep radio silence until our safe return. I sensed there were more agents out to kill us."

Nicholas nodded, appearing defeated. "You did the right thing." He turned his attention back to Alexandra and Alexei as Trepov neared.

"What's wrong with them?" asked Trepov.

"They've both grown extremely ill. I believe from the shock," said Rasputin. "Alexei is in dire need of a blood transfusion."

"My poor Alexandra," said Nicholas, kneeling to her and caressing her face. "Everyone, I must have some privacy with Father Rasputin."

Rasputin waited until they were out of earshot, then knelt to Nicholas.

"What ails them, Father?"

"I can cure them both, but you will be required to obey me in all I say."

"Whatever it takes, I will give my life for them."

Rasputin nodded. "Good ... we must wait until after dark."

Nicholas was alarmed. "I don't understand ... my family is dying. We must help them now."

"Emperor. God has spoken to me. If you abide, I can save them."

Chapter 22

Rasputin stood. They stared into each other's eyes until Nicholas looked away.

"They need rest," said Rasputin. "For now, my Emperor, you must stand strong. Attend to your plans. See to it your armies draw the Bolsheviks into the heart of the city. When Alexei wakes, I will cure him and Alexandra. And victory will shine upon us from the skies above."

"Thank you, Father," said Nicholas, embracing Rasputin. "You are our savior."

He let go the embrace and returned to his cabinet members.

*

СОВЕРШЕННО СЕКРЕТНО [TOP SECRET]
Clipping from the Bucharest *Adevărul*:

Flash Riot Ravages Bucharest

Bucharest, Dec. 16—Unexplained riots erupted in Bucharest on the evening of December 15, causing its worst destruction since the 1847 fires consumed a third of the city. Little is known about the perpetrators or the cause. During the first several hours, the revolt was thought to be targeted at the German occupying forces, but it soon victimized inhabitants across all areas of the city.

The havoc erupted promptly after dusk, beginning in Romanian police precincts and German militia depots. No officials could be reached for comment; however, it has been reported that most police precincts and military posts in Bucharest and the surrounding provinces have been destroyed. A large number of police and soldiers are missing.

A peculiar phenomenon surrounding the riots was their cessation promptly at dawn, and the rioters vanishing from the city streets. No perpetrators have been apprehended, and much of Bucharest is still burning.

A few survivors have reported mangled and gored bodies littered throughout the streets along with the smell of burning flesh hanging heavy in the air. Reports state

Part III: Sfârşitul Lumii

tens of thousands of citizens are fleeing the city, creating a dire refugee situation. Citizens who are staying have begun boarding themselves inside churches and mosques.

[Cont. A-10]

*

December 16, 1916 (OS), afternoon

Felix and Denis arrived near the outskirts of Saint Petersburg at 3:19 p.m. They had spent the previous forty-eight hours on what Felix would come to realize was the most harrowing trip of his life. Despite their precautions to fight the cold—no exposed skin, layers of animal fur draped over their bodies, and Denis's low-altitude flight patterns—both men suffered from near hypothermia by the time they reached Saint Petersburg. Felix swore his heart might stop. Many times during the flight, he looked to the barren, snow-patched landscape below and wondered if a train full of vampires was preferable.

Denis landed near a farm about sixteen kilometers south of Saint Petersburg and convinced the farmer to trade him his diesel passenger truck and some dried meats for the plane. Felix thought it an audacious maneuver.

Still shivering as they approached the city outskirts, they came upon a large military encampment.

"What about our canisters?"

"Say they're for gardening," said Denis.

"In the dead of winter. Great. Best to say we're exterminators."

A dour officer motioned them to stop. Eight soldiers surrounded the vehicle—all of them holding bolt-action rifles across their chests.

"State your purpose."

"We're meeting my brother."

The officer looked them over, noticing Denis's gas canisters.

"What are the canisters for?"

"Oh," began Denis. "We're exterminators."

The officer squinted.

"These are bug spray. My poor brother has roaches." Denis reached around with his hand and tapped the nozzle.

Chapter 22

The officer scrunched his face and looked to Felix, who smiled and nodded.

"Cockroaches in winter? Do you think me stupid?" asked the officer.

Denis paused. "My brother lives … poorly. He's a filthy man."

The officer looked them over for another moment. "And you are aware of the riots?"

"Yes, we know."

"And you still want in?"

"Yes."

"We cannot guarantee your safety. Once you enter, we are on strict orders not to let anyone out of the city. This is a one-way pass."

"Understood."

"Proceed." The soldier motioned to the empty road ahead.

Denis pressed the gas, and the truck clanked along.

"Hard to believe he accepted bug spray," said Felix, shaking his head.

"I'm not certain he really cared. This is strange," said Denis, peering into the rearview mirror.

"It's strange they're letting people in but not out," said Felix. "You'd think it would be the other way around."

"For certain."

Denis peered again into the side mirror and watched the soldiers as they loitered about, kicking stones and conversing with one another. "They seem unusually relaxed."

Felix looked through the back window and shrugged.

They drove along the dirt road for a few miles until reaching some low-lying buildings just outside Saint Petersburg. Denis pulled the truck to the roadside and stopped the engine.

"What are you doing?"

"Walking," said Denis.

Felix appeared surprised.

"I'm not driving us into the middle of a riot zone. Nobody knows whose side we're on."

Felix considered the statement as Denis exited the truck. He moved to the cargo bay and pulled out his canvas satchel. After another moment, Felix followed him.

Part III: Sfârşitul Lumii

"How do you suppose we find Rurik?" asked Felix, staring at the Saint Petersburg skyline.

"His apartment is about two kilometers from here—we'll start there. Best to use side streets. I don't want to be caught in the open for any reason."

"Agreed."

*

Denis and Felix slipped undetected through the back streets of Saint Petersburg. They were hindered only by the intermittent spatter of gunfire and echoes of militiamen dashing between city blocks, and Denis's several long breaks to ease the chafing and soreness of his leg.

It was nearly dusk when they reached Rurik's home, a plain, multilevel apartment complex a few blocks from the city morgue. Denis started up the stairs, followed by Felix. The building was quiet.

Felix scurried up three flights and waited for Denis to make his way. They came to a short hallway extending to the right. Denis limped to Rurik's door and noticed it was ajar. He shook his head toward Felix.

"This could be grim." Denis knocked on the door. "Rurik?"

He knocked once more, then pushed on the door. They entered the midsized apartment to find it ransacked.

"Rurik?"

Felix walked down a hallway, then into Rurik's small bedroom. Every piece of furniture had been overturned or destroyed. "Bedroom's the same," yelled Felix.

He walked back to the living room. Denis was busy sorting through spilled papers.

"Vampires?"

"I don't know," said Denis, shaking his head. "Burglary is odd behavior for the undead."

Felix crouched at the window and looked out onto the fire escape. He heard a small explosion in the distance and saw a plume of black smoke rise behind a squat building at the end of the block.

Chapter 22

Several men ran around the corner and up the street just as ten of the tsar's soldiers appeared at the intersection and gunned them down. The soldiers yelled among themselves, then sprinted toward the fallen bodies.

Felix stood back from the window and listened as the soldiers opened fire once more on the limp bodies. Denis peered over his shoulder, watching the soldiers shuffle down the block.

"That is why we're sticking to side streets."

"This is a side street."

Felix righted an overturned chair and sat in it. "Do you think Rurik would still carry his penchant for vodka in times like these?"

Denis smiled. "I imagine it would increase."

Felix shot from the chair. "Follow me."

*

Nighttime had settled over the city when they arrived outside the Imperial Pub. A large sign reading "Closed" hung across its front door.

"There goes that idea," said Felix.

Denis looked more closely to see a light emanating from behind the stained glass. He moved to the door and opened it slightly, peeking into the crack. The door flung open, and two uniformed men pounced on him. Several others emerged and wrestled Felix to the ground as handcuffs were clasped upon him. Three police stood over them with guns drawn while two others searched through Denis's coat pockets.

"No papers!"

Another officer searched Felix.

"Same."

"Who are you?" demanded the commanding officer.

"We're exterminators."

"I am Prince Felix Yusupov," said Felix, with an air of command in his voice. "Unbind me immediately."

The officers laughed.

"You're lucky we don't shoot you in the back," said the commanding officer. "Search their bags."

Part III: Sfârșitul Lumii

Two officers dumped the contents of their canvas satchels onto the street.

"What the hell are these?" said one of them as blackwood stakes and the rest of their equipment clanked upon the cobblestones.

The officer subduing Denis rapped a baton on his gas canisters. "Boss, looks like they have mustard gas."

"Look at these," said a policeman, holding up a gas mask and machete.

"Are you Bolsheviks?" yelled the commanding officer.

"No sir," said Denis. "We're scientists."

"I thought you said you were a prince," said the officer, kicking Felix in the gut.

A few more police exited the pub with mugs of ale in their hands.

"Bring me my beer," said the commander. A moment later he stood with his stout in one hand and a lit a cigarette in the other.

"What should we do with them?" asked an officer. "That one's only got an arm and a leg."

"Run them in," said the commander. "I don't want to see them coming back at us later tonight. Hold on … Hedrina!"

He looked back into the pub until Hedrina emerged at the door.

"You know either of these men?"

She peered down to them. "Rurik?" Her face brightened, and she knelt to Denis until she saw the burned portion of his face. She gasped. "Sorry, I thought you were someone else."

"Rurik's my twin."

"Oh! How wonderful. He's my best patron … I was—"

"Enough," yelled the commander.

Hedrina stood and shook her head. "I recognize the other—he was in here with Rurik not too long ago."

"They Bolsheviks?"

"No, sir. Not Rurik anyway. He's just a hardworking fellow, so far as I know."

The commander stood over Denis and Felix for another moment. "Run them in anyway."

Three police moved in and led them away.

"Hedrina," shouted Felix. "Have you seen Rurik?"

Chapter 22

She shook her head. "Not for few days. He came in one night. Seemed really spooked. Drank a bunch, then left without saying goodbye."

Denis and Felix were led down the block to an unmarked car and shoved in the back.

"Keep your heads down, boys. We're likely to get shot at." The policeman in the passenger seat cocked his rifle, holding it in his lap as they drove off.

*

Hedrina and the remaining officers watched as the car disappeared from view.

"Commander? How much longer you suppose the Metropolitan Police will use my pub as a command post?"

"Well, dear, you're no longer talking to police. We're deputized Russian army now, and we're keeping your ale safe from the wretched specter of communism. Now how about another?"

He patted her on the ass as she walked inside. The other officers followed, eager for more complimentary stout.

*

Denis and Felix were stripped of their possessions and taken to a cellblock consisting mostly of smaller, single-person cells. Toward the block's end was a larger conjoined cell, brimming with rough and haggard inmates. Denis hopped down the hall with his right arm wrapped around Felix for support—the police had confiscated both his fake limbs.

"Look," said Felix. "Just tell Petrov who I am. He knows—"

The officer shoved him in the group cell, followed by Denis, who fell to the floor. The bars clanked behind them.

"Turn around," ordered the officer.

Felix turned his back to the bars, and the officer removed his handcuffs. Upon removal of his fetters, Felix bent down and assisted Denis from the floor. As he took in the rest of the cell, Felix noticed an inmate jump up from the floor and run to them.

Part III: Sfârşitul Lumii

"Felix!"

Rurik's face was so badly bruised that Felix barely recognized him. Rurik greeted him with a warm hug and looked to his brother, who was leaning against the cell bars.

"Denis! I can't believe it's you!"

He reached to hug Denis, who deflected him.

"Nice to see you too, brother," said Rurik flatly.

The three stood for a moment as the rest of the inmates' eyes moved upon them—bruised and dirty faces were everywhere.

"Mostly Bolsheviks," whispered Rurik.

Felix looked to him. "What happened to your face?"

"I was beaten by the police. Here, sit."

The three sat near the bars. Rurik reached his hands to each man's shoulder, squeezing them tightly. "It is so good to see you both! A miracle we're all here."

Denis forced a half smirk. "So why were you beaten by the police?"

"Oh," began Rurik. "Well, after I sent Denis that letter, I was attacked by a female vampire the Sleepwalker had slipped into the morgue. Which I staked, by the way." He pointed his thumbs to his chest in a self-congratulatory fashion. "And after the attack, I realized ... hey, I'm in big trouble ... I needed a safer place. I went for some vodka, and then it occurred to me—what's safer than jail? So I stashed my equipment, then walked to town and decked a policeman!"

Rurik seemed disheartened by their silence.

"I punched a policeman ... in the mouth!"

"Why did you do that?" questioned Denis.

"To get in jail. Where it's safe."

The three were quiet.

"Are you still drunk?" asked Felix.

Rurik smiled. "A bit," he said, pulling a flask from his pocket.

"How'd you get that in here? Put it away," said Felix, looking down the block to see if any guards had noticed.

"This place where you stashed your things, is it big enough to fit a person?" asked Denis.

"Sure, it's big enough for ten people."

Chapter 22

"Why didn't you stay there?"

Rurik considered the question. "Well, now that you mention it. I … well … hey! I was drunk, so what? We're all here now!"

Rurik reached in once more and embraced them both. Denis caught Felix's eyes.

"I got the brains too," he said.

They sat huddled together. Felix occasionally looked behind him to see if any other inmates were listening. Nobody appeared bothered.

Felix looked to Rurik. "So the Sleepwalker is with the royals. Everything he needs is before him. I want to kill him."

"We must wait out the revolt," said Rurik. "It's not safe anywhere but here."

"That's not good enough. Isn't Petrov trying to hide the Sleepwalker murders from the royals?" asked Felix.

"Yes. He felt it was embarrassing to the police."

"Well, what if we could use him to get close to the Sleepwalker? Just explain who I am and what we know, except for the vampire part. We'll tell him he can nab the Sleepwalker and be a hero to the tsar."

"That's a terrible plan—you're wanted for murder," said Denis.

"Don't forget who I am. Petrov's certain to take that into account. The man who interrogated me had nothing to do with the police. I'm sure of it. I believe Petrov will listen."

"Stupid," said Denis.

"That's it? Stupid? I'm racking my brain here, and you two are looking at me like a couple of dimwits!"

"Easy, Felix," said Rurik. "It's not wise. Even if Petrov goes for it, the Sleepwalker will kill him. Then it won't take long for him to find us sitting nice and confined in this cell."

"Not if I'm there."

Denis and Rurik laughed.

"What?"

"You can't be serious," said Rurik. "It's too powerful for you."

"I survived multiple vampire attacks on the train to Bucharest."

"You did?"

"He blew up Gara de Nord in the process," said Denis.

Part III: Sfârşitul Lumii

"Incredible! I'm so proud of you, Felix," said Rurik, patting his shoulder.

"Keep your voice down," said Felix. "Yes, but it wasn't my fault. Listen, up front we have canteens filled with giant hogweed sap, the gas canisters, and blackwood stakes."

Denis shook his head. "It's foolish. You'll never get close to him."

"Bet me."

Felix stood up, removed his belt, and started banging his buckle against the bars.

"Hey! Officer! Here. Down here!"

The rattling continued until a policeman came to the bars.

"What's the problem?"

"Officer, it's imperative that you put me in touch with Constable Petrov. The lives of the royal family depend on it."

The officer glared at him.

"Officer, please. If you do not help me, the blood of the tsar will be on your hands."

Rurik stood and whispered into Felix's ear. "This is very dangerous. You're in a cell full of the tsar's enemies—"

"Stop," said Felix, looking back to Rurik. "I've done it your way long enough." He turned to the policeman. "Officer, I am Prince Felix Yusupov. I am wanted for a murder I did not commit. Tell Petrov who I am. Tell him I can prove it all and that I will make him a hero. The royal family is in grave danger. I beg you."

The officer stared at Felix with an obvious sneer. "Are you certain?"

"Yes, tell Petrov. Tell him the Sleepwalker is a guest at the Winter Palace. Tell him he murdered my fiancée, Irina Alexandrovna, and I was framed for it. He'll know from the state of the bodies that I couldn't have committed the crime. Tell him the Sleepwalker plans to murder the royal family. You must help me. Think of the tsarevich. Can you live with the murder of a little boy?"

The officer stared at him for another moment. "Wait here," he said, then moved down the cellblock.

Felix sat with his back to the rest of the inmates. Denis leaned into him. "That is the stupidest thing you could have done. You're

Chapter 22

surrounded by men who want the tsar dead, and you're shouting off about being royalty!"

"Shut up, Denis."

Denis fanned his hand toward Felix and turned his back. Rurik slid closer.

"He's right, Felix," whispered Rurik. "This is very dangerous. We'll be out in—"

"Today's the sixteenth, Rurik. This is the day. The Sleepwalker has everything he needs at his fingertips. You're the one always saying we have to act quickly. Now you want to wait?"

"Felix—"

"This is the only shot we have, damn it. I won't let this pass."

Rurik shrugged. Felix stood and faced the bars.

"Felix?"

"Skip it."

Felix heard the cellblock open, followed by the sound of officious wooden heels clicking on the cement floor. A moment later, the policeman returned with a red-faced officer who glared into the cell.

"Constable Petrov?"

"Prince Felix, I presume."

"It's me."

Petrov looked him over, then noticed Rurik. "Kozlov. You sober up yet?"

"Mostly," said Rurik.

Petrov gave him a disdainful glance, then let out an annoyed sigh. "This situation is a nightmare. I have Bolsheviks running rampant, the city coroner beating police, and now a wanted murderer in my jail. What am I supposed to do with this nonsense?"

"Let me out," said Felix. "Rurik can vouch for me."

"Him?" yelled Petrov. "A drunk who assaulted one of my officers? Not a very strong character witness."

"The lives of the royal family are in your hands," said Felix. "At least let me out so we may talk. The Sleepwalker is a guest at the Winter Palace. I can give you all the proof you need. Help me and you'll be a hero to all of Russia."

Part III: Sfârşitul Lumii

Petrov was silent. "Is it the starets? From the newspapers? He's a new guest at the palace."

"Yes. It is him."

Petrov nodded and turned away. "We can handle it."

"Constable, Constable! You can't do it alone. You'll need my help."

"What are you doing?" interjected Rurik.

"You've seen the bodies of his victims," yelled Felix. "He'll do the same to you without my help."

Petrov stopped. He leaned toward the officer and mumbled a few words. Petrov continued down the hall, and the policeman returned to the cell. He pulled Felix out and locked the door.

Denis and Rurik stood at the bars.

"Felix! Stop! You cannot do this," yelled Denis.

"Felix, I beg you," beckoned Rurik. "He'll rip you to bits. Take your own advice, remember the bodies. He'll do the same to you!"

"Look at me, Felix," shouted Denis, extending his nub through the bars. "I'm half a man thanks to this killer!"

The cellblock door slammed closed, silencing them. Denis gripped his hand tightly around a bar, squeezing it until his knuckles turned white. Rurik slumped to the floor with his head in his palms.

Denis looked to Rurik. "This is dire," he said and hung his head.

*

Denis stood on his leg, leaning against the bars for nearly an hour with a lost, listless expression on his face. He looked to the ceiling where the bars met the plaster. He leaned heavily on the bars for a second, then released, noticing the corrosion around the paint give ever so slightly. He turned to the other prisoners.

"Gentlemen, how many of you would like to break free?"

*

Felix sat in a varnished wood chair at the front of Petrov's desk.

"And that is how I believe it is him," said Felix. "There is cause. Certainly you can arrest him."

Chapter 22

Petrov twirled his tongue about inside his cheek. "Circumstantial evidence at best. You've tied him to none of the murders. The only coincidence is they started around the time he apparently came to Saint Petersburg. I need more."

"But I saw him in the room when Irina was murdered. Yes, I was drugged, but I'll never forget that gleam in his eye."

"As much as I'd like to—unfortunately I cannot simply arrest people with gleams in their eye. I need evidence."

"Constable. Martial law has been declared. Do you not have the right to detain anyone you suspect might be a threat to the royal family?"

"I do. But the protocol is messy. This is cause for sensation if Grand Duke Pavlovich is involved."

"No worse than having me implicated."

Petrov nodded. "Rasputin—as he is named in the papers—is an official guest of the royal family. Technically I must have it approved by Okhrana, who would handle the arrest. But …"

"But?"

"As you stated, since the Bolshevik revolts, the Metropolitan Police are deputized into the tsar's militia. And I do have the right to apprehend anyone I suspect a threat to the royal family."

Felix slammed his palm onto the desk. "Then let's go!"

Petrov curled his chin and shook his head.

"Constable. You're going to be a hero for this. It's easy. We take forty of your best men and move in. Surely we can overpower him. I'll even direct it, and you can stand outside and take credit for everything. Think about it! Once it's proved that you apprehended the Sleepwalker and cleared my name …"

Petrov leaned in.

"Imagine the praise. Not just Russia. You'll be internationally famous—a hero who made history. I'll even reward you. Name your price."

Petrov nodded. "You'll come with us? As a representative of the imperial court?"

"Yes, you merely have to stand in the room and look angry and official. I'll cuff him myself."

"And I can take credit for it?"

Part III: Sfârşitul Lumii

"You can have a sworn statement typed before we leave. I'll sign it."

"I'd like that," said Petrov with a big smile on his face.

"It's yours. There's just one small thing."

"Tell me."

"When I was arrested, I had a large canvas satchel. I'll need to take that with me."

"Fine," said Petrov.

"And there was also a back harness with some gas canisters that I'll need."

Petrov cocked his eye. "I don't think so, Prince Felix. That sounds—"

"The satchel's great then … How long will it take to wrangle the men?"

"Twenty minutes."

Chapter 23

Part III: Sfârşitul Lumii

23

December 16, 1916 (OS), night

Felix and Petrov exited the Metropolitan Police Station. Outside, a mass of forty heavily armed officers stood in front of fifteen police automobiles and wagons. They walked to an automobile as its exhaust rose into the frigid night. Just as they climbed inside the car, Petrov looked to the full moon and noticed several large shadows cross it.

"Did you see that?"

"What?" questioned Felix.

"Up there. Giant shadows. Big birds or something."

Felix looked up to the moonlight. "I don't see anything."

Petrov looked upward once more. He shrugged and jumped into the back seat. He ordered the driver to go, and they were off to the Winter Palace.

*

The police convoy sped through central Saint Petersburg. With sirens blaring, they cut directly through the barricades across Palace Square and drove right to the foot of the Winter Palace. The automobiles rounded the circular driveway and parked in a long, neat row. Petrov and Felix exited their vehicle, and the remaining officers waited for Petrov to signal the ascent.

"Draw your weapons, men," he yelled as they marched toward the palace's south entrance.

Petrov was stopped by a military officer backed by a surly crew of soldiers.

Chapter 23

"What's your business, Constable?"

"I am here to place Father Grigori Rasputin under arrest."

"I cannot allow you to pass," said the officer.

Petrov nearly thrust his chest into him.

"I have an official from the royal court," he said, motioning to Felix. "And suspicion to believe Rasputin is a grave threat to the royal family. Under martial law you are ordered to stand down and allow me passage or you will be tried for treason."

The soldier stepped aside, and they continued up the stairs toward the entrance of the Winter Palace. The force of forty police officers entered the grand lobby and moved toward the east wing. They were greeted by a royal liaison who walked with them as they climbed the Jordan Staircase.

"Constable, may I be of assistance?"

"We believe Father Rasputin is a grave danger to the royal family. Can you direct us to his location?"

"Father Rasputin has just risen. I believe he is still in his study. Is this arrest sanctioned by the tsar?"

"Of course it is," said Petrov, nearly yelling.

The liaison bowed and led the way.

The force marched down the sweeping, ornate halls in single file. As they marched toward Rasputin's quarters, servants poked their heads into the hallway and ducked away, sensing their deliberate intent. The liaison led them to a nondescript door, then bowed to Petrov.

"This is it," he said and shuffled away.

Petrov looked to Felix. "You ready?"

Felix appeared agitated. "You're goddamn right."

Petrov nodded and turned to his troop. "I want fifteen of you in with us. The rest wait here, guns drawn. If you hear the slightest bump, I want you inside immediately."

The men nodded down the line.

Petrov turned to the door and motioned to two burly policemen. "Kick it down on three."

"Wait," replied Felix.

Felix leaned in and turned the handle—the door creaked open. He turned to speak to Petrov and was almost knocked over by the

Part III: Sfârșitul Lumii

force of rushing officers. All fifteen burst into the room with guns drawn.

Petrov looked to Felix. "After you."

Felix moved inside.

The bedroom was beautifully furnished with gold trim accentuating alderwood finishings. Felix looked across the room where a large window sat in a study area that receded from the main floor. Several officers stood atop the shallow flight of stairs with guns drawn. Felix took a deep breath and walked with Petrov toward the study. Seated peacefully behind a carved desk was Grigori Rasputin with a pen in hand, staring forward with a sense of bemusement. Felix's guts tumbled inside him as he looked at Rasputin.

"Prince Felix! We meet again." Rasputin clasped his hands. "I presumed you were still in Bucharest."

Felix fumbled inside his canvas satchel and crept down the stairs, his eyes never moving from Rasputin. Petrov followed Felix with his revolver drawn.

"Grigori Rasputin," said Petrov. "I hereby place you under arrest in the name of the tsar. For suspicion relating to the murders of—"

"Rodion Kvoss, Anna Taneyev ... and ... oh, let's not forget the very delicious Irina Alexandrovna. You remember her, Felix?" Rasputin appeared suddenly focused, his eyes taking in the slight movements around him. He watched Felix move alongside Petrov. As Rasputin's eyes looked him over, Felix unscrewed one of his canteens and pulled a lean blackwood stake from his canvas satchel.

"How quaint." Rasputin unclasped his hands and placed them behind his back.

Petrov looked to the stake, and then to Felix. "What are you doing?"

"Nothing," said Felix. "Just follow my lead."

"Gentlemen," began Rasputin, turning to the policemen. "If you care to live, turn now and go."

Petrov cocked his gun and pointed it at Rasputin.

"Stand your ground, men. You're completely surrounded," he asserted. "There's another twenty-five armed men outside that door waiting for my signal."

Chapter 23

Rasputin threw back his head and laughed, revealing large fangs growing from his canines. He glared back at Petrov with black eyes and ridged bones defining his forehead. "Then call them. I'm terribly hungry." A deep guttural echo carried in his voice.

Petrov was visibly shaking as Rasputin stood.

"Oh, Felix," said Rasputin. "You didn't tell him?"

Felix jumped toward Rasputin and flung his canteen at him. A glob of giant hogweed sap landed upon Rasputin's chest. He fell back in the chair, hissing at the liquid. Rasputin tore the smock from his body and threw it on the floor. He stood up once more, his gruesome jowls fully apparent.

"Shoot him!" yelled Petrov.

*

The remaining officers waited outside the door, listening for Petrov's signal.

"Shouldn't we go in?"

"Not unless we hear something," said the sergeant.

"Sir, it's been too long."

The sound of breaking glass came from the room.

The officers burst through the door and rushed to the study. Entrails and bony meat from their comrades were strewn about the room. Several police threw their hands to their mouths, others vomited. One fallen policeman, whose throat was torn from his neck, lay on the floor gurgling, his last moments of life in him.

The sergeant ran to him and looked about the room.

"Petrov? Prince Felix? Where are they?"

The police sergeant held the dying man, who gagged on the blood clogging his windpipe. He raised his mangled hand and pointed to the large bay window that was nothing but shards of broken glass. The sergeant lowered him to the ground and motioned the rest toward the window. They steadied their guns.

"Constable Petrov? Prince Felix?" he called, looking to the broken glass.

The police crept toward the window and slowly peered over the sill to see a sheer three-story drop to the concrete below.

Part III: Sfârşitul Lumii

"They down there?"

"No, nothing."

"Where the hell are they?"

The police stood at the window, scanning the night sky.

"Hey, Sarge. You see that?" said an officer, pointing upward.

"Yes. I see them. Christ, they're everywhere."

They stared into the night, squinting and trying to make out the flying objects.

"Shhh. Listen. It's like a squealing … clicking."

"What the hell are those things?"

The sergeant looked for another moment, and his face relaxed in a sullen amazement.

"Giant bats."

Chapter 24

Part III: Sfârșitul Lumii

24

December 16, 1916 (OS), 9:36 p.m.

"As you have requested, Emperor, a large majority of the Bolsheviks are now trapped within central Saint Petersburg. There is no escape. They will be drawn toward Palace Square per Father Rasputin's advice. Victory will be ours. A toast, gentlemen! Na zdorovye!" General Dragunov's white teeth shone as he raised his wineglass into the air.

"Na zdorovye!" said the party in unison, clinking their glasses together.

Dragunov eyed Nicholas's every motion as the tsar raised the wine to his lips. Nicholas swirled the red liquid around in his mouth, trying to place the taste. He swallowed it and closed his eyes as the wine seemed to take him under for a brief moment. Nicholas took another sip and coughed.

"Something wrong, Emperor?" asked Dragunov.

"Hmm? Oh, nothing. Where did you say you found this wine? It tastes quite peculiar."

"It was a gift from Father Rasputin. He said it was the finest from Siberia."

"Siberian wine," interrupted Prime Minister Trepov. "I don't believe I've ever tasted such a thing. Please allow me," he said, extending his empty brandy glass.

"Ahh. Ahh," said Dragunov. "Father Rasputin was firm on saying that he blessed this bottle personally, and that only the tsar and myself were to drink from it."

"Then why aren't you drinking yours?" demanded Trepov.

Chapter 24

"I like to let my wine breathe, Prime Minister. Thank you for inquiring." Dragunov bowed slightly at the waist.

Nicholas brought the glass to his nose and wafted deeply. He swirled the viscous liquid around in his glass and held it to the light. Nicholas's eyes watched as the wine's legs settled along the hull. After deciding the settling time was acceptable, he tipped it to his lips.

"It's quite good," said Nicholas, bringing the wine to his nose once more. "Now wait just a moment. This isn't wine at all!"

The group turned to Nicholas. Dragunov's face flushed as he waited for Nicholas to continue.

Nicholas grinned. "Why ... it's fermented cherry juice!"

Unnoticed by the group, Dragunov's shoulders relaxed.

"Ahh, Siberia," interjected Trepov.

"Quite good though. A bit more, please."

Dragunov tipped the bottle to Nicholas's glass. He downed nearly the entire serving.

"Simply delicious. I must ask Father Rasputin why he didn't share this with me earlier."

At that moment, a young soldier burst into the hall. He ran to the tsar's group and stood at attention.

"What is it?" asked Dragunov.

"General, police have stormed the palace and placed Father Rasputin under arrest."

The cabinet slowly lowered their glasses and looked to Nicholas.

"An outrage!" yelled Nicholas. "Are you certain? I gave no authorization."

"Yes, sir. They barged in only moments ago."

The group was silent as Nicholas searched for a reply.

"And there's something else, Emperor," said the soldier, stuttering as he spoke.

"What is it?"

"Something in the sky. Over Saint Petersburg. I cannot explain it. I request that you all see it for yourselves." He pointed toward the window.

Part III: Sfârșitul Lumii

Nicholas and his cabinet relaxed with a pleasant curiosity as Trepov led the way toward the window. Nicholas leaned into Dragunov for more wine.

"Here, have mine," whispered Dragunov as he poured his red liquid into Nicholas's glass. He looked up quickly to see if anyone else had noticed.

They opened the tall, wide window, and the sound from above overwhelmed them at once.

"What's that horrid clicking?" questioned Trepov, placing his hands over his droopy ears.

Each man leaned against the windowsill and peered into the Saint Petersburg skyline. It was overrun with flying creatures, dipping downward, then soaring high, seemingly with no reason at all to their movements. The moon occasionally broke through the thick shadows, and the creatures came into better view as they dipped closer to the gas lamps of the city night.

"What are they?" questioned Nicholas.

The men stood silently, taking in the sight.

"They're bats," said the soldier. "It started about an hour ago. They keep coming."

"Holy heavens," said Trepov. "I've never seen such a thing. Emperor, what should we do?"

Nicholas looked up to the sky. "Shoot them. I don't ... know," he stammered. "Gentlemen, you must excuse me. I must lie down."

The group looked to Nicholas.

"Emperor, you are safer with us. We need to assess the Rasputin situation," said Trepov.

"I'm not concerned about that right now. I'll tell you how to assess it when I awake."

Nicholas stumbled off.

"I'll see to him," said Dragunov, helping Nicholas stand upright.

Trepov watched them for a moment until the noise from outside distracted him once more. He swung around and stared back to the skyline.

"It's incredible. Listen to the sound!" With his finger, Trepov traced the bats' flight path to a circular motion. "That's odd," he said.

"What is it?"

Chapter 24

"They're circling. Look. Follow my hand."

The group watched as Trepov traced the bats' flight path.

"I see it," said the soldier.

"Me too."

Trepov leaned outward a bit over the windowsill.

"Look there," he shouted. "Directly above us!"

The rest of the party leaned outward to see an open portion of the night sky directly above them. The camp of the bats encircled it, churning about some invisible focal point.

"The vortex of it is right above us," said Trepov. "What do you make of that?"

The men continued to stare, watching the bats twist and dive toward the Saint Petersburg skyline.

*

Several Okhrana followed Dragunov as he walked with Nicholas.

"To my quarters," said Nicholas, leaning on General Dragunov. "That was some strong stuff. I feel invincible!"

"Yes, Emperor," said Dragunov.

"Just a moment," said Nicholas. "My quarters are back that way. This is the empress's wing."

"I know," said Dragunov. "I'm taking you to Alexei's room. Father Rasputin has insisted you be present when Alexei awakes this evening."

"I like Father Rasputin," said Nicholas with heavy eyes and a drunken smile.

"I know you do, Emperor."

By the time they reached Alexei's door, Nicholas was nearly unconscious. Dragunov turned to the soldiers.

"I can take it from here. I'm just going to put him to bed next to the boy."

"I'm sorry, sir. I can't allow it," said the commanding officer. "We are not to leave his side under any circumstances."

"Very well," said Dragunov. "Can you at least get the door?"

Part III: Sfârşitul Lumii

The Okhrana opened the door, and Dragunov moved Nicholas toward Alexei's bed. He placed Nicholas next to the sleeping boy, then sat in a chair along the far wall.

*

Felix woke with a terrible aching sensation in his wrists and shoulders and saw that his hands were cuffed over his head. Petrov slouched next to him, unconscious. Felix's eyes followed Petrov's arms to see them also bound by handcuffs to prison bars. He looked around the dimly lit cell and noticed a figure asleep in a bed along the back wall. Felix's head hurt badly, and he almost passed out once more. He looked toward a large, gaping hole that had been ripped from the side of the prison cell. Rasputin, as vámpir, emerged from the shadows. He walked slowly toward Felix and transformed into his naked human state. Rasputin knelt before him. He asserted a cold, clammy grip on Felix's face.

"Do you recognize the man on the bed? That's your old pal Minister Makarov. He will wake soon, and you're in for quite a show when he notices your plump friend. Tonight is the night, Felix. You are about to learn something very important about yourself. All truths shall be revealed. But first, I must finally ensure that you are under *my* control."

Rasputin opened his jaws and globulous spit flew from his mouth. The viscous liquid splashed across Felix's face, and his appendages went numb. He felt Rasputin move more closely to him, then move away.

Rasputin stood over Felix, then turned his back.

"Good night, my Prince. I look forward to working with you in the very near future."

A fierce gust of wind surged through the cell, and Rasputin was gone. Felix's neck slumped as Rasputin's venom dripped from his face. He shook his head, trying to stay present. He looked to Petrov, who was still unconscious. Felix breathed out and managed to blow some spit from his mouth. His body was entirely numb.

"Petrov, wake up!"

Felix flung his leg toward Petrov and bumped him. Petrov stayed limp. Felix grew overwhelmed by the tingling sensation coursing

Chapter 24

through him. He glanced up to Makarov who appeared asleep. A creaking noise rang out from down the hall, followed by a loud bang. Felix craned his neck as the sound of stampeding feet rumbled toward his cell. Petrov opened his eyes slowly.

"Where are we?"

"Don't ask."

Felix leaned back, positioned his face between the bars, and watched the inmates run past, the feeling in his arms returning slightly. He cocked his jaw, trying to regain fluid speech.

"Rurik, Denis!" he yelled as each inmate passed by. "Rurik, Denis!"

After a few more tries, an inmate with thick glasses and a bruised face stopped at the cell. Denis clung to his side.

"Felix? How did you get back here?"

"No time. Get us out."

"You're lucky to be alive," said Denis.

"Am I?"

"In my pocket," said Petrov. "Keys to the cell and cuffs."

Petrov leaned backward, and Rurik fumbled through his pocket until he pulled out a large key ring. Gunshots and yelling emerged from the station's foyer as Rurik fumbled through the ring.

"Which key?"

"The biggest for the cell," said Petrov.

Rurik inserted the key and pulled open the door. Felix and Petrov came with it, still bound to the bars.

"Which one for the handcuffs?"

"Let me see the ring," said Petrov.

Rurik held the key ring, sliding each key by him.

"That one!" said Petrov.

Rurik reached to unlock Felix's cuffs. "That's not the one!"

Rurik knelt and shuffled the keys past Petrov.

"Uhh, Rurik?" said Denis, tapping him on the shoulder.

"Yes?"

"Hurry." Denis pointed to the prison bed.

Rurik turned to see Makarov sitting in bed. His black, hungry eyes glared at them as sharp silvery teeth grew from his mouth.

Part III: Sfârşitul Lumii

Makarov sat still and watched them with a sense of curiosity, seemingly confused by their actions.

"Now, Rurik," said Felix, noticing he began to regain feeling in his limbs.

Rurik slid the keys faster.

"It's that one!" said Petrov.

Rurik twisted the key inside Felix's bindings, and the cuffs clinked open. Felix slumped to the ground and crawled from the cell. His motions agitated Makarov, who stood and started walking slowly toward them. Rurik fumbled with the keys, looking between the cuffs and Makarov to judge his timing.

"Let's go!" yelled Denis.

"Rurik, hurry," said Felix.

Petrov closed his eyes. "Oh please, God."

Rurik dropped the keys and snatched them up.

"Which is it?"

Makarov crept toward them, hissing softly—his eyes entranced by their erratic actions.

"Found it!" Rurik attempted to place the key inside Petrov's cuffs. "The keyhole is bent."

Petrov opened his eyes. He looked to Rurik, then to Makarov. "Try again!"

"It won't fit," said Rurik, struggling to make a match.

"Rurik," yelled Denis. "Shut the door!"

Makarov extended his hands and moved in quickly.

Felix pulled Rurik from the cell door, and Denis shoved his weight against it, slamming it closed with Petrov locked inside. Makarov reached through the bars and grabbed Denis, desperately trying to pull him into his sharp fangs. Rurik pushed forward and locked the cell as Felix pulled Denis from Makarov, who gnashed his fangs and thrust his arms through the cell bars. Rurik wound up with the key ring and forcefully swung the metal shards into Makarov's face. He recoiled, hissing at Rurik.

"Good shot!" yelled Denis.

Petrov writhed upon the ground, trying to free himself.

"Help me! Don't leave me! Please, don't leave me!"

Chapter 24

Makarov turned his attention downward to Petrov, seeming to inhale his panic. Makarov lunged at Petrov.

"Run!" yelled Felix, sliding under Denis's arm. He pushed Rurik from the cellblock, dragging Denis with him.

They ran down the station hall as a chilling gurgle and infantile murmur followed them. Rurik turned to see a puddle of blood spilling from the cell as Petrov's screams silenced.

They emerged into the police station foyer. Thick smoke hovered everywhere. Other than multiple police officers and Bolsheviks who lay dead on the floor, the station was deserted. Felix hopped over the front desk and walked into a back room. He emerged a second later, his arms loaded with their equipment satchels.

"What about my—"

"One second, Denis."

Felix went back into the storage room and returned with Denis's prostheses. Denis sat upon the floor and strapped himself into the harnesses. "What about the gas masks? Should be three."

Rurik rummaged through a satchel and pulled out three gas masks—only two of them had Denis's custom viewing glass.

"Who gets the crappy one?" asked Rurik.

"You do."

Rurik frowned and handed out the others.

Felix strapped his hogweed canisters to his back, then fumbled with the hose and trigger. He handed the other canister harness to Denis.

"You remember how to use it?" asked Denis.

"Well enough," said Felix.

They pulled on their gas masks and jumpsuits, and Felix crept toward the window at the front door.

"Anything?" asked Denis, his breathing already fogging his mask.

Felix shook his head. "Looks clear."

"We should make a dash for it," said Rurik. "Just follow. Safe house isn't far."

"Wait . . . hang on." Felix looked to a dead policeman on the floor. "Grab that rifle," he said, pointing to the policeman's gun. He hung the hogweed nozzle from its holster upon his backpack.

Rurik handed the rifle to Felix. He cocked it, then ensured it was loaded. "Follow me. Denis, can you keep up?"

"You know I love that quest—"

"Fine. But we can't get separated. I'm shooting anything that moves."

"Be mindful," said Rurik. "That vampire is certainly free of the cell by now."

"Got it," said Felix. "Denis, back me up with the hogweed."

Felix turned away and peered out the window once more. In the reflection, he saw Rurik and Denis distance themselves from him by several feet. They slid their gas masks to the tops of their heads. He turned to them and noticed their faces looked unusually pale.

"What is it?" questioned Felix.

The brothers stood silently.

"What's wrong with you two?"

"Um, Felix?" began Rurik. "There's a problem."

Felix flipped up his mask.

"What? Come on, let's go."

"It's you, Felix. You're bitten."

Felix slowly raised his hand to the back of his neck and felt the fang marks. His face grew pale. He closed his eyes and fell limply to the floor—the rifle falling at his side. Rurik ran to him.

"Kill me," Felix said, looking to Rurik.

"Felix, we—"

"Son of a bitch!" yelled Felix, slamming his fists into the floor.

"Felix," said Rurik. "You're still with us."

Felix reached to his neck to feel the bite mark.

"I'm a goddamn vampire! You have to kill me."

Denis and Rurik stood and whispered to each other while Felix remained upon the floor—the sound of occasional gunfire rumbled from outside.

"Well," said Rurik, "for someone who didn't believe in vampires a week ago, I'd say becoming one is incredible!"

"What?" said Felix, looking up to them.

"You're coming with us, Felix," said Denis. "We'll figure something out."

Chapter 24

"I don't think—"

"Let's go," said Rurik, extending his hand to Felix. "Don't worry. One foul step and we'll stake you."

"Wonderful," grunted Felix as Rurik pulled him from the ground.

Felix bent down and grabbed the rifle. He leapt toward the exit.

"I can't believe this," he grumbled. "You two ready?"

The brothers nodded and repositioned their gas masks. Felix did the same.

"Hoods up, everyone!" said Denis. Each man pulled up his hood, securing it around his gas mask.

Felix burst through the door and ran past the circular drive. He jumped over a raised cement barrier with Rurik right behind him. Denis hobbled along a short distance away. They sprinted across the street, ducking at the sound of gunfire rattling in the distance. Felix swung around the street corner and dove into a stairwell alongside an apartment building. Rurik followed. They sat for a long moment, waiting for Denis.

"Was he shot?" asked Felix, his gas mask fogged.

Rurik shrugged, his goggle eyes staring blankly at Felix. Denis suddenly made a clumsy attempt at rounding the corner.

"Thought we lost you," mumbled Rurik.

"What?"

Rurik pulled up his mask. "I said, thought we lost you."

Denis cast an angry glance at him.

Felix was still breathing heavily, his viewing mask completely fogged. He pulled it from his face.

"These won't work. I can't see a damn thing."

Denis pulled his mask away from his face. "You probably don't need it."

"He's right, I can't see anything," said Rurik, sliding the mask to his forehead.

"Your choice," said Denis. "I for one don't want vampire spit in my face. No offense, Felix." He pulled down his mask.

Felix looked to Rurik. "How long before I'm one of them?"

"Sit," said Rurik, motioning to the cement stairs.

"I don't want to sit," he said, deflecting Rurik's hand.

Part III: Sfârșitul Lumii

"Your only salvation is to kill the vampire who turned you before its venom overtakes your own blood. Also if you kill a person and drink their blood—you're forever damned."

Felix bit his lower lip. "There's something else. Rasputin said something—"

"Who?" asked Rurik.

"Grigori Rasputin—I learned through Petrov that's the Sleepwalker's name. He was in the cell right before you found me ... spit at me ... that's when I must have been bitten. He said that I'm about to learn a lesson about myself. There's more to this." He gazed at Rurik. "So what now? I'll wake up tomorrow like Makarov back in that cell?"

Rurik considered the question. "Yes. At nightfall tomorrow."

Felix's face flushed red. "Look, the second we get to a safe place, you put a stake in me. You got it? I'm not going to become one of them." He glared at Denis for a moment.

"Of course," said Denis. "Whatever you like."

"Good ... where's this safe house?"

He looked up to Rurik, whose eyes widened, his finger slowly rising to the sky. Felix and Denis followed Rurik's hand, and their hearts twisted inside them.

"It's happening," said Rurik.

Denis hobbled from the stairwell and stood in the street with his head craned upward. The entire night sky was filled with giant vampire bats.

"This is bad, gentlemen," said Denis.

Felix shook Rurik. "Safe house!"

"Oh, sure. Good idea. But first we must warn Hedrina."

Rurik pulled down his mask and ran from the stairwell. He sprinted past Denis with Felix fast behind him.

"Where are we going?" asked Denis.

"To save Rurik's girlfriend, believe it or not," shouted Felix.

Denis watched his brother's figure sprint away. He looked to the sky once more and shook his head.

"Always Rurik and the women."

Chapter 24

Alexandra burst into Alexei's room in a desperate panic. Her eyes shot to the bed to see Nicholas lying unconscious next to her son.

"Oh my God!" She dashed toward Nicholas with several soldiers following her.

The Okhrana attending to Nicholas leapt toward them. "What is it, Your Highness?"

"Hurry. We must get Nicholas out of here."

"Alexandra, this is a mistake!" said General Dragunov, as the guards lifted Nicholas from the bed and pulled him away.

"And arrest him," she said, pointing to Dragunov.

Dragunov huffed and rolled his eyes. "On what grounds?"

"Arrest him immediately," yelled Alexandra.

The soldiers looked to one another, moved behind Dragunov, and restrained him.

"What of the tsar, Your Highness?" questioned the commanding guard.

Alexandra's eyes searched for an answer.

"How many soldiers in the Room of Coins?"

"At least thirty."

"Take him there. Do not allow anyone to enter. Under no circumstances! Shoot anyone who enters the hall!" Her voice near hysterical. "Do you understand me?"

The soldiers nodded.

"Put as many available men as you have there."

"Highness, what's happening?"

"The unthinkable. I order you—take him there now. Protect him with your very lives!"

The Okhrana sprung from the room, carrying Nicholas in their arms. Dragunov stood with two soldiers behind him. His face appeared stern as his eyes caught Alexandra's.

"Alexandra, you can't win."

"You traitor!" She lunged toward him, her right hand outstretched. Alexandra forcibly clawed his face, scratching him across the cheek. Dragunov tried to hide any semblance of pain, but his eyes watered as small splotches of blood filled the fingernail marks on his face.

He bowed. "Highness."

"I will not let this atrocity happen. Even at the cost of my life!"

Dragunov was calm. "You've already lost. I'll be freed by night's end."

"Imprison him!" she yelled.

The guards cuffed Dragunov's hands and shuffled him from the room.

Alexandra looked to the remaining soldiers.

"You five, are you armed?"

They nodded.

"If anything enters this room, anything at all, you shoot it dead, do you understand me?"

"*Thing*, Highness?"

"Just shoot! Here, stand around the bed. Don't let anyone but me near Alexei."

The soldiers clicked their heels and stood around Alexei's bed. The child was still asleep, his chest rising and falling in slow rhythmic lulls.

Alexandra ran to Alexei's bathing quarters and turned on the faucets to the large bathtub. The water poured in and filled the basin. Alexandra leapt toward an ornate vanity. She searched through the drawers until she found a box of razors and placed them on the stairs to the tub.

She ran back into Alexei's room and moved past the soldiers at his bedside. She leaned to him and stroked his face—his skull bones still pronounced on his forehead with small fangs poking from behind his lips. Alexandra kissed him on the forehead, and tears streamed from her face.

"His temperature is too high. We need to get him into the cold bath."

"Yes, Highness!"

Two soldiers gently lifted Alexei and followed Alexandra into the bathing quarters. They placed Alexei into the tub—the water covered his body up to his face.

"I can finish from here," said Alexandra.

"Highness, are you sure? We're not—"

"Go!" yelled Alexandra, thrusting her finger into the air.

The soldiers clicked their heels and filed out of the bathroom.

Chapter 24

"Anything enters, you shoot it," echoed behind them as Alexandra slammed the bathroom door and locked it.

She dragged the vanity in front of the door, then stood at the small stairs that led to the bath. A single razor blade sat on the rim. She climbed into the tub, still in her nightgown, and sat behind Alexei, his arms floating freely in the ever-deepening water. Alexandra wept audibly as she hovered over Alexei. She looked at him once more and clasped her hands together. Alexandra leaned forward, wrapped her hands around Alexei's neck, and forced his face below the waterline.

The child was still for a moment, then grabbed on to her arms with both his hands. He flailed about under the water, thrashing and kicking as Alexandra pressed her hands firmly onto his throat. The sound of pouring water masked Alexei's struggle, and she leaned over him, thrusting downward with nearly enough pressure to snap his fragile neck.

"I'm sorry, my baby. I'm so sorry."

Alexei struggled for only another moment, and his body fell limp. Alexandra flipped him on his belly and he floated facedown. She let out a great wail. The soldiers began banging at the door.

"Everything's fine, I slipped on the tiles," she yelled.

The door continued to rattle and shake as the soldiers tried to break it down. Alexandra reached for the razor, then slit both her wrists upward upon her forearms. She did not wince, and there was no pain. She lay back—her blood turning the water a royal crimson. Alexandra pulled Alexei to her breast, wrapped her arms around him, and cupped him tightly. She exhaled all the air in her lungs and slowly slipped beneath the red water, the only sound apparent a muffled banging at the door.

Alexandra's consciousness faded as the banging grew louder. For a brief moment she believed there were gunshots. A cracking sound ripped through the bathroom, and the vanity flew across the floor. Alexandra sat up and looked to the doorframe to see Rasputin as vámpir standing over her.

"It's over," she yelled. "I won't allow it!"

Rasputin seized her arm, forcing her to watch the slash wounds heal. He pushed her back into the tub, and she held Alexei's lifeless body.

Part III: Sfârşitul Lumii

"He's gone! It's over," she cried.

"Awake," spoke Rasputin.

Alexei stood fiercely upright, knocking Alexandra toward the back of the tub. Bloody water dripped from his pale face as he looked obediently to Rasputin, gasping in short, controlled breaths of air. Alexandra leaned forward to grab him, and Rasputin swung his wing around the boy. They vanished from the room.

Alexandra struggled and flopped out of the tub. She ran into Alexei's bedroom to find the soldiers' mangled bodies strewn about—blood splatter was everywhere. She screamed, sprinting toward the Room of Coins in her blood-soaked nightgown.

*

Nicholas lay unconscious on the sofa in the center of the room. His cabinet ministers sat around him like a group of doting handmaidens. Forty soldiers lined the walls with another two rows of soldiers, ten men long, standing at the main entrance to the hall. Prime Minister Trepov sat next to Nicholas, fanning him with a piece of thick parchment.

"Do you think he was poisoned?" questioned Trepov.

"He's breathing," replied Ambassador Sazonov. "I believe he's merely drunk."

"Perhaps, but Dragunov was so peculiar about the contents of that wine bottle. And now that Alexandra has ordered his arrest, what are we to think?"

"I'm sure Nicholas is fine. We must wait until this emergency has ended, then we can get him to his doctor."

"I dearly hope so," said Trepov, returning to his fanning duties.

"Look out there!" Sazonov pointed to the window.

The group looked to the massive bay window to see the bats flying about over the city.

"Incredible!" said Trepov, rising to get a closer look.

The cabinet members crept to the window to see the bats flying haphazardly across their field of view.

"The size of them is astounding—"

Chapter 24

At that moment, a giant bat swooped down and crashed into the window, leaving a large crack across the glass. Trepov and the remaining three cabinet members backed up as several other bats rammed themselves against the window.

"I think it's best to stay away from the windows," said Sazonov.

The men backed away, never taking their eyes off the large panes of glass.

"It seems the whole world is coming to an end," spoke Trepov.

The remaining cabinet members ignored the comment and sat around Nicholas as explosions and gunfire erupted in Palace Square. Prime Minister Trepov moved to a window and hid behind the curtain as he tried to peer downward. He cupped his hands against the glass to see the tsar's militia engaging what he believed to be the last of the Bolsheviks moving into Palace Square.

"Where are the binoculars?"

Sazonov retrieved them and handed them to Trepov, who rubbed the frost from the window and looked outward, studying the rebels engaging the tsar's militia.

Trepov shook his head. "Those men aren't Bolsheviks."

"How can you tell?"

"I can't for sure, but they're dressed like Stovâjįk."

*

The row of soldiers at the hall's main entrance stood dutifully still, each scanning the long shadowy hallway for the slightest movement. They became aware of a small figure moving toward them. The front row knelt and aimed their guns. The second row also targeted the figure.

They realized it was Alexei and relaxed their guns.

"See if he's harmed," said the commander.

Two soldiers walked to Alexei.

"Are you hurt, young master?" asked one.

"He's soaking wet. And I think he's bleeding," said the other.

"Have you been cut?"

Alexei looked to the soldier and shook his head.

Part III: Sfârşitul Lumii

"I'm here to see Father," said Alexei with a dazed look on his face. The bone protrusions in his forehead were no longer apparent.

"Come with me," said the soldier, picking him up.

He carried Alexei to the threshold.

"Wants to see his father."

The commander nodded, and the soldier continued with Alexei seated upon his hipbone. He carried the boy to the cabinet members. Trepov rose to greet them.

"Alexei, my boy, you're soaking wet!"

Alexei stared at him with a haunting, empty gaze.

"What's the matter, boy?"

Alexei looked down to Nicholas and started breathing heavily.

"He wanted to see his father," said the soldier.

"Fine. Let him."

The soldier placed Alexei on the ground, and he crept toward Nicholas. He crawled on top of his father and lay down on his chest, placing his face at the side of Nicholas's neck.

Alexei lay still for a moment.

Trepov stood behind the couch and looked over them, aware of a slight bobbing motion of Alexei's head. The rest of the cabinet members returned to light conversation. Trepov looked more closely and noticed the peach-colored fabric turning a deep red around Nicholas's head.

"Alexei?"

Trepov moved in closer still, aware of a small sucking sound as dark crimson bloodstains seeped into the satin fibers.

"Dear God!" yelled Trepov, reeling away.

"What is it, Alexander?" questioned Sazonov.

Trepov pointed to Nicholas's body, and the rest of the cabinet members looked to see a puddle of blood dripping from the sofa onto the floor.

"Child!" yelled Sazonov. He ran to Alexei and seized him by the shoulders.

Alexei sat up and gnashed his fangs at Sazonov. The ambassador stepped backward, holding his heart at the sight of a gaping bite on Nicholas's neck. Alexandra's screams echoed from the hallway as massive explosions from Palace Square shook the room.

Chapter 24

"Dear God! Help us!" yelled Trepov, trying to take cover underneath his chair.

Alexei returned to his father's neck, continuing to feast upon the last of his blood.

*

The *draculae* bats swirled about the invisible vortex high above the Saint Petersburg skyline. Below them, the city was alive with struggle. Gunshots and grenade blasts echoed through the streets as the remnants of the Bolshevik militia and Russian army engaged one another in every section of central Saint Petersburg.

At the foot of the Winter Palace, the Stovâjįk mercenaries had finally overtaken the palace guard as a great wail resounded from above. A blue luminescence began to radiate from the bats circling in the night until the entire skyline swirled like a galaxy of blue and white lightning, appearing to absorb the bats in an ominous thundercloud. The remaining Stovâjįk fell to their knees, raised their hands to the sky, and began to pray.

The light in the sky circled with dense turbulence as the bats within transformed to Nosferatu. Their bones cracked into position and their skin bubbled as if some unholy monster were trying to claw its way through their flesh. Their piercing screams rang out for only another moment, and the sky fell to black.

Wind whipped through the streets of Saint Petersburg as Bolshevik and soldier alike stood dazed, staring into the night and watching the shadowy figures descend upon them from above.

*

The windows encasing the Room of Coins imploded with a fierce gust of wind.

The palace went dark.

By moonlight, those inside watched the Nosferatu gather along the ceiling, hanging for a moment as an uneasy stillness settled over the room. Sazonov and the others dove to the floor. They looked upward to see the fanged monsters staring back at them. And without

Part III: Sfârşitul Lumii

another heartbeat, the Nosferatu sprung from the ceiling to feast on the remaining soldiers and cabinet members.

*

The Imperial Pub emanated playful candlelight from behind its stained glass. As they stood outside, Felix became aware of a clicking noise at their back. He turned and looked down the alleyway. "Uh, fellows? We should go in. Now."

Denis swung around, then stood rigidly upright. He tapped Rurik on the back and motioned to the street. Four Nosferatu stood scattered about the long alleyway with their winged appendages raised to their chins like a group of praying mantises. Dozens more began crawling up the alley, clicking and squealing as they neared. Rurik turned and pushed on the door. Denis and Felix followed.

A gaggle of police officers sat around the bar, too drunk and boisterous to notice the intrusion.

"Rurik!" yelled Hedrina as she ran to him. She kissed him on the cheek. "What are you doing here? What's on your head?"

"No time to explain," he said. "We have to go out the back way."

Rurik pulled her arm and dragged her with him—Denis and Felix flanked them. They moved behind the bar, and a drunken officer tried to tug upon Denis's jacket. Rurik took Hedrina through a curtain that led to the back storage room.

"What's this about, Rurik? Are you drunk?"

"I can't explain everything. Just promise me you'll follow us and listen to everything I say."

Hedrina threw her arm down, breaking Rurik's grip. "Now, look here," she said, raising her finger to him. "I'm not going anywhere until you tell me what's going on."

"No time!" yelled Rurik, tugging on her sleeve.

Hedrina folded her arms and stood firmly.

"Well," began Rurik, "the city is being overrun by ancient vampires, and we've come to save you because I'm secretly in love with you. Can we go?"

Rurik grabbed her wrist and attempted to pull her with him.

"Is that so?" said Hedrina, standing in place.

Chapter 24

"Uhh, madam?" said Denis. "We really should be going."

Hedrina considered Rurik's statement, and a broad smile appeared on her face.

"Oh, Rurik! You're so sweet," she said and threw her arms around him. "But you didn't need to make up all that vampire stuff—"

The bar erupted in gunfire and breaking glass. Hedrina turned to see an officer fall into the storage room as a Nosferatu gouged out his rib cage.

Hedrina screamed and held on to Rurik.

"Let's go!" she said.

They dashed out the back entrance and ran along the darkened alleyway. A terrible ruckus rose from the corridor as they plowed through a mess of trash cans. They emerged from the alley with Rurik and Hedrina in the lead. Denis was hobbling far behind.

"Rurik? Which way?" yelled Felix.

Rurik spun around and gathered his bearings. "This way," he said, pointing up the street.

They ran, continually stalked by Nosferatu fluttering overhead, their high-pitched squeaks and squeals growing ever louder.

"Can you feel that?" yelled Denis.

"Yes," said Rurik.

"Me too," said Hedrina.

"Feel what?" yelled Felix.

"They're using echolocation to hunt us. I can feel it in my chest."

Felix looked up and saw three Nosferatu gliding overhead, positioning themselves for the kill. As the group neared the boulevard, the Nosferatu descended.

Felix felt a strong blow to the back of his head, and dropped his rifle as he dove for the ground. Dazed, he stood quickly and twisted the nozzle on his gas canister while readying the spray rod. Behind him came a horrid screech, and he turned to see Denis on the ground, spraying hogweed gas onto his Nosferatu attacker. The pressurized gas enveloped the ghoul—its flesh emitted an eerie green glow as it melted to nothing.

"You see! It works!" yelled Denis.

Part III: Sfârșitul Lumii

Felix looked to Hedrina and Rurik, who were unconscious on the street with noxious spit dripping from their faces. Felix turned and pulled the hose trigger. Nothing. He looked down to see his hose wrapped around itself.

Two Nosferatu crawled toward Rurik and Hedrina. Felix removed his gas mask and threw it at them, hitting one in the head. The Nosferatu let out a great shriek, and turned its gaze to Felix. It recoiled from Rurik and bowed to the ground. The other followed.

Felix watched as both Nosferatu huddled low and crawled toward him, their black eyes staring through him as quiet echolocation clicks emanated from their heads. Dread surged upon him as he looked to their faces—slight and nearly human faces but sucked of their life. Black, dead eyes rendered terrifying by a grotesque pug nose, pointy ears, and fearsome jowls that jutted from their otherwise slim, hauntingly feminine features.

Denis hobbled behind Felix, aiming his nozzle at the Nosferatu. They slithered closer to Felix, their bony heads bowing deeply to him. He and Denis stood still, enveloped by the sounds of carnage in the distance. The echolocation noises from overhead had grown deafening.

"What should I do?" whispered Felix to Denis.

"Move so I can get a clear shot."

Felix's body shook nervously as the Nosferatu neared. Their pure white bodies appeared to sparkle against the backdrop of the dark city streets. They reached him, raising their claws as if expecting some blessing from Felix.

"Go," he said, shooing them with his hands.

The Nosferatu looked to him. Their soulless eyes conveyed no semblance of understanding. Felix shrugged his shoulders and looked back to Denis.

Denis nodded. "Keep distracting them."

"Be gone!" said Felix more assertively.

The Nosferatu retracted their claws.

"Out of the way!" yelled Denis.

The Nosferatu hissed at him, then threw their attention back to Felix. "I said go!" he yelled.

The Nosferatu cowered like obedient dogs. Denis bumped Felix out of the way and shot his hogweed gas upon the Nosferatu.

Chapter 24

They let out great wails as their bodies disintegrated into a sinister green glow that melted onto the street, flooding around Denis and Felix's feet.

They took a few steps backward to avoid the toxic muck.

"Nice work," said Felix.

They rushed to Hedrina and Rurik.

Felix picked up his gas mask from the ground, then wiped the spit from Hedrina's mouth. Rurik sat up, swaying a bit from the dizziness. He reached over to care for Hedrina, and helped her sit upright.

"What happened?" asked Hedrina, barely able to hold her head up.

"They obeyed me," said Felix. "Maybe they sensed I've been bitten."

"It's something more," said Denis. "It is written that they only obey the Bloodchild." He paused, considering Felix. "They're gone, that's all that matters."

Rurik moved in between them, placing his gas mask on his head. "Remind me to keep it on next time," he said, and pulled it down.

"Here, put this on." Felix slid his gas mask over Hedrina's head and tightened the straps. He looked to her and she smiled through the glass. His blue eyes stared sullenly upward, taking in the shadows of the Nosferatu flying above. Then Felix looked to his friends.

"Let's get the hell out of here."

*

Rurik led them along the dark city streets until they reached a recessed stairwell. At the bottom was a rickety blue door.

"That it?" questioned Denis, an air of disappointment in his voice. He looked upward to Nosferatu shadows fluttering in the sky —havoc still echoed through the city. "They'll find us."

"Be patient," mumbled Rurik as he reached to the top of the doorframe and ran his fingers along it until he found a metal button. A click sounded from the other side of the wall to his left. He positioned his shoulder against the cement and thrust his weight into it.

Part III: Sfârșitul Lumii

The wall slid backward about three feet, revealing another stairwell descending to a dim corridor.

"Go," he said.

Everyone shuffled down the poorly lit stairs, a naked bulb overhead their only beacon. Rurik moved to the other side of the fake wall and forced himself against it until it was once again flush with the outer stairwell. He clasped a lever that locked the false wall from inside and joined the rest, who stood huddled together, removing their gas masks.

"I thought you said ten people," said Denis.

Rurik pulled up his mask. "Give the man a minute!"

Rurik reached up and yanked on a string that ignited another naked bulb, revealing a row of shelves stacked high with wine bottles. At first inspection, the room could have passed as a wine cellar. Rurik looked over the bottles and began counting out aloud. After running his fingers over several bottles, he looked to Hedrina.

"My dear. How does a '93 Château Léoville suit you?"

Hedrina smiled and nodded.

"Ahh, a woman of exquisite taste."

Rurik pulled the bottle from the shelf and bowed, holding it to Hedrina as the shelving system slid away. Behind it was a sizable room with humble furnishings.

"Complete with a working toilet," said Rurik.

He held on to the wine bottle and walked into the room. Three tugs of a string and the room was flush with light. The rest followed him into the smuggler's paradise. An array of stolen items were stockpiled against the room's walls: canned goods, endless cases of wine, stacks of fine china, trunks of random clothing, boxes of cigarettes, and a large crystal chandelier leaning against a pile of brand-new patent leather boots.

Hedrina sat in a chair and began shaking and sobbing. "What is happening, Rurik? What are those things?"

Rurik knelt to her side and held her hand. "I told you—the city *is* being overrun by ancient vampires—Nosferatu."

"That's impossible," she cried. "It goes against God."

Chapter 24

Rurik placed his hands on her shoulders. "You're safe here, Hedrina. And for what it's worth, the part about me being secretly in love with you is true too."

Hedrina looked to him and tried to dry her tears. She nodded a yes as her chin quivered. The two embraced.

Denis cleared his throat. "Nice place," he said, and threw himself onto a sheet-covered couch.

"Hey!" yelled the couch.

Denis leapt away.

A young kid sat up and threw the sheet to the ground.

"Watch where you sit," he said. His eyes shot to Denis. "What happened to your face?"

Denis glared at the kid. "Mind your business."

"You're the smuggler kid from the train," said Felix, pointing to the boy.

"That's me!"

Rurik pulled on a lever that closed the shelving system. The group collectively sighed as the mechanism stopped to a soothing silence.

"Everyone, this is the kid," said Rurik. "The kid, meet Hedrina, my brother Denis, and you've already met Felix."

Everyone nodded their hellos.

"Felix has been turned into a vampire, just so you know. I'd keep my distance."

"Whoa! You were bit?"

"Yeah," gruffed Felix.

"Can I see?"

Felix appeared bothered.

"Come on," said Rurik. "Let him see."

Felix turned around, exposing the back of his neck.

"There's nothing there," said the kid.

Felix moved his hand to the wound. "It's gone." He looked to Rurik. "So what's it mean?"

"Don't know. Probably a part of the process."

"Am I going to grow fangs soon?"

Part III: Sfârşitul Lumii

"From my understanding you will sleep tomorrow, and when you wake, you'll be a little randy."

"Randy?"

"You know, all agitated. Looking for love and blood and that kind of thing." Rurik cast a smirk to Denis.

"Will you please take this seriously?"

"We do take it seriously, but what can we do?" said Rurik.

"You'll have to kill me."

"Not an option, Felix," said Rurik. "Not yet."

"Agreed. If you act out of hand, only then will I keep my promise to stake you," said Denis. He sat on the couch and massaged his thigh before loosening his leg harness.

"That's disgusting," said the kid.

"Should have seen the real one come off." Denis relaxed and threw his arm over his face.

Felix slumped on the floor.

Rurik took a corkscrew from a nearby table and uncorked the wine. He handed a wineglass to Hedrina and another to Felix.

"No thanks," said Felix.

"Come on," said Rurik.

"Yes, Felix. It's your birthday in a manner of speaking—you should celebrate," said Denis, sitting forward and yawning.

Felix swatted the glass from Rurik's hand. It shattered on the cement floor. Rurik stood over him. "That is not helpful."

Felix shook his head. "Neither is drinking when we should be planning."

Rurik pulled another chair from the wall and sat next to Hedrina.

"May I ask a favor?" asked Hedrina.

"Please," said Rurik.

"My mother. She's out there." Hedrina pointed to the ceiling. "Is there any chance we can find her?"

The room was silent. All eyes turned to Rurik. Hedrina placed her hands to her face and wept. Rurik knelt to her.

"We can't. I'm sorry. We have to wait until sunup."

Rurik threw a blanket around her shoulders. He moved to the far wall, where three large trunks sat along the floor. He opened one to reveal a trove of blackwood stakes and garlic vials.

Chapter 24

"Wrong trunk," he said.

He walked to another and pulled out a thick rope. He tossed it to Felix.

"What's this?"

"A precaution," said Rurik.

"Oh, no—"

"Sorry, friend. You're outnumbered on this one," said Denis.

"It's only till we leave. Early morning," said Rurik. He sat in his chair and looked to the group. His face was somber. "When the Nosferatu have finished feeding."

"You have to escape the city," said Felix. "If you can't or won't kill me, then leave me behind. I'll just walk into a fire or something."

Denis winced. "Not as fast a death as you might think. Besides, we're not leaving the city. We will stay and fight."

"Fight for what?" asked Felix. "We're doomed, remember?"

"We have one last chance," said Rurik, looking to Felix. "How well do you know the Winter Palace?"

"Very well."

"Empress's wing?"

"Certainly."

Rurik sat back, tipping his chair a bit. "It's my guess that's where they'll roost. Is it true she keeps it free of light?"

"Yes," said Felix. "Can we draw them into the sunlight?"

"It won't kill them fast enough," said Denis.

"Sunlight made both Alexandra and Alexei terribly sick."

Rurik leaned forward. "As it will any vampire. Direct sunlight will disorient them, burn them horribly, and kill them if the exposure is long enough. But if they're well-fed, human blood fresh in their veins, they can withstand sunlight—it's a mere deterrent at that point. We'd have to starve them first, otherwise it only buys us time." Rurik paused for a moment, reflecting on his comments. "Hogweed sap acts as an ultraviolet light accelerant. It will destroy them instantly, but—"

"We'll never get close to the palace," interjected Denis.

"It's our last stand," said Rurik. "We will. If we can't get inside, we'll get close enough to torch it to the ground."

Part III: Sfârşitul Lumii

Denis thumped his wooden arm. "We have to kill the boy."

Rurik raised his hand to Denis and motioned toward Felix.

"It's fine, Rurik. I know," said Felix.

The room was silent.

"We must act immediately at dawn," said Denis. "Surprise them. The Nosferatu will guard the Bloodchild with incredible voracity, but none can stand against us with my hogweed gas. We'll fumigate the whole roost."

"Will it work?" asked the kid.

Denis looked to him. "Most certainly."

"And when you run out of hogweed?" asked Felix.

"Well." Denis took a long pause and let out a heavy breath. "Let's hope we kill the Bloodchild in the process."

"*Let's hope*? That's your plan?" Felix was agitated.

"Yes," said Denis with a scowl. "We're entering the hornets' nest to kill the queen—expect a swarm."

Everyone save Denis hung their heads.

Rurik unbound a rolled-up mattress near the wall and tossed it on the floor.

"We should rest."

*

Rasputin and Alexei stood upon the sweeping rooftop of the Winter Palace, their cloaked figures defiant against the full cold moon. Rasputin's eyes slowly traced each section of the city. Fires burned below in Palace Square and across the city, consuming the architectural might of Saint Petersburg. He watched the Nosferatu flutter about the skyline, and reveled in panicked screams echoing from the streets below.

Rasputin closed his eyes and concentrated on the pleasant pulsing sensation that swelled inside his head. The night was his. It beckoned to his very soul. He opened his eyes once more and looked out to Saint Petersburg—dread and destruction budding from every cranny of the city.

The world will follow.

Chapter 24

His eyes moved to the full moon as the earth's shadow crept across it. He and Alexei patiently watched the shadow envelop the moon, turning it to hues of deep crimson. They huddled together over the panoramic skyline as the moon finally fell to black.

Alexei closed his eyes, taking in the disquieting sounds. A wondrous sensation swept him. The screams resonated through his entire body—the carnage lifted him into the air. He opened his eyes and looked to Rasputin, absorbing him as the image of sternness, power, and intent. Alexei's heart surged. His eyes traced the long dark shadow of Rasputin's cloak to the stark paleness of his face and pointy ears. Fangs emerged from Rasputin's mouth, and Alexei reached to his cold hand and squeezed it tightly.

"Father," said Alexei.

Rasputin closed his eyes at the sound of the boy's voice and leaned forward, pulling Alexei with him. Their figures fell from the rooftop terrace and transformed to black mist against the palace's gorgeous façade. They fluttered gracefully into the sky, through the wispy white clouds of the crisp winter night. Together they soared into the darkness—hearts enraptured by the call of fresh blood.

Part III: Sfârşitul Lumii

25

December 17, 1916 (OS), 6:42 a.m.

Rurik opened his eyes and listened—nothing but silence from the streets above. He sat up and looked about the candlelit room. Everyone was asleep. His eyes moved to Felix, who lay on the floor bound in ropes—his chest rising and falling peacefully. Rurik heard Denis sit up and slide behind him.

"We should stake him," he whispered.

Rurik shook his head. "I can't."

"I believe I can."

Rurik turned to him. "We'll all be dead by sunrise anyway," he said, trying to lower his voice below a whisper. "What's the difference?"

They sat in silence, staring toward each other's chests. Denis looked to the ceiling. "Seems quiet. We should move."

Rurik knelt to Felix, whose face dripped heavy with sweat.

"I heard it all," said Felix, opening his eyes.

"How are you?"

"Terrible. Itchy inside. Hungry."

Denis knelt next to them. "What do you think, Felix? Will you harm anyone if we untie you?"

"No. Not now. But I will. I feel outside myself—like I'm looking in. If I slip away any more, I'm not certain what I'll do."

Denis looked to Rurik. "We should stake him."

"Not yet," said Felix, breathing deeply. "You'll need my help. He's sleeping now ... Rasputin. I can sense him. In my veins. Alexei too. Asleep with him." Felix closed his eyes.

Chapter 25

"We must go," said Rurik. He patted Denis on the back and walked to the false wall. "Don't wake them." He motioned toward Hedrina and the kid, then activated the false door. He crept up the stairs.

Rurik wrapped his hands around two circular iron rods fastened to the cement wall and pulled on them, allowing only the slightest crack to the outside. He peered upward to the street. The buildings cast stark shadows against the early morning astronomical twilight.

Several mercenaries, who appeared to be Stovâjįk from their loose-fitting garments and sikke hats, corralled a group of scraggy citizens into the back of a cargo truck. Rurik heard the mercenaries yell to one another but couldn't understand what they were saying. The truck lurched into motion and drove from view.

One mercenary remained behind. Dread filled Rurik as the man carefully inspected the surrounding buildings. He loomed over the stairwell. Rurik froze. The man cocked his head, then descended toward the blue door. A voice beckoned to him from above, and he looked upward. Rurik followed the voice to see the shadow of another guerrilla standing atop a flat roof on the building across the street. The man in the stairwell yelled to him, then ascended from view.

Rurik relaxed.

He continued to watch the man who rested his foot on the corner of the building's roof and peered down into the street like a vulture searching for prey. He slung his rifle from his shoulder, rested it across his knee, and yelled down to the street once more. A voice called back to him, and he laughed. He mockingly aimed his gun at whoever was below, laughing once more. After settling, he continued to keep his stern eye on the streets below. Rurik pushed the false door closed and headed to the basement.

"Things are worse."

Denis sat up looking extremely tired, even angry. The kid rolled awake and appeared disheveled about every portion of his body.

"What's wrong, Rurik?" asked Hedrina, yawning and scratching the back of her head.

"Everyone, you need to listen."

Each person shook the sleep away and looked attentively to Rurik.

Part III: Sfârşitul Lumii

"We can't leave. The vampires have enlisted mercenaries as their day keepers. I watched them pack a truck full of people and ship them away. A sniper is perched atop the roof across the street. I can only assume this is true of other buildings."

"What then?" asked Denis.

Rurik held the rifle and looked it over. "Four bullets," he said with a breath of disappointment. "Well, I can try for the sniper, but I don't know how many more there are. There could be another on top of our building. It's been a long while. I don't know if my marksmanship is what it used to be."

"I can do it," said Felix.

"That he can," said Denis. "Quite the marksman, our prince."

"Really?" said Rurik, looking to Felix. "I didn't know your skill with guns extended beyond losing them in snowbanks."

"Hilarious, Rurik. But it's true—I should be the one to take the shot."

Rurik sat on a chair and strung the rifle across his lap as he considered Felix's offer. "Here's what I think. We should—"

"Forget it!" said Denis, rolling his eyes. "Marksman or not, how the hell do you envision we sneak four people and a vampire past snipers?"

Rurik glared at him. "We're better off against Gypsy mercenaries than vampires. I'll take my chances. Besides, Hedrina and the kid stay."

"If you think you're leaving me behind, you're crazy," said Hedrina.

Denis laughed and fell back on the mattress, cupping his hand behind his head. "Disastrous already."

"Let me finish. We open the false door, Felix shoots the mercenary on the roof, and we move for it."

"Move for what? The palace is over twenty blocks away!" yelled Denis. "We have no idea what's up there or how many of them. You think shooting one of them isn't going to inflame the rest? Gunshot rings out? They'll be all over us."

"Well, brother!" screamed Rurik. "It's our only way, and I'm not going to stick around for dusk and fall victim to worse."

Chapter 25

"Keep your voice down," commanded Denis. "Fine. We'll do it. But I'm telling you—this is a bad plan."

Hedrina and the kid looked to one another for comfort. "But can't we all last down here for a bit? We have enough supplies," she said to Rurik.

"I don't think so," said Rurik. "We're hidden, but not well enough. It's only a matter of time before they find us."

Denis sat up. "And what about our marksman?"

The room was silent as all eyes fell on Felix, who was now keeled over, twitching about on the ground.

"Stake him," said the kid.

"Agreed," said Denis. "It's what he wants, anyway."

Rurik shot his finger to the kid. "Stay out of this." He moved to Felix and shook him.

Felix opened his eyes, taking a moment to focus. "Sorry, I … something took hold of me."

"Are you better now? Can I free you?"

Felix stared at him. "I feel … strange … angry all over."

"Great idea, Rurik. Unbind him immediately," said Denis.

"Shut up," he said, turning his attention back to Felix. "Felix, look at me. Denis and I are leaving. We won't be coming back. I need you to take this shot—can you do it?"

Felix grunted, then looked to Rurik. "Yes."

A moment later, Felix was free. He sat up and patted Rurik on the shoulder. "Thank you, my friend."

"Come with me, Felix." Rurik helped Felix from the floor. "Denis and the kid will pack up our things." He handed Felix the rifle and they walked up the stairs.

Hedrina appeared worried and placed her face in her hands.

"It's going to be fine," said Denis to Hedrina. He slid toward his satchel and strapped on his hogweed canisters.

*

Rurik pulled open the cement door ever so slightly. Felix huddled near the crack.

"See him?" asked Rurik.

Part III: Sfârşitul Lumii

"Yes. Shooting him will attract too much attention."

Felix watched for another moment until a truck pulled in front of the building. The driver opened the door and stood on the seat, extending his arms over the truck's roof. He yelled to the sniper, who motioned upward. The driver hopped on the ground, closed the door, and jogged around the front of the truck.

"What's happening?" asked Rurik.

"Can't tell."

A few moments passed, and the driver's shadow emerged next to the sniper. The next moment, their faces were illuminated as they lit cigarettes. They relaxed and casually looked about the skyline. Felix noticed the truck's tailpipe was still puffing exhaust into the air.

"He left it running," he said, turning to Rurik. "Get Denis."

Rurik ran to the basement.

"We're going," said Rurik, picking up two medium-sized canvas duffel bags. Denis pulled himself from the ground, his equipment already strapped to him.

"Grab the canisters," said Denis.

Rurik slung them around his shoulders as Denis limped from the room and slowly made his way up the stairs.

"No way are you leaving us," said Hedrina.

Rurik knelt to her. "We'll be back. I—"

"That's not what you said earlier."

"We're coming too," said the kid, slinging a satchel of blackwood stakes around his shoulder.

"It's too dangerous," said Rurik.

"Come on, Rurik," began the kid. "If you get killed, we're stuck down here by ourselves for who knows how long."

Rurik looked to Hedrina, who folded her arms and raised her eyebrows.

"All right, but you have to listen to everything I say."

"Fine," Hedrina and the kid said almost in unison.

They came to the bottom of the stairs. Rurik looked up to Felix. "Still good?"

Felix nodded.

Chapter 25

"Oh, no!" said Denis, looking to Hedrina and the kid. "You want to get them killed?"

Hedrina stood in front of Rurik. "We're not staying down here to starve if you don't come back."

Denis, surprised by her vigor, nodded and smiled. "Suit yourself, my lady."

Felix pulled on the false door until his back was against the wall. Denis hobbled outside.

"Go," said Rurik.

Hedrina and the kid ran up the stairs.

Felix waited for Rurik to pass before following him around the false wall. They stood in the stairwell, peering up to the mercenaries, who were still smoking and inspecting a portion of the street perpendicular to their position. Rurik and Felix moved to the street level.

Denis and the rest crouched behind the truck.

"Come on," said Denis as Rurik approached. "Get in."

Denis helped Hedrina into the back of the truck as the kid threw the duffel bags over the gate. Felix jumped in and pulled Denis inside.

"Guess I'm driving," said Rurik. "Felix, hand me the rifle. I'm on point now."

Felix slid it to him. Rurik then ran to the front and hopped into the driver's seat. A second later the passenger side opened and the kid jumped in.

"No way!" Rurik scowled at the kid. "Never mind … shut the door." Rurik threw the truck in gear and slammed on the accelerator. The vehicle growled as it punched into motion.

The men on the roof yelled and threw down their cigarettes. The driver ran from the roof as the sniper fumbled with his gun, pulling the truck into his sights. By the time he'd targeted the driver's cab, the truck had disappeared behind the building in front of him. Several snipers on other rooftops looked to him. He yelled, motioning to the streets below. A sniper several blocks in the distance motioned that he understood and positioned himself as the truck drove past his building. He fired off two rounds. After a moment of stillness, he stood and indicated a misfire. The others readied their rifles, looking for any other commotion below.

Part III: Sfârşitul Lumii

Rurik inspected the bullet hole that pierced the cab, then looked down to the kid.

"You hit?"

"No, sir!"

Rurik swung a hard right onto Nevsky Prospekt, the whole of Saint Petersburg opening before him. The city was in ruin—pillars of smoke rose into the purple twilight, entire portions razed to the ground. Charred skeletons of once-great buildings surrounded them. Rurik barreled down the deserted street toward the Anichkov Bridge. Small fires and gored bodies were strewn everywhere as Rurik did his best to avoid the carnage.

"Can you shoot?" yelled Rurik, moving the rifle to the kid.

The kid took the weapon. He placed it between his legs, the barrel aimed toward the ceiling. "Aye, aye, Captain," he said, and gave an exaggerated salute.

"No. I'm serious. Can you handle the weapon?"

"My dad was a hunter. Hell yes!"

Rurik looked forward. "Good. If we reach any checkpoints—you're the gunman. Fire at will. I'm not stopping for anything."

The kid nodded, then looked over the gun. "Will do, Commander!"

The words were barely out of the kid's mouth when the windshield exploded from two bullets—one missing Rurik just over his left ear, the other shattering the small glass window behind the kid's head.

"Get down!" screamed Rurik. He slid downward and grabbed the kid's jacket sleeve, pulling him below the windshield.

Felix peered through the cab window. "What is it?" When he saw the kid and Rurik crouched below the windshield, Felix ducked low into the bed of the cargo hull, pulling Denis and Hedrina with him.

Back in the cab, Rurik's entire body was crammed below the steering column, straddling it with his right foot on the gas. He pressed the pedal as far as it would go, and the truck crept toward its top speed of thirty kilometers per hour. Rurik poked his head above the steering wheel to see a group of six men standing at a barricade just before the Anichkov Bridge. Three stood with their rifles raised—the others knelt at the entrance to the bridge.

Chapter 25

Rurik crouched once more, and a flurry of bullets tore through the top of the cab.

"One of those hits the engine and we're done," he said. Rurik pushed open the driver's side door and looked to the curb, using it as a visual cue to ensure they stayed on path. "Stay down, kid. It's coming up quick."

The kid leapt up and leaned out over the hood. More bullets whizzed by the truck, some tearing through the roof.

"Get down," yelled Rurik, clutching at the kid's pants.

The kid fired off a shot and quickly cocked the weapon. "Missed!"

Rurik pressed all his weight into the gas.

More bullets ripped through the truck, two striking the open door just below Rurik's hand. He recoiled, and the door closed. He positioned his left foot to the edge of the door, keeping it slightly ajar. He peered through the small gap, aligning the truck with the curb. "Kid, I said 'get down'!"

The kid fired off a shot and then another. He looked in the distance to see a red mist splatter around the head of a kneeling mercenary.

"I shot one! I shot one!"

The fallen man's comrades, hardly fazed by the kill, positioned themselves and sighted the kid. Rurik heard the sound of gunfire rattle once more, and from the corner of his eye watched the kid's body fall limp. He listened to the sound of the rifle slide from the hood.

"Kid?" Rurik reached to him. "Kid?"

At that moment, the truck barreled through the checkpoint. More bullets tore into the cab. Rurik felt a sudden burning in his right thigh. He looked to his leg—a bullet had grazed him. His hand flew to the wound. He winced and sat back up into the driver's seat.

The first image that greeted him was the sight of the kid's wide eyes staring back at him. A bullet hole gushed blood above his left eye. Rurik reached forward, grabbed the back of the kid's jacket, and pulled his lifeless body into the cab. He fought tears as winter's nip blew fiercely into his face.

"Felix!" he yelled. "Felix!"

Felix poked his head through the cab's window.

Part III: Sfârşitul Lumii

"The kid's dead!"

"Hedrina's shot too," shouted Felix. "Pull over!"

"We can't," screamed Rurik, using his sleeve to wipe the tears from his eyes. "Denis hit?"

"Just Hedrina."

"Goddamn it! Is she alive?"

"Yes, but she's shot in the neck."

Rurik slammed his fist into the steering wheel.

"You?" shouted Felix.

"Nothing serious ... get back to Hedrina."

Felix's face disappeared from the window. Rurik focused on the road, repeatedly wiping the wind-whipped tears from his eyes.

*

Hedrina propped her back against the front of the cab. She held a bloodied rag to her neck, continually gagging and expelling grumes of blood from her nose. She looked wide-eyed to Denis, who was kneeling to her, holding her hand.

"You're going to make it, Hedrina," said Denis.

Hedrina forced a smile, revealing bloodstained teeth. Denis pretended not to notice. He removed his sable coat and draped it over her torso.

"You'll be fine," said Felix, reaching out to her. He looked to the blood spilling from her neck and intense shivers shot through him. He looked away, hoping to curb his oncoming craving. "I can't be near her."

"Then get away," yelled Denis.

Felix slid to the cargo door and watched central Saint Petersburg roll past. Mutilated carcasses of the Bolshevik militia lay strewn about the street, leftovers from the Nosferatu attacks. He tried to focus on the passing buildings as his mind obsessed over the blood spilling from Hedrina's neck.

They sped past the Kazan Cathedral, a large portion of its roof entirely destroyed. Rurik hung a sharp right just as the truck passed over the Moika. He drove along the General Staff Building and stopped at its easternmost corner—just before it opened up to

Chapter 25

Palace Square. He jumped from the vehicle and ran to the cargo bay.

Denis glared at him. "Don't look, brother."

Rurik looked beyond him to see his brother's sable coat draped over Hedrina's head.

"She's gone," said Denis.

Rurik punched the cargo door, then walked toward the front of the vehicle. He slumped upon the front bumper. Felix ran to him.

"This wasn't supposed to happen," said Rurik softly. He hung his head.

Felix placed his hand on Rurik's shoulder.

Denis limped toward the building's corner and peered around to Palace Square. "Gentlemen," he said, looking back to them. "You'd better see this."

Palace Square was encased with barbwire. Across the square, several cargo trucks lined up near the wall encircling the palace's west lawn. Stovâjįk mercenaries yanked people from the backs of the trucks and shoved them into the compound.

"Where are they moving them?" asked Felix.

Denis studied the enclosure for a long moment. "Nowhere ... it's a feeding pen."

They continued to watch.

"How close you think we can get before they realize we're a stolen truck?" asked Rurik.

"Forget that," said Denis. "See there." He motioned with his hook. "Middle and eastern portions of the compound are empty."

Rurik looked near the Alexander Column to the front of the palace. The entrance to the empress's east wing was just ahead of them.

"Alexandra's wing is right there," said Felix.

"Then that's where we're going," said Denis. "Right through the front door."

He spun around and hobbled toward the truck. Felix and Rurik watched the mercenaries force more people into the enclosure.

"Gentlemen," called Denis.

They turned to him.

Part III: Sfârșitul Lumii

"I meant now." He opened the passenger door as the kid's limp body fell partially from the seat. "Put him in the back," he said, motioning to the kid.

Rurik and Felix lifted the kid, trying not to look down as they carried him. They slung him over the cargo door while Denis pulled himself into the hull. He sat up and looked at Rurik.

"I'll ride with the dead," said Denis. "See you inside." He looked away and reached inside one of the duffel bags. "Here," he said, handing a gas mask to each.

"I don't need it," said Felix.

"You will when we start spraying ... unless, of course, you prefer to melt to death."

Felix took the mask.

He and Rurik ran to the front cab. They threw on their gas masks and pulled tight their hoods, leaving no exposed skin. Rurik cranked the truck into gear and slowly turned the corner. He aligned the front of the truck with the east wing's door and floored the accelerator. The truck smashed through the wire encampment, then swung right and barreled toward the southeast entrance. In the distance, the encamped prisoners perked up their heads like a gaggle of frightened quail. A group of seven or more Stovâjįk who were huddled near the Alexander Column ran toward the vehicle. Rurik and Felix ducked as the truck barreled onto a small flight of stairs and crashed through the southeast entrance.

"Jesus!" yelled Felix. He sat up and watched the grand lobby sail past.

Rurik poked his head over the wheel. He pressed the accelerator and steered toward the main staircase. The front tires blew out as they struck the stairs. Rurik slammed the brakes and turned a hard left, losing control and crashing into the stair wall.

"Get out," yelled Felix, pulling Rurik with him.

Felix and Rurik jumped from the vehicle as smoke filled the cab. They moved to the back of the truck.

Denis crawled toward the cargo door.

"You all right, Denis?"

Denis shot his hand to Felix, who pulled him forward. He plopped onto the carpet that ran up the stairs and took a quick moment to reposition his false leg. Felix helped him up.

Chapter 25

They looked upward at the long row of dark Doric columns that surrounded the stairwell. Denis aimed his spray device at the coffered ceiling.

The upper peristyle was empty.

"Where are they?" asked Rurik.

Felix looked down to the lobby. "They're not following us."

"I meant the vampires." Rurik knelt and positioned his back against the truck's rear tire.

Denis limped next to Felix and stared down the massive stairwell to the debris left from their entrance. "It doesn't seem they are coming after us. We'll worry about them later." He nudged Felix's shoulder and shuffled back to the truck—its engine spilling black smoke into the expanse as a fire kindled on the carpet beneath the engine block.

"Everyone takes a satchel," said Denis, reaching for a duffel bag. He paused for a long moment and stared at the shadowy figures of Hedrina and the kid. He turned and dumped the duffel bag: blackwood stakes, flashlights, hand mirrors, and machetes on the red carpet that ran the center of the stairs. Several hand mirrors shattered upon impact.

"Careful not to touch the stakes with your bare hands, Felix. The blackwood will burn you. Everyone put on your gloves."

They picked through the weapons and stuffed them into their satchels. Rurik ascended the stairs, and Denis flung his arm around Felix for support as they followed. They moved into the grand peristyle on the second floor and stood before tall double doors that led into the next hall.

Felix faced the doors and closed his eyes. Rurik and Denis crouched with their backs to him as they inspected the long row of giant columns that ran the length of the room.

"It's empty," said Denis.

"They're here," said Felix. He suddenly buckled over and clutched his stomach.

"Where?" shouted Rurik and Denis, as they turned around with their spray weapons. Each hastily turned the dials on the canisters—the hoses snapped taut.

Part III: Sfârşitul Lumii

Felix stood slowly. He looked to Rurik and Denis as a faint red glow illuminated their blood passages. Felix closed his eyes, fighting the urge to feed upon them.

Rurik lifted his mask. "What's wrong, Felix?"

"Nothing. Forget it." He walked to the center of the high double-door that separated the peristyle from the next hall.

"You sure?"

"Yes. I'm fine."

Denis and Rurik walked to his side and stared at the looming door. Denis took a quick second to pull up his gas mask and allow in fresh air.

"They're on the other side," said Felix. "Several hundred Nosferatu."

Rurik pulled down his mask.

"Why aren't they attacking?"

Felix closed his eyes and placed his hand on his head. "I can hear them. They're asking me …"

He fell silent.

"Asking what?"

Felix looked to Rurik. "Why I haven't eaten you."

All three slowly turned their heads and stared at the tall, rectangular door—a sullen paleness about each of their faces. A small light flickered from the distance as the truck fire crept up the stairwell.

"Several hundred?"

"Yes. More are coming."

Denis gripped his spray rod and positioned his hook on its trigger. "You on, Rurik?"

Rurik reached to his canister dials, ensuring they were fully open. He nodded and steadied his spray rod.

"What should I do?" asked Felix.

Denis looked to him. "Stay low. Grab a machete and start swinging."

Smoke filled in all around them as Felix fumbled through his satchel and pulled out a machete. He stood behind Denis.

Chapter 25

Rurik nudged Denis when he noticed smoke filter underneath the opening at the bottom of the door. Denis nodded. They knelt at the door and shoved their rods underneath.

"Now!" yelled Denis.

They squeezed their triggers and unloaded the gas to the other room. High-pitched shrills erupted as the door burst open. A sea of Nosferatu crashed through the door, knocking Denis and Rurik to the floor as a shower of wood splinters fell around them. Felix dove and rolled on his back, trying to get his bearings through the thick cloud of hogweed gas filling the expanse.

The Nosferatu echolocation rang through the fog.

A mass of Nosferatu crashed through the windows that ran along each side of the peristyle and escaped into the morning twilight.

Rurik lay on the floor, spraying wildly into the next hall. Dark shadows and horrid screams swarmed all around him. Nosferatu flesh sizzled and glowed green as the gas devoured them. Denis limped from the gas cloud and positioned himself at the top of the grand staircase—a few dozen Nosferatu crawled along the coffered ceiling. They looked down and hissed at him as their echolocation clicks rang through his heart.

Denis aimed his nozzle upward and enveloped the entirety of the ceiling in thick gas fog. Felix stood next to him as globs of glowing green flesh and bits of bone littered the marble floor. More hunks of burning flesh fell from the ceiling onto the stair's carpeting. The fire spread across the staircase.

Rurik backed toward them and watched the smoldering body parts plunk from the ceiling. The hissing and echolocation stopped—hogweed gas cloud swirled about the hall.

"Everyone alive?" yelled Denis.

"Check," said Rurik.

Denis looked to Felix. "How many left?"

Felix closed his eyes. "Can't tell. We've only killed a few dozen."

Denis turned and hobbled into the next hall, spraying a cloud of hogweed gas before him. Rurik followed, spraying toward the vaulted ceiling. They huddled near the room's center behind a large pedestal. The gas settled around them as the palace fell silent.

Part III: Sfârşitul Lumii

Felix noticed a dense frost forming on their gas canisters. "How much do you have left?"

"Plenty," said Denis. "Anything coming down the halls?"

"No. They've retreated," said Felix.

"You see!" Denis shook his spray rod in victory.

Denis and Rurik stood back-to-back, each staring down opposite sides of the massive hall.

"Can you sense Rasputin or the boy?" asked Denis.

"No. But there are others—asleep," said Felix. "This way."

Denis looked to Rurik. "How the hell could they sleep through that?"

Rurik shrugged. "Too much to drink?"

He ran after Felix.

*

"Felix," whispered Denis.

Felix stood at a heavy oak door, his palm planted upon the wood.

"Two in here. Both vámpir."

"Rasputin?"

"No. But he's about."

Felix stood silently with his palm still against the wood. "Makarov!" He thrust open the door and disappeared into the black room.

Rurik pulled up his mask and looked to Denis.

"Follow him," said Denis. "I'll cover here."

Rurik pulled down his mask and slipped into the room.

Denis moved to the room's entrance and leaned against the wall just next to the doorframe. He positioned his spray nozzle outward and continually looked back and forth, scanning both entrances to the expansive hall.

Doctor ...

The whisper came to him from the opposite hall.

Doctor ...

Denis peered into the darkness, noticing a wispy black fog materializing in the distance. He limped to the hall's center.

Chapter 25

"Is it you?"

The fog poured in from the next room and formed a column before him. Denis positioned the spray nozzle underneath his armpit and reached up to open the hogweed canister. He felt something brush by him followed by a sudden tug on his arm.

The spray rod clacked upon the marble floor.

Denis looked down to see the nozzle lying next to a severed arm. His eyes shot to his biceps—blood spurted from his torn limb. Panic and confusion stabbed at him. He stood silently, watching the fog slither about.

"That's three of your limbs I've taken, Doctor."

Denis spun around to see Rasputin standing before him.

"Shall we make it four?"

Rasputin smiled. His massive teeth shone in the darkness. Alexei stood behind him, poking his head around Rasputin's waist.

Denis caught the child's dead stare, and a nervous shiver surged upon him. He tried to yell but produced only a small grunt. His eyes moved to his arm lying on the floor, then to his blackwood limb.

The hook glimmered.

He pointed it toward Rasputin and lunged for him.

Rasputin gnashed his great claws and ripped through Denis's neck, gripping his spine. Cracking bones and tearing ligaments snapped as Rasputin split Denis's head from his spinal column. He plunked the bloody mass onto the floor.

Denis's last vision was his own headless body, standing boldly before Rasputin—if only for a moment—until his leg buckled and the rest of him fell limply onto the marble.

I am madness maddened.

*

Rurik followed Felix's footsteps through the pitch-black.

"Felix, stop. Where are you?"

"Over here," came Felix's voice. Felix flipped on his flashlight. He stood in front of an ornate brushed-metal bed frame. He pointed the beam toward Rurik, who guided himself closer.

"They're here. Under the bed," said Felix.

Part III: Sfârşitul Lumii

"Shut the light."

"It's fine. They're asleep."

They stood at the foot of the bed. Rurik bent over, trying to catch a glimpse. Felix placed his flashlight on the floor, aiming the beam slightly away from the bed.

"Gas ready?"

Rurik reached up and ensured his gauges were open. He nodded.

"After I lift. Don't spray until my command."

Rurik nodded and steadied himself as Felix crept to the side of the bed. Felix's fingers gripped underneath the mattress and he tilted it upward, peeking under the bed—nothing but bare hardwood.

Felix stood fully upright with the mattress leaning against his palms. He stared at the vacant hardwood floor, shaking his head.

Rurik moved closer. "You sure about this?" he mumbled through his gas mask.

Felix stepped into the frame and pushed the mattress away. It thumped onto the floor, sending a small curtain of air upward.

Felix pulled off his mask. "I don't get it," he said, turning to Rurik. "I can sense them right he—"

The floor beneath Felix's feet splintered to pieces as two hands punched through the wood and grabbed him by the ankles. Felix lost balance and fell backward into the hidden compartment, breaking the rest of the false floor with his fall.

Rurik's foot bumped the flashlight as he ran forward, sending the beacon spinning in circles. The light settled on him as he crept toward the rectangular hole in the floor. Growls and struggle filled the room.

"Felix?" yelled Rurik. He positioned his finger on the nozzle trigger, ready to fire. At that moment Felix rose from the chest-deep compartment with a limp body in his grasp, and slammed it to the floor.

"Don't shoot!" yelled Felix, staring at Rurik with black eyes and blood dripping from his gloved hands. Rurik noticed sharp fingernails protruding through Felix's gloves.

Rurik retrieved the flashlight and shined it on the body.

"It's Dragunov," said Felix. "One of Nicholas's generals."

Rurik shined the light on Dragunov's fanged face.

Chapter 25

"Christ, Felix," said Rurik as blood spurted from Dragunov's neck—his throat completely ripped away, revealing his spine.

Dragunov lay still, wheezing and coughing on his own blood.

"Should I spray him?"

"No! Wait." Felix disappeared into the compartment and produced his satchel. He pulled himself from the hole and knelt to Dragunov, who lay still, staring vacantly at the ceiling. Felix reached his gloved hand into the satchel and pulled out a blackwood stake. He drove it deep into Dragunov's heart, then dumped his body back into the secret compartment. Smoke and an audible squeal rose from the hole.

Felix stood and looked to Rurik with a gaunt, angry face. Rurik raised his spray weapon.

"Stand back, Felix."

"Don't," he said, grunting a bit. "There's more here."

Rurik lowered the nozzle, keeping his light on Felix, who swung around and stood over another hidden compartment in the floor.

Rurik traced the light to a rectangular groove cut into the hardwood. Felix stood over it.

"Makarov?" yelled Felix. "Makarov!" Felix slammed his bootheel onto the floor.

"Don't kill me." The voice rose softly from underneath the floorboards.

Rurik shuffled behind Felix and positioned his spray nozzle.

"Careful," said Felix. "I'm not covered anymore."

Felix slammed his foot into the wood once more. "Unlock it or I'll smash through."

Felix stood back, and a clicking came from the floor. The door swung downward, and Makarov's bony hands appeared from the shadows. He stood until his upper torso was visible—his face was pale, his eyebrows mussed in every direction.

Makarov shivered.

"Please, don't kill me. I can help you."

Felix jumped into the compartment and shoved Makarov to the back.

"Where's Pavlovich?"

"I ... I ..."

Part III: Sfârşitul Lumii

Felix asserted his grip around Makarov's neck. "I'll rip your throat out. Where is he?"

Makarov panted heavily. "In Bucharest. He ... he was converted ... then sent there for reasons unknown to me ..."

Rurik shined the light on them both to see Felix's sharp, bloodstained fingernails poised to tear through Makarov's neck.

"Spare me, Felix. I'll lead you to Dmitri Pavlovich."

"I don't need you."

Felix shoved Makarov and pulled himself from the hole. He walked past Rurik.

Makarov looked upward, nodding his head submissively. "Don't hurt me," said Makarov. "I'm on your side now." He smiled with bloodstained teeth.

"Gas him," said Felix from the distance.

Rurik pulled the trigger and a stream of hogweed gas enveloped Makarov. His high-pitched wail was audible only for a moment. The gas settled, and Rurik walked to Felix.

"I think you're going to have to kill me soon. I can't control this much longer."

"Just a bit more, come on." Rurik took Felix's arm and they ran from the room.

They entered the next hall to see Denis's headless body sprawled out on the floor.

"Denis!" shouted Rurik and ran to his brother's body.

Felix followed and knelt to Denis.

Rurik felt his gas mask tear from his face as something powerful pinned his arms. "Felix?" he whimpered.

Felix turned to see Rasputin holding Rurik, hulking over him. Rasputin moved his clawed hand around Rurik's neck and held him outward. He ripped the canister harness from Rurik's body, then threw the device down the hall.

"It's time, Felix," said Rasputin, pulling Rurik back into his grasp.

Rurik fell stiff, unable to speak. Felix looked to Rasputin's waist to see Alexei peer around his back.

"Don't fight it, Felix," said Rasputin.

Chapter 25

A lucid sensation swept Felix. His mind was alive with a terror-tinged anger as he watched Rurik struggle in Rasputin's grasp. A new sensual awareness pulsed through him, darkness became day, and sound seemed to reverberate off his skin. The blood inside Rurik's body shone toward him, nothing but red entanglements—beacons of glimmering sinuous delight. Fangs grew from his mouth, and he moved in toward Rurik.

Rasputin ran his sharp fingernail across Rurik's cheek, and blood spilled down his face and onto his neck. The redolent smell overwhelmed Felix as he leaned in slowly toward Rurik, whose panicked heart enticed him further.

"Felix, stop!" murmured Rurik.

"He is yours," whispered Rasputin.

Felix's brow and jawline protruded as saliva dripped from his jowls. He grew entranced by the glorious shower of glitter-red cells pulsating through Rurik's jugular vein and the vascular network of ruby-colored liquid flowing through his torso.

He placed his face next to Rurik's neck.

Rasputin held the back of Rurik's head, lengthening the striking point of his jugular vein.

Felix licked his teeth, then moved in for the kill. He lashed upward over Rurik and lunged for Rasputin's neck. Rasputin blocked Felix's attack with his forearm, then dropped Rurik to the floor and smashed his boot into Rurik's face, knocking him unconscious. Felix bit down hard upon Rasputin's arm, and a loud grunt echoed through the hall as he pushed Felix to the floor and ripped his arm from Felix's jowls. Rasputin placed his knee into Felix's sternum and pinned him on the floor while wincing from the pain surging through his forearm. Felix struggled, but Rasputin's strength proved too much for him.

Rasputin wrapped his hands around Felix's neck.

"Listen to me, Felix," said Rasputin as Felix continued to squirm beneath him. "Felix, stop. You need to understand your place in all this. I have no desire to kill you."

"Get off me," huffed Felix. "You murdered Irina!"

"Felix, you must listen. I needed to isolate you from all these happenings. Pavlovich's carelessness was responsible for Irina's death. I merely eased her pain."

Part III: Sfârşitul Lumii

"Liar!"

"Stop resisting," said Rasputin as he applied more weight onto Felix's sternum. "I injected my venom into you to awaken you, Felix. But you are stronger than I expected. Now you must submit to me or die."

Felix stopped struggling, and Rasputin shifted some of his weight to make him more comfortable. At that moment, Alexei rushed to Rasputin.

"Don't hurt him!" exclaimed Alexei as he looked to Felix. "Uncle Felix, Grigori is our friend. He cured my sickness."

Rasputin looked to Felix. "Now then, Felix. Shall we listen to your godson? Else I fear this will have to go another way. I cannot allow you to live unless you submit to me."

Felix peered to his left to notice one of Denis's blackwood stakes was within his grasp. He looked back to Rasputin and nodded.

"Very well," said Rasputin, casting a warm glance to Alexei. "It looks like we're all family now."

Felix snatched the blackwood stake with his gloved hand. He shot upward with the stake, aiming for Rasputin's chest.

Rasputin easily deflected it and disarmed Felix while pushing Alexei away. Rasputin's grasp began to smoke as he held the blackwood stake, but he showed no semblance of pain.

He pinned Felix once more.

"Well then," said Rasputin. "If I cannot control you, then I guess our story ends here."

Rasputin raised the stake into the air and drove it toward Felix's chest.

"No!" screamed Alexei, lunging toward Rasputin.

Felix knew his time had come. He gripped the stake as the tip of it cracked his sternum. Rasputin's weight was too much. Felix moaned and pushed back as hard as he could while the stake slid farther into his chest, nearly at his heart.

Just as he was done for, Felix heard a fierce growl, then felt Rasputin's weight shifting off him. Rasputin rose and took a few lumbering, clumsy steps away before falling onto the floor next to him. With all his might, Felix pulled the blackwood stake from his chest and threw it on the ground as Rasputin slumped next to him.

Chapter 25

Felix was stunned to see Rasputin missing an arm and part of his neck chewed away. He looked before him to see Alexei standing with blood running down his chin.

"I'm sorry, Uncle Felix. I had to. He was going to kill you." Alexei began to cry.

Rasputin sat up and slowly backed away to the wall, holding his neck wound. He huffed and snorted as he looked down to his severed arm.

"Well, my Prince?" he said, staring at Felix.

Rasputin pulled his hand away from his gaping wound, and Felix noticed it begin to heal. Without another thought, Felix reached down to the blackwood stake and lunged for Rasputin, who proved too disoriented to defend the blow. Felix held the stake tightly and shoved all his weight into Rasputin, sending the blackwood stake through his heart and out his back. Rasputin let out a great wail.

Felix looked into Rasputin's eyes. "For Irina," he said.

Rasputin tried once more to mutter something, then resigned himself to his fate as his body dissipated to a dusty ether. The blackwood stake clacked to the ground.

Felix turned to Alexei as a new sense of pain flashed all over his body. His sudden screams echoed through the hall as he writhed upon the floor and his chest wound began to heal. His veins seemed to boil as Rasputin's venom dissolved inside him. A flash of intense pain surged through him and then it was gone. He crawled to his knees with snot and blood dripping from his nose. After rubbing his eyes, he saw Alexei, who was curled up in a tiny ball on the floor. Felix could hear him whimpering.

"Alexei, come," he said reaching out to the boy.

Alexei came toward him and the two embraced. Felix looked to Rurik, who was now conscious and crawling along the floor. As he reached Denis's headless body, his fingers gripped the back of his brother's shirt. He buried his head into the small of Denis's back. "Oh, my brother. My brother …"

Felix watched him and held on to Alexei. The boy lifted his head and looked to Felix.

"He made me do everything, Uncle Felix. I'm sorry. I didn't—"

"Be calm, child. Where's your mother?"

Part III: Sfârșitul Lumii

"Asleep."

Rurik removed the hogweed canister from Denis's body and strapped it on his own back. He stood just before them and pointed the spray nozzle at Alexei.

"Get away from him, Felix."

"Put that down, you moron."

"Out of the way, Felix. My brother is dead!"

Alexei turned to seek refuge in Felix's embrace. He stood with the boy latched on to his hip.

"You'll have to kill us both," said Felix.

"You're not a vampire anymore ... it—"

"It will scar me permanently."

Rurik thumped his foot into the ground. "Damn it, Felix! We can end this right now. The Nosferatu are still alive."

Felix reached out and pushed the spray nozzle away.

"Then gas them." Felix placed Alexei on the floor and held his hand. "We're not killing an innocent child."

"Innocent?" yelled Rurik.

Felix ignored him and knelt to Alexei. "Alexei, can you hear those people talking in your head?"

"Yes." Alexei pointed down the hall. "You mean them?"

Felix and Rurik turned to the sweeping hall to see a mob of Nosferatu standing before them—some crawled along the ceiling and walls.

Alexei closed his eyes. "They want to kill you. I told them to stay away."

Felix looked to Rurik. "We're safe as long as he's with us."

Rurik grimaced. "Think of—"

"I don't care if I have to kill every last one myself. We're not hurting him."

Felix picked up Alexei and moved toward the Nosferatu. Rurik positioned his spray nozzle and followed.

"Those voices will obey you. Just keep telling them to stay away from us and let us pass," said Felix.

Alexei nodded and held on to Felix more tightly. They walked toward the Nosferatu. A gap opened, and the monsters bowed to the

Chapter 25

ground as they pressed through. Rurik reached forward and placed his hand on Alexei.

The surrounding Nosferatu stared silently at them as they walked by.

"Can you lead us to your mother?" whispered Felix.

Alexei yawned. "Yes. This way."

They walked through the hallway as the Nosferatu continued to shoot their echolocation sounds into Rurik and Felix, staring at them both with their gaunt, dead eyes.

As they made it to the end of the hallway, Rurik ensured both Felix and Alexei were in the clear in front of him. He then turned to the hall full of Nosferatu.

"For Denis."

He pulled the trigger on his nozzle and filled the hall with hogweed gas. He turned and followed Felix and Alexei as the screams of the Nosferatu rang out behind him.

Part III: Sfârșitul Lumii

26

December 17, 1916 (OS), 8:48 a.m.

Alexandra was lying facedown in her bed. Alexei's hand reached up and shook her.

"Wake up, Mama."

She shot up. "Oh, my baby!"

Alexei jumped on the bed and hugged her. Felix sat next to them. "Hello, Alex."

"Felix?" She reached out and pulled him closer. "Please tell me it's really you." She wept.

Felix hugged her. "It's me … Rasputin is dead."

"Thank God," she said, holding him close. "Oh, how I've prayed for you. I know you would never hurt Irina."

Rurik stood at the foot of the bed, and Alexandra looked to him. "Who's this?"

"My friend Rurik. He's … he's saved us all."

Rurik nodded. "Hello, Your Highness."

Alexandra bowed her head to him, tears streaming down her face.

"Oh, my boy." She hugged Alexei deeply. "What about the others … the monsters?"

"They've overrun the city," said Felix. "Most are still roosting here to protect Alexei."

"What are we to do?" she questioned. "Alexei is their—"

"I know. We'll figure it out. We have to leave—the palace is burning."

"This way," said Alexandra, rising from bed.

Chapter 26

*

Felix and the rest exited from Alexandra's secret passage to the grand lobby on the first floor. The flames from the truck fire had spread downward across the stair, consuming large portions of the lobby as parts of the ceiling crashed onto the floor. The main entrance through which their truck had crashed was completely caved in—a large pile of debris burning before it.

"There's no escape!" yelled Rurik.

They ran by the main staircase as flames whirled about the charred skeleton of their truck. Felix looked up to the peristyle to see the fire consuming the walls and ceiling.

"This way," said Alexandra, motioning to a slim corridor next to the stairs, its walls beginning to be engulfed in flames.

"We can't!" shouted Felix. "It's too hot."

"We must," she said.

She held Alexei and dashed down the hall with Rurik quick on her tail. Felix waited and watched their figures move toward the corridor's end. He took a deep breath and ran after them.

They reached the end of the hall as the corridor's ceiling caved in, trapping them.

"Where does it go?" asked Felix.

"The wine cellar," said Alexandra. "There's a door to the sewer system. You can—"

A large crash resounded behind them as more of the ceiling caved in. Alexandra placed Alexei on the floor and reached in her gown pocket. She produced a key and opened the door.

"Go!" she yelled.

"You first," said Felix.

"Don't be stupid. Go!"

"Alexandra."

Her eyes filled with tears, and she pulled Alexei close. "You know we can't come. Leave us."

Felix embraced her and then knelt to Alexei.

"It's OK, Uncle Felix. Mama will protect me."

Felix ran his fingers through Alexei's hair. "I love you, little one."

Part III: Sfârşitul Lumii

"I love you too."

Felix stood and took one last look at Alexandra. He and Rurik stood back from the door as Alexandra closed it. There was a click as she locked it from the other side. Felix shook his head. "No. They're coming with us." He lunged forward and thrust his weight into the heavy oak door.

"Alexandra!" He banged on the door. "Open it!"

"I must end this, Felix! I am sorry," she said through the door.

Rurik reached to him. "Felix."

Felix kicked the door once more. "Alexandra!"

"It's over, Felix." Rurik flicked on his flashlight, illuminating the stairwell. "Let them go."

"What's she going to do?"

Rurik looked to him. "You know."

Felix frowned. He placed his hand on the door once more. "I love you both," he said with tears in his eyes. He added softly, "You were the last family I had."

Rurik reached to Felix and squeezed his shoulder. "I'm sorry, my friend. It's over."

Felix nodded and they descended into the wine cellar. They walked through an open circular door, and eventually emerged into Saint Petersburg's sewer system.

*

Alexandra pulled Alexei to her as they sat against the door. She held him closely as the fire moved near.

"Why didn't we go with Uncle Felix?"

"We can't. Be calm, my son. The fire will set things right."

"Do we have to die because of those monsters?"

"Yes. We have to be brave. It will only hurt for a moment."

"I'm scared."

"Don't be, my child. Hold on to me."

They huddled together as the fire crept onto Alexandra's gown. Alexei's pants started to burn, and he winced.

"I'm so sorry, baby," said Alexandra.

Chapter 26

Alexei looked up to her and smiled a bit. "It doesn't really hurt," he said as he buried his head into her breast.

"I love you, my son."

"I love you too, Mama."

They embraced one another as the fire swirled upon them. Within moments, their hearts were mere ash.

*

Morning's twilight cast deep hues of purple and cobalt over the burning city. Wispy clouds swirled their way through the charred frailty of Saint Petersburg's once grand skyline. A domineering quiet rang over the bulbous spires and rigid towers, imbuing them with a sense of penitence and defeat. The frigid wind was the only song resonating through the city streets until the harrowing cries of the Nosferatu echoed over the calm. Their existence, tied to the mortal plane by the Bloodchild, disintegrated into the ether evermore.

Part III: Sfârşitul Lumii

27

December 17, 1916 (OS), 10:24 a.m.

Felix and Rurik broke through a corroded iron grate and walked onto the frozen Neva River. Dawn was upon them. They spent the next half hour hugging the walls along the icy canals, avoiding militiamen, until they made it to the Moika River. Their freezing feet carried them across the ice until they reached the foot of the Yusupov Palace.

"That's better," said Felix, kindling a fire in his bedroom's hearth. He handed Rurik a plate full of crackers and caviar.

"Fancy!" said Rurik as he warmed his freezing digits.

"It's all I could rummage up. I'll embarrassingly admit I don't know where the servants keep the food."

Rurik laughed. "Suits me," he said, cramming a cracker full of caviar into his mouth.

"I'm sorry about Denis, Hedrina, and the kid," said Felix. "Denis was my friend."

Rurik continued to munch on his crackers. "I'm trying not to think of it," he said with his mouth full. "But thank you. I'm sorry for your losses as well."

Felix hung his head. "I guess we're all each other has now."

Rurik swallowed. "I have always wanted a prince in the family."

Felix walked to his dresser. "Funny if you think about it," he said, rummaging through his clothing.

"What's that?"

"Breaking into your home, stealing your own clothing and money."

"Desperate times, my friend. Desperate times."

Chapter 27

Felix paused and looked to Rurik. "I have to wonder, though—what did Rasputin mean when he said I needed to understand my place in this?"

"I don't know, Felix. He certainly had some plan for you."

"There's something more here. Something bigger. I understand he converted me to try and control me. But it didn't work."

Rurik paused. "I honestly do not know. But for now—it is done."

"Is it ... done?"

Rurik glanced to him. "With Rasputin dead and the Nosferatu gone ... yes—our chances are great."

Felix let out a relaxed breath.

"All that's left is exterminating any vámpir in Saint Petersburg," said Rurik. "There are likely some converted by Rasputin."

Felix turned his back.

"Well ... good luck with that. It's not going to take long for the Bolsheviks to figure out the door to the throne is wide open. Sticking around to see how the army sorts out this disaster is madness."

Felix dumped a full duffel bag onto his bed and pulled the straps shut. He lumbered to his bedroom door and dropped it on the floor.

Rurik walked to him. "Where will you go?"

"Eventually? Paris, I suppose. Depends on how well the kaiser fares ... For now—Bucharest." Felix flashed his confident grin. "I have a score to settle with a vampire."

Rurik cocked his head. "I hope you aren't intent on traveling alone?"

Felix bowed at the waist and clicked his heels. His arm swung wide toward the door.

"After you, my good Mr. Kozlov."

PART III: SFÂRŞITUL LUMII

TO BE CONTINUED IN
THE NOSFERATU CONSPIRACY, BOOK TWO:
THE SOMMELIER

Felix and Rurik travel to Bucharest to destroy Charles Vondling and Dmitri Pavlovich. Upon arriving, they discover an ancient secret that far worsens their predicament.

Aided by a new band of supernatural allies and hunted by terrifying forces of extreme darkness, they set off on a harrowing adventure across war-torn Europe. When the true cause of World War I is revealed, our heroes race to stop Kaiser Wilhelm from carrying out his ultimate plan of global genocide.

To succeed, they must locate a mysterious Parisian sommelier who harbors the genesis of the unfolding events—a wine bottle containing the last remnants of Vlad Drăculea's blood. If the bottle is not destroyed before German special forces can obtain it, Felix and his friends will face a foe even more powerful than the Nosferatu: the reincarnation of Vlad Drăculea himself.

The Nosferatu Conspiracy: Book I

CONTACT THE AUTHOR

The author's site:
http://www.brianjamesgage.com/

The book series' site:
http://www.nosferatuconspiracy.com/

The author's Instagram Profile:
instagram.com/brianjamesgage

The book series' Instagram Profile:
instagram.com/nosferatuconspiracy

The Nosferatu Conspiracy: Book I

ABOUT THE AUTHOR

Brian James Gage was born and raised in Youngstown, Ohio, and has been living in Los Angeles, California most of his adult life.

In addition to writing, he is an entrepreneur, investor, fitness enthusiast, and aspiring classical pianist enrolled at The French Conservatory of Music in West Los Angeles.

For more info, please visit:
http://www.brianjamesgage.com/

The Nosferatu Conspiracy: Book I

Made in the USA
Columbia, SC
16 September 2020